Mary McNamara has worked for the *Los Angeles Times* for seventeen years, writing extensively about the inner workings of Hollywood. She lives in Los Angeles with her husband and three children. This is her first novel.

OSCAR SEASON

MARY McNAMARA

POCKET
BOOKS

LONDON • SYDNEY • NEW YORK • TORONTO

First published in the USA by Simon & Schuster, Inc., 2008
First published in Great Britain by Pocket Books UK, 2009
An imprint of Simon & Schuster UK Ltd
A CBS COMPANY

1 3 5 7 9 10 8 6 4 2

Simon & Schuster UK Ltd
1st Floor
222 Gray's Inn Road
London WC1X 8HB

www.simonsays.co.uk

Simon & Schuster Australia
Sydney

A CIP catalogue record for this book is available
from the British Library

ISBN: 978-1-84739-109-4

Designed by Karolina Harris

Printed by CPI Cox & Wyman, Reading, Berkshire RG1 8EX

For Richard,
with constant love and gratitude

OSCAR
SEASON

High above Los Angeles, the pool on the roof of the Pinnacle Hotel glowed azure. Tiny whorls of steam rose from the water, maintained precisely at eighty – two degrees, into the cool night like hairs on the arm of someone suddenly frightened. Rows of empty lounge chairs stood in silent ranks around the pool, pale and open – armed, sheltered here and there by a ficus tree or a planter bristling with calla lilies. At one end, a cluster of café tables; at the other, a line of cabanas. On three sides, wings of the hotel rose another eight stories, windows alight in odd and even formations against a long, dark sky.

In between, nothing but gently shining water and fine white stone. No figures lay entwined on a lounge, no sweet funky smoke rose from the cabanas, no private party writhed in any of the half dozen spas. Juliette stood alone for a moment in the symmetrical solitude. Only a few stars were ambitious enough to penetrate the urban murk above her; below, the tide of traffic began to ebb to its late – night sigh.

Squaring her shoulders, Juliette turned to leave, when something, a shadow of something, caught her eye—a darkness gathered in one corner of the pool, rumpling the smooth skin of the water. "Hello?" she said, listening for the sound of a stifled laugh, a held breath. Nothing. Juliette took two steps toward the pool, then stopped as the silence transformed into tension.

Had she heard the scraping of metal against concrete? Was that a rustle through the greenery on her left? She considered calling security, but the nature of her visit made that unwise. Instead, she retraced her steps until she was outside the pool director's office, which was locked and empty. Feeling her way along the wall, she flipped a switch that bathed the area in high-wattage security light.

Floating in a far corner of the pool was a man, fully clothed in a dark suit, spread-eagled and face down. For a moment she was transfixed by the serenity of the scene; it looked so perfect, like a scene from a movie. But then a breeze blew by, rucked up the surface of the water, and the body began to slowly spin. Reality struck and, heart pounding, Juliette raced toward the pool with the wild hope that whoever it was had just this second fallen in, that that wasn't blood she saw swirling under the body like a cloud, that security, which she was dialing even as she ran, would somehow get to the body before she did, and that they'd all be able to figure something out long before the police came.

1

Staff members of the Pinnacle Hotel in Los Angeles received their Oscar Night Survival Kits at their annual Oscar Season Summit, held three days before nominations were announced. The black leather fanny packs (donated by Coach) contained the following: two pairs of cufflinks, two bow ties (one clip, one traditional), one set of tweezers, three makeup brushes, two compacts each of eye shadow and blush (donated by M.A.C), three lipsticks (one gloss, one matte, one shimmer, all Chanel), four tubes of concealer in various skin tones, a dozen tiny safety pins, a roll of toupee tape (for preventing wardrobe malfunctions), a sewing kit, a tube of hair gel, a lint brush, a tin of breath mints, a bottle of ibuprofen, and a small vial of Xanax.

"The Xanax is, of course, for guests only," Juliette Greyson said as she handed out the packs. "And only in case of emergency."

"Where are the cyanide capsules?" asked Gregory Bridges, director of rooms and entertainment sales. "Where are the tranquilizer darts?"

"You will see in the small outside pocket a laminated card

with a list of names and phone numbers for anyone you might possibly need," Juliette continued, pointedly ignoring Gregory. "Hair, jewelry, handbags, physicians, pharmacies, yoga instructors, personal trainers, psychiatrists, *animal* psychiatrists," she said with emphasis, aiming her words at Gregory, who, with a gleam in his eye, had opened his mouth to remind her of what the staff now referred to as *The Strange Incident of the Dog on Oscar Night*, when a nominee's Labradoodle had howled from the time she left the hotel until the moment she won her award, "cosmetic stores, perfumeries, aromatherapists, and, of course, the concierge service at Saks, Neiman's, and Barneys. These are all culled from last year's debriefing session and if you have a number you think should be added, please see me after the meeting."

"You're kidding, right?" said Louisa Halston, the head concierge. She hefted her bag without opening it, then tossed it onto the table. "I don't need this, Hans certainly doesn't need this." Louisa nodded at the head chef. "Unless you think he's going to be doing dress repairs in the kitchen. We have all of this available at the concierge desk, except," she added with a smirk, "the mints. But who needs mints during Oscar season? They're in every pocket of every publicist in town."

"Not in adorable tins with the Pinnacle logo," said Gregory sweetly. "Not created from an award-winning recipe by our world-famous pastry chef."

Juliette nodded at him and again ignored the sarcasm in his voice. God knows she was used to it; as the person who decided who got which room in the hotel, Gregory was treated like a prince by every publicist in town and he never let Juliette, or anyone else on the staff, get away with one single thing. But Juliette knew that his sharp tongue was just a camouflage. He quietly doled out the mountains of swag he

4

received to room attendants and bellhops, waiters and custodians, while loudly complaining about the worthlessness of just about everyone. It was what Juliette valued most about him; he kept the staff from taking themselves too seriously.

"These," she said, pulling the tin out of her pack and holding it up so the entire group could see, "are the crack cocaine of breath mints. Everyone will want them and they are only available in one place—the lobby of the Pinnacle Hotel. As for the packs, Louisa, you were the one who . . ."—she paused for a moment; "complained" would have been accurate, but no Pinnacle staff member complained; it was against company policy—"*observed* that your staff spent too much time running up and down the stairs last year. While the aerobic fitness of our staff is legendary, these packs will allow each of us to provide our guests with basic support, which should allow Oscar night to run with even more efficiency."

White winter sunlight flickered through the poplar and oleander that grew outside the two-story-high windows of the private dining room, hung like haze over the long Louis XIV dining table around which the staff members were gathered. Christmas had been recently banished from the hotel, the holly and white roses giving way to sprays of orchids, here in a golden forest, there in ribboned clusters of pale pink and violet. The dining room was rose and gilt, with the table at one end and a cluster of velvet- and silk-upholstered chairs and love seats at the other. With its pale pink walls, the room looked like the inside of a jewelry box just opened.

Juliette surveyed the group gathered around the table with quiet satisfaction. Bathed in the forgiving light, her co-workers looked like people in a painting, or, more appropriately, a movie: there sat Hans and Rick, the chef and pastry chef, in their kitchen whites; beside them Louisa, her hair as sleek and black as her concierge uniform, her impossibly handsome assistant diligently taking notes—Louisa always insisted on having an impossibly handsome assistant, to make up for, Juliette assumed, all those hours she spent negotiating dinner reservations and hair appointments. Farther down was Gregory, tan and tense in his inevitable Armani, flirting with Marta, the head bartender, whose combination of Eurasian beauty and lyrical profanity made the Pinnacle's bar the hottest, and most photographed, in town.

Across the table, the head of housekeeping looked more dignified than all of them put together in her toast-colored pantsuit, while the head doorman, a young man from Ohio named Barney, was, in his morning gray with his cap on the table, the picture of ruddy-faced mid-American friendliness. *We all look so precisely our parts,* Juliette thought, considering her own linen skirt and pale blue cashmere sweater, her auburn hair clipped into a demure ponytail. *Like the people in that board game, Cludo—Miss Scarlet did it in the library with the lead pipe.* Off duty, Juliette assumed, everyone wore jeans and T-shirts, went grocery shopping, and got their oil changed. But as she looked at them now, such things seemed almost impossible. *Impeccable,* Juliette thought. *How* do *we do it?*

"Um, Juliette," said Doug Barnes, head of security. "You want us to wear those too? Cuz I'm carrying enough gear as it is, but if you think it will help . . ."

Juliette smiled at "Dog," who had started work at the Pinnacle on the same day she had, and for the same reason. He was not a physically imposing man for a security head; in her heels, Juliette towered over him. But he had the uncanny ability to read guests—to know precisely how much exposure they wanted, how much privacy they really needed, no matter what their overly cautious publicists might claim. She had also seen him escort invading photographers and insistent fans off the premises with gentle chatter that belied the firmness of his grip and left the intruder feeling like he had indeed been "escorted" somewhere.

"No, Dog," she answered. "I don't expect you to wear one. But take one anyway. It's a nice bag and your wife might like some of the makeup. God knows, we could all use the Xanax. In fact," she said with a glance at Louisa, "the bags are optional for all of you. I would suggest we try them out this year to see if they help. But you are professionals, and of course we trust your judgment."

"I'll certainly be wearing one," said a voice from a doorway, "though I expected mine to have gold trim, or my initials in diamonds." General Manager Eamonn Devlin never entered a room without a line. The brogue, however, came and went depending on the audience and the need. After working with him for a few months, Juliette had warned him that it was a "tell"—the higher the stakes, the thicker the Irish. "This is exactly why I hired you," he had said with a laugh, and afterward Juliette did not hear the hills of Mayo nearly so often in his voice.

Now Devlin headed straight to the sideboard and loaded a plate with spring rolls, crab cakes, and brownies. "Carry on," he said, waving a fork, his mouth full. The room relaxed. Down to the room service runners, the staff of the Pinnacle had been chosen for their friendliness, their flexibility, their dedication to service, and their ability to intuit the needs of their high-profile guests. While this made for a lively, intelligent group of workers, it also meant there wasn't an automaton in the lot, so suggestions carried much more weight than demands.

Juliette had called the first summit three years ago in order to see exactly what she was dealing with, and that was still true. It was good to gather the group in one room, to see that Louisa and Gregory still hissed at each other amicably enough, that Hans and Rick were still joined at the hip, that the food and beverage director had gotten over his crush on Marta, that everyone still circled each other, synchronized but at a proper distance and with distinct personalities, like the planets. This delicate balance was what made the Pinnacle the best hotel in town. Maintaining it was the keystone of Juliette's job.

Juliette's title was Director of Public Relations, but when Devlin hired her he had promised her free rein. They had met ten years before at the Plaza in New York, and since then he had tried to hire her at every hotel he had run, from Bali to Paris. But circumstances, mostly in the form of Josh Singer, Juliette's now ex-husband, never allowed it. Until Devlin came to Los Angeles, where Juliette had been working at the Mondrian.

Devlin was determined to make the Pinnacle *the* Industry hotel in a town where every major hotel, from the Four Seasons to the Bel Air, had staked out its celebrity territory with the precision of the Conference of Yalta. The Peninsula had the Brits, the Four Seasons the brats (young stars who didn't quite know how to behave), the Bel Air had old Hollywood, the Beverly Hills Hotel drew the money men, dot-com millionaires and trust funders who still believed that movies were a good investment and the Polo Lounge the place to be seen. Raffles L'Ermitage had somehow cornered the rock and rap market, the Chateau Marmont was still first choice among hipsters with the Standard a close second, the Beverly Hilton usually scooped up TV, and the rest of the big hotels just picked at the crumbs.

In less than four years, Devlin had turned the Pinnacle into the hub of it all—press junkets, Industry parties, and, most important, Oscar season. Last year, they had hosted more of the Golden Globe and Oscar nominees than any other hotel in town. And though Juliette would not take the credit Dev constantly tried to give her, she did know that her ability to think on her feet and to apply common sense to even the most overwrought situations had helped. Like the survival kit, which would undoubtedly find its way into *InStyle* and become the standard of every big hotel by this time next year. Louisa would bristle because Louisa always bristled at innovation that did not come directly from her own imagination. She hated the fact that while Juliette and Gregory were known by their names by the hotel's high-powered guests, she was, in most people's eyes, just a lovely uniform or, even worse, a helpful voice on the phone. She didn't like Juliette, whom she saw as direct competition for advancement in the hotel and, perhaps more important, the heart of the general manager.

Watching Louisa pick up the fanny pack, so clearly torn between her irritation and her desire to please Devlin, Juliette smiled to herself. Juliette had no interest in running the hotel and there was no evidence that Eamonn Devlin even had a heart—she pitied the woman who would waste her time mounting a search party for it. Not that she didn't like Devlin. She knew her boss as well as she knew this hotel and she found both very comforting. As insane as the weeks ahead would be, there was order here, familiarity. Safety. From the kitchen, there was the faint clatter of the lull between breakfast and lunch, from the lounge the soothing constant tide of voices.

"So," Juliette said. "What do we need to know to make this year even better than last?"

"Well, Lily Mathews had her triplets early this morning," said Gregory matter-of-factly, referring to an A-list actress whose well-documented pregnancy had been difficult and tenuous. He pulled a huge congratulations card from the leather folder he always carried and pushed it to Barney. "I want everyone to sign, and not just names. Sweet little notes. We're sending a Bugaboo built for three, which I had custom-made, full of goodies, including the promise that if she stays here for the Oscars, we'll put aside the Presidential Suite so she'll have room for the babies and the nannies."

"Good God, she wouldn't be coming to the Oscars two months after giving birth to triplets," said Louisa. "She was on bed rest for, what, the last three months?"

Gregory snorted. "They're pushing for her to present Best Picture. If she can wedge herself into a black dress, she most certainly will. Did you see the cover of *People* a month ago? 'Is Lily's Career Over?' Or *Newsweek:* 'The Last of the Superstars?'"

"Lord," said Louisa, shaking her head with disapproval. "If she lets them push her around like that, her career really is over."

"I could fire you for that, you know," said Devlin amiably. "No, no, I've sent my own," he said, passing on the card. "Along with a box of Cubans for the new daddy. We'll have to discuss the Presidential Suite, Greg, there may be a situation with that. But we'll make it work," he added, holding up a mollifying hand, "no worries. What else?" He looked around the room.

"We're going to need an extra seamstress this year," said Elena, the head of housekeeping, consulting a list she had in her hand. "Perhaps two."

Juliette nodded. Last year, a nominee had tried on her crystal-encrusted dress four hours before showtime and discovered she had put on some weight. Crystals flew everywhere—the woman's stylist took one in the eye that scratched her cornea—and Elena had spent three hours sewing them back on while Gregory had filled in as head of housekeeping.

"Don't forget to put the chocolate pudding and risotto back on the menu," said Gregory with a twinkle in his eye. "For the Crew." Hans and Rick groaned, while Juliette and Louisa laughed.

"What crew?" said Devlin.

"The Skeleton Crew," Gregory explained. "All them boney bones with their pointy hips and their pointy shoes. Pudding makes it easier for them to bring their dinners up."

"No," said Hans. "No. I am going to take it off just for that. For that reason alone. It is an insult."

"Now, now," said Devlin, "your worry is how it tastes, not how, or if, it digests. And the person who uses the term 'the Crew' within earshot of any guest will be fined five hundred dollars."

"We're going to need a few more bellmen to run flowers and gifts," said Louisa, adroitly changing the subject. "We'll need to use the banquet room to store them; they were just sitting around in the lobby and hallways last year, which looked terrible."

"And someone needs to act as a gift basket adjudicator," Gregory added righteously. "Some of the things people sent for the Golden Globes were just pathetic. One box of muffins I could not let pass—I threw in some of my own Belgian chocolate and an orchid, but I can't be responsible for everything around here."

Juliette listened and took notes and watched the time. The meeting had to come in under an hour or the hotel literally would grind to a halt. Gregory had heard that one longtime movie star couple was splitting, so they would require two rooms, on different floors, in separate wings. Devlin confirmed that two New York–based studio executives currently suing each other would also be staying during the month between nominations and the Oscars, so similar accommodations would have to be made, including constant surveillance by the staff to avoid unpleasant encounters.

About forty-five minutes into the meeting, everyone's cell phones, set on vibrate, were ringing so insistently that the room itself seemed to buzz.

"It sounds like we are under attack from some very large hummingbirds," Devlin said. "I'd say we're on solid ground here. Thanks for coming, everyone. J.," he said, pulling Juliette aside, "I need you for about half an hour."

"Now?" she said, glancing at her BlackBerry, its screen solid with e-mail messages.

"As soon as you ever can."

"Five minutes," she said. "No, ten. I need to do reconnaissance."

"Take fifteen," said Devlin, shouldering his survival kit. "Just because I absolutely love the mints."

At any given time, there were at least a half dozen interviews and photo shoots taking place in the Pinnacle and Juliette did not like any of them to happen without her at least momentary presence. Photographers had to go through her to set up; cameras were allowed only in certain areas of the hotel—the garden, the banquet rooms, the guest rooms—though photographers, desperate for a different environment, sometimes conveniently forgot this. She had less control over interviews—the public rooms, the restaurant, the bar were, after all, public—but if the subject was a guest, or a potential guest,

Juliette wanted to make sure he or she felt comfortable and safe. On more than a few occasions, she had gotten calls from frantic publicists asking her to make sure that a journalist did not go over his or her allotted time unless the star or Industry exec involved seemed to be enjoying it. Once or twice, she had had to intervene, delicately introducing herself and bringing the interview to a close by drawing the subject away. Juliette was surprised at how shy and uncertain some of the most famous actors and actresses were when caught without their various handlers.

Today, Natalie Portman was being photographed in the garden, Brian De Palma in one of the banquet rooms, while Dames Maggie Smith and Judi Dench were holding court in the Orchid Suite. In the lounge, a model and a producer were discussing their engagement; at the pool, the cast of an Emmy Award–winning television show was goofing it up for a reporter, throwing a beach ball around and shouting.

"Are they bothering you?" Juliette asked a young man lying on a lounge reading a script.

"Hullo, darling," he said, squinting up at her. "I haven't seen you in ages. I heard you had defected to the Four Seasons." Juliette laughed. David Fulbright had been staying in the hotel for almost six weeks—he was shooting a movie over on the Universal lot—and wherever Juliette went, he seemed to be. They had closed the bar down last night, testing some of the new drinks the head bartender was trying out for Oscar season.

"Have you recovered from the currant Bellini?" she asked.

"Up at dawn for a run," he said. "My British constitution. I don't suppose," he added after a pause, "that there's any truth to the rumor that Sean Bean has checked in."

"We cannot discuss the identity of our guests," Juliette said primly. "Why? Is he a friend of yours?"

"Well, yes and no." David looked out over the pool. His dark hair was grown out for the role and hung in his eyes, making him look like a high school student. A very sexy high school student, Juliette thought. "I think he's here to replace me," he said. "I think I'm going to be sacked."

"Aaron loves you," Juliette said soothingly. "He told me so not three days ago." Aaron was the film's director, also staying at the hotel, who was currently having breakfast with Sean Bean, who had checked in yesterday.

"I am," David said, watching her face. "Oh, God, I am. And you know it." He pulled himself to a sitting position.

"I don't," she said, reaching out her hand—to what? to brush the hair out of his eyes?—then letting it fall. "Okay, he is here, and he and Aaron did have breakfast, but Aaron's casting that other movie now, I think, the one about the tennis players. And they were having breakfast in the main dining room. Why would they do that when Aaron knows you're in the hotel?"

David fell back in his chair. "You're right. I hope you're right. Oh, God," he said. "First I lose the lead to Colin bloody Firth, and now this. I cannot bear it." He caught Juliette's hand. "You must help me to bear it."

Juliette reluctantly drew her hand away. "There's nothing to bear. And I've just broken about fifty Pinnacle rules, some of which I wrote myself, so I'd appreciate you saving the dramatics for the camera."

"I do love you," David called out after her. "No matter what happens, my darling, you must remember that."

Juliette ducked her head as she walked, so no one would notice the smile on her face, and ran right into the large and manly chest of Phillip Ramirez, the pool director. "What?" she said, seeing the furrowed brow, the dark eyes almost black with concern.

"She's at it again," Phillip said with an almost imperceptible gesture to the running track that circled behind the pool area. "For the last two hours. I swear to God, she is going to die. On that track. Right in front of my eyes."

"She" referred to a young starlet who had checked in about two weeks before, the daughter of a software billionaire (who always seemed to be financing the films in which she starred) and clearly a card-carrying member of the Crew. At first, the staff had assumed she was a drug addict and hoped she knew better than to check in to the Pinnacle for a spree. "That's what all those Comfort Inns in Palm Springs are for," Gregory had said with a shudder. But it soon became clear that Melissa, or Lissy to her friends, was a bona fide anorexic.

"Listen," Phillip said, "I did something that might be wrong, but I just can't watch her . . . I don't know . . . die. So I put some protein powder in her Diet Coke. And some lime syrup. I told her it was Diet Lime Coke. I think they have that now. Anyway, she drank it. Could I get fired for that?"

Phillip was supporting his mother and two younger sisters. Juliette had hired him six months ago; he had been a bellman at the Beverly Regent, so this was a huge leap up the ladder for him and he was obsessively concerned with maintaining Pinnacle standards. Part of Juliette wanted to laugh, but another part knew that if the woman found out, she would surely complain, not only to Devlin but also to Daddy. "I don't think," she said carefully, "that mixing up a drink order is a fireable offense. And you know how I love my Diet Coke with protein powder and lime syrup." She put her hand on Phillip's shoulder. "Just be careful. Protein powder has a pretty noticeable taste. Especially to an anorexic."

She was five minutes late in meeting Devlin, who was standing in the lobby chatting with a PGA champion and his new

wife. Dev raised his eyebrows; he was not accustomed to waiting. She shrugged slightly. After introducing her to the couple
and then excusing himself, he put a hand under Juliette's
elbow and guided her to the elevator.

"It's a good thing you have red hair," he said, pressing the
button. "Otherwise you wouldn't get away with half of what
you get away with."

"Sorry," she said. "Had to do damage control. David
Fulbright heard that Sean had checked in, and he thinks he's
going to be sacked."

"He is," said Devlin, stepping into the elevator.

"I know," said Juliette. "I just feel so badly for him. It's been
a hard year; this was supposed to be his big comeback after
the breakup." David had been engaged to a supermodel who
had left him, literally, at the altar, and run away with her personal trainer who was, not that it mattered in the least, a
woman.

"Don't get emotionally involved with the guests, J. It's not
good for business, and it's not good for you."

"Thanks, Mr. Roarke," she said. "Now, where exactly are we
going?"

The elevator stopped at the top floor, which was occupied
by three enormous suites, including the Presidential Suite.

"We have a special guest who has requested your personal
attention," said Devlin, walking slowly down the hall. "He is
receiving medical treatment. Officially he's doing preproduction work in Morocco."

"Treatment for what?" Juliette asked suspiciously. "You are
not going to ask me to hold someone's hand after lipo and a lift
again, are you? Because that's what Eden Hill is for."

"Cancer," Devlin said shortly. "He has a round-the-clock
nurse here, so you won't be expected to deal with anything

medical. But he says he knows you from your days at the Plaza and that you are, and I quote, 'one of three people I could stand having in the room, and the other two are dead.'"

Juliette's heart started to pound; she had not talked to Josh, her so recently former husband, and still, despite her best efforts, the love of her life, for months. But she would have heard, wouldn't she? Someone would have called. Wouldn't they?

"Who on earth are you talking about?"

Devlin stopped outside the door to the Presidential Suite. "Now, Juliette, I know as a hotel professional you will not make our guest feel at all uncomfortable about his appearance, which is somewhat . . . altered."

Juliette put her hand on the door and blocked Devlin. "You are not opening that door until you tell me who is in there."

"Michael O'Connor," Devlin said, and suddenly Juliette could see the lines around his mouth, his eyes, see how tired her boss looked. "And he is in pretty bad shape."

Michael O'Connor. Juliette couldn't believe it. Two-time Oscar winner, megastar, and perpetual ladies' man, with three ex-wives . . . or was it four? At fifty, he was one of the few bona fide movie stars still standing with better box office than just about any other actor. Action pictures, romantic comedies, psychological dramas—there wasn't a role he hadn't tried, nothing, it seemed, he couldn't do. He was an acrobatic pilot, raced sailboats, and rode one year on the Olympic equestrian team. Michael O'Connor had cancer. Jesus. But hadn't she just seen him, beaming up from the pages of *Vanity Fair* or *People*, walking down the red carpet in Cannes, or hosting some charity event for, what was his cause, pediatric AIDS? Or was it the rain forest? Didn't he have two movies out this very moment? Michael O'Connor remembered her from the Plaza.

God, that was ten years ago, maybe closer to fifteen, though she still remembered it clearly. He had a hit movie out that summer, was doing Shakespeare in the Park, *Hamlet* or *Othello*, one of the big ones, and every time he entered the hotel it was as if a meteor had landed. "'And he glittered when he walked,'" Juliette murmured now.

"What?" said Devlin.

"Nothing. God, that's terrible. But I have no idea why he wants me; I haven't seen him except to say hello across a crowded room in fifteen years." Well, there was that night, Juliette thought, that one night when "yes" might have made a big difference in her life, but she had chosen "no" because "no" had seemed to be the only real option.

"Fifteen years is not so long in Juliette time," Devlin said with a grin. "I met you fifteen years ago and look how it changed my life." He knocked softly on the door. A tall bald man in a teal nurse's uniform opened it. "Can you tell Mr. O'Connor that I have Ms. Greyson?"

"Well, tell her to get the fuck in here," called a voice from the depths of the darkened room. "Because life is shorter for some than for others."

"I'll leave you to it," murmured Devlin, withdrawing. Juliette walked through the door. It took a minute for her eyes to adjust to the light, but then she saw him clearly enough, sitting on a hospital bed, an IV on one side, a box with a monitoring screen on the other. It made a strange silhouette, jarring in the otherwise opulent setting. But that was nothing compared with the man who lay in it. His famous dark curls were smashed and greasy and streaked with gray, his face was lined and hollow around the eyes, and his broad shoulders seemed nothing but bone beneath his pajamas. He watched her watching him and cocked a famous eyebrow.

"Well, you look pretty good for a woman who's been dumped by a hack for a dewy young thing," he said. "Still tall and tawny and the match of a thousand men. I hear you're running this hotel, which is why I came. In the past, I've always preferred the Peninsula."

Any thought of tender loving care had disintegrated at his first words, which she assumed was his intention. His face, that beautiful, utterly famous face, was a ruin. How long had he been sick? How bad was it anyway? She looked right into his eyes, afraid of what she might see there, afraid of the blue gone gray, the milky film that she knew from experience preceded death. But his eyes were clear enough. Amused. Anxious. Angry.

"The Peninsula doesn't have suites with this kind of floor space," Juliette said. Lightly. "And you seem to be requiring even more floor space than usual."

That made him laugh, a strange barking sound that led to a fit of coughing. He held up a hand when she moved toward him. "But enough about you," he said when he could talk. "How about me? Did you miss me? Don't lie, now, I've been lied to by the best and I'll know it." When he spoke, she could hear a dozen of his performances behind his words, the cadence of his speech, was unsure if this was a performance right now, though surely no makeup artist could render his wrists so thin, his skull so pronounced. This was what she hated about actors—you could never tell when they were acting. The good ones didn't even know themselves, fiction having melted completely into fact, and life was complicated enough. Which was why she had stuck with the writer. Through thick and thin for all those years, never complaining, even when she came home at night to find him still sprawled on the couch, the only pages written balled up in the trash. And see how wonderfully that turned out.

"You look like hell," she said, trying to meet him on equal ground. "I mean, Jesus, you might have cancer, but surely you also have a comb. Or have you lived in the hands of groomers so long you've forgotten how to shave?"

The actor stared at her and Juliette wondered, for a moment, if this was, perhaps, the wrong tact—she remembered him as being a tough-talker who liked women who tough-talked back. But that was a different era, when there were not many rules at all and very different medications involved.

O'Connor stared at her a little longer and then he smiled. A wide-open, sunrise-after-endless-night movie magic smile. The smile that took a handsome man and turned him into a superstar.

"Well, look at that," Juliette said softly. "You haven't forgotten a thing."

"I certainly haven't forgotten you," he said, leaning back. "Have a seat, my Juliette. Rest your long and weary bones."

She sat and kept looking at his face; he seemed to be daring her to look away, daring her to make a sound or a gesture . . . Of what? Pity, maybe?

"Oh, 'bare ruined choirs, where late the sweet birds sang,'" he said softly.

Juliette shrugged.

"I've seen worse," she lied. "Hell, since Josh left, I've dated worse," she added, lying even more. "When did you get here anyway, and why did you ask for me?"

"Last night. The extra-sneaky, secret way," he said, raising his eyebrows, widening his eyes. "Officially, I'm doing preproduction in Morocco. We even hired a double to fool the paparazzi. There's already been a picture of 'me' doing shooters at some bar with girls all over my lap. Which I guess beats

20

a picture of me and Rory, the new love of my life." The nurse appeared from the next room. "You remember Rory, don't you?" Michael said. "He was on *The Playground*, remember? He played the kid with the funny laugh."

"Oh, sure," Juliette said, looking at the man with his salon tan and shining scalp, not remembering at all. *The Playground* was the television show that had been Michael's breakout role all those years ago; as the jock with the heart of gold, he had launched a cottage industry: T-shirts, lunch boxes, a million posters plastered on the bedroom walls of a million girls— Michael O'Connor's face had been everywhere. So when he then took as his first movie role an alcoholic lawyer with an overbite and a missing eye, everyone thought he was crazy. That had led to the first Oscar nomination. The rest of *The Playground*'s cast had, as far as Juliette knew, faded into obscurity. "So you became a nurse?" she asked.

"Honey, I became many things," said Rory, tweaking the IV line. "But I seem to have wound up a nurse."

"I ran into him about a year ago, right, Ror?" Michael said. "So when this whole thing went down, he was the first person I thought of. He quit his job at Huntington Hospital to take care of me. And they say there's no loyalty in show business."

"The half mil doesn't hurt either," said Rory complacently.

"So if you have Rory, what is it you need from me?"

"Juliette, how can it be you even have to ask?" Michael put one hand on his heart. "After all we meant to each other? Or almost meant to each other. Could have meant to each other. Do you know, Rory," he said, raising his voice so the nurse could hear him, "I tried to seduce Miss Juliette way back in the way back and she said no? *No.* Can you believe it? And me in my prime."

"I had a boyfriend," Juliette said.

"Everyone I knew had a boyfriend," said Michael, "and it didn't stop any of them. You married that boyfriend, didn't you, and now look at what happened."

"Where is your wife, by the way?" asked Juliette. "Sally? Or is it Madeline? It's hard to keep them straight. Is she in Morocco with the double?"

"You need to catch up on your tabloid reading," he said. "We are sep-ar-ated. Irreconcilable differences. Do not press for details. I'm saving them for my autobiography."

"Okay," said Juliette, rising. "For a very sick man, you seem to be having a pretty good time, whereas I have about seven thousand phone calls to return. I'm sure you know that we are all at your disposal. If you need anything at all, just call down and ask for me."

"I understand," Michael said, "I understand. You are very busy, very, very busy. It's *Oscar* season. I certainly don't want to keep you from your publicists and reporters and nominees who want *organic* egg whites and *seedless* watermelon. I am just hoping that you can spare a little time now and then to come visit an old man on his bed of pain, bring him news of the big wide world. Or even just the sight of your pretty face." He sat up, grimaced, and lay back down. Juliette leaned over him, automatically pulling the pillow more firmly under his head, smoothing the blankets, tucking in the sheets. "The chemo I can take," he said quietly, putting his hand on her wrist. "It's the loneliness that's killing me."

"Don't any of your friends know?" she asked, ignoring how large and warm his hand was, how it engulfed her wrist. "Your wife? I mean, how bad could the differences be?"

He shook his head. "My agent, my lawyer, and I only talk to them when I have to in the best of times. You know the drill," he said, cocking the eyebrow again. "If you're going to get sick in Hollywood, you might as well die, because you'll never work again. I intend to work again and without the pleasure of a post-recovery appearance on *Oprah*."

"Oh, come on," Juliette said lightly. "If anyone's big enough to get sick, you are."

"It's breast cancer," he said after a moment. He laughed shortly. "See, I can't even say it with a straight face and it just may kill me. Because, interestingly enough, it is not only rare in males but incredibly aggressive. But I leave to your sturdy imagination how me and my pink ribbons would play in the trades. I could live my whole life not being the poster boy for male breast cancer, and I intend to do just that, one way or another."

Juliette kept her face steady, holding on to what Dev called her "don't worry, ma'am, the engines are supposed to be on fire" look. She had seen and heard extraordinary things behind hotel doors, had built a career on knowing how to react, but she was at a loss here. Breast cancer. Jesus.

"Green eyes," Michael said, watching her carefully. "Now, you don't see those every day. Though I suppose you do . . . Juliette." He whispered her name, enunciating the *t*'s so that it sounded like the wind shaking the branches of icy winter trees. He had always been good with *t*'s, she thought, with consonants in general; it was one of his signatures. Then he closed his eyes. She could see the silver bristle of his beard, smell the sour sickness of his breath. The room already seemed more like a hospital room than a suite.

I should send some flowers up, she thought. Lilies, freesia, fragrant flowers. Why didn't Dev do that? Or Gregory? Did he even know O'Connor was here? Turning away, Juliette sighed. Three days until Oscar nominations were announced, so much she had to do, so many needs to meet, and now this. Beneath

Michael O'Connor, the world he ruled moved on, churning, anxious, self-centered, and oblivious.

"I'll try to come up around dinnertime," she said as she pulled the door closed behind her.

"You know where to find us," he said.

2

Juliette took the stairs down, figuring sixteen flights would let her put a little distance between what had just happened and the rest of the day, and help build the stamina she would need for the next month. She put her phone back on ring and it promptly rang—the head of housekeeping on the other end.

So instead of returning to her office, Juliette found herself in the bowels of the hotel, in the housekeeping annex, listening to a young room attendant recount her morning's adventures, which, unfortunately, involved Forrest Hughes. For the past ten years, Hughes had been the hottest funnyman in town, commanding astronomical fees, and just about everything else he could think of, for the movies in which he starred. Lately, however, several of his projects had stalled and the celebrity press leapt on this with glee, speculating endlessly that Hughes had finally priced himself out of the market. Far from being humbled or even noticeably worried, Hughes had given pretty much everyone the finger, calling certain studio executives assholes and blaming his longtime, long-suffering writing staff, who many considered the secret of the comedian's success.

Hughes had been at the Pinnacle all of twenty-four hours, but already there was trouble. Apparently he had seen one of the housekeeping staff servicing other rooms and requested extra towels; when she brought them in, he and his female companion had backed her into the bathroom. The woman had tried to kiss her while the star had unzipped his trousers and begun masturbating in front of her. The woman, whose name was Maria, had handled the situation beautifully, Juliette noted, extricating herself from the room and reporting the incident immediately to her superior. There were tears still shining in her eyes now, but she spoke calmly and with an air of professional detachment—she knew that what happened would be dealt with accordingly.

Juliette took notes and spoke kindly. "I am very sorry this happened to you, Maria," she said. "And we will ensure that it will not happen again. Do you want us to press charges?" She looked at the young woman, her face blank. Maria answered instantly, if a bit haltingly—her English had not been good when she had been hired and she was only halfway through the class the hotel provided for new hires with language barriers. "No," Maria said, "I trust that this hotel will handle the matter . . . appropriately." Juliette nodded again. "Please feel free to take the rest of the day off," she said. Again the woman shook her head. "I would rather get back to work," she said. "We are very busy." Juliette smiled and nodded, made another note—Maria would be receiving a nice bonus in the coming weeks and she wouldn't be working any hours she didn't want to.

Back in her office, Juliette immediately dialed the actor's publicist, Arnie Ellison, a reigning prince of MDB, one of the two biggest agencies in town. Consigliere to Lisa Javelin, one of Hollywood's most powerful and loathed publicists, Arnie had once told Juliette that if she would sleep with him, he would take Josh on as a client and "make magic happen." Juliette had refused, as lightly as possible, and the two had spent the subsequent years pretending it had never happened. When Josh had left her, Arnie had been one of the first to call with condolences.

"Juliette," he said when, after she spent five minutes on hold, he finally got on the phone. "What can I do for you?"

"Well, darling," she said in her sweetest tones, "we've got a bit of a situation and I wanted you in the loop before it gets out of hand." In calm and measured tones, she described what had happened, pausing for a moment to let the ramifications sink in.

"Our employee," she said at last, "is a very discreet and responsible woman and you know how strict we are about protecting the privacy of our clients from the press. Now, we have assured her that should she choose not to press charges, we will make certain the behavior will not be repeated. That"— she paused again—"won't be a problem, will it?"

"Not at all," said Arnie brightly, as if they were discussing a table arrangement or a birthday party. "That will be no problem at all. I'm sure there was miscommunication on both ends—"

"No," said Juliette firmly, "there was not. In fact, it bore all the hallmarks of that incident with the Australian tennis instructor. Your boy seems to think everyone owes him a 'happy ending,' doesn't he?"

Arnie fell silent—his client had paid through the nose for that one and still it was all over the Internet for months.

"But I don't think we need to go to such extremes here," Juliette said. "If you would just speak to Mr. Hughes and let him know that while we appreciate the stress he has been under lately, we will not tolerate the abuse of our staff. Devlin," she added, "is very clear on that. As I think you know."

"Yes, yes," said Arnie, suddenly businesslike. "Of course. It won't happen again. And what else do you want?"

"I beg your pardon?" Juliette said coolly.

"Juliette," said Arnie, switching gears yet again, "I really do appreciate the concern you are showing for my client. You know I think the world of the Pinnacle, which is why I've sent so many of my clients and friends your way over the past year."

"And we appreciate that, Arnie," she said as the conversation fell into precisely the track she had laid for it. "We hope you keep that in mind in the next few days—it certainly looks like John and Bill are shoo-ins for Oscar nominations this year, and I don't believe we've had the pleasure of their company. Yet."

For a moment there was silence on the other end. The publicist sighed. "Funny you should say that," he said. "I was just about to call Gregory to see how we could work together. I know John is a big fan of the hotel."

"And the feeling is completely mutual," said Juliette. "I can transfer you to him right now. I'm so glad we're going to be seeing more of you in the next few weeks."

Arnie laughed. "You're something," he said. "You know that, don't you? Has Devlin bought you that Mercedes yet? If he hasn't, I'll give you a job any day of the week."

"Ta, Arnie," Juliette said, smiling into the phone as she hit the transfer buttons. "Merry Christmas, honey," she said when her co-worker, who had been trying to get an in to John and Bill for two years, answered.

After a four-minute phone call with a pair of BBC reporters about whether or not they could follow a famous photographer as he made the pre-Oscar rounds through the hotel, Juliette headed to the kitchen to talk to Hans about the menus for the weekend of the awards—Hans had gained a reputation for creating dishes that somehow echoed either the themes, the time period, or the location of those films nominated for Best Picture. He was happiest when at least one was set in Italy or France, though Asia did just as well. This year the front-runners were two Depression-era films and a box office smash set almost entirely in a prison and Hans was a little concerned. "There is only so much one can do with mushroom soup," he said anxiously. "Even my very good and fresh mushroom soup."

To get to the kitchen, Juliette threaded her way through the lounge with its tang of tomato juice and Grey Goose, past the library where the gas fire burned cheerfully and with absolutely no heat. The books, their red leather spines an impressive sight at two stories high, were real, though if you looked closely enough you would see that there were at least a dozen copies of *The Iliad* and other highly sought-after titles like Pearl Buck's *The Time Is Noon* and John Steinbeck's *The Red Pony*. The original decorator had ordered the books by the foot, and Devlin could not be persuaded to change them. ("How many people look on the top shelves, love? And can one honestly have too many copies of *The Iliad*?") Juliette could not walk by the room without a shiver of disgust.

As she headed across the black marble floor of the lobby, she was struck by the sweet soothing scent of roses and the pleasant front-door buzz of the driveway, where every sort of high-end luxury car purred to a halt with seamless regularity. Only now there seemed to be a bit more buzz than usual; through the beveled glass of the entrance, Juliette could see a woman with long blond hair banging on the window of a large

SUV. Stifling a sigh, Juliette made a quick left turn to investigate.

Outside, she realized the woman was Leslie Newcomb, an actress who had just had a baby; her husband, the actor Ted Norman, had been filming in L.A. during the past two months of her third trimester and she came out to be with him, hoping that maybe the sight of an enormously pregnant woman on set would speed up production. It didn't. She wound up giving birth at nearby Cedars-Sinai and bringing the new baby—an adorable little boy—home to the Pinnacle. Where, of course, he was showered with all manner of gifts, including the hotel's new infant massage and facial. Still, Juliette felt bad that anyone would have to bring their baby home to a hotel, even one as nice as the Pinnacle. The demands the entertainment industry put on even its biggest stars seemed at times outrageous; Juliette regularly saw children and spouses relocate to L.A. for weeks, for months, to be close to the working parent; often they rattled around the hotel, and the city, like trapped tourists. And she liked Ted and Leslie, who had been married for ten years and seemed as down-to-earth as a pair of multimillionaire movie stars could be.

Except right at the moment, Leslie was throwing what could only be described as a tantrum, banging her fists on the glass of the SUV's back seat, pulling at the door handle.

"Relax, sweetheart, relax," said her husband, anxious behind his aviator shades, reaching out to put his hand on her shoulder. She shook it off. "Get him out," she ordered, her voice rising with each word, "get him out of there now. I want my baby out."

"The doors locked automatically when he shut them," said Barney sotto voce to Juliette. "The keys are still in the ignition. We tried the slide on the lock, but it didn't work. There's a locksmith on the way." Raising his voice and speaking to the couple, he said, "We'll have your baby out of there in no time." Ted smiled, but Leslie had her eyes glued on the baby in the back seat. "At least it's not summer," Barney added softly.

Juliette could see the new baby blinking in his car seat. He opened his mouth in a perfect circle, smacked his lips, waved his tiny fists, and began to howl. As if electrified, his mother began to bounce, slapping her hands against the glass. "Why did you shut the fucking door?" she screamed at her husband. "Why did you buy this fucking car with its fucking automatic locks? I hate this car. It's not even a car. It's a fucking death trap! Someone get him the fuck out of there."

As the actress turned toward her, Juliette could see that her breasts were damp with milk. Leslie noticed this as well, pulled her tank top away from her body, and began what could only be described as keening. "Oh, my God, oh, my God, oh, my God," she wailed.

There were at least a dozen people in the midst of arriving or departing the hotel, and a small crowd was knotting itself around the pillar just inside the doorway; Dog appeared out of nowhere, his hand reaching to lower a camera a guest was raising to eye level. It was only a matter of time before the paparazzi appeared and Leslie and her wet breasts would wind up in *Us Weekly*.

"Okay, this is not good," Juliette said. She bent over and reached beneath one of the miniature cypress trees that twisted away from the hotel's entrance. She picked up one of the imported river rocks that lay around them in a winding Zen-ish design. She unhitched her Hermès scarf and wrapped it around her hand and with a fluid, almost unnoticeable gesture, broke the small side window on the passenger's side, reached in, and unlocked the door.

"Being a new mother is hard enough," she said to Ted, who stood openmouthed as his hysterical wife leapt into the car to reclaim the infant. "Barney," she said, "send the car down to Al's. It will be back to you within the hour," she explained to the actor. "If you need it before then, we'll be happy to provide a car and driver."

"Thank you," said Ted, finding his voice. "And please, just send me the bill."

Juliette held up her hand. "Not at all. We break it, we buy it. That's the Pinnacle policy. Being a new father," she added with a friendly pat on his shoulder, "is pretty hard too."

Then she put her arm around Leslie and the baby and guided them all firmly into the fortress of the hotel.

"That was pretty slick," said Gregory, appearing out of nowhere. "Where'd you learn to do that anyway?"

She looked up at him and grinned.

"Before I got into hotels," she said, "I was a car thief."

"Did you really?" said Michael O'Connor when Juliette told him what had happened.

"Did I what?" she asked, rolling a spear of asparagus in butter, then raising it to her mouth. "Break the window? I can produce witnesses, if you need them."

"Steal cars," he answered, watching her eat the spear, then lick her fingers. His own dinner—clear soup, broiled chicken breast, and unbuttered peas—lay on its plate, picture-perfect and untouched. "And do you always eat your vegetables with your hands?"

Juliette smiled, rolled another spear in butter, and raised it in the air so that she had to tilt her head back to eat it. It was going on eleven and she was very, very tired.

"'Dear Abby' says it's perfectly polite to eat asparagus with your fingers," she said. "Which is why I love asparagus."

"Makes your piss smell funny," said Michael dryly.

"And your semen," she said, eyes level with his.

"Oh, how I love it when you talk dirty," he answered. "But will you put the maid's uniform on later? That is the question."

"Please," Juliette said, holding up her hand. "After today, no jokes about maids." She told him the story, leaving the names out of it; she had worked with big stars long enough to know that they loved nothing better than gossip. As long as it wasn't about them.

"Let me guess," O'Connor said. "Forrest Hughes."

Before she could catch herself, Juliette blinked—how had he known so quickly?—and that was all it took. "I knew it," he said. "That guy is such an asshole. I mean *such* an asshole. I did a cameo on one of his pictures a few years ago, and he spent two days screaming about the temperature of his bottled water. It had to be precisely forty-five degrees. He had three assistants whose sole job was to oversee his water. He had this thermometer that he would dip in the bottle and if it beeped he would go into this screaming fit. It was embarrassing. And expensive. I think the director went about a month over schedule. And took all the heat. Pardon the pun."

"Well, his excesses seem to be catching up with him," Juliette said. "I just read in the trades that he's got yet another film shutting down because the script 'needs rewrites.'"

O'Connor snorted. "He's a greedy bastard—he gets twenty million and half the back end and everyone else gets scale plus ten. You should have pressed charges."

Juliette barely suppressed a laugh—Michael O'Connor had

been one of the first actors to hit the twenty-million-dollar mark and his back-end deals set the industry standard. It was always funny, and a little frightening, to hear stars trash other stars for shared foibles.

"Maria didn't want to press charges and that wouldn't have gotten us anything anyway," she said, shrugging.

"Yes, you neatly seemed to turn the whole situation to your advantage. But," he said, his eyes brightening for a moment, "you are avoiding the original question, aren't you?"

"There was a question?"

"You're doing it again," he said, sitting up and taking a sip of juice. "You did steal cars before you got into the hotel business, didn't you?"

Juliette stared at him, clearly amused.

"Or something else," he said, undeterred. "I remember now. Alex hired you off the street, didn't he?"

"Mr. O'Connor, you say the nicest things."

Michael rolled his eyes. "I mean, you hadn't ever worked in a hotel before, right? Didn't you, like, break up a fight in the lobby?"

At this Juliette laughed out loud. "Is she a hooker or a bouncer? Only her hairdresser knows for sure."

"Well, something, there was something. God," he said, flinging himself back against the pillows, "my memory is just shot to hell. I hope it's the drugs. It better be the drugs."

"It wasn't a fight," Juliette said. "It was a misunderstanding. A problem some guests were having. Which I was able to solve."

"Oh, right, right," Michael said. "You got some poor rich tourists backstage to *Cats* or something and all was forgiven."

"Something like that."

"And Alex hired you on the spot."

Juliette shifted her gaze to the window. "Something . . . like that." She was suddenly aware of the silence all around her, the muffled light from the nightstand, the steady hum of the monitor, the drip of the IV. The fragrance of the lilies and roses she had had sent up, welcoming when she had first walked in, were now making her queasy and anxious.

From the bed, Michael watched her.

"You were with Alex when he died, weren't you?" he asked.

"I was," she said, remembering her old boss, who for so many years had been her best friend. "Well, not the moment he died, but . . . a lot. At the end." She kept her eyes on the window and the blanket of lights twitching out there in the pale city darkness. How long ago had it been? Had it been ten years?

"I don't have AIDS, Juliette," Michael said softly.

She looked back at him, startled. "I didn't think you had."

"And I'm not going to die," he said.

"I know," she said, shaking off the memories. She reached for another asparagus spear; rolling it in butter, she held it up to his mouth. "Because we don't allow that sort of thing here at the Pinnacle."

It was almost one when she left the hotel. For a few moments, she treaded water at the entrance to the bar, where a respectable number of guests were gathered, some with female companions of, perhaps, the very expensive hourly variety. She waved to Marta; Marta could tell a hooker at twenty-five paces, tipped by clues Juliette never even saw. The Pinnacle rules regarding what staff called "the rentals" were simple—only if the women, or men, were already on the clock. If they came in alone, looking for business, they would quietly be asked to leave. Otherwise, they were just considered one more form of business partner. Tonight, the hotel was fairly quiet, full of suits and families, the lull before the Oscar storm. Juliette shook her head when Marta raised a vodka bottle in small salutation, and then glanced around for David; he wasn't there, so with a nod and a smile to the night doorman, she got in her car and headed home.

Juliette lived about twenty minutes away from the Pinnacle in the Hollywood Hills. The house was large and lovely, Spanish—"Early Screenwriter," Gregory had called it—with a walled-in front yard, a back veranda, and a swimming pool. Punching the security code into her gate, she was overwhelmed with the smell of jasmine. December had been warm this year, tricking many of the flowering plants into early blooms that would die in the next cold snap. Without turning on any lights, she headed up to the bedroom, her eyes straight ahead, her shoulders tense until she came to the master bedroom and turned on the light and relaxed. It had been more than a year since Josh left and still she hated coming home to this empty house, especially at night. He had taken very little when he had gone—"You can have everything," he said, his face pale and tight with his need to be away, his need to start his new life—and that had just made it worse. Juliette was left with all they had owned together, left in the house they had bought in the delirious first days in Los Angeles, when he had finally, finally sold a script, and the script had led to rewrite work, and then he sold another script and suddenly the bank accounts they had pored over so carefully for so many years doubled and trebled and overflowed with cash.

They had just celebrated their tenth wedding anniversary when *A Touch of Summer* began shooting, had just made the decision that it was time to have a baby. For so many years, Juliette had supported them and could not see how she could do what she did and have a baby too. But here he was with a shooting script and a development deal; it seemed like they would never have to worry about money again. They had fucked like beavers during the week before he left for location, hoping it might take the first time. They had kissed and kissed outside the terminal at LAX and then he got on a plane to Toronto and never came back.

Or at least Juliette's husband never came back. Josh Singer came back, after six weeks, nervous and thin, so bursting with emotion that he couldn't even wait until they were in the house to tell her; he broke the news in the car. He was in love with Anna Stewart, the star of the film, and wonder of wonders she was in love with him too. Juliette would never forget the look on his face when he told her, the hyper, twitching joy, as if he half expected Juliette to be happy for him, to exclaim over his good fortune that this British acting goddess, with her dark smudgy eyes and perfectly disheveled ringlets, had become his lover. He was so clearly thrilled by it all that he couldn't even summon the appropriate emotions—guilt, remorse, sorrow, even confusion—which left Juliette with nothing to do, really, but give him two hours to pack his shit and get the hell out of what had suddenly become her house.

"I want you to know, you can have everything," he said as he went. "The house, the furniture, whatever. I won't even get a lawyer. We can do it through arbiters. Because you deserve it, you really do."

Every word he said was like a bullet through her skull, shattering bone and brain, grinding her jaw into shards. For a month, Juliette walked around as if she had a concussion; it didn't seem real, it didn't seem possible. Not when she saw Josh and Anna holding hands in *People,* or being interviewed together at the premiere of the movie. Not even when Devlin took her to the opening of a sister resort in Cancún and tried to seduce her "just to get your mind off him." She and Josh had never been like that, never been temporary or distracted. Josh didn't even want to be a screenwriter; he wanted to be a novelist. When that didn't happen, he had taken a friend's advice and turned two of his much-rejected books into scripts, which, as it turned out, was what they really were. But Josh had always hated the entertainment industry, especially actors, hated any woman who made her way on looks and seduction; he loved being with Juliette, he said, because of the thoughts "that streaked like brilliant fish through her brain." That was what he said, more than once. Did Anna Stewart have brilliant fish streaking through her brain? Juliette thought not.

Now she was at least used to it, the sense of loss, the confusion. The fact that ordinary people occasionally lost their minds, along with their marriages and families, when in contact with fame and fortune was just another odd but predictable feature of the Los Angeles landscape. Like earthquake weather and fire season or the purple explosion of the jacaranda in June.

Pulling off her clothes and letting them drop to the floor— Josh had been a neat-freak and Juliette still delighted in this small freedom—she got into bed. "I have to sell this house," she said. "As soon as the Oscars are over, I am going to sell this house."

Turning off the light, she tried to not think of what she was waiting for. *A Touch of Summer* had picked up several Golden Globes—Best Actor, Best Director—and the odds were good that it would receive its share of Oscar nominations, including Best Actress and Best Original Screenplay. That would mean Josh would have to leave the safety of Anna's London home and come back to Los Angeles. At least for Oscar week. And during Oscar week, there was no avoiding the Pinnacle—the Brits had their big party there, the Writers Guild had its awards event there. Juliette had not seen her husband since that trip back from Toronto almost a year ago. She needed to see his face one more time. Then she would know what to do. Then she could let it all go.

3

Two days before the Oscar nominations, the Academy of Motion Picture Arts and Sciences had a luncheon for Bill Becker, the producer of this year's show. Becker was a former studio executive recently ousted by the company's board, who felt he was too free with the funds. The subsequent trial, in which he sued the board for wrongful termination and defamation and they countersued to retrieve his twenty-million-dollar separation package, kept the press busy for the few months in between the celebrity breakups and breakdowns. Becker somehow managed to keep hold of his golden parachute and immediately formed his own production company, snapping up, among other things, the rights to a first-time script by a hot blogger that had everyone buzzing. The story followed a writer who goes into seclusion after his teen-angst novel makes him a cult figure. When the project became public, J. D. Salinger sued. He lost, but Becker could not have asked for better publicity. The script was currently in rewrite and between that and Becker's bad-boy reputation, the Academy apparently felt he had enough sizzle to help the show's dwindling ratings.

Juliette had no idea if that would work or not—she had also heard rumors that Becker had used dirt he had collected on various high-profile Academy members throughout the years to snag what would undoubtedly be a "comeback" story that would play big in every media outlet.

What Juliette *did* know was that today the *Los Angeles Times* wanted to shoot Bill Becker standing, all 280 pounds of him, fully clothed but soaking wet, in the middle of the hotel's ten-foot-high fountain. To show just how unpredictable and madcap he was.

This required much more effort on the part of the photographer, and the stylist, and the groomer, and their assistants, than one would think. Becker himself seemed too busy achieving the perfect ratio of cream cheese and salmon to bagel while fingering his way through the pastry basket in search of a raspberry Danish "like the one I had here a few weeks ago" to bother getting his picture taken. His publicist nervously mentioned "carb points" and "fat points," dug in her purse for Becker's nicotine gum, which he managed to chew even as he ate, and made ineffectual suggestions that perhaps they should get started.

In answer to the photographer's anguished stare, Juliette stepped in and moved the food cart out of sight and arm's reach. "I'm just going to send this back to the kitchen for a freshen-up," Juliette said. "I know you must be incredibly busy, Mr. Becker. How can we help this go more smoothly? Do we need more towels, do you think?"

"What he needs is a couple of naked girls," said a voice right behind her. Juliette turned and smiled into the face of Max Diamond, the comic actor and one of her favorite guests. He had been gone for almost a year, doing a stint in a musical remake of *The Odd Couple.*

"Max," she said, embracing him. "It's so good to see you, it's been ages. How was New York? The play was a smash, of course."

"It was okay," Diamond said, kissing her neck. "Not great, but okay. I'm thinking of doing a one-man show, though, next fall. Like Billy Crystal did, only funnier. Maybe at the Taper or the Geffen. You think people would come to see me still?"

At sixty-five, Diamond still had the sweet face of an anxious teenager; his self-doubt seemed bottomless and perhaps even sincere. It also was an impenetrable defense that allowed him to say whatever he wanted about anything or anybody.

"In droves," Juliette said, meaning it.

He squeezed her hand. "This guy giving you trouble?" he asked, jerking his head toward Becker. Juliette allowed herself a small grimace.

"What are you waiting for, asshole?" Diamond shouted at Becker, with a wink at Juliette. "If you had any balls at all, you'd pee in that fountain. I dare you. I double-dare you. Whip it out, man, give the *Times* a picture worth printing for once."

"They'd have to use a wide-angle lens, motherfucker," Becker said, straightening himself up with a grin. The photographer began snapping furiously as the producer finally began to pose.

"You mean telephoto, don't you?"

Diamond snorted and turned back to Juliette, peering into her face. "How are you anyway? I heard what happened, that little shit. He's a hack. That movie of his is a piece of crap. And that girl? That girl tried to sleep with *me*, for chrissake, five years ago; remember she was in *The Stampede* with me and Anjelica? She couldn't even read her lines. You're better off, you know that, right? Of course you do. You should come out to the Malibu house with us some weekend. Say you'll do that, okay?"

"Okay," Juliette said, suppressing a smile. Over the years, she had been invited to Diamond's Malibu house, his house in the Hamptons, his apartment in Paris, and his yacht in Greece. But somehow little details like dates and addresses had never been filled in. "Are you here for the luncheon? Are you going to host this year?"

Max Diamond had hosted the Oscar ceremonies a legendary ten times, twice more than Billy Crystal. Every time, Max swore it would be his last, and he often took a year or two off, but he always came back, in part because no other host ever quite measured up.

"NO," he roared. "*Nein, neyet, non,* nonononono. I am done, through, kaput, finished. Never again. I told them. Never again. Do they listen? No, they don't, but I mean what I say. I'm too old for all this craziness. What, I still need to work that room for four freaking hours while Kate Winslet sits there tugging at her corset and Johnny Depp sneaks out in the middle of my opening for a cigarette? I don't think so. This year, I'm just going to watch from home. Someone else can worry about who's going to piss off the president or the censors. I'll be getting a nice blow job from my girlfriend. You hear that, Becker?" he shouted.

"I hear that, Diamond," the producer shouted back from the fountain as the stylist applied more glycerin to his hair. "Can we wrap this up?" he said to the photographer. "Because I don't know how long it's going to take to get this shit out of my hair."

"Just a few more," the photographer murmured from his crouch.

"It looks great, Bill," said the publicist, a young woman with long straight hair and a wide band of midriff showing. "Doesn't it?" she said, turning to Juliette and Max. "Doesn't it look great?"

"You need to put a sweater on or something," Diamond said,

looking at the waistline of the pants, which dipped below the young woman's hipbones and certainly required a bikini wax. "It's ten o'clock in the morning, for chrissake. Jesus. Here," he said, pulling off the blue cashmere V-neck he wore, revealing a black T-shirt stretched tight over a surprisingly impressive chest, "put this on and go buy yourself a real shirt. He's gotta be paying you enough so you can afford clothes that fit."

Juliette turned away so no one would see her laugh.

"So I hear you're attached to the Salinger project," she said, covering.

Max held up a finger. "Now, now, now," he said. "It has nothing to do with Salinger. Who is one of this country's finest writers and whom I would never in my life offend."

"Sorry," Juliette said with a grin. "I understand you are going to play a writer who bears no resemblance to J. D. Salinger. I heard that's why Becker bought the project in the first place."

Diamond gave a small shrug of false modesty. "There has been talk, there have been discussions. But it's early days yet." He leaned in and lowered his voice. "Frankly, I don't know if the sonofabitch can afford me. Hey, Becker," he said, pulling away and taking a few steps toward the fountain, "I'm coming in there with you." And while everyone, including the photographer and the stunned but now-sweatered publicist, laughed in shock, that's exactly what he did.

"Kiss me, you fat fool," Max said with a dead-on Groucho, gathering the producer into his arms. And as the photographer clicked away in delight, Becker chose photo-op over irritation and dunked the comedian playfully in the water.

Passing through the dining room, Juliette saw David Fulbright huddled over egg whites with his director; the young actor did not look happy.

45

Shit, Juliette thought, looking steadily and purposefully at her BlackBerry just in case he glanced up and saw her. It was one thing to be fired, it was another to be fired in public. Why had they been seated in the middle of the dining room? There were special tables the staff reserved for just such meetings, in corners, camouflaged by plants. La Guillotine I and La Guillotine II.

There was a movie junket on the tenth floor, which meant a procession of journalists from across the country slouching through the lobby, their eyes peeled for signs pointing them to the hospitality suite, where they would scarf up lunch and as many swag bags as the publicists would allow them to carry before crowding into a room to shout questions at "the talent"—the film's actors, director, and writer. Because most of the movies released during Oscar season were nonstarters, the crowd was small but irritating.

At the doorway to the kitchen stood a tall lovely woman with long black hair and wearing a pink linen dress. Juliette recognized her as Therese Salvatore, the young Colombian actress who was causing much conversation this year. Discovered in a fruit market, she had been cast as a young prostitute who is brought to New York essentially as barter material but who, through pluck and some really fortuitous plot points, winds up exposing and shutting down a sex slave ring. The film was a festival darling, and she had been nominated for a Golden Globe. She hadn't won, but still the studio had Oscar hopes and so they had installed her at the Pinnacle for almost two months.

Now she was chatting animatedly with the assistant room service manager. "We are from the same town," Therese said as Juliette drew closer. "I think our sisters, they know each other."

Juliette smiled and nodded and gently moved the actress

away from the door. "Ricardo is probably the busiest man in this hotel," she said as the assistant manager slid back into the kitchen. "But it is amazing how many people it turns out you actually know in this place."

"Only him so far," said Therese a little sadly. "This is a lovely hotel," she added quickly, "and everyone is very nice. But I feel like I have been here for so long and it is . . . lonely."

Juliette smiled and put her arm lightly around the young woman's shoulders. According to Gregory, she was on the "short list" of a recently divorced star in the market for a new wife, somewhere between Scarlett Johansson and Claire Danes. The star had indeed shown up at regular intervals in recent weeks, each time in another gorgeous vintage car and matching leather jacket. "But I think her good Catholic uncle is a drug lord or something," Gregory had said. "And he's let it be known she is not on the market."

The source being Gregory, Juliette wasn't sure she believed either part of this tale. What she did know was that Therese had never been to Los Angeles before and her handlers had essentially dumped her here; they only showed up when there was a party or a press event.

"Let me talk to Ricardo," Juliette said. "He must be due for some time away from here. Why don't we get you a car and he can take you around the city? Go down to Long Beach, even, see the aquarium or the *Queen Mary*. You could go out to Catalina or just down to Manhattan Beach."

Therese's eyes lit up. "I would like that," she said. "I do not like to be alone so much."

Unable to resist, Juliette raised an eyebrow. "Alone? What, don't you like guys who collect antique cars?"

She felt the actress stiffen, and a sincere smile slid over her face like a mask, disguising, what? Anger? Fear?

"I have made many very good friends in the past few months," Therese said with a laugh that echoed a hundred press junkets. "I feel very fortunate. It is just nice to connect with someone from my . . . old life."

Juliette nodded and gave the girl a reassuring squeeze around her shoulders. As she walked toward her office, her cell phone rang; it was Devlin. "I've got Russell Crowe and Colin Farrell on their way in tomorrow. They arrive at around nine p.m. Together. I want you to meet them. Nah-ah-ah," he murmured as she began to point out that there was a whole group of people whose job it was to settle guests into their rooms. "I want someone on hand to make sure that those two don't burn the hotel to the ground. And don't let Crowe throw a television at room service."

"Telephone," Juliette corrected him. "He threw a telephone. At an assistant manager. But that was ages ago."

"Whatever. The movie is hot, I'm pleased they're having the junket here, but I want my telephones to remain stationary."

"On the day before nominations? God, Dev, I'll be dead by nine p.m."

"Listen to her, the only woman in the world who would whine about spending an hour with two of *People*'s Sexiest Ten. Ask them to massage your feet. I'm sure they'll oblige."

"If it's such a plum, why don't you ask Louisa? I'm sure she'd be happy to accommodate."

There was a brief pause. "Louisa?" Devlin asked as if she had suggested one of the housekeepers, and for a moment Juliette felt a twinge of sympathy for the concierge and hoped that Louisa didn't love Devlin in any real sort of way.

"Well, why don't you meet them, then?" she asked, suddenly irritated on Louisa's behalf, and even more irritated at herself for caring what the woman thought at all. "You can all smoke cigars together and rank the girls in the bar . . ."

"I would. I would. But I am"—Devlin's voice tripped into an uncharacteristic falter—"otherwise engaged. Just settle them in, Juliette. How difficult could it be?"

Difficult enough that you're not asking the people whose job it is to do it, Juliette thought, lengthening her stride across the lobby. Maybe it was time for her to move on. Maybe, Juliette thought, she was finding an end to these years. Jesus, she thought, this was great timing; smack in the middle of the busiest weeks of the year and here she was contemplating burnout. *Breathe deep,* she reminded herself, *pace yourself.* The year before, Gregory had given them all T-shirts around this time that read: LIFE IS SHORT, OSCAR SEASON IS LONG. She needed to find that shirt.

Passing the small waiting area outside the patio restaurant, she nodded a greeting to two burly men seated uneasily on a delicate-looking divan. They were the security detail for a studio executive who regularly held his meetings in the hotel. Mutt and Jeff, staff members called them. Everyone was too intimidated to communicate with them beyond a nod and a smile—the men looked like mob consultants for *The Sopranos.* One of them even had what Juliette was fairly certain was a cauliflower ear. Stopping to check on a seating arrangement for the Academy luncheon, she had almost forgotten they were there until she heard them speak.

"I don't speak to you in that tone, Douglass," said Mutt to Jeff in an injured voice. "I don't see why you have to speak to me in that tone."

From the corner of her eye, she could see Jeff stiffen. "You really are the limit, you know," he said, standing suddenly. "I can't even be here right now." And he strode off.

A wild gulp of laughter rose in her throat. Seriously, she thought, how could she ever work anywhere else?

"So what else do you do to prepare for the big night?" Michael asked her later that evening.

"Lift weights," she said. "Go into psychotherapy. Drink a lot and have indiscriminate sex. Because for four weeks, this hotel owns our very souls."

She had brought him a plate of risotto and a dish of chocolate pudding to replace the bland doctor-recommended meal that she could not believe even came from their kitchen. While he struggled to eat it, she told him some of the revelations of the Oscar Season Summit and the tale of Phillip's attempt to keep the software skeleton alive on his watch—at the suggestion of the pastry chef, he had lately added ground pecans and brown sugar to her oat bran, and crème fraîche to her lowfat yogurt, telling her that it was just a little Splenda and cinnamon.

It was eleven p.m. The room was dim and warm. From the adjoining bedroom, she could hear Rory snoring softly. Michael rolled his eyes. "What else?" he said, taking a bite of food. "Besides ordering extra champagne and caviar."

"And towels and sheets and lamps and bathrobes and curtains and hair dryers."

Michael raised an eyebrow and Juliette laughed. "I don't know what it is about fame that turns you people into kleptos, but we never see so much stuff walk out the door as we do during Oscar week. Last year, one guest, who shall remain nameless though you do know her, intimately, packed up her sheets, her comforter, and her bedspread. And when we added the cost to her bill, her assistant called us in a snit and said that she had been asked, specifically, what colors and fabrics her boss had liked and so had assumed these items were part of the welcome package. Right along with the fruit and complimentary pedicure."

"You are shitting me," O'Connor said. "I know exactly who you are talking about—little Miss Let's Save East Africa, one resort at a time—and you are shitting me. Took the bedspread. Oh, my Lord. Did she leave the curtains? Or send them out to her dressmaker to be turned into her Oscar gown?"

"Wouldn't surprise me," Juliette said. "Did you see what she wore to the Golden Globes? I didn't think they made that shade of yellow anymore."

"I did, and it was not yellow," he said. "It was yell-er. Pure yeller. And she probably dreamed of that dress all her young trailer-park-challenged life."

Juliette snorted and she put her hand to her mouth. "Oh, God," she said. "Dev would fire me if he heard me talking like this. I would fire me if I heard me talking like this. I don't know why I said that. A lovely woman, really, a generous woman and one of our finest actors." Michael hooted and leaned back against the pillows. Juliette fixed him with a sideways glance. "You know what?" she said, looking at his flushed cheeks, his ready grin. "I don't think you look sick at all. I am wondering if this isn't a setup entirely."

"Don't worry," he said. "I'll be getting another treatment soon and then I'll be plenty sick for you. They let me get just well enough to feel human and then they strike me down again. But right now," he said, "I feel wonderful. Just wonderful. And I really like that lamp," he added, motioning toward the corner. "Could you box that up for me when I go?"

Juliette shook her head, laughing, and got to her feet. "I have to go," she said. "Tomorrow's a big day and it starts at five a.m."

"You could sleep on the pullout," O'Connor said. "And we could watch the nominations announced together. Just think of how romantic it would be. I heard Diamond was in the hotel today; is he hosting this year?"

"He says no."

"As he says every year."

"I think he means it."

"As he does every year. Oh, well, he probably does. He's even older than I am and God knows I'm sick of it, and I've actually won the damn thing."

"He could still win," Juliette said defensively. She felt very maternal toward Max. "This Salinger movie sounds like it's got awards potential."

"Harken to her," O'Connor said. "Devlin said you're so good at picking winners you're not allowed to even enter the Pinnacle Oscar pool."

"I have a certain talent," Juliette conceded.

"So what odds do you give *Bluebird* for a nomination?" he asked, peering up at her sharply. She opened her mouth, then shut it again; O'Connor's latest performance had not been, in her opinion, one of his best. "Never mind," he said, waving his words away. "Just remember, Max Diamond is no pussycat. I know two directors who named their first heart attacks after him—he may have mellowed with age, but back in the day, he was a holy terror."

"I don't believe it," Juliette said; she had heard the rumors about Max's early career, about the drinking and the bar fights, the vendettas that played out for years, but they did not jibe with the Max she knew.

O'Connor shrugged. "Keep in mind that the man has had more wives than even I have." He leaned back against the pillow as if suddenly exhausted. "Well, we're none of us angels, are we? Just next time you see Max, tell him to sign the Salinger deal already? Becker keeps bugging me to read it."

"Have you?" Juliette asked, suddenly curious; rumor had it, the script had been through the hands of some of the best writers in town, all of whom had been sworn to secrecy.

"How can I?" he asked. "According to my agent, I'm booked through 2010, and anyway, I'm in Morocco if you haven't noticed."

Juliette laughed. Swiftly checking to see that her cell phone, BlackBerry, and notebook were all in their proper places, she turned to go.

"Juliette," O'Connor called softly just as she reached the door, and something about those consonants made her shiver. "I am feeling better," he said when she turned. "Could you arrange for the pool to be closed sometime day after tomorrow? I'd like to take a swim before the next treatment. If," he added softly, "it's not too much trouble."

The very day nominations were announced he wanted her to close the pool. "Shall I fill it with rose petals?" she almost snapped but in the golden light, he looked sincere and almost sad. *What a strange thing this is,* she thought, her shoulders sagging, though she wasn't sure what precisely she was referring to.

"I'm sure we can arrange that, Mr. O'Connor," she said.

4

And so, at a little past midnight, after a day filled with Oscar nomination madness, Juliette knelt on the roof of the Pinnacle Hotel in Los Angeles, tugging at the foot of a man who lay suspended in the gentle blue waters of its pool. As the body bumped the side, she saw long dark hair fan out around the head like a halo. *No,* she thought. *No. No. No. No.* Kneeling, her skin scraped raw against the concrete, she managed to scoop one shoulder up so the man's face was lifted from the water and then the scream, the real true scream she should have let loose about five minutes ago, began its siege against her throat. It was David Fulbright, his handsome face pale and strangely peaceful. She felt for a pulse in his neck, found nothing. His skin was warm, but of course it would be; the pool was heated. Why would someone kill David? She could see crimson staining the white shirt where the jacket drifted open—no point in mouth-to-mouth even if she could get him out of the water herself, which she couldn't.

From across the terrace, she heard a door open and close and she could see an outline at the edge of the light, tall and angular, moving slowly, carefully. *Michael. Christ,* she thought, letting David's body slide back into the water, face up this time, and hurrying over to where O'Connor was standing.

"What the hell?" he said as he took in the floodlit tableau, her damp clothes.

"It's David," she said, taking his arm, drawing him away, out of the light, back into the safety of the hotel. "Someone's shot him, I think. I don't know, he was floating in the water when I came up here, just floating." Her voice was growing high and tight with hysteria. "Can you believe it? Can you fucking believe it? We've got a floater. On the day of the Oscar nominations." Realizing exactly how terrible that last sentence sounded, she shut her mouth with a snap.

O'Connor put his hands on her shoulders, dug his fingers in hard, and shook her. "Juliette," he said quietly. "Settle down. Did you call the police?"

"The police?" she said. "Are you crazy? I called security. They should be here any minute. Oh, my God," she said, seeing Michael finally, gaunt and unsteady in his white robe. "You need to get out of here, get back to your room."

Just as she spoke, there was the sound of the door at the far side of the pool opening, the light clatter of high heels followed by a series of screams. "He's dead, oh, my God, he's dead," said one woman loudly as a throng of partygoers, the women in glamorous gowns, the men in tuxedos, pushed their way into the pool area. Right behind them swarmed a cluster of photographers; the flashes glinted and gleamed like sudden bursts of lightning. The women clutched at each other, the men smote their brows and tried to pull David out of the water, while, oh, dear God, Juliette couldn't believe it, a man with a video camera captured it all.

How had they all gotten up here? Juliette wondered. She had asked Dog to close off the pool area himself to ensure

Michael's privacy. Who were they? She didn't think there was a party going on in the hotel tonight; she certainly would have noticed a group of people who looked like they had just stepped out of the Coconut Grove. And where was Dog? She had called him minutes ago.

Along the two side towers of the hotel that rose beside the rooftop pool, lights went on and French doors banged open and guests began appearing on terraces, their faces hanging concerned and curious over the rails. Torn between caring for the sick man and trying to contain what she realized was probably an uncontainable situation, Juliette took a deep breath and pushed the actuality of the dead man out of her mind, turning the event into a simple problem of logistics. If she didn't get the press out of here, Devlin would kill her. Juliette steered Michael to a lounge in a dark quiet corner. "I'm sorry," she said, pushing him down onto a chaise.

"Please," she said calmly, walking over to two of the photographers and grabbing them by the shoulders, "no photographers in the pool area." Even to her own ears it sounded absurd, given the circumstances, but the men seemed to obey. Then, over the keening of the women, she heard murmured male voices, and footsteps spilled across the walkway toward the pool.

She hurried toward the pool, where three police officers were tugging David's body out of the water; two paramedics appeared out of nowhere, pushing a gurney. The photographers went wild, but the crowd began to disperse.

"Ma'am, I'm Detective Cassidy and this is my partner, Detective Kidd. Are you the one who discovered the victim?"

Detective Cassidy was tall and broad, with a handlebar mustache and a backwoods accent, as handsome as any TV cop she had ever seen. "Yes," she said. "Yes, I came up here to . . .

check on things, and there he was. I pulled him toward me—he was floating face down at first. But then I . . . I heard something and went over to see if someone was there, but he wasn't. I mean . . . no one was there. Who called you anyway?" she asked, as the man took notes into a tiny notebook and the two paramedics heaved David onto a gurney. "I didn't have a chance to call the police."

"We got a call about fifteen minutes ago that there was a gunshot heard up here, followed by a splash. One of the guests called, I assume," said Cassidy. "Not rocket science to figure out what happened. And here we are. Did you know the deceased?" he asked, as another man appeared, this one in a trench coat with a camera and a tape measure who proceeded to take pictures of the pool and the corpse and to measure the depth of the water.

"It's six feet," Juliette told him. "At this end, it's six feet."

The man in the coat blinked and Detective Cassidy cleared his throat. "Did you know the deceased?" he asked again.

"Yes," Juliette said, drawing her professional persona around her. Out of the corner of her eye, she saw Dog finally emerge from the hotel. He came up quietly and stood behind her. "His name is, was, David Fulbright. He was, is, a guest at the hotel. An actor."

"What's happened here, Officer?" Dog asked, taking in the now-sheeted figure on the stretcher.

"Looks like someone's shot one of your guests," said Cassidy with a small tight smile, as he flipped his notebook closed. "Can I get business cards from both of you?" he asked. The paramedics were rolling David toward the main elevator. Both Juliette and Dog leapt to stop them.

"Right this way," Dog said firmly, steering them toward the service elevator, which would lead them down to a back entrance. "If you would call your driver and tell him to pull into the alley behind the hotel. We don't want to disturb any of the other guests."

Hearing his words, Juliette looked up; on at least a dozen of the balconies overlooking the pool, people stood. As she watched, someone's flash went off. *Shit!* she thought. She glanced over to where O'Connor sat but could see nothing in the darkness except a small pinprick of light. He was smoking. *Unbelievable*, she thought, *cancer and he's smoking.* Again laughter threatened, but as she watched the men maneuver the shrouded figure through the elevator doorway, it died. Part of her wanted to follow David down, as if he were still alive. Dog gave her a little wave and she nodded; he would make sure things went as smoothly as they possibly could. She looked up again at the balconies. People were beginning to drift back into their rooms. Both her phone and her BlackBerry began buzzing as if on cue; the front desk must be freaking out, she thought. But first she would have to get O'Connor back into the hotel somehow, and soon—he was only wearing trunks and a robe and the breeze had gained a little heft, turned cold.

"Ma'am," said the detective as she handed him her card. "We'll be in touch." And then they were all gone, leaving Juliette again in silence, wondering at the brevity of it all. She looked around for the women who had initially screamed, in hopes of talking them down from spreading what they had seen, but they too were gone. Strangely, everyone was gone. Murder scenes seemed very different in the movies. But then this was real life. A real-life nightmare. Making her way across the terrace, she hit the speed-dial button for Dev. Wherever he was, whatever he was doing, his night, like hers, had just taken a turn for the worse.

*

A guest had apparently gone for an unexpected late-night swim and, being perhaps a little merrier than usual, had miscalculated a dive and hit his head. He was taken to the hospital, where his condition was not yet known.

This was the story Juliette and Devlin crafted in about five minutes and relayed to the front desk, Louisa, Gregory, the head of room service, and every staff member they could get in touch with at one in the morning. This was what Juliette told the local television crew and *Daily News* reporter who showed up, breathlessly investigating rumors and images that were somehow already all over the Internet. This was what Juliette quickly wrote in response to an item, complete with images, that showed up on several Hollywood gossip blogs within minutes of the police leaving.

"Look," she said at around 2 a.m. "Defamer says someone was found dead at the Griffith Observatory. And," she said, double-clicking, "TMZ is reporting a shooting at the Sky Bar." She turned around in her chair. "But there's nothing on latimes.com or MSNBC. What the hell is happening?"

"No doubt we will find out soon enough," Devlin said grimly; he had already called in extra security. "Right now we have our own fire to fight."

When the last seemingly frantic but mostly curious guest had been calmed, the two of them sat in Devlin's office and waited. For follow-up calls from the police, for more television camera crews, the metro reporters, the Hollywood press. Juliette called David's publicist and then his agent, but neither answered and Devlin's phone remained silent.

"Something's not right," said Juliette as an hour passed, then two, and nothing had happened.

"Maybe the angels are smiling on us," said Devlin. He had seemed momentarily stunned by the news of David's death, but that was quickly consumed by his strategies for damage control—a dead actor in the pool was not exactly good for business.

"Jesus, Dev," Juliette said, pushing his head off her lap. At some point she had collapsed, exhausted and shaky, onto the sofa. Comforting her, Devlin had automatically begun his effective, if a bit distracted, methods of foreplay, which she just as automatically declined. But somehow he wound up lying with his head in her lap anyway.

"Sorry," he said, struggling to a sitting position. "Sorry. I know how much you liked him. Me too. What a terrible thing, a terrible thing. But we have to be prepared. Too many people depend on us, after all."

Juliette couldn't even bring herself to reply to the sanctimonious look or the first-person plural.

"It just seems strange we haven't gotten a call from the *Times*," she said. "Or AP. I don't know how those pictures got on the Internet so quickly. Or why they looked so much like a fashion shoot. Didn't you think that was weird?"

Devlin shrugged. "I don't know. I am just holding my breath that it somehow blows over. Maybe somebody truly important died somewhere else and we just haven't heard."

"All the same, it seems very strange." She stretched and looked out the window; the light was pale and halfhearted. "I guess I'll go home, maybe get some sleep, and change," she said, glancing over at her boss, who was now standing shirtless in front of his closet in which three or four dark suits hung. He grinned at her and she had to admit that there was a legitmate reason Louisa and half of the Pinnacle's female clientele had a crush on her boss—Eamonn Devlin certainly stripped well.

"Don't bother," he said, opening the other side of the closet to reveal an assortment of women's clothing—his famous "morning after" supply. "I'm sure you can find something in here," he said with a wink.

"I worry about you," she said, pushing aside a short leather skirt, a gauzy gold dress, and fingering a pale silk sweater she suspected had been chosen just for her. "It's all going to catch up with you someday."

"Ah," he said, expertly knotting his tie. "By then I'll be too old to care."

"I wouldn't be too upset," said Michael, when she stopped in to check on him before she left. He was lying in his bed while Rory moved around him, setting up the various bags and tubes that would administer the chemotherapy and the machines that would monitor its impact.

Juliette stared at him. Was he really that self-centered? "Why not?" she said sharply. "A man is dead, for God's sake. David Fulbright is dead. And someone killed him. Someone who might still be in this hotel."

"Someone who might be in this very room," Michael added dramatically. "You know what they say—in the majority of cases, the one who found the body turns out to be the murderer. Did he spurn your advances? Or take a part in your ex's next picture?"

"It isn't funny," she said, not bothering to watch her tone. She went over the scene beside the pool in her head—the detective hadn't even bothered to question her all that much. Surely that was strange.

"There was something about that cop that seemed familiar," she said almost to herself. "I wonder if he's stayed here before."

"Cops can't afford these rack rates," O'Connor said. "Maybe

your crime-ridden past is catching up to you." He shut his eyes and waved her away. "Now go away while I am slowly poisoned to death." Juliette opened her mouth, closed it again. She was suddenly so tired her eyes felt grainy and her hands were numb, suddenly so tired that nothing seemed quite real and everything made sense, sort of.

"What are you doing anyway?" she asked. "I thought your treatment was tomorrow."

O'Connor didn't open his eyes. "Well, since I didn't get my swim I thought I might as well get started."

Juliette stared; she couldn't think of a thing to say so she turned to go.

"Wait," O'Connor ordered, turning his face toward her. "Come kiss me. For good luck."

Obediently, she lowered her face toward his, grazed his lips with hers. His breath was sweet and minty; a tin of the Pinnacle mints was open on the night table. "Don't you worry, my Juliette," he said softly in her ear. "It will all come out right in the end."

Then he waved her away, nodded to Rory, and closed his eyes.

"Commence countdown," he said as the nurse opened the IV drip.

On the drive home, Juliette imagined herself falling right into bed; the adrenaline of the evening had worn off, and she felt limp and wrung out. The actual events, which for several hours had swirled into a brew of anxiety and shock and fear, now lay separate and startling in her mind: David's body suspended in the foggy blue, the pallor of his face, the blood on his shirt, the women screaming, then vanishing—had the police managed to talk to them? She couldn't remember—Michael's calm silence as she helped him back to his room; Devlin's stunned, and stunning, efficiency.

Her ears ringing, she wandered around the house, touching things—the pitcher she and Josh bought in Siena, the photos of the High Crosses Josh had taken at Monesterboice in Ireland, the candlesticks she had found in a shop in Barcelona. No matter how poor they had been, she and Josh had always traveled; her connections meant they always had free or cheap lodgings and they were happy to bike or walk if they couldn't afford the car rental, the train ticket. Happy. They were happy. For so many goddamn years, they had been happy. Would she ever feel anything like that again? She remembered the bubble of delight that rose in her belly when she was talking to David Fulbright, how much she enjoyed hearing his voice, seeing his animated face. And now he was dead. It seemed ridiculous, impossible.

She hadn't seen him that day—the Oscar nominations eclipsed everything. She, Devlin, and Gregory had spent most of the day on the phone with publicists, calling in favors and pitching packages that would draw the nominees to the Pinnacle. A few surprises sent them scrambling—a small film about a pair of elderly bird-watchers was nominated for Best Picture and Best Director and no one had any idea who the contacts were; Eddie Izzard, the transvestite comedian, whom Juliette and everyone at the hotel adored, was up for Best Actor, which meant convincing the studio that usually stuck with the Peninsula to switch. And, of course, *A Touch of Summer* got the nod for Best Picture, Director, Actor, Actress, Screenplay. Devlin had kindly suggested that everyone would understand if she wanted to "release" the talent to the Beverly Hills Hotel, but she didn't even let him finish his sentence. "That would be even worse—Josh sleeping with another woman *and* in another hotel. I'm fine," she said to her boss, and for a moment she believed it.

But amid all the insanity, she hadn't had a chance to talk with Fulbright. The night before, she had seen him in the bar. He had told her it was official, he was off the film, but he seemed all right about it. His agent had him lined up to fly to New York to meet with Woody Allen, who was planning to shoot another movie in London in the spring. Juliette had sent a bottle of champagne up to his room with a note saying, *Woody Allen wins Oscars,* but she hadn't seen him since. She tried to remember where the blood had been coming from, his chest it had seemed, a person couldn't shoot himself in the chest, could he? But who would kill David Fulbright? And how could whoever it was do it without anyone seeing or hearing anything? Dog had just double-checked the pool area for her. Hadn't he?

Standing in front of the refrigerator, Juliette ate three containers of yogurt before finally climbing into bed. Just before she slept, she remembered the feeling of Devlin's lips on her neck. Not even a murder could shake Dev—seduction was his default setting, that's why he was such a good hotelier and precisely what kept her from getting too close to him. He was dangerous in his own way, as were most men of great charm. As she had reminded Josh time and again during that year of endless meetings with directors and producers and actors, charm is just a form of enchantment, a blurring of reality. It was almost always accompanied by an equal measure of ruthlessness. Devlin was charming but would stop short of nothing to preserve his hotel. Michael was charming and fighting as much for his career as his life. David was charming and now he was dead. What reality had he been trying to blur?

At last she slept, though uneasily. Caught in a dream in

which she and David were lost at sea, adrift on a hospital bed, Juliette managed to get about two hours' sleep before both her cell phone and landline rang. Simultaneously. "How do you do that?" she murmured, hitting the speakerphone by the bed.

"It was a Mother of God fucking publicity stunt," said Devlin's voice, as hoarse and Irish as she had heard it in a while. She sat up.

"What are you talking about?"

"When you come in, drive down La Brea. And come in now."

Dipping down from Sunset toward Third, she saw it, rising above a nail salon and a Subway—a billboard plastered with a photo of David Fulbright, soaking wet, blood staining his shirtfront, his face arranged in a sexy sideways glower. Beside him ran the words: ON SUNDAY, FEBRUARY 26, WE WILL RAISE THE DEAD. In the bottom right-hand corner was the little gold statue—the trademarked image of the Academy Awards.

5

"There were 'murders' all over town," said Devlin, who had been waiting for her in the lobby, chatting with guests and generally providing an image of unruffled and, perhaps more important, complicit good humor. "We got off easy," he said, steering her into one of the small private dining rooms where coffee and breakfast waited for them, "because you closed off the pool. So the only people who saw David dead were the ringers. Oh, yes"—he nodded—"all those people were part of the act. Elsewhere, things occurred on a much more public level. Three guys were machine-gunned at the Sky Bar, a woman was found stabbed multiple times in the spa at the Peninsula, there was even a guy who staggered into a restaurant in Chinatown with his nose slit." Juliette looked at him sharply and he twisted up a smile. "Film murders. We were either *Sunset Boulevard* or *The Great Gatsby*, depending on who you ask."

Now Devlin's face was pale, with fatigue and something even more unfamiliar—anxiety. Bill Becker had called him a few minutes after Juliette left last night, laughing as if Devlin had been in on the joke even as Becker explained it. Twenty famous cinematic murders had taken place all over Los Angeles the night before—well, nineteen; the scene from *The Birds* didn't work out at all—the birds just flew away, leaving a Tippi Hedren look-alike screaming on the Santa Monica pier at nothing.

"But the cops," Juliette said.

Devlin shook his head. "Weren't cops. Actors."

Juliette swore. "That's why that guy looked so familiar. But how did the real cops let them get away with it?"

In most cases, Devlin explained, the fake cops showed up before the real ones were called. But Becker had assured Dev—"as if this would make me feel better, mind you"—that the new police chief, recently arrived from Chicago, had been in on it from the start. Becker had somehow convinced him that what was good for the Oscars was good for L.A., and promised him and his wife a seat between Charlize Theron and Warren Beatty. Some of the newspapers and TV stations had been tipped too. "Becker said he wanted to 'do the responsible thing,' didn't want to cause widespread panic," Devlin said. "He assured the chief that all the 'venues' involved were more than happy to be part of the project. Which might have been the case if the sonofabitch had bothered to let any of us in on it. I was on the phone with Francoise at the Polo Lounge—they had a poisoning—and Richard Mac at Molly Mallone's. Poor Mac, he had some guy come staggering in, bleeding all over the place, and saying, 'Frankie, your mother forgives me.' They're both just beside themselves."

"So what did you say?"

Devlin shrugged and rolled his eyes. "What could I say? *Entertainment Tonight* was on its way over, the *Times* was on the phone, and we've got personal assistants having meltdowns all over the country, stars wondering what the hell is going on. I laughed and told him what a brilliant stunt it was and thanked him for including the Pinnacle. It was rather brilliant," he conceded grudgingly. "'The Hoax of the Century,' they're calling it all over the Internet. There's about four dozen roses in your office from Fulbright," he added. "I think he feels really bad you found him—I guess there was a whole shooting scene we missed because you closed the pool. Then they sent those girls up to find him and make a fuss, maybe bring some guests in. Fortunately"—he smiled warmly at her—"my J. was on hand to keep things contained. What were you doing up there anyway? Why was the pool closed?"

Juliette explained. Devlin groaned. "Brilliant. God. Did O'Connor survive?"

Juliette narrowed her eyes. "He wasn't fazed at all. That sonofabitch," she said, realizing he had let her run around like a crazy person, let her feel all those horrible feelings, and the best he could do was tell her it would be all right in the end. "He knew."

"As did we all," said Devlin. "Send out a memo to the entire staff and don't let anyone talk to anyone until they've memorized it. Officially as of this moment, the Pinnacle staff was in on it from the start."

"It's all about the ratings," Gregory explained later that day. "Apparently the network told the Academy that if they didn't see at least a five percent rise this year, they were going to cut the show down to two hours, with a half hour for arrivals."

"They always say that," said Juliette.

"Yes, well, this year they meant it, apparently. Which would mean only the above-the-line talent would get their awards on television. Which would mean all sound editors and cinematographers and costume designers would be downgraded to technical status. Which would wind up with the unions up in the face of the Academy and picketers at the Oscars."

"So what's a few murders, then, between friends?" said Juliette. She looked at the room director sharply. "Did you know?"

"Honey, if I'd known," he drawled, "I would have made sure David Fulbright was buck naked and you would have been forced to give him mouth-to-mouth."

Juliette punched him in the shoulder.

"You're too cool by half," she said. "I think it was a ridiculous thing to do. They're just lucky no one had a heart attack."

"It's just the beginning," he said, lowering his voice. "Becker has promised a ten percent ratings hike or he will personally pay the network a hundred thousand for each point it falls short. He's bringing in all the big guns—people are saying he's convinced Woody Allen to accept the Thalberg, that Paul McCartney's playing, or Sting, that Paul Newman and Joanne Woodward will present together. He's going to announce the host tomorrow, and the money is on Forrest Hughes."

"Jesus," said Juliette. "I can't believe Forrest Hughes would agree to host the Oscars. It's far too beneath him. And it doesn't pay."

Gregory shrugged. "He says he's been wanting to get back to his 'comedy club roots.' And he's gotta do something to get back in everyone's good graces; he's one bomb away from being box office poison."

"His comedy club roots, yeah, I can see that," Juliette said sarcastically. "And I can see the censors having a field day. The guy doesn't know how to make a joke that doesn't involve at least three 'cunt's, sixteen 'fuck's, and a 'faggot.' Which," she said, "doesn't even make sense."

Gregory shrugged. "Becker just pretended to murder nineteen people. I don't think he's going to be swayed by the network censors. Although," he added, his eyelids drooping, "at times I think the censors are the only people with any real power in this town. They're the only ones still capable of saying the word 'no.'"

Bill Becker had accomplished one thing. He had managed to outshine the actual nominations in the media—"and when you can push a transvestite nominated for Best Actor off the front page, you've entered a whole new level of media whoredom," said Gregory. The murder stunt was the only thing anyone was talking about, from Larry King to the girls pushing latte at Starbucks. People were shocked, horrified, amused, outraged, gratified. People thought the Oscars were a joke, sacrosanct, overblown, meaningless, the epitome of Hollywood insanity/glamour. The *L.A. Times* quickly put together a five-part series on the economics of awards season with a history of network coverage and mini-profiles of all involved in the stunt, while *The New York Times* just had an L.A.-bashing field day. "But Can They Fake an Earthquake!" ran the headline of one editorial.

In less than three days, Devlin, Juliette, and Gregory managed to speak with each of the 350 nominees, presenters, or other Oscar-related celebrities who was a confirmed or potential guest of the hotel, assuring them that "the stunt" had been all in good fun and promised a very exciting awards season. Halfway through the first day, they all began to believe it. When she started getting envious calls from hotels that had been murder-free, Juliette realized that Hollywood had outdone itself.

"The Beverly Regent is furious," said Devlin as they passed

in the lounge, "and I heard that Wolfgang Puck spent a half hour screaming at Becker—he's catered the Governor's Ball for years now and none of his restaurants were picked."

By the end of the day, it was clear those commercial venues that had been scenes of the murders were leapfrogging up the A-list, and the actors who participated were filling the late-night couches and posing for the covers of *Time* and *Newsweek*. Devlin had somehow assumed the mantle of venue spokesman; reporters from all around the world were calling him and he was soon recounting the events as if he had been there, as if it had all been his idea because, of course, "the Pinnacle is the heartbeat of awards season."

Juliette refused to answer the seventeen phone messages she got from David Fulbright—she hadn't decided if she could ever forgive him for the hours of horror and fear, even if it had not been part of the original plan. She disposed of the roses he sent by having them delivered to O'Connor's room, with the original note. She was convinced that Michael had known exactly what was going on. Still, when she got a call from Rory asking her to come by before she left for the evening, she went. As it was way past dinnertime, she knocked softly and was surprised when Rory told her to come in.

"He's pretty doped up," the nurse said, ushering her into the dim room. Michael lay motionless on the bed. "But I know he wanted to see you. Can I get you something? Coffee? A sand-wich?"

Juliette shook her head, taken by surprise that someone was offering her something for once. "I'm good," she said.

"You're better than good," said a low voice from the bed. "Thank you for my flowers. I've never had roses from a corpse before, though the irony did not escape me. Irony can be fatal, you know, in certain cases."

"Everything can be fatal," said Juliette. "In certain cases. Why didn't you tell me? You knew that night, why didn't you just tell me?"

"I didn't *know*. I *suspected*." He looked at the anger in her eyes, and even perhaps the hurt, and laughed. "Oh, come on, it was so unbelievably stagey. Who would kill that kid? He's done nothing worth being murdered for, unless you count that western—Brits should never attempt Texan. So someone lured him up to the pool for an after-hour assignation and shot him down? Or did you think he had killed himself?"

Juliette flushed. "He had just gotten booted off his film," she said defensively.

Michael laughed and tried to sit, but collapsed in the attempt. Juliette moved to help him and he pushed her away. "Anyone kills themselves for getting fired from a picture deserves to be dead. People get fired all the time. I got fired from *Rain Man*—Tom Cruise and Dustin Hoffman as brothers. With what? A thirty-year age difference? Please."

"Well, I can see you're feeling okay," Juliette said evenly. "You're talking about yourself again."

"And I will continue to do so until something more interesting appears. Which does not include David Fulbright doing *Sunset Boulevard*."

"Or *The Great Gatsby*."

"Trust me, it was *Sunset Boulevard*. Who would you rather sleep with? Bill Holden or Redford?"

"Well, since one of them is dead . . . and what do you have against Redford? He can't have beat you out of a role."

"*The Horse Whisperer*."

"Big loss," Juliette said. "Sounds like Hollywood Alzheimer's—forget everything but the grudge."

"And yet, of the two of us, I was the one with enough

presence of mind to know that the police never move the corpse before the detectives arrive. Don't you watch *CSI*?"

"The Hilton and the Bel Air have a lock on the Emmys," Juliette said automatically. "So I don't watch television."

"Well, fuck me." O'Connor looked at her with a mixture of admiration and concern. "When I get better, I am going to take you to Majorca or somewhere. You are in serious danger of taking this much too seriously. I didn't tell you, my Juliette, because I wasn't sure."

As he finished his sentence, O'Connor grew even paler and Juliette could see the shine of sweat on his face. His voice suddenly lowered to a whisper. "Can you get Rory, oh, Christ, can you hand me . . ." Just before he began to vomit, Juliette figured out what he wanted and was able to grab the plastic basin from the nightstand and hold it in place. "I'm sorry," he said as he vomited again and again. Juliette shook her head and kept her eyes on the seascape painting on the opposite wall. One hand hovered over him. Pity welled up in her and she so wanted to touch him, his shoulder or the back of his neck, to comfort him like you would a child. But something told her he would not welcome that sort of physical contact, so she willed herself into what she called visible invisibility, a talent she had perfected over the years: *I am a pillar, I am a plant, I am that painting on the wall,* she thought.

Finally, Rory appeared from the next room and took the basin from her; she went into the bathroom and got a warm, wet washcloth, which she handed to the nurse. She moved away from the bed, carefully examining the roses she had sent up, plucking a brown leaf there, an overblown petal here. When Michael was once again lying flat, she drew nearer and smiled down at him.

"I should let you get some sleep," she said.

"No," he groaned. "I can't sleep when I feel like this." Rory appeared again, with a can of Coke that he fed to Michael carefully through a straw. "Talk to me," the actor said after he had taken a sip. "We never had a chance to discuss the most important thing that happened yesterday, the undeserved nomination of those associated with *A Taste of Summer.*"

"*A Touch of Summer,*" Juliette corrected.

"Whatever," O'Connor said. "The Academy has a strange soft spot for films about British people in Mediterranean climates. Also," he said, watching her closely, "the fact that the lowly screenwriter wound up with the girl probably didn't hurt either. Never mind that he already had a girl at home." This last was said with the faintest hint of malice, as if he needed to punish her for seeing him in such compromising circumstances.

Though not surprised, Juliette was disappointed by this. She realized she liked O'Connor well enough to expect better. "I thought the film turned out very well," she said calmly. "Josh deserved to be nominated. So did Anna. It was a good performance, a great screenplay. It ought to have been," she said, grimacing. "We rewrote it often enough."

"*We?*"

"He," she said quickly. "He. I mean, I helped, the way you do when you're married to a writer." All those hours, all those days, the weekends, the vacations fractured by working through dialogue, rearranging plot points. He couldn't get the women's voices right, they all sounded the same, and there was no chemistry between the lead characters. She had helped, the way you do when you love someone and he can't quite seem to do what he so wants to do.

"I *don't* know," he said, suddenly interested. "I've never been married to a writer. What exactly does that entail?"

"I don't know," she said with a shrug, remembering how Josh had offered to give her credit, to put her name on it, even after it sold. But she could tell he was only saying it because he thought it was the right thing, not because he wanted to, so she had said no. "Act as a sounding board, make a few suggestions."

"Why do I have a hard time visualizing this?" O'Connor said. "You making a *few* suggestions. Look me straight in the eye and tell me you didn't write at least half that damn thing. Don't lie. Because I've been lied to by the best and I'll know it."

She looked him straight in the eye. "I thought you didn't like the movie."

"I liked about *half* of it."

Juliette kept on looking at him because she couldn't quite quench the pleasure his words brought her, the relief of having someone else at least *know*.

"I'll be damned," he said softly after a moment. "Well, this should be interesting. They aren't staying here . . ."

"They most certainly are," Juliette said. "Are you kidding? It got, like, nine nominations. They're all staying here."

"And that won't bother you at all."

"What *bothers* me is that he left me," she said. "For an *actress*. Everything else is just what happened next. It won't bring him back."

"He'll be back," Michael said. "You can count on that. She'll get bored, he's undoubtedly been bored for months now."

"I hope not," Juliette said quietly, looking at the floor. "The only thing that makes this bearable is the thought that they really, truly love each other. I mean, that can happen, and then I can sort of stand what he put me through. I don't *like* the idea of him loving someone more than he loved me, but at least I can understand it." Her eyes grew hot and for a moment she concentrated on widening them just enough to keep the tears from falling. "If it was just because of on-set lust, or who she was, or Hollywood politics," she said, raising her chin and forcing herself to grin, "I'd have to kill him."

"Give Bill Becker a call," O'Connor said, closing his eyes. "If he thought it would help the ratings, I'm sure he'd take care of it for you."

6

Like most displaced New Yorkers, Juliette had initially found L.A.'s endless cycle of drama baffling, irritating, and yet somehow compelling. Far from being the land of the lotus eater, as she had been led to believe, Los Angeles was fueled by superlatives. It was the crime of the century, the biggest blaze in history, the department's worst scandal, the biggest box office opening ever. Phones rang perpetually with the most important call of the day, people rushed from one key meeting to another, propelled by an intensity that never flagged and more coffee than Juliette had ever seen consumed in her life. She had come to California expecting mimosas and tequila shooters; instead she found hourly lattes and more cocaine use than she would have thought possible post-1985.

After a few months of fighting the current, Juliette had simply surrendered. When she took Devlin up on his offer at the Pinnacle, it was a matter of days before she too was ratcheting up the monologue in her head, convincing herself that all of the guests were so talented, the staff was so lovely, the town was so exciting, and what they did so important. In one way it was easy for her, but still she wondered if her ability to compartmentalize her life with such efficiency was healthy.

Within a few days, everything at the hotel was back to normal—Devlin was storming around because he had heard the hotel's florist was pitching his life as a series to HBO ("He knows who's in love, and who's in trouble, before anyone else," read the pitch). Under any other circumstances, Devlin would have fired him on the spot, but they couldn't very well go into Oscar season without a florist. Hans was obsessing because one of his sous-chefs was pregnant and too stricken by morning sickness to cook; Phillip was still worried about his skeleton, although Juliette had to admit it looked like she had put on a few pounds; Gregory was closeted away going over diagrams of studio hierarchies, the year's guest accounts, and old *Entertainment Weekly* and *Fortune* magazines, trying to figure out who should go in which room, while Louisa huddled with the head of the spa and local merchants, putting together gift baskets that would be special but not so special they would upset anyone's tax status. Within a few days of finding David Fulbright floating in the pool, Juliette was telling the story with a light laugh.

"I guess I should have told Becker I'd host," said Max Diamond, who had stopped Juliette as she passed to hear all the details. "I mean, the Academy must be flipping out to okay a stunt like that, not that I believe for one minute they actually okayed it. It's ridiculous—he'll never be able to pull off ten points. We always managed to do just fine without killing anyone, for chrissake."

Diamond was holding court poolside, chatting now with Robert Duvall, with Morgan Freeman, with Hilary Swank, with Hugh Grant. The celebrity quotient was high, and although Juliette would have liked to attribute it to the season, she was afraid curiosity had a lot to do with it.

"I, for one, wish you had," Juliette said with a smile. "It would have saved me quite a shock."

"You seem pretty shock-proof to me," Max said, pulling her down onto his lap, a hand resting on her waist, just below her breast. "I hear your ex is staying here, is that true? You should leave town when he's here. Come down to my Palm Springs place. I'm driving down this weekend; hell, I'm thinking of moving down there full-time. This town is starting to get on my nerves. I can't believe how nutso everyone is getting over Becker's stunt—it isn't healthy. Seriously, I never thought I'd say it, but Hollywood is getting too crazy for me."

"Just don't stay away too long," Juliette said, extricating herself with a kiss on the comedian's preternaturally tanned cheek. She loved him because he was so relentlessly himself, always with the grin, that reluctant grin that seemed twisted out of him, as if he were perpetually surprised he could find humor in the situation. It was utterly at odds with the blank-faced nihilism that ruled comedy today, old-fashioned but charming, like Dean Martin or early Johnny Carson. Nothing seemed to faze Max or even surprise him much. He smelled of Fred Segal's lemon verbena soap and expensive cigars, and he always looked at her as if he thought she was the prettiest thing he had ever seen. It didn't bother her at all that he looked at most women this way; somehow she felt he always meant it.

"They wanted to give me an honorary Oscar this year, you know, the lifetime achievement whatever," Diamond said. "Don't tell anyone, I wouldn't accept it, so really don't mention it. I mean, how crazy is that? I'm, what, sixty-five, they're so sure I'm never going to be nominated again? Not that the Academy ever recognizes comedy, but still, you never know.

Look at Jack Palance, look at Art Carney. He beat out De Niro, for chrissake. I told them thanks but no thanks. I think it's time for a little time in the desert."

"Max, my life has been a living hell and I am blaming you entirely," said a short, dark-haired woman in black, coming up behind the comedian and putting her hand on his shoulder. "You see what happens when you don't agree to host?"

"Hello, Sasha," Juliette said as Diamond pulled the *L.A. Times* reporter into a faux-lascivious kiss.

"I am feeling a tiny bit guilty," said Max when he was done. "I was just telling Juliette that. But fuck 'em. They should have given me the Oscar for *Incognito* if they need me so much, right?" He grinned self-effacingly. "Not that losing to what's-his-face is anything to be embarrassed about."

"And there's the Salinger movie," Sasha said. "I know, I know," she added, answering his look. "It's not Salinger. Whatever. That's an awards vehicle if I've ever seen one."

Max smiled. "From your mouth to God's ears," he said, "not that you heard it from me because, of course, no announcement's been made because Becker's got his hands full killing half of Hollywood and keeping Hughes under control. He should take a lesson from you, Juliette," he said pointedly. "You seem to know how to get the man to behave." Before Juliette could react, much less find out where Max got his information, Diamond's attention had moved farther into the room. "Well, look who's here, Johnny T," he said, gazing over the women's shoulders and catching sight of Travolta parting crowds. "Call me," he said as he moved toward the star, "we'll have dinner at the beach."

"Was he talking to you or me?" Juliette asked.

Sasha shrugged. "He was talking to himself. As usual. Becker told me he didn't even ask him to host because he was sick of Max panting over the Salinger project. If Max wanted the part so bad, he should have just bought the rights himself, but he's too damn cheap. But who knows? Becker could be lying. They all lie. It's part of their allure. How are you, anyway," she said as the two women embraced, "besides dredging corpses from your pool? And what did Max mean about knowing how to control Hughes?"

"I'm well," said Juliette brightly. Last year, Sasha had done a big piece on the hotel during Oscar season that management had been, by and large, happy with, but Juliette viewed all members of the press warily; like stars and publicists and just about everyone else, they always wanted something. "How are you? Can I get you some coffee?"

"Exhausted. Fed up. The usual. And yes, a nonfat latte would be great." The two women sat at a corner table. "Nothing like spending a day on the phone getting nominee reactions. 'Congratulations,'" she said in a high-energy enthusiastic voice. "'So, were you surprised?' Like Meryl Streep or Leonardo DiCaprio is surprised to get an Oscar nomination. Like every actor, director, screenwriter, and composer out there doesn't think he deserves an Oscar as a birthright. Like it matters for more than fifteen minutes anyway—look at Halle Berry. Can she even open a movie now? No, she cannot. I swear to God, this is the last year I cover this. Seriously. It is not a real job for an adult."

Juliette smiled; every reporter she knew said this every year, as if it were a mantra, as if by saying it they could then be excused for flinging themselves into the glamour of the whole thing.

"Well, it was great about Eddie Izzard," she said. "That was a surprise anyway."

"Yeah, yeah, that was great." Sasha's face brightened. "I love him. And that Russian girl, Natasha Whatever, that was good—she has a pretty amazing story. She doesn't even speak English; she had to learn her lines phonetically. It's good to see Travolta up too, he's so nice. Though I'm surprised Michael O'Connor didn't get it for *Bluebird*."

Juliette stiffened at the mention of O'Connor's name. What would he have done if he had been nominated? she wondered.

"I'll tell you who was genuinely, and almost pathetically, surprised was Alicia Goldstone," Sasha was saying. "I mean, everyone thought she was just dead in the water—she was doing reality TV, for crying out loud."

Juliette nodded. "It's hard for women over forty."

"Forty? She's pushing sixty. And it's pushing back. She's had some bad surgical advice, but I have to admit her performance was really good. I can't imagine she'll win—not over Meryl or Naomi—the Academy has been dying to give Naomi an Oscar for years and she certainly is owed. But you better believe Alicia'll be the fiercest campaigner out there. It's too bad about Therese, though. I thought she was a shoo-in. But then, it never pays to piss off the studio matchmakers."

Juliette too had been surprised that Therese had not gotten a nomination, and it was always alarming to see how fast the talent could be dumped when they didn't live up to expectations. Within an hour of the nomination announcement, Gregory had gotten a call from the studio that Therese would be checking out. That day. Juliette had felt so bad she sent Ricardo to help the actress pack; she found out later he had driven her to the airport and that, far from being disappointed, Therese had seemed relieved. As had Ricardo.

"She really missed being home," he had said. "And she is too nice a girl for Hollywood, I think." Something in his tone made Juliette look at him again, more closely, but he just smiled and gave nothing else away.

"You know," Juliette said now, "I think she was just as happy."

Sasha shrugged, gulped down the last of her coffee. "Well, one non-English speaker is probably the Academy's limit in any category anyway. God, just listen to us. How do they get us to care about their careers so much? I mean, really. Do you think Meryl Streep is worried if I ever get nominated for a Pulitzer? Not that that's likely—catch them giving a Pulitzer to an entertainment reporter; that would be like a comedian getting an Oscar . . . oh, Ma-ax," she called softly. "Or do you think Michael O'Connor's worried about you getting a raise? I don't think so. I swear, I am not covering the Oscars next year." She sighed and hooked her hair behind her ears. "So who's staying here, pretty much everybody? I mean, besides *A Touch of Summer* . . ."

Ah, Juliette thought, here it was, the point of the conversation.

"Pretty much everybody," Juliette said smoothly, "including *A Touch of Summer*. I'm really proud Josh is getting the credit he deserves."

She held the reporter's gaze for a long moment and just when she thought she would not be able to continue, Sasha shook her head and looked away. "You are a braver gal than I, Gunga Din," she said. "But good for you. I hope it goes well. They're going to be all over the place, though, just so you know. Her publicist is pulling out all the stops."

Juliette gave a small shrug. "It's Oscar season, after all."

"Four weeks of pure hell," said Sasha, returning to her prayer wheel of complaint, as Juliette hoped she would. "I'm following Becker around for two of them. Lucky, lucky me. I wonder if he'll kill anyone. Or maybe someone will kill him. That'd be worth a Pulitzer nomination anyway. Some good may come of this yet. Well, thanks for the coffee," the reporter said, pulling her bag toward her, checking her cell phone for messages. "And would you mind validating my parking?"

Juliette found that the more often she acknowledged Josh's nomination, the easier it was to think about him, to put him in a category of "them" rather than "us"—a guest, a celebrity, a nominee, someone not quite real.

Or at least it was until he called her. She was standing in the pastry refrigerator with Hans, going over the various complimentary sweet trays that would be given to the guests, and trying to decide between the gold-dusted truffle and the gold-dusted praline as the centerpiece when her BlackBerry rang and she answered it. Unthinking.

"Hi," he said. "It's me. Josh," he added, and for a horrible moment she thought he was going to say his last name.

"Hello," she said quickly to stop this from happening.

"Are you busy? I mean, you're always busy. But I . . . is this a good time to talk?" Behind the ringing emptiness of long distance, she could hear the sound of traffic—he was calling from the street, or maybe his car. It was late at night in London. Was he not allowed to call her from home?

"It's a fine time," she said, pointing to the truffle.

"Okay, good, good," he said. "How are you? I mean, besides busy."

"I'm well," she said, and something in her tone brought Hans's head up with a jerk. She made a gesture that she hoped meant "looks good" and quickly headed out to the kitchen pantry, where the enormous tins of canned tomatoes and jars of mayonnaise surrounded her like a fortress. "I meant to call to say congratulations," she said, "but things were a little insane around here on nomination day."

"I know, I know," Josh said. "It was all over the news here. Anna said David felt really badly that it was you who found him . . . That must have been terrible."

"Oh, it was pretty obvious," she said, feeling a rush of emotions—Anna, how easily he said that name—crested by the shame of being a topic of his casual conversation, of their casual conversation. "And it happened so fast it was all just a blur. The whole thing is just so hilarious; Bill Becker is out of his mind, but business has never been better. And we're all happy New Line has decided to put you all here," she added lightly.

"Yeah, right," he said, "well, that's why I was calling. I guess I just wanted to touch base and make sure that that's okay with you."

If I were better at this, Juliette thought, *I could take this opportunity to say something nasty, like: Since when have you cared what was okay with me?* But the best she could do was smile sadly and say, "Oh, it's fine, Josh, really, but thanks for checking. That was nice of you."

"Julie," he said, then stopped himself. "I know it sounds terrible, or maybe it doesn't, but I really am glad, I mean, I'm really looking forward to seeing you. Even," he added quickly, "if it's just, you know, in passing. But maybe we could have coffee, or lunch, or something. We haven't talked in so long, and I know that's been my fault, but still maybe we could."

"Of course," she said, "sure. You know, I'm going to put the house on the market after these bloody awards are over, so if there's anything in it you want . . ."

"No," he said, sounding stung. "I mean, maybe, yes, but no, that's not what I wanted to talk to you about. You're selling the house?"

"I thought I would, yeah. It isn't exactly a happy place for me. Anymore."

There was silence on the other end of the phone and for a minute Juliette thought she had lost the connection, but then Josh sighed. "Christ, Julie, I'm sorry. I've got to go." In the background she could hear a car door slamming followed by fluty laughter and female British voices. Josh's voice changed, got louder and more formal. "I'll call you when we get in, which should be in a week or so—we're coming in early, which I guess you knew. The weather here is frightful and Anna wants to lie by the pool for hours, don't you, darling? So I'll talk to you soon.'Bye."

He was gone. And Juliette was left to read the labels of the enormous jam jars—raspberry, strawberry, marmalade, apricot—over and over until her heart stopped wringing itself out and she felt well enough to move on.

The month between the announcement of the Oscar nominations and the Academy Awards ceremony was filled with parties, luncheons, various other awards ceremonies, and general mayhem. While the Academy had banned the sort of high-priced media campaigns that brought several small studios to the brink of destruction, nominated films had DVD release parties with gift bags from Tiffany and Hermès, studio heads opened their art-laden homes to the media, and star-studded lunches and cocktail parties kept voting members out and about until the wee hours of the morning while their screeners—the videos of the actual films they would be voting on—piled up next to their plasma screens. This year, several studios had gotten around the rules by doing their high-end marketing before the nominations were announced—*A Touch of Summer* arrived to members of the Screen Actors Guild, the largest voting bloc in the Academy, in a portable DVD player that members were free to keep. Not to be outdone, the sound-track for *Willa*, Alicia Goldstone's movie, came to Directors Guild members preprogrammed into iPods emblazoned with the film's name. Those who didn't want the bother of declaring the gifts at tax time were encouraged to return them. No one did.

Still, there was much discussion on the Internet and in the trades about the morality of these moves, even more about the "artistic integrity"—several directors were outraged that Academy members would view nominee possibilities on such small screens. "Sometimes," wrote one in an op-ed in the *Los Angeles Times*, "I think the point of Oscar season is to keep voters from actually seeing the films."

In a way, that was true. Yes, the Academy screened the nom-inated films on rotation, and theaters around Los Angeles were dotted with white-haired members laden with colored pencils and notebooks and a rare sense of duty, but many of the votes were inevitably cast by people who had not seen the movies. Their choices were often based on an incalculable combination of adoration, allegiance, pity, goodwill, gratitude, and a desire to back a winner. Studio marketers knew there was nothing they could do to alter the actual product, so their job was to create a suitable substitute. This director was owed, that actress had just had a terrible personal year, this actor was in his seventies—who knew if he had another nomination in him?

The entertainment media went into overdrive trying to find news in what was essentially a marketing campaign, while the publicists pressed the stars to drag out their children, aging parents, beloved pets, their vacation tips, anything, anything to keep their names and faces in the news.

Much had been made over the choice of Forrest Hughes, who held a press conference after the announcement to inform the world that the NBC censors could go fuck themselves if they thought he was going to submit a draft of his opening like every other spineless host in the history of the show. "I am the reason God invented the five-second delay," he said, and two days later appeared on the cover of *Vanity Fair*, head shaved, completely naked, painted gold, and holding one very well-placed, very long envelope.

Meanwhile, designers were competing to dress Eddie Izzard, who had announced he would be going all-out couture "with plenty of leg," he said. And Bono had agreed to perform the nominated songs after a consortium of stars headed by Barbra Streisand and Angelina Jolie agreed to donate a hundred thousand dollars each to end world hunger.

"It isn't enough to be famous anymore," Michael said when she brought him an armful of magazines, "now you have to be a fucking freak show too. It used to be different, you know. It used to be special. Now you paint yourself and you're a star."

He was thinner now, if that was possible, and pale. The magazines slid from his lap and he made no attempt to stop them. Juliette watched them fall.

"I'll tell you one thing," he said peevishly. "Bill Becker is a goddamn barracuda. If Hughes thinks Becker is doing him a favor, he'd better watch his back. Everybody involved in this show better watch their backs. Because that asshole would kill, cook, and eat his own grandmother on TV if he thought it would move his name up the power list half a notch. The things I could tell you about Mr. Bill Becker . . ." He waved his hand in disgust and threw his head back against the pillow, waiting for Juliette to ask him for details. When she didn't, he struggled back into a sitting position.

"One time, he tried to fire this actress off his movie because she wouldn't sleep with him. You remember, the one he practically broke his arm patting himself on the back for hiring after she got busted for possession. Anyway, he figured she should show her gratitude in blow jobs or whatever, and she wouldn't. So he tried everything to get her off the set and when he couldn't do it, because she had a contract, because she was a *professional*, he laced her water bottle with OxyContin and then demanded a drug test. So she gets fired and goes off the deep end and last I heard she got arrested in some alley in Atwater Village. And that's not even the worst of it," he said, falling back again. "This town is just so fucked."

"You need to stop reading these magazines," Juliette said soothingly, surprised by the bitterness she heard in his voice. She thought somehow he was above bitterness. "I'll bring you a book tomorrow. Or I can have someone run out now if you'd like."

"Don't you have a library downstairs? The famous Pinnacle library, with its wall of books? Or are they too erudite for the likes of me? I may not have gone to college, but I have done Chekhov, you know. God," he said, his tone becoming less querulous, "did you hear that? I can't believe I said that. Maybe it's better if I die and be done with it. 'I have done Chekhov, you know.' Ah, but never Hamlet, nor yet Lear. It's the end, I feel the end drawing near. 'Why,'" he said, doing a passable Bette Davis as he reached for Juliette's arm, "'it's grown so dark I can't see my hand.'"

Juliette looked at him quizzically, shook her head. He made a sound of impatience. "*Dark Victory*. Jesus. You are the most cinematically illiterate person I have ever met."

"And you know more about Bette Davis than most straight men I know."

"Who says I'm straight?" He mustered up a grin. "You were there in the late eighties, the good old days, remember? When it was more about whoever got in the cab with me first than a silly old issue like gender. Don't you remember all those Page Six items? Don't you remember the story about the hamster?"

"I thought it was a guinea pig," she said, because she did remember—back in the day, it was said O'Connor had sex with just about everyone and everything.

O'Connor made a face. "Too butch for me. Is that what kept you from my bed, lovely Juliette? Were you afraid of what you might find there?"

"Well, I never have been one for crowds."

"And here we are, alone at last."

"Don't mind me," said Rory, who was, as usual, hovering in the background, straightening up the pillows on the sofa.

"You could have the night off," O'Connor said. "I'm sure you'd be happy to get out of here. Come on," he said to Juliette. "If nothing else, the bed's got five settings."

"Stop," said Juliette, picking up the magazines O'Connor had let drop and wondering if she was talking to herself—she was starting to enjoy this man too much, starting to worry, starting to wonder how much of his fondness for her was sincere. "I can bring you a book from downstairs if you want to read *The Iliad*, *The Scarlet Letter*, or *The Time Is Noon*. Because the dirty little secret of the Pinnacle is—" She leaned in close and whispered, "Books by the yard."

He laughed, a sound weak but still true enough to make Juliette feel a bit better. "'I love books, they're so decorative, don't you think?' That's *Auntie Mame*, by the way."

"It is my bête noir," she said, ignoring him. "But Devlin is too stubborn or too cheap to get a real library in. It makes me crazy. I can't even go in there. I won't let photographers near it. It's the only thing in the hotel that is truly fake."

O'Connor eyed her dubiously. "No," she said. "I mean it. The Pinnacle is what it is—a hotel catering to people who are used to being catered to. And it doesn't pretend to be anything else. You may not like it, but it is sincere. Except the library." She shivered. "Our heart of darkness."

"If a fake library is as bad as it gets," he said, as Rory came in with a syringe, "you are doing all right."

She looked down at him, at his hand plucking fretfully at the sheets, at the strength still in his jaw, the gentle humor in his eyes. Ill as he was, he was still seductive. But like with Devlin and his automatic kisses or Max Diamond and his endless invitations, it was a default setting, a side effect of celebrity. It meant nothing. Which, Juliette constantly reminded herself, was why you could never let men like these get too close.

"What?" Michael said. "You've never seen a movie star get a sedative before?"

As Juliette smiled down at him, her BlackBerry buzzed. It was Devlin. "Get down here," he said. "Natasha Coleman just OD'd."

Natasha Coleman was the Russian model nominated for Best Actress for her film debut as a Ukranian girl brought to the U.S. for an arranged marriage to a mobster who winds up taking over his territory after kicking some serious ass. And she managed to do most of it wearing only a negligee. She was scheduled to check in to the Pinnacle in a few days, but at a party in New York had apparently mistaken heroin for cocaine and snorted herself into oblivion.

"What, didn't she see *Pulp Fiction*?" Gregory said as a group of the staff huddled around the television in Devlin's office. "Sor-ree," he said when Louisa gave him a disgusted look.

"All I can say is thank God it happened at the Plaza and not here," said Devlin. "It's a terrible tragedy, such a lovely young woman, but we've had enough corpses for one awards season."

"Maybe it's not real," said Juliette. "Maybe it's another one of Becker's ploys."

Devlin shook his head. "He was just on the local news, looking pretty shaken for Becker, with the president of the Academy. No, this one's real. I wonder if they'll have to give her the award posthumously. Has this ever happened?"

Gregory shook his head. "But you better believe the publicists are moving on it now; the film has three other nominations—I'm sure we'll be hearing from all the above-the-line talent shortly."

"It really is terrible," said Juliette as the screen flashed a close-up of the young woman's face. "Look at how beautiful she is. I wonder how it happened. It seems so odd . . ."

"Just another casualty of the lack of education about drugs in this country," said Gregory. "What?" he said when everyone stared at him.

"You are going to hell, you know that, don't you?" said Juliette.

Gregory shrugged. "This is my ninth Oscar season. How different could hell be?"

7

For a day or so, the mood in Los Angeles was somber, as the actress's short career and strange death were examined. Fellow party guests, including Will Ferrell, Parker Posey, Al Pacino, and a welter of other A-list names were interviewed, and the obligatory stories about drug abuse in Hollywood were churned out with the inevitable matching sidebars on historical overdoses—Janis Joplin, John Belushi—and famous recoveries—Dennis Quaid, Robert Downey, Jr. But as usual, the fluid nature of Los Angeles triumphed. "I guess we can raise the flag from half-mast," muttered Gregory as he and Juliette watched one limo after another pull up and disgorge laughing groups in formal wear for the *InStyle* cocktail party.

"Life goes on," she said, rushing over to help Martin Scorsese, who seemed to be having some trouble with his scarf. As she bent, smiling, to help him, a woman brushed by; looking up, she saw it was Sally Gardens, Michael O'Connor's latest although now apparently ex-wife. She was beautiful, as all his wives were beautiful—model-tall and model-thin, high-breasted, with long hair and longer legs. Sally was dark, which set her apart slightly—the other three had been blond. Juliette felt a wash of jealousy—what would life be like if she were that beautiful, if she hadn't had to conjure up all the special skills she had created for herself, skills that had gotten her where she was today. "What did you do before Alex found you?" O'Connor had asked, and Juliette had almost told him the truth; he seemed so harmless, so needy lying on that bed.

Watching Sally, Juliette felt her stomach grow tense as if she had been caught in some secret, which made no sense. She wasn't O'Connor's lover. She wasn't even his friend. She was part of the service he hired when he checked in to the hotel. So why did she feel so guilty? Because, she thought, his wife should be with him, it was his *wife* who should be comforting him. How far could the man's pride extend, to keep the woman he had married from knowing how sick he was? Even if the couple were separated, it seemed wrong that he was lying some sixteen stories above, thin and shivering, while this woman thought he was cavorting in Morocco.

Juliette tried to imagine what she would feel if she discovered that Josh was not living with Anna in London but instead suffering in some hospital, alone, in secret. Impulsively, she took a step to follow the woman—O'Connor would be furious, Devlin might well fire her, but still . . . She watched Sally's perfectly toned back disappear into the crowd. It wasn't her business anyway. She turned away and found herself confronting Devlin's immaculate shirtfront.

"I think you've earned an evening off, my dear," he said. "Why don't you run along now? We can take it from here."

Juliette looked up into Devlin's wide dark eyes with surprise and suspicion. "What are you talking about?" Behind him she could see Louisa, juggling a cell phone and two gift bags in her hands, as Barney, the head doorman, rushed in the door with a worried expression. "Five minutes," he said to

Louisa, then, catching sight of Juliette, smiled in a most unconvincing manner. She felt herself get cold and still inside.

"Josh is coming," she said. Devlin nodded. "He wasn't supposed to be here till tomorrow."

"They hitched a ride with Harrison Ford," he said. "We just got word. Now there's no need for you to be here, no need at all."

"I won't have them chase me out of my own hotel," she said, surprising herself with her fierceness. "I'll be in the Wisteria Room," she said, nodding toward the flow of party guests, "if anyone needs me."

Moving along the periphery of the party, Juliette nodded and embraced and allowed herself a wide, cold martini. She could see them in her mind's eye getting out of the limo, Josh looking anxiously around as they moved through the lobby, though maybe Anna would request the more private entrance from the garage. She could see Devlin and Louisa greeting them, handing them their gifts, showing them around their room with the flowers and fruit and pastry tray that she had helped choose, could see them alone in the room then, throwing open the window—Josh always hated to have the windows closed—embracing, drawing a bath, calling down to room service, safe and served in the perfect cocoon. Juliette closed her eyes tightly. The martini had rushed to her head—it probably hadn't helped that she swallowed it in three gulps. She headed for the bathroom, closed one of the cubicle doors behind her, and leaned her head against the wall. "Nothing has changed," she told herself. "Just because they are here, nothing has changed at all."

When she finally came out, she winced against even the soft light of the powder table. There, fixing her lipstick, was Sally Gardens. Juliette smiled at her in the mirror. Sally smiled back—she really was so pretty, and much younger than Juliette had realized. When did everyone become so *young*? Before Juliette could think about it, she was talking to Sally in a soft urgent voice, telling her about O'Connor, how ill he was, how he didn't want anyone to know, how he was in the hotel at this minute and she, Juliette, could take her up to him if Sally would like that.

Sally pursed her now-crimson lips together and fluffed her raven hair. She did not take her eyes off her reflection for a moment.

"There is nothing you can tell me about Michael O'Connor that I don't already know," she said in a soft reasonable voice. "Why do you think we separated?"

Seeing Juliette's shocked expression, Sally smiled again, a little sadly perhaps, and turned to face her. "In case you hadn't noticed, the position of Mrs. Michael O'Connor has a high turnover rate even in the best of circumstances, though the pay's pretty good while it lasts." She looked Juliette up and down and shook her head. "I wouldn't suggest it as a career move, if that's what you have in mind. You'd do better with Dev. Though I imagine the working conditions would be similar." She turned back to the mirror. "Tell Michael I said hello," she said as she made her exit. "And I hope he pulls through. I really do."

Juliette quietly counted to twenty and then left the ladies' room, threaded her way through the party, and then out into the clean silence of the lobby. "Tell Devlin I took him up on his offer and went home," she said to Louisa, who looked up in surprise from the concierge desk. "I'll see you in the morning."

At home, she went for an hour-long walk, hard up the hills, and tried to think of nothing. She came back and drank two more martinis and tried to think of nothing. She turned on the evening news, heard that a schoolgirl had been killed in a drive-by shooting and an *L.A. Times* reporter had died of food poisoning at the paper's downtown office. She turned off the television and tried and tried to think of nothing, but all she could see behind her eyes was Josh, how happy he had been, how much he had loved her, before the money and the success and the movie business ruined their lives just like it seemed to ruin everyone's lives. And even though she knew it changed nothing at all, she cried herself to sleep.

The next morning, Juliette was surprised to see Rory having breakfast in the garden café. Catching his eye, she did an exaggerated double-take and the nurse obligingly laughed.

"He lets you out of the room," she said. "I am amazed."

"He told me I was looking too pasty, I was depressing him," Rory said, rolling his eyes. "I actually have a nine o'clock appointment for a bronzing in the spa—the man is impossible, but at least he ponied up for a massage and a pedicure. Join me?" he said, gesturing to the chair across from him.

"For a moment, sure." Juliette slid into place. The waiter hurried over and she ordered a cappuccino and some scrambled egg whites.

"They should just stop offering eggs," said Rory. "I don't know anyone who eats the yolks anymore. When I was a kid, my mother used to force us to eat the yolks. She said they were the part with all the good stuff. But then she took diet pills and smoked a pack a day when she was pregnant with me, which probably explains quite a bit if you think about it."

Juliette studied Rory's face. He was aging well, the shaved bald head became him, and his face was as expressive and engaging as any other successful TV star she knew.

"Why did you quit acting?" she asked. "I mean, you can tell

me it's none of my business, but I'm just curious—you were so good, and I remember you did some movies too, didn't you? After the show got canceled."

"TV movies," he said, grimacing. "Me and Valerie Bertinelli." He sighed. "I don't know, it just got old. The magic didn't happen and it got too hard to keep hanging around watching it happen for other people."

"People like Michael?"

"Oh, Michael made his own magic. We all knew it from the first episode." Rory's face grew soft with something hovering between admiration and adoration. "No, he was born to be a movie star. It was just some of the others, people I knew who got series or won awards and my quote just got lower and lower until I was working for scale, which didn't seem worth it."

"So you went to nursing school."

"Well, first I had to get sober, but then I went to nursing school."

"And have you worked with many of your former colleagues, many stars?"

"Oh, dear God, no. Can't stand them. For most people, celebrity is like a disease—the bad attitude rises off them, airborne, like the flu or something, and I wasn't having any of that. I had had enough. Of that. But then Michael called and I couldn't say no." Again that dreamy look came into the nurse's eyes. "I couldn't believe he remembered me after all these years. Not that I ever forgot him. Never. How could you?"

"Pays well," said Juliette, remembering Sally's comment.

"Yes, indeed," he answered with an eye-rolling laugh. "But I would have done it even if it hadn't. He's one of those people you just want to be around. For as long as they'll have you."

The eggs and cappuccino came, but Juliette was not hungry.

She pulled a corner off a triangle of toast and dipped it in the small bowl of jelly. "He's going to be okay, isn't he?" she asked. "I mean, the treatment seems to be helping."

Rory looked up at her quickly. "Yes, it does," he said in measured tones. "The doctor seems quite confident. Speaking of doctors," he said, obviously steering the conversation away from the topic of Michael's health, "did you hear about that reporter who died at the *Times* yesterday?"

"The woman who got food poisoning? I've heard the food in their cafeteria is pretty bad . . ."

"Uh-uh. Now they're saying it wasn't food poisoning. Officially, it was a heart attack. But I heard they're doing a toxology screen. That's right," he said when Juliette opened her mouth. "It might have been poison-poison. Like an Agatha Christie novel. Someone apparently sent a box of doughnuts to the Calendar section, and you know how those journalists are when it comes to free food."

Juliette flashed a wry smile; that she did know—as Gregory said, if you want to clear a room of reporters, let them know there's lobster and an open bar next door.

"Well, this one woman—she writes some column called 'The Hollywood Life' or something—she ate three. And dropped dead. Right at her desk."

"Jesus," Juliette said, thinking of Sasha and the other reporters she knew. "Did anyone else get sick?"

Rory shook his head. "Not that I've heard. Unfortunately, there weren't any doughnuts left to test . . . at least that's what I heard."

"But a heart attack," she said. "If it were poison, wouldn't she have, I don't know, had convulsions or something?"

"Not necessarily," said Rory, his eyes narrowing with the pleasure of inside knowledge. "Cyanide looks like a heart attack, cocaine could cause heart attack. In Sherlock Holmes it was always nicotine, pure nicotine," he added. "Which leaves no trace."

"Yeah, but this isn't Sherlock Holmes," Juliette said, dubiously. "This is L.A. People have heart attacks all the time. Do they know who sent them?"

"That's the good part," Rory said, digging into the jelly pot. "Apparently, the card said, *Compliments of the Academy,* but the Academy is denying it, of course. And why would they poison a reporter when they can just blacklist her?"

Out of the corner of her eye, Juliette could see Devlin bearing down on her. "I owe you," she whispered to the nurse as she rose, now fully informed, to meet her boss.

"I just spent an hour in my office with a hysterical starlet who claims that staying in this hotel has made her fat," Devlin hissed, steering her toward a quiet corner of the back garden. "And after exerting considerable effort to calm her down"—he unconsciously checked the line of his shirt buttons and the neatness of his hair—"I have made a few inquiries and discovered that indeed there seems to have been a campaign among my staff to increase the caloric intake of this particular guest. And that you had full knowledge of it."

"I think 'campaign' is a bit of an overstatement," Juliette said, buying a little time. This was Eamonn Devlin at his most unpleasant—if you crossed him, he could be brutal.

"I've already given Phillip the sack, and I've let Hans and Rick know I am not well pleased. But it's you I am most disappointed in—if I can't trust you, Juliette, then you are of absolutely no use to me."

Fuck you, Juliette wanted to say. *Fuck you and this hotel and all these fucking people who think they deserve the moon and the stars and sugar-free chocolate shavings on top.* But she didn't.

Because she couldn't. Without this job, she was back where she started all those years ago, and that was a thought not to be considered.

"Eamonn," she said quietly. "Did you see that girl? Phillip saved her life, I swear to God he did. If we saw a guest put a gun to his head, we would pull it away, wouldn't we? She was running that track for hours every day and I'd try to talk to her and she was essentially incoherent. Yes, I was aware that the boys were slipping a little crème fraîche into her yogurt or whatever, but Jesus, did you want a real live corpse turning up in this hotel?"

She could see Devlin's face settle back into lines less fierce, so she pressed the advantage. "And that is exactly what Phillip said to me when he put a little protein powder in her Diet Coke. He was worried about the reputation of the hotel—imagine if we let a guest starve to death under our roof. Imagine if the press got ahold of that in the middle of awards season? Like things aren't strange enough?"

"Okay," Devlin said, holding up his hand, "I see your point. But we are not an intervention program for eating disorders and if we get the reputation of making women fat, we're dead. She's threatening to sue; she's already complained to her father, who mercifully is somewhere in the Aegean on his yacht, or no doubt I'd be dealing with him."

"Let me," Juliette said firmly. "I will set it right, I swear to you." Devlin looked relieved and Juliette realized it wasn't so much the nature of the complaint as it was that he had had to deal with it—Devlin liked receiving praise, not criticism. That was why he had hired Juliette: to ensure there was never any criticism, or if there was, that it never intruded into the sanctum of his office. "And the boys. I will talk to the boys. But you can't sack Phillip. Not now. Think about it. The New Yorkers, the Brits, they spend their entire days at the pool. They don't understand that it's freaking February, all they know is the sun is out. And they love Phillip. He knows how to keep everyone happy—you should see the system of lounge chair assignments he made up after the nominations. It's a work of art."

Devlin thought a moment, then nodded. "Okay. You make the problem disappear and he's back, but on notice. Another complaint and he's gone. Do you hear me? I'll run the pool myself if I have to."

"Well, hang on a second," Juliette said, closing the deal good and tight. "Does that mean you'll spend your days in your Speedo?" She hitched her eyebrows up suggestively, thought of the sisters Phillip was supporting and tried not to despise herself.

Devlin's face surrendered the last line of anger. "Is there any crime you can't talk your way out of, I wonder?" he said, pinching her chin. "All right, the issue is yours. Deal with it as you will. I just don't want any more angry anorexics rattling around in my office."

"What have you heard about that reporter who died?" she asked as they headed back toward the lobby.

"Nothing more than what was on the news," he said. "Why? Do you know something?" He scanned her face quickly.

"No." She shook her head. "What's the Academy saying?"

"That they don't know a thing about it. I think the reports must be wrong. Why would any woman in her right mind eat three doughnuts?" With a shiver, he dismissed her and strode off, leaving her standing in the lounge so irritated and amused by his comment that it took a minute to register the fact that Josh Singer was hurrying past the silent, empty bar toward her.

When it did, she felt trapped in a moment that she hadn't expected. Everything loomed around her suddenly, vibrating as if in a dream. She could smell the lilies from the arrangements that bloomed on every tabletop, see how the morning sun streamed through the drawn blinds of the bar in tiny shreds of light, how the bottles gleamed like soldiers at attention. The thick gold carpet devoured the sound of Josh's footsteps. He looked just as he had when he had been her husband, and yet not—his jawline was sleeker somehow, his trousers more expensive, his linen shirt perfectly pressed, and he walked with a loose confidence she didn't remember at all.

"Julie," he said, looking so happy to see her she thought she might cry, might fling herself into his arms and burst into tears and somehow make all of it, all of the past year, vanish, dissolve into rumor and misinformation.

"Josh," she said instead, not moving but smiling her best greeter smile. "Hi. I was just going to ring your room. Make sure you both got settled properly last night. Where is Anna?"

"Oh, still asleep," he said, blinking at the professional tone in her voice, at the fact that she did not step forward to meet his embrace. "I wanted to see you alone, you know, first, because it's been so long and I just hoped we could maybe talk for a minute or two. Sometime. Like now, if you can, or later. You look wonderful," he said, putting his hands on her shoulders. "Just wonderful. I know you won't believe me, but I've missed you. I really have."

Juliette opened her mouth to speak and closed it. Why wouldn't she believe him? she wondered. Because it was such a stretch that he would even think of his wife of ten years while in the presence of a movie star?

She shook her head; she wasn't ready for this after all, not here, not now. She reached out her hand and squeezed his wrist. "Of course, I'd love to talk to you, Josh," she said brightly. "But I can't right now, things are just insane. You know. The hotel business. Maybe later on today. Or before dinner. Can we get you reservations anywhere?" she asked, noting with satisfaction the look of pained surprise on his face.

He shook his head. "I think Anna is going to want to spend pretty much the whole day by the pool," he said. "It's been raining for a month in London. I have a meeting at two, but otherwise I'm free."

"Why don't we try to grab a drink around five, then? If that's all right with Anna," she added, enjoying seeing him off balance—had he really expected her to feel nothing but joy at seeing him?

"Five o'clock will be fine," he said. "I'll meet you down here."

"Perfect," she said. And, flushed with her success, she leaned in and kissed him on the cheek. "You look wonderful as well, Josh," she said. "And you smell nice too."

He shrugged. "Guess it's the mints," he said, holding up a tin of Pinnacle mints. "From the gift basket. Your idea?"

She allowed herself a small nod.

"I figured," he said, smiling into her eyes. "They're really good. Just like everything you do."

Michael was restless and irritable when she stopped by around lunchtime.

"I'm just going to run downstairs for a minute or two," Rory said when she came in. Juliette nodded. "I have my cell if anything happens."

"I heard my ex was here the other night," Michael said by way of greeting. "Did she have her blond bimbo boyfriend with her? The twenty-two-year-old?"

"I didn't notice," Juliette said. She sat down and pulled a copy of *To Kill a Mockingbird* out of her purse. "I brought you this—I like reading it when I'm not feeling well . . ."

He stared at it. "You know, I spent ten years trying to get a remake of that off the ground—don't you think I'd make an admirable Atticus Finch? But no one would fund it." He waved it away. "So I heard Lisa Javelin went off the deep end at MDB," he said, referring to the hot topic of the day—that Arnie Ellison's boss had abruptly taken an unexpected leave of absence. "It's getting harder and harder to find a publicist over the age of twenty-seven anymore. But then I guess the years of managing Lindsay and Britney would get to anyone. Or did Arnie mess with her meds? That guy's a fucking shark."

"There was some commotion, I believe," Juliette said. "The official line is that something went wrong with her flu shot; she's being hospitalized with 'flulike symptoms.'"

"'Flulike symptoms,'" he mocked. "I love that. That woman worked the Oscars while she was in labor, for chrissake. Remember? She practically gave birth in the limo. And she was up the next morning making sure Hilary got on *Oprah* before Julia. It would take more than a flu shot to hospitalize her. A gunshot, maybe, but only if it hit a vital organ. And how about that dead reporter? Did she have flulike symptoms?"

"No, just a heart attack."

"Rory is convinced it was *mur-der*," he said. "But I think he's just bored. God knows I'm bored. Bored of being sick. And sick of being bored. What have you heard?"

"That they're doing an autopsy," Juliette said, pretending to be better informed than she was. *Why,* she wondered, *am I trying to impress him?* "And the Academy is issuing about a thousand denials and offering to get her a star on the Walk of Fame—"

"Rory says this year's Oscars are cursed," Michael said, interrupting her. "Of course, I thought the same thing when I didn't get nominated. Not that I wanted to be nominated. Not that I didn't go to great lengths to avoid nomination . . ."

"'If nominated, I will not run. If elected, I will not serve . . .'"

"You laugh, but can you imagine? There aren't enough flu-like symptoms in the world to explain away this"—he gestured to his thin, still form.

There was a hopelessness about the gesture that disturbed her, the way his hand fell, like the joke, weakly onto the bed. "I saw Josh," she said, offering it up like a parent might distract a sick child with a new toy. "He was so glad to see me you just can't imagine."

She described the encounter in detail, trying to keep a savage good humor in her voice, that pitch-perfect narrative tone that let the listener know the teller was in on the joke though the joke was completely on her.

"What do you want from him?" O'Connor asked when she was done, and the gentleness of his voice surprised her. "Because he clearly wants something from you."

Juliette shook her head. What could Josh want from her? Something small and thrilling took hold in the pit of her stomach.

"Would you take him back?"

She looked at her hands, at the emerald engagement ring she still wore though she had taken the wedding band off—had Josh even noticed? "I want what I had," she said. "I want it to go back to the way it was before."

"Women always say that," O'Connor said disdainfully. "But they don't mean it. Because, inevitably, they're the ones who pushed for things to change. 'Let's get married.' 'Let's buy a new house.' 'Let's have a baby.' 'Why do you need to work so much?'"

"I didn't want things to change," she said. "I was happy the way things were. I didn't care if he didn't make a lot of money or got published or whatever. It didn't matter to me at all."

The actor looked at her and there was both pity and contempt in his eyes. For a moment, she was afraid of what he would say next because she couldn't imagine it was going to be kind. But then his face changed, grew waxen and beaded with sweat. He groaned, drew himself onto his side, and tried to rise from the bed. He suddenly could not seem to catch his breath.

"What?" she said, startled, frightened. "Michael, wait, let me help you." He staggered out of the bed, stretching the IV line that ran from his wrist. She tried to support him and pull the IV along with them. He began to vomit, weakly, and fell to his knees. She knelt beside him, put her arms around his shoulders, and stroked his head. "It's okay, it's all right," she murmured, and he vomited again and shook with fever; she could feel the sudden heat of his skin against her arm, her cheek. "You're going to get through this, you're going to get better."

As soon as he stopped retching, he shook her arm off his back and pushed her away. "Just get the hell out," he said, wiping his mouth with the back of his wrist. "Jesus. What is wrong with you anyway?"

His shove had been surprisingly strong, had sent her sprawling, legs splayed and ridiculous. For a moment she was furious, for a moment she considered just leaving him there, hunched on the floor in his own vomit. But the sight of him on his hands and knees, the once-powerful shoulders so frail, dissolved her; she would help him, she had to help him, she would will him to health if she had to. And then she would tell him off.

"You need to ask yourself why it is you won't let anyone who cares about you help you," she said, pulling herself to her knees, straightening her skirt, and then moving to help him up.

"And *you* need to ask *yourself* why it is you can only love a man when he needs your help," he said, his head still hanging, sweat now dripping down his face. "I bet *that's* why he left you, you know. I bet Anna had nothing to do with it." He raised his face and grimaced. "You're the kind of woman who can only love a man when he has to lean on her every minute of the day. Even if you have to trip him yourself to make sure."

As if struck, she pulled her hands away from him, rocked back onto her heels, and stood. Rory appeared in the doorway, dropping papers and packages to hurry over and help O'Connor to his feet and to the bathroom. Not that Juliette remained to make sure everything was all right. For once in her life, she just didn't care.

8

Threading her way past all the public areas of the hotel, Juliette headed for her office, where she shut the door. Methodically, she began answering her phone calls, organizing photo shoots and interviews, answering publicist requests. The highlight was a conversation with the software billionaire who called to thank the staff of the Pinnacle for helping his daughter—apparently the validation she received from her family and friends when they saw her at a marginally normal body weight convinced her to enter a treatment program. "Whatever I can do, whenever I can do it, you just let me know," he said. "Meanwhile, I think you can plan on hosting our parties and conferences for the foreseeable future."

In a soft voice Juliette asked him if he would be kind enough to repeat these sentiments to her boss, and with a laugh, he agreed to be transferred. "Merry Christmas to me," she said as she heard Devlin's "Hullo" and hit the transfer button; as soon as Oscar season was over, she was going to call this man back and get a job with his company. Sell her house and move to Seattle and life would commence anew once again. Less than four weeks. A little month.

This decision—and she considered it a decision, not a desire—was what allowed her to keep her date with Josh. The bar was quiet enough that she was noticeable when she walked in. He was already seated, tossing a few mints from the Pinnacle tin into his mouth like peanuts. Marta nodded her way and raised her eyebrows, grinning when Juliette made a gesture with her hands indicating a big drink. "If you're hungry, we should order the crab cakes," she said to Josh. "They're the best in town."

Startled midswallow, he half rose and choked.

"Death by breath mint," he said, coughing, his eyes streaming. "You know, I just used that in a script I finished. A guy gets poisoned by a breath mint because . . . well." He broke off with a boyish smile. "I won't bore you with the details."

She smiled dutifully and sat down; her martini arrived and she received it in both hands. "Booze in a bucket," he said, nodding in approval. "I imagine you've earned that."

"You have no idea."

He fixed his eyes on her, those big brown eyes with their almost feminine fringe of lashes; his hair, she noticed, was carefully mussed and his face was so unlined she wondered if he had gotten a lift. Certainly dermabrasion and facials had been involved. "Julie," he said quietly, "please say you've forgiven me. I know I don't deserve it, but you have to anyway."

Juliette felt the vodka wash down her throat, as if each inch of her esophagus were being illuminated until her empty stomach glowed. She took another sip, felt the glass cool and smooth against her lip, heard it clink against her teeth. She noticed that missing from his little pitch were the words "I'm sorry." An apology without an apology—he really had gone Hollywood after all. She missed those lines around his mouth, the crease between his eyebrows. God, she had loved him, the fretful untidy longing of him. Would she really even want him now? So sleek, so successful? So easily categorized?

"There's nothing to forgive," she said, putting down her glass. "You fell in love. There is no good way to tell your wife that you've fallen in love with someone else. At least your way was quick and definite. No vacillating, no wavering in purpose. I appreciated that. You were there, then you were gone. Like magic."

She smiled at him, hoping the sarcasm hadn't been too biting, but he leaned forward, took her hand in both of his.

"It was," he said, "it was like that. Like I was bewitched. I can't explain it. I felt like it was fate, like I had no other choice, but . . ." His eyes fell and his hands too, fell away and clasped each other. "It isn't quite like I thought it would be. Anna and I . . . there's so much other stuff to cope with. The fans, the photographers, her meetings, her publicist. God, her publicist alone is a full-time job."

"Oh, come on, Arnie's got enough on his plate that he can't be bugging Anna too much," Juliette said, irritated by his seemingly boundless self-absorption, by the poor-little-starlet song she had heard so often.

"You'd think," said Josh. "Can you believe what happened with Lisa Javelin? I heard she was on drugs, I mean nasty drugs, like crystal meth. How trashy is that? But Arnie, well, Anna's like his pet project. Especially with this film. He is bound and determined she is going to win this award—she's been up twice before and I guess he feels like it's getting embarrassing. I told her she should fire him. I've always felt he was highly overrated . . ."

Of course you did, Juliette thought, *ever since he refused to take you on as a client.*

113

"And now that he's the head of the firm, he's just impossible," Josh said. "He's always hated me, as you know. He hates all screenwriters except the ones who aren't really, like Tom Stoppard. Before, I figured it was because he had the hots for you, but"—he suddenly seemed to remember Juliette was actually there—"he's none too pleased with you either these days. I heard he was furious about the hand-slapping you gave him over Hughes. I heard he was out for your hide. Good for you, Julie. You never did take any crap." He was smiling at her now. "That's one of the things I loved best about you."

Juliette felt her face grow warm under his gaze. For a moment Josh looked almost like the man she had loved for all those years, the man she had married. *Goddamn him*, she thought miserably. *Goddamn me.*

Oblivious to her thoughts, Josh took a sip of his drink. "What was I talking about?"

"Anna," Juliette said, barely able to keep viciousness out of her voice. If Josh heard it, he gave no sign.

"Right," he said. "It's been quite a learning experience, I must say. People like Anna are not so much people as they are their own private economies. You have no idea," he said, "how many people make money off her. It's unbelievable—she's like an industry and sometimes I feel like I'm the vice president or CEO or something."

"Nice work if you can get it," Juliette said lightly, reaching again for her drink.

"Oh, I'm not complaining." Now the hands were back, on hers, the eyes, on hers. "But I see now what it isn't." Josh squeezed Juliette's fingers, turned her left hand, saw the engagement ring, ran a fingertip over it. "It isn't us. I miss us. I know I can never have it back," he said, looking up at her, his

114

face open and self-recriminating. "I know that I have made that impossible. But I just wanted you to know . . . I guess I just wanted you to know that I do understand what it was I left behind. That I do know how valuable and rare it was. And if I had it to do all over again . . . " He dropped her hands as the waiter approached; Juliette held up two fingers and he vanished.

"I'm sorry," Josh said, sitting back in his chair, shaking his head. "It isn't fair, is it, me coming in after all this time saying this? It's ridiculous. I'm ridiculous."

"No," Juliette said. "No. I appreciate what you're saying. I do. Look, healthy marriages don't dissolve in six weeks, not even on location. Obviously, we wanted different things. I might not have realized it at the time"—here she allowed herself one wry laugh—"but it would have come out sooner or later."

"Do you think so?" he said, leaning in again, his eyes dark and liquid. "I wonder. Are you really going to sell our house?" he asked softly. "Our beautiful house."

"It's a little big for one," she said a bit harshly. "And I don't find it quite so beautiful anymore."

"Well, you'll make a fortune in this market," he said. "Really, I had no idea how much values have skyrocketed."

Juliette kept her gaze level—Josh had signed the house over to her a few months after he left. Because, as he had said so many times, she deserved it. If he thought he was going to weasel out of that, he was seriously mistaken.

After a moment, Josh smiled and again laid his hand on Juliette's. "I'm glad," he said. "I'm glad I did something right for you. You should use the money to take some time off. You're wasted here. You could do so much more, whatever you wanted."

Juliette looked away, torn between shame, at having suspected him, and pride that she was handling this better than she thought she would, and something else, something that left her feeling more uncertain than she had in years. Fortunately, the next round of drinks came and Juliette changed the subject. They talked about the Oscars, about Josh's nomination, about Becker and his schemes, about the dead reporter and the flipped-out publicity head. They talked for an hour, two hours, about places they had been, and the months that had gone into *A Touch of Summer*.

"It's as much your movie as it is mine," Josh said. "I wish you had taken credit."

She shook her head. "No, you just thank me when you win."

"I will do that. Not that," he added quickly, "I think I'll win. You know, I really do miss your ear. I've got these two scripts I'm working on and, man, I wish I had someone like you to take a look at them."

Flattered, she smiled.

"Maybe I could send you copies and you could, I don't know, let me know what you think."

"Sure," she said. "I'd like that."

"You'd have to be discreet," he said, rolling his glass between his hands, then looking up at her through his lashes. "Some of the balls are still in the air." She nodded and he grinned. "But of course there's nothing I can teach you about discretion."

The conversation moved on. Juliette told Josh about some of Devlin's shenanigans, relayed the story of finding David.

"And you still haven't called him?"

"No." She grinned. "And he keeps sending me flowers. I think he's in Toronto now. He's pretty cute. I imagine at some point I will soften."

Josh smiled, but still he looked slightly pained. Glancing at his watch, he made a sound of surprise.

"Good Lord, we've been at it for more than two hours," he said. "I really need to . . . well, that is, I think Anna may . . ."

"That's all right," Juliette said. "I have things to do as well." They stood and looked at each other awkwardly. "Thank you for . . . what you said before," she said, leaning in to kiss his cheek.

"Oh, Julie," he said, and enfolded her in a long and close embrace. "I'm so glad we're talking again. I can't tell you how glad." He pulled away and looked down at her with tears in his eyes. "Well," he said, composing himself. "I'm sure we'll be seeing each other soon." He waved and turned to go, then stopped and turned back around. "Oh," he said, "I'll get you copies of those scripts tomorrow. It would be great if you could give me notes on them by, say, Tuesday. Maybe we could have lunch. You know. Talk them through, like the old days." He looked down at her again, and his smile was wistful. "I really miss the old days," he said.

And then he was gone, walking his new walk toward the elevators.

Watching him, a word came into her mind, unbidden: *Perfect*, she thought. *That was so perfect.* Then, like a religious vision, it dawned on her, filled her head with clarity and light—that's what this was all about. The scripts. He couldn't write the scripts without her. He wasn't sorry. He didn't miss her. He just still couldn't do female dialogue, still couldn't figure out how to end a scene. He never could figure out how to end a scene. That was why he had brought up the house, to seem magnanimous, to make her feel like maybe she owed him something. "Talk them through . . ."

Unfuckingbelieveable. Mr. Oscar Nominee.

"Why, you sonofabitch," she said. "You lying, starfucking sonofabitch."

Juliette hadn't meant to speak as loudly as she had. From behind the bar, Marta looked up, shock plain on her face. Several patrons turned their heads. Juliette flushed, grew angrier still when she realized two of them were Max and Becker, startled from deep conversation. Max rose and walked toward her and she debated hurrying out. Deciding that would draw more attention, she chose to move slowly toward the door, obviously allowing the comedian to fall into step with her. "You all right?" he asked in a low voice. She nodded, mouth in a tight smile. "I told you you shouldn't let that bastard stay here. What is Devlin thinking?"

"It's not that," she said, pulling herself together. "It really isn't. I'm just very tired and something he said . . . well, I just took it the wrong way." She shrugged and allowed tears to gather in her eyes. "Divorce . . ."

Max nodded and embraced her, putting his cheek for a moment against hers.

"Sometimes," he said, "you have to let what you have be enough. This is what I have learned and what I think you know and he is too stupid to realize. My second wife . . ."

Juliette smiled and gently extricated herself from his arms. He nodded, his face assembled into compassion, and let her go. Was there nothing in the world, she wondered, that these people could not apply directly to themselves?

She strode out of the hotel and got in her car. She could not go home, not to that house. If she went home, she would burn it to the ground. Instead, she drove through the night to figure out what to do next . . .

*

Juliette was late for work the next day, a fact that registered on the surprised looks she got from Barney and Louisa on her way in. "Devlin's looking for you," Louisa said. "He's called you about twelve hundred times."

"Look at me," she said, throwing her hands in the air. "I turned my cell off and I haven't checked my BlackBerry. So sue me."

"Unfortunately, that's not my job," Louisa said. "But you might think about getting a lawyer." And, turning on her heel, she headed toward the concierge desk.

"Bitch," Juliette said to herself as she pushed open the door to the administrative offices, which propelled her firmly into the arms of Phillip, the pool manager.

"Juliette," he said, hugging her so hard he lifted her off the ground. "I've been waiting and waiting for you. I called and called. I just can't thank you enough. I thought I was fired, and then I found out about the raise, and I know it was all your idea. I don't know how I can ever thank you."

Juliette smiled and extricated herself from his grasp. "By leaving me alone," she said. "You just keep making the divas happy," she said before his face could register hurt. "During Oscar week, you are the most important man in Los Angeles. How would we function without order and serenity around the pool?"

She pushed him gently out the door and headed toward her office, where, surprisingly, Rory was waiting for her.

"Did you see it?" he asked with a strange mixture of envy and excitement on his face. "No? Well, here, go to the library and read this." He thrust a cream-colored card into Juliette's hand.

"What are you talking about? God, I'm one hour late and this place is like an insane asylum."

"The library," Rory said, steering her out the door. "You have to open it in the library. I have my orders."

"Devlin's looking for you," Gregory muttered as he passed her in the lobby.

"I know," Juliette muttered right back, adding as if it were a secret password, "I'll be in the library."

Gregory didn't answer, but as she passed, she felt him pinch her right buttock. "On your toes, missy," he said. "On your toes."

The library was empty when Juliette reached it, the fire flickering dutifully, the lilacs that were this week's theme flower drooping likewise from vases on the mantel and the table, the mahogany writing desks properly gleaming, the stacks of white notepaper arranged on their sleek surfaces as if by Mondrian himself. *So?* she thought, looking around, unconsciously squinting her eyes against the sight of the hateful red leather spines.

Only they weren't there. The shelves were filled instead with books of every shade and size, real books, good books, classic and modern. Juliette took a few steps forward, began reading titles. Shakespeare bumped shoulders with Margaret Atwood, Milton with Marcel Proust. Agatha Christie and Dorothy Sayers comfortably occupied an entire shelf, here was Wharton and Forster and Martin Amis. Here were Waugh and Willa Cather, Capote and Mailer and entire sets of Austen, Dickens, and Trollope. Juliette felt the breath leave her body as she stroked the spines, pulled down this one and that one, felt their fine heavy weight, smelled the musty mouthwatering perfume of leather and paper and ink. This was a library, someone's wonderful, well-chosen, much-treasured library. How did it come to be here?

She looked down at the card in her hand and opened it. On a plain ivory card a few words were scrawled:

Now you know why I have four ex-wives. Please forgive me because I am so very sorry. Love, Michael.

How had he done it? In only one night? It seemed impossible that he had remembered their conversation, that he had listened and remembered something that was so important to her. For the first time in almost a year, Juliette Greyson felt something like happiness shake loose in her chest, felt the misery that had coated her heart crack and peel away in great flaky pieces. She saw Josh as he walked away from her, saw him as he really was, and she didn't care that he was gone. Finally, she didn't care that he was gone.

It's over, she thought, closing her eyes to better find the smell of lilacs, the warmth of real books, the relief of a heart she could actually feel beating after all these months.

"I'm sorry to spoil what is clearly a very special moment for you," said Devlin's voice, startlingly close to her elbow. "But where the hell have you been? I've been calling you since last night."

"I was out," she said, opening her eyes. "Finishing up some old business. You know anyone who wants to buy my house, Dev?" Her boss was glaring at her and the glare went unchecked. "What?" she said. "I was out of pocket for ten hours and the world has come to an end? It's not enough that we now have all of Prophet's entertainment business and a brand-new million-dollar library? What? Did Cate Blanchett not get the room she wanted?"

"Josh Singer is missing," Devlin said.

"Missing? What do you mean, 'missing'?"

"I mean he was supposed to meet Anna and some friends at Jar at eight o'clock, and he never showed. She says he was supposed to be having a drink with you at five. Marta, who was behind the bar last night, says the two of you were talking till almost seven-thirty."

"Yeah?" Juliette said. Devlin raised his eyebrows. "He said he had to meet Anna, he went, and I left."

"And you didn't hear from him again?"

"No."

"Have you checked your messages?"

"No."

"Well, maybe you should do that."

"What are you trying to say, Dev?" She looked at him with irritation.

"I'm not trying to say anything, Juliette," he answered. "All I know is Miss Stewart is damn near hysterical, I've got agents, publicists, and studio heads calling me every fifteen minutes, so if you could possibly shed any light on your ex-husband's whereabouts, I would sure as hell appreciate it."

Juliette pulled out her BlackBerry, first scrolling through her e-mail, then listening to her voice-mail messages, the last ten of which were from Devlin. "Nothing," she said. "Except my boss, who's obviously not having a very good morning."

The attempt at humor fell flat. Devlin looked so upset that Juliette, still insulated in the pleasure of Michael's apology, put her hand against his neck. "I'm sure he's fine," Juliette said. "Is his car still here?"

Devlin shook his head. "Doesn't have a car. The studio was supplying the limo and Anna had it."

"Did he call for a cab?"

"No record of it," he said.

"Could he have walked to Jar?"

Devlin stared at her incredulously. "It's two miles from here; and why on earth would he do such a thing?"

Juliette shrugged; tiny claws of concern began tearing at the corners of her sense of well-being. "Well, maybe he ran into a friend and went out drinking," she said, but even as she spoke she realized that wasn't a real possibility—Josh might have reneged on his wedding vows, but he was fairly scrupulous about keeping dinner engagements.

"Was he upset when he left you? Did you have an argument? What did you talk about?"

"Jesus, Dev," she said. "We talked about all sorts of things, if that is any of your business. We hadn't seen each other in, like, nine months. But no, we didn't argue, not at all. We had a pretty nice chat, for a divorced couple, and then he went off to meet his girlfriend for dinner. If anything, he was slightly concerned that he was running late. The last I saw was the back of him."

Devlin nodded.

"He'll turn up," Juliette said, not liking how uncertain her boss looked, not liking the concern that was quickly turning into anxiety. "He has to—he's nominated for an Oscar."

Devlin nodded again and turned away. Juliette stood still and watched him leave, just as she had watched Josh leave, so she saw how white Louisa's face was as she came around the corner, how she grabbed hold of Devlin's arm, how she glanced Juliette's way with shock and disbelief in her eyes.

"What?" Juliette said loudly, thinking she should join them but suddenly unable to move her legs. "What's happened?" She saw Devlin shake his head, motion Louisa back into the lobby, and hurry back to her. He put his hand under her elbow and guided her to a chair, keeping his dark eyes on hers, unblinking.

"Josh has turned up," he said in a voice she had never heard before. "He's dead, sweetheart." His eyes were still on hers.

"Some joggers found his body in Griffith Park. His throat was cut."

Juliette made a strangled sound; she could feel the blood leave her face. Devlin's hand came up behind her head, pulled her into his shoulder. "Stay with me, Juliette, stay with me. I'm right here, we're all right here. You're going to be fine. It's going to be fine. Just stay right here with me." Juliette felt her hands clutching the front of his shirt, felt her forehead press hard against his chest. Above the beating of his heart, she could hear the sounds of the hotel: the front door opening and closing with the gasp of outdoor life, the clatter of heels on marble floors, the chink of a room service cart running by. "When you're ready, we'll go to my office. Are you ready? Can you walk?" He pulled her away from him, peered into her face, smoothed his shirt. Juliette nodded, drew herself away, pressed her palms against her cheeks. "Good girl, see, you're doing fine."

Taking a deep breath, she stood.

"Do they," she said, "do they have any idea ... who ... why?"

Devlin shook his head. "I don't know anything more than I just told you. The police are here now," he said, his voice low, his hand steady and comforting on her arm. "They want to talk to you."

The next hour was even more surreal than the night Juliette found David Fulbright floating in the pool. This time, though, there could be no mistake about whether or not she was dealing with the actual police. There was nothing heroic or handsome about the detectives who introduced themselves in Devlin's office. The man, Detective Harrison, was thin and stooped, with white stubble that stood out unnervingly against his dark skin; the woman, whose name Juliette didn't catch, was red-faced and built so broad and solid it was difficult to tell where her breasts ended and her waist began.

They asked many of the same questions Devlin had asked. When she had met Josh, how long they had talked, the tenor of the conversation.

"So no arguments over the divorce, no disagreements over, say, the house or division of property?" asked Detective Harrison.

Juliette shook her head. "We had worked that out months ago."

"Your lawyers . . ."

She shook her head again. "No, we didn't use lawyers," she said. "Josh didn't want anything. We divided up the bank accounts ourselves. He was very generous."

"So who filed for divorce?"

"I did."

The woman wrote this, or something, down in her note-book.

"So you talked about, what, the weather for two and half hours?" the woman asked, a little sarcastically.

"No," Juliette said quietly. "We talked about a lot of things. We talked about the Oscars, we talked about the other films nominated. We talked about people we both know, we reminisced . . ."

"And you didn't argue about anything?"

"No," she said.

"Really?" Detective Harrison said. "According to the bartender, you were noticeably angry when he left. You called him"—he glanced at his notes—"'a starfucking sonofabitch.'"

"But he didn't hear me," Juliette said. "I said it to myself."

"You said it loudly enough for the bartender to hear."

Juliette swallowed. She couldn't bring herself to look at

Devlin, so she kept her eyes on the detective's carefully bland face. "I was standing very close to the bar at the time. And I'm sure Marta also told you that Josh gave no signs of hearing, that he kept right on walking."

Grudgingly, Detective Harrison nodded.

"If you didn't argue, Ms. Greyson, then why were you so upset?"

"It's hard to explain."

"Try." His tone was firm.

"He asked me to read his scripts," she said after a moment.

The two detectives exchanged glances. "Read his scripts," Detective Harrison said.

"Scripts he was working on. It wasn't exactly what I had been expecting."

"What had you been expecting?"

"Not to be asked to read his scripts."

"And this bothered you because . . . ?" the woman asked.

Juliette shrugged. "I don't know. I guess because I thought we were just having a friendly talk and then at the end he wanted something from me."

"And had you helped him with his scripts before?" asked Detective Harrison.

"Well, yes," she said. "I mean, I was his wife."

"The script that he was nominated for, did you feel you had helped him on that one?"

At this point, Devlin, who had been sitting quietly behind his desk, put his hand on her back. "Juliette, you don't have to answer them if you don't want to. Detectives, I am increasingly inclined to call our lawyer."

"No need, no need," said Detective Harrison, "though that is, of course, your right. So after your husband left you last night, what did you do, Ms. Greyson?"

"I left the hotel."

"Did you go home? Did you stop for dinner? Call a girl-friend?"

"No," Juliette said. "I just drove."

"Where did you drive?"

"To the beach. I drove to the beach and I sat for a while and then I drove up the coast for a few hours."

"Did you stop at a hotel? Did you stay overnight?"

"No," said Juliette, her voice deadening. "No. Just drove."

"Your colleagues say you were late to work. So we are to believe you drove from approximately eight p.m. until ten a.m.?"

"Well, no," said Juliette hastily. "I mean, I stopped at beaches, I stopped and slept, and around, I don't know, seven or so, I got back home, took a shower, changed . . . and came in."

"And you were during that time, again according to colleagues, unreachable either via your cell phone or BlackBerry. Is that usual, Ms. Greyson?"

"No," she said, confused. "I mean, I don't usually drive all night either. I was upset. I hadn't seen Josh in months, and when he asked me to give him notes, it was upsetting."

The two detectives were now both writing furiously.

"Is there anyone who can corroborate your story, Ms. Greyson?" asked Detective Harrison. "Did you stop for dinner? To get gas? Did you meet anyone while you were sitting on the beach?"

"Corroborate? What do you mean? No, I mean, I don't remember if I met anyone, I might have, what are you saying?" Juliette's voice was rising tight and high as she looked from one detective to another. "Do you think I killed Josh? That's absurd . . ."

"Detectives," said Devlin firmly, standing behind Juliette. "I think that's enough for right now. Ms. Greyson has had quite a shock, and she has answered your questions."

"I understand your concern, Mr. Devlin," said the woman. "But if Ms. Greyson doesn't feel comfortable answering our questions here, perhaps she should join us down at the station."

"Now, you wait one bloody minute," said Devlin, his voice deepening.

"No need to take that tone, Mr. Devlin," said the woman, rising from her chair.

"This can't be happening," said Juliette, as much to herself as to anyone. "Tell me this isn't happening."

"I am going to call my lawyer right this minute," said Devlin. "And you aren't taking her two steps out of this office unless you charge her with something."

His hand reached for the telephone just as Detective Harrison also stood, saying, "We will do what is right for this investigation, Mr. Devlin," when the phone rang right under Devlin's hand. Taken by surprise, Devlin let it ring twice before he answered it.

"Yes, yes," he said, "well, we're a bit busy at the moment. What? She was? You're sure? He's sure? All right. All right. We'll be right up."

He put the phone down slowly, his back to the detectives, and Juliette could see him deciding something, could see him arranging his features back into those of the smooth hotelier.

"Detectives," he said quietly when he turned back. "If you will follow me, I think we can shed some light on Ms. Greyson's whereabouts last night. Juliette," he said as she opened her mouth, "I know what you're about to say. But it's all right. You can tell them the truth."

128

9

"She was with me," said Michael, propped into a sitting position by innumerable pillows, as the detectives shifted about uneasily, eyes wide, mouths trying to work themselves away from ingratiating smiles. "As you can see, I am, shall we say, experiencing technical difficulties." He smiled at the female detective. "I'm sorry, I didn't catch your name."

"Florence," she said. "Abigail Florence."

"My favorite city in the entire world," he said. "Have you been? Oh, you should go. I proposed to my second wife on the Ponte Vecchio. At sunset. Unfortunately"—he allowed himself a small laugh—"L.A. proved not quite as magical as Florence."

His consonants clipped and sighed with quiet precision. Juliette felt the hairs on the back of her neck rise. From the look on the detective's face, so did she.

"I checked in to this hotel several weeks ago with the understanding that no one but my friends Eamonn and Juliette would know I was here. You understand," he said to Detective Harrison. "Show a little weakness in this town and . . ."

The detective narrowed his eyes in sympathy.

"So Ms. Greyson has kindly spent several hours a day, sometimes more, holding my hand and keeping me company. It's very lonely," he said simply. "I feel so helpless, and I'm afraid I'm not used to feeling helpless." He smiled with chagrin. "Juliette has sat with me through the night on several occasions, including last night. I had a particularly difficult night last night," he said.

"I am sorry, sir," said Detective Harrison, "to hear you're sick. And may I just say how much I enjoy your films, especially *Dark Hawk* and *Never Again*."

O'Connor nodded; his smile dazzled briefly. "Those were fun, weren't they? My favorites too. I'm so glad you liked them."

Looking pleased, the detective struggled to bring himself back to his question. "So, Ms. Greyson was here from about when to when?"

O'Connor's eyes did not leave the detective's face. "From about eight till, oh, six a.m.? I was up much of the night and we both fell asleep, I think around three, wasn't it, Juliette?" He turned to her briefly and smiled. "Poor thing, at one point she was asleep in the chair, but I got Rory to put her on the couch."

"So you have a nurse here 'round the clock," said Detective Florence, attempting a certain firmness. "Why, then, would you need Ms. Greyson?"

O'Connor looked at her, eyes wide and very blue. "Well, as fond as I am of Rory"—he nodded toward the nurse, who stood beside the sofa—"two grouchy old men can get on each other's nerves pretty quickly. And Juliette is a bit easier on the eyes, wouldn't you say? Besides, Rory's stuck in here with me. I need my daily dose of gossip, Detective Florence. It's as vital as the chemo, you know, and much more fun."

If she hadn't been almost completely numb from the morning's events, Juliette would have laughed out loud. Or applauded. He was so charming, so utterly convincing that she began to remember being in the room all night herself. The detectives certainly seemed to have no doubts. After chatting with them for several more minutes, O'Connor made it clear that he was exhausted, begged them to use their own best judgment and discretion, and assured them he would cooperate in any way. "You have to understand Juliette's extreme loyalty to the hotel and the guests," he said. "I only wish I had been able to speak with her before all this began so she would not have felt obligated to . . . well . . . dissemble." He smiled again, a pull-out-all-the-stops smile. "I'm glad we were able to clear things up right away, aren't you?"

Devlin soon ushered the detectives out the door; they seemed to have forgotten Juliette was even there. She watched the door close, and the sudden silence seemed like a sort of death.

"Did you kill him?" O'Connor asked from the bed. She turned and looked at him. His face gave nothing away save curiosity. "Not that I care if you did—he probably deserved it, all things considered, and actually it would be more fun if you had. I'd just like to know exactly how diabolical I'm being. For the record."

Juliette shook her head, her eyes filling, her hands so cold, her arms so cold. After a few moments, O'Connor threw back a portion of the blanket and Juliette crawled in beside him.

In the fragrant quiet of the room, Juliette eventually stopped shivering, but still she lay with her head in the crook of his arm. She could hear the silence give way to the murmured blips of his heart monitor, the steady hum of the machine that delivered the self-administered pain medication, and the occasional cough from Rory in the next room.

"Peaceful, isn't it?" Michael said. "Sometimes I just lie here and listen to all my machinery breathe."

Juliette raised her head to look at him, but he pressed it back down. "No, no, not yet. Stay awhile. God, just to feel the weight of a woman's body . . ." He kissed the top of her head.

Thinking of how long it had been since she had felt the weight of anyone's body, how long since she had lain next to a man on a bed, Juliette fell back, put her hand on his chest, watched it rise and fall with his breath. She could imagine the hotel beneath her moving likewise. Despite the seeming serenity of the whole, every floor continually pulsed with movement, along corridors, behind closed doors, in soft or silent communication, like the constant work of the body, the perpetual electricity in the brain. She had always felt safe here, not just at this hotel but in this life. She knew how it worked, what it was supposed to do, she knew how to fix it when it didn't. For the past fifteen years she had comforted herself with the idea that even if it wasn't perfect, even if it wasn't quite what she had wildly dreamt of when she was young, this world would protect her, cushion her from the life outside, which she knew to be cruel and uncontrollable. All the hotel asked in return was devotion, and Juliette had always been good at devotion.

She started to shake again, and O'Connor pulled her closer. "What?" he said. "What are you thinking?"

In a split second, she thought of a million things she could say, a million things that were close enough to pass for the truth. "I never thought it could get us in here," she said instead. Then, embarrassed by her words, she tried to explain. "This place is like a fortress, like a castle—that's why people like you come here. In a way your whole world is like a fortress, yours, and Anna's, and I guess Josh's. With a million walls, a million secret doors, a million people between you and . . ."

"And real life?"

She nodded.

"And now the walls have been breached," he said.

She nodded again.

"But it didn't happen here," he said.

"I know," she said, "but it feels like it did. He was on his way to Jar, for God's sake, to meet his famous girlfriend who's in town for the *Oscars* . . . if that doesn't protect you, what does?"

"What is it you're afraid of, Juliette?" O'Connor asked after a moment.

It seemed too big a question, the way he asked it, and she could not even begin to answer. She thought of the hotel, dug her mind deep into the hotel—lunch being ordered, the lounge filling up, people crowding onto the back patio to smoke, people in their rooms, talking and fucking and watching TV, the concierge desk phone ringing, guests lying by the pool, ignoring the breeze-lifted goose bumps, resolutely feeling only the sun. Life was going on; that was the beauty of a place like this, the beauty of a city like this. She pushed any thought of Josh out of her mind. The events of the morning seemed impossible, unreal, while here O'Connor was substantial, not half as frail as he seemed. The arm beneath her head was strong—she could feel the muscles flex and move.

"I wonder what would have happened if I had slept with you all those years ago," she said instead of answering, allowing Josh to fade into nonexistence, forcing Josh to fade into nonexistence.

O'Connor laughed quietly. He stroked her hair, twirled a strand around his finger. "Probably nothing good," he said. "I was an asshole back then. An even bigger asshole," he amended. "Back then I thought I somehow deserved it, you know. That I was special, that all the attention and the money proved I was special."

"And you don't think that now?" she asked, with a small doubtful click of her tongue. "When it might possibly, actually be sort of true?"

"More and more, I realize it has nothing to do with me," he said softly, ignoring her sarcasm. "That it never did. The work, that's me, for better or worse, and there's plenty of both. Just like anyone. But the rest? That's something else, something way beyond my control."

He paused and she could hear him swallow, feel him shift so the curve of her hip pressed against him. "Fame isn't like a fortress at all, you know," he said. "It's more like an earthquake or a ten-car pileup. It's abnormal, like a hurricane. Some people walk away, some people do okay, but most of us are damaged one way or another. Look at me," he said quietly. "No children, few friends, or real friends anyway, calling on a woman who worked in a hotel where I once stayed to hold my hand while I try not to die."

Juliette lifted her head, just a little, turned onto her side, and it was easy, after all, to kiss him. She began with the cheek, the neck, heard the unmistakable small gasp of pleasure, found the soft surprised mouth, the tender soft spot behind the earlobe, then back to the mouth, focused, unhurried, feeling strength return to both of them.

"You shouldn't have lied," she said, when she finally raised her mouth from his.

"I didn't," he said, putting his hand deep into her hair, pulling her back to him. "You were here. All night long."

"People saw me leave," she said, her breath coming quick and shallow.

"You came back," he said, and his kisses grew deeper, his hands cupped her face.

"Rory knows I wasn't here," she said.

"I gave Rory the night off." His mouth slid down to her neck and she closed her eyes, wondered for a moment, as pleasure washed over her, how far this could go, how far she wanted it to go. "He's the one without an alibi, not you. Who knows what he was doing last night? You were here. Where you belong."

Juliette arched over him now, her hands on either side of his chest, her hair falling around them. His hands slid along either side of her waist, then cupped her breasts.

"Oh, God," he groaned, and she knew she was falling, away from thought and decision, but then she felt him pushing her, saw the sweat on his face, felt a heat rising from him that she knew wasn't desire. Pulling herself off the bed, she quickly reached for the basin.

"Fuck, fuck, fuck," he said when he was done. "God forbid I feel like a human being for two fucking minutes." He caught her hand as she turned toward the bathroom to empty the basin. "I'm so sorry," he said. "You were, you are, wonderful, amazing, miraculous . . ."

"I have this effect on many men," she said, jerking her head at the basin. But then she smiled at him and pushed the hair off his forehead. She turned to go again, but he held her hand tightly, pulled her back.

"You didn't do that just because of what I said to the police," he said, "did you? Because I would have said it anyway. For the hell of it."

She looked at him, his face flushed, hair matted like a child's. She had no idea what the truth was, but she said exactly what he wanted to hear because that was what came most easily.

"I did that because I wanted to," she said. "For a very long time."

Hearing her enter the bathroom, Rory discreetly poked his head out of the adjoining bedroom door. "Everything okay?" he asked, his eyebrows only slightly raised.

"Juliette has to get back to work," O'Connor said, collecting himself quickly. "So you're back on the clock, Nurseman. Listen, sweetheart," he said as she reappeared, straightening her sweater, smoothing her hair. "Why don't you take the keys to my Brentwood place? Seriously. You aren't going to want to go home and you shouldn't stay around here today . . ."

"Thanks," she said, holding up her hand. "I'll be okay . . . Michael. I'll look in on you later," she promised, taking a deep breath and preparing to return to whatever was occurring in the hotel below.

"Just be careful," he said. "I think there's more to it than Josh's death, not," he added hastily, "that that's not bad enough. Think about it, two nominees dead, and that reporter, even poor old Lisa whacked out on the wrong flu shot. I mean, Hollywood is a dangerous place, but there is something seriously strange going on. And I don't like the thought of you being anywhere near it."

So says the movie star being secretly treated for cancer, Juliette thought. *He is sick but still very handsome and I kissed him with great pleasure less than an hour after he lied to police who seem to suspect me of killing my ex-husband who was found this morning in Griffith Park with his throat cut.*

How much stranger could it get?

"Here at the Pinnacle," she said, popping a breath mint into her mouth, "we pride ourselves on being the center of it all."

"That's exactly what I'm afraid of," O'Connor said.

*

Many things had changed in the short time Juliette had been in O'Connor's room, and Gregory was happy to describe them in breathless detail. After escorting the police out of the hotel, Devlin promptly had Marta transferred to the Pinnacle in Bali. Effective immediately. When the bartender threatened to tell the police, he laughed and told her to go ahead—he was sure the police would be more interested in Marta's crack-dealing past than a staff reorganization. "If I had known it would get me to Bali," Gregory sniffed to Juliette, "I'd have ratted you out too."

But Marta's dismissal was not the most important development. Upon hearing of her lover's death, Anna Stewart had suffered what appeared to be a grand mal seizure and was rushed to Cedars-Sinai. When the police were finally able to question her later that day, her story was slightly different than the one she had told Devlin and the staff of the hotel. Josh had indeed shown up at the restaurant, a half hour late. They had quarreled and she had left him there, at around nine o'clock, and gone on to the Sky Bar for several hours before returning to the hotel. He had called her cell phone twice, just after she left him, but she had shut it off and had not received the messages until she got back to the Pinnacle.

"I went to bed," she said, sobbing. "When he wasn't there when I got home, I was very upset, so I took some Halcion and went to bed. I assumed he would come in during the night."

She had given Devlin a different account because she wanted Josh found as soon as possible but didn't want the kind of "rumor-mongering publicity" a tale of a restaurant quarrel would generate. "It was nothing," she told the police. "A lovers' spat. I was pretending to be jealous because he was with his ex-wife. It was silly. He knew that. We both knew it was nothing."

When police examined Josh's body, they found that his wallet and cell phone, as well as his watch and rings, had been taken. The manager of Jar remembered that Josh had finished his dinner, paid, and then walked out of the restaurant, quite calmly, talking on his cell phone. She did not remember seeing him get in a cab, and none of the waiters remembered him asking for one to be called.

At a press conference early that evening, the police chief said the murder seemed, on the face of it, to be a case of simple robbery. Officers were trying to find any witnesses who might have seen Josh walking down the street near the restaurant, or any cabdrivers who might have taken him elsewhere. In answer to a question from an E! reporter, the chief said there was no evidence linking Josh Singer's death to that of Natasha Coleman or reporter Marie Stanton. He pointed out that Singer and Coleman had died in very different ways on two different coasts and the reporter's death, though still under investigation, seemed to be of natural causes.

"There is no hard evidence to suggest that these are anything but isolated incidents," he said as the cameras clicked like frenzied insects. Still, E! led that night with a story about the new "Oscar curse."

Meanwhile, after offering Anna every comfort known to man, Devlin informed Gregory and Juliette that in the unlikely event he would survive this Oscar season "that bitch" would never set foot in the Pinnacle again. "Not if she wins ten Oscars and the Congressional Medal of Honor. She almost single-handedly brought down the reputation of this hotel."

"Not to mention putting our Juliette behind bars," murmured Gregory. "Though I do appreciate the supersexy visual."

"Can you imagine what would have happened if people thought he had gone missing from here?" Devlin said, not listening. "It's bad enough he was staying here, a fact every news report seems determined to mention. Oh, right, sorry, love," he said to Juliette. With a nod to Gregory, he drew her into his office. "You look exhausted. What you need is a good feed and an early night. Why don't you come home with me? I'll make you dinner and tuck you in. And that's all. On my honor. I mean, unless . . ."

She remembered the brief improbable longing she had felt kissing Michael, the hope that somehow the tubes and the monitors would disappear and he would flip her over on her back and make everything else insignificant. At least for an hour. As disturbing as it was to think she had felt desire while Josh's body lay cooling in a morgue somewhere, Juliette couldn't help but take some comfort from the fact that at least she was still capable of desire.

"You sound like Max," she said to Devlin. "He was in this afternoon, on his way to the desert, to offer me moral support and a place to stay if I needed 'sanctuary.'"

And I'll keep my hands to myself, he had also said, *not that an old man like me would stand a chance with a girl like you, but just so you know.*

"Of course, he wanted the blow-by-blow," she said now. "Even in a time like this, he is such a gossip."

"I'm offering because I care about you, J.," Devlin said. "Sure, and you must know that by now," he added softly but with his broadest brogue.

"Thanks," she said, kissing him softly on the side of the mouth. "For everything today. For shouting at the detectives and letting me wrinkle your shirt."

"If I had known you were with O'Connor, I wouldn't have let you lie, you know," he said. "No hotel is worth that. He was an idjit," he went on, as if it were something he had been saving up. "Josh, I mean. Not that I would have wished such a thing on him or anyone, God knows. But be careful you don't love him now just because he's dead. It's even easier to love a lying bastard when he's dead."

He spoke so heatedly that Juliette stopped and stared at him. There was such a sadness in his face, she thought. Deep and inextricable, carved almost into his bones. Surely it was not for Josh. Had it always been there?

"I won't," she said, feeling a rush of fondness for her boss. What was it Sally had said? *You'd do better with Dev, though I imagine the working conditions would be similar.* She couldn't imagine being brave enough to let herself really love Devlin. That was too perilous an occupation. Where had he been last night? she wondered. And with whom?

Back in her office, Juliette played catch-up with the few journalists she hadn't spoken to during the day, including Sasha, who filled her in on the security frenzy and general paranoia now ruling the *Times* newsroom and Hollywood at large. "Someone said they heard DiCaprio's brakes went out on Mulholland yesterday, and that some actress got a chemical burn from some face cream in the gift bag she picked up at the SAG luncheon, though we haven't been able to confirm. And the whole Lisa Javelin thing has everyone talking—apparently she told a few of her friends that she was going to take her clients and start a new agency. Next thing you know, she's having a psychotic breakdown at Morton's, dumped a Caesar salad in Ed Limota's lap. People are freaking out all over town," she said excitedly. "It's been really awful here; everyone is just in shock and horribly sad," she added dutifully. "Which I'm sure you can understand. How are you holding up, anyway?"

"Oh, you know, adrenaline is a powerful drug," she said.

"So can you tell me what happened?" Sasha said in an intimate "between girlfriends" voice. "I mean, I'm sure you've been talking about it all day, but we really feel there's something bigger going on here, and it would help to know as many details as possible."

Which was her way of saying everything was on the record. Rubbing her forehead as she spoke, Juliette told Sasha pretty much what she had told the police—she and Josh had had drinks, it had been pleasant enough, and then he left. She left out the part about the hotel being turned upside down looking for him, about Anna's lies, about the police's initial suspicion of her.

"It just doesn't seem real to me," she said, giving the reporter what she hoped would be her quote. "I mean, I know it is real. This time. But it seems so senseless—the idea that Josh was just in the wrong place at the wrong time is so ironic considering why he was here. He was on the top of his game, just everything going for him."

She could hear Sasha typing away, with the occasional muttered, "Mhmm-hmm."

"Great," the reporter said when Juliette finished speaking. "Thank you so much. Listen," she added as if she had just remembered. "I'm probably going to be over there tomorrow, maybe you could carve out a tiny bit of time to talk to me more, just about how all this is affecting the staff and the guests, about your take on its impact on the Oscars."

When the reporter at last hung up, Juliette realized that the real irony of Josh's death was that it wouldn't be about Josh. As horrifying as it was, his murder was morphing into just another part of a larger picture, in which the milieu was more important than the actual events. Just like Michael had said—when you're famous, it isn't about you. Strangely enough, it's about everyone else. It wasn't so much that he had been killed, or even how he had been killed, but that he was a nominee killed during what was becoming the strangest Oscar season in history.

With this thought came a wave of overwhelming sadness, the sense of loss she had been groping for—that she had to grope frightened her, but here it was, with the chest-rattling tears, the blinding disbelief. Whether she was crying for Josh himself or for the belated cold reality of the world he had chosen over her, she didn't allow herself to answer. It was enough that she was crying, like any normal woman would. Like Anna Stewart had.

When Juliette finally sat up and wiped her face, it was going on eleven and there was really only one thing for her to do. She took the elevator up to Michael's room, quietly let herself in, and, stripping down to her camisole, navigated her way around the tubes and the wires and curved herself quietly beside his sleeping form.

"It took you long enough," he mumbled, turning onto his back and drawing her once again into the comforting crook of his arm.

10

Juliette woke up alone, to the whoosh of curtains, sudden sunlight, with the smell of coffee and lightly burnt toast.

"Your thing is buzzing," O'Connor said from across the room. Squinting and pushing the hair from her face, she sat up in the bed and turned toward the voice. He was sitting in a chair a few feet away, pouring coffee from a silver carafe into a white china cup.

"You're out of bed."

"It happens." He pulled a silver dome from off a plate of scrambled egg whites and zucchini. "We asked the kitchen what Ms. Greyson preferred for breakfast and this is what they sent. With a strawberry Pop-Tart."

Her BlackBerry was indeed buzzing. The digital clock icon informed her it was seven-thirty. O'Connor gestured to the coffee and she rose from the bed to join him, gathering the sheets around her like a cloak.

"Please," he said. "Women only do that in movies." There was a robe lying over the back of the chair he was sitting in. He tossed it to her. "I sent Rory down to get you some clothes. I guessed a six."

"On a good day," she said.

"I have a feeling this is going to be a very good day." He dug his fork into what looked like a bacon and cheese omelette and ate a large bite. The transformation was remarkable—his skin was flushed and healthy-looking, his hair wet and slicked back, his chin smooth and regaining its trademark jut, and he was looking at her with an expression of immense satisfaction.

"Did something happen last night of which I should be aware?" she said.

"Why do you ask?" His eyes gleamed with their famous mischief.

"Because if I didn't know better, I'd say you just got laid," she said.

"You should take it as a compliment," he said. "This is the effect you have on men, and you don't even have to put out. No, I'm afraid all you are seeing are the effects of a very, very lovely night's sleep."

His grin was so infectious that Juliette couldn't help laughing. "Stop it," she said. "I liked you better when you were shoving me across the floor."

"No, you didn't," he said. "You like me now. Admit it. Admit you like me."

"Well, I trusted you more then. Now I'm just wondering what's up with your medication."

"What's up with his medication is he's not taking any," said Rory, coming in with his arms full of bags from Saks.

"How did you get into Saks at seven-thirty in the morning?" Juliette asked.

The nurse rolled his eyes. "Don't ask me, ask him."

"I had to put in a long-distance call from Morocco for a friend of mine," Michael said, slathering butter on toast.

"I went with grays and blues," Rory said, handing Juliette a small stack of skirts and sweaters. "They seem to suit you. And I got two sizes because Chanel runs small," he added kindly.

"You're not taking any medication?" Juliette said.

"I'm in between treatments," Michael said. "So I'm going easy on all the other stuff. Too much is happening right now. I need to have my wits about me."

"I don't see why you should worry about them, when they don't seem to be too worried about you," Rory said.

"Rory is still upset that I didn't get a nomination."

"And Pacino did? He doesn't even act anymore," Rory said disdainfully. "He just lurches around and shouts. He thinks stressing every third word somehow translates into meaning. It's a travesty."

"Rory feels very strongly about Pacino," O'Connor said.

"And Alicia Goldstone—what is that about? I know Becker said he wanted to raise the dead; I didn't know he was planning to do it literally."

"Rory feels very strongly about Alicia Goldstone," O'Connor said.

"I swear they should just clear out the Academy and start all over again," Rory said. "When was the last time someone who actually deserved an Oscar won anyway? It's nothing but a big popularity contest. Worse than that, it's just a big marketing competition."

"Rory feels very strongly about the Academy," said O'Connor. "Though I felt I deserved my first Oscar. Possibly not my second, but certainly my first."

"I think it is a curse," said Rory. "I do. I think they have tainted the process so much that someone or something is fighting back. I just hope we learn something from the tragedies that are unfolding around us. Can I get you anything?" O'Connor shook his head. "Okay, I'll be next door if you need me."

"Well, okay," said Juliette as the door closed behind him. "He is a very interesting guy, your nurse."

"Devoted."

"Obviously."

"Slightly demented, but devoted."

"Just the way you like them."

"How can you say that, Juliette?" He drew out the syllables as if each were a separate delicious word. Shaking the crumbs from her napkin, she stood.

"As strange and seductive as it is here in the alternative universe of you, I have to go to work." He grabbed her hand as she passed and she thought, *If he pulls me down, I may never get up,* but he didn't. He turned her hand over and kissed her palm, lightly. Unconsciously, she drew it back along the line of his jaw. God, he was handsome, unbearably handsome even now, and there was something, a softness in his eyes, that she thought had not been there before. But she did have to get back, return to the life she had left on the floor in splinters, put the splinters back together, see what was really missing.

"Go," he said, nodding toward the bathroom. "Let's see if Rory has the makings of a professional shopper."

It turned out that Leonardo DiCaprio had experienced car trouble on Mulholland Drive, though it had been his transmission and not the brakes of his electric car and there was never any thought of danger except to his publicist's highly calibrated schedule. Josh's face was everywhere—in the papers, on the television, invariably arm-in-arm with Anna, who was granting an interview to Barbara Walters at the hotel the next day. Juliette was mentioned as a biographical aside, when she was mentioned at all, and footage of Anna leaving Cedars last night, stunningly sorrowful in a black veil, somehow made it onto the morning news.

"I would suggest avoiding all screens for at least the next forty-eight hours," said Gregory, who was the reason Juliette's BlackBerry had been buzzing at seven-thirty in the morning. "Arnie is going to milk this for all it's worth—one of his underlings actually had the decency to call me for the sole purpose of warning you. An MDB publicist going out of her way to do something nice, I don't know. That may be the strangest thing that's happened yet. Although, Arnie taking over at MDB may trump it. Oh, you didn't hear? Yeah, after Lisa flipped out, good old Arnie simply took over her client list. So now he's overseeing something like half the nominees. Arnie Ellison, king of the Oscars. At least someone is benefiting from all this mess."

Gregory had been on the phone all morning doing damage control, checking in first with Europe, then with New York, and finally with points west to make sure that everyone was clear that Josh had not disappeared from the hotel, that Anna was still at the Pinnacle, where she planned to stay now until the Oscars.

"They're nervous," he admitted. "But they're not waffling. They're all still coming. It's not like after 9/11 or when the war broke out. And we've still got three weeks. In three weeks, it will all be forgotten. Oh," he added slowly, patting Juliette's arm, "you should know that Arnie's first move was to issue a press release, in Anna's name, saying that Josh's memorial service will be held in London next month. 'So as not to interfere with the awards Josh valued so highly.'"

Juliette felt the top of her head grow cold and distant, as if someone had lifted away part of her skull. Josh's memorial service. What sort of words were those anyway? She nodded mutely.

"God forbid he cast a pall on the proceedings," Gregory said. "I'm sorry, honey. I figured you'd rather hear it from me."

"Thank you," Juliette said, and, turning her attention to her BlackBerry, she walked away.

At the hotel, everything was in overdrive. Bill Becker and Forrest Hughes, along with several of the Oscars production team, had lunch with the president of the Academy, taking the most visible table in the restaurant so everyone who came in could see them talking seriously, yet with the occasional good-natured laugh—stars dropped by, and tourists, and all were welcomed with equal goodwill. Juliette was surprised to see Hughes's signature blond mop top very much in evidence—so he hadn't actually shaved his head for his *Vanity Fair* cover. Two tables over, Juliette spied Arnie, ostensibly having lunch with another publicist but clearly there to keep an eye on things, more specifically Hughes. Not that he needed to, or so it seemed. The comedian's green eyes were clear and bright and the mobile face that had made him so much money over the years was set firmly on Charm. Hughes greeted everyone who stopped by with a smile that swore he had been waiting all day just for the chance to say hello to them. *Amazing*, Juliette thought as she watched Hughes and Becker move through the room as if they were Red Cross rescue workers or beloved local politicians rather than the high-strung, high-paid powermongers that they were.

Devlin too was very present, greeting guests and visitors, all the while ensuring that no one made a false step or in any way got out of hand. When he saw Juliette passing, he motioned her over.

"Mr. Becker, Mr. Hughes, I think you know Juliette, the heart and mind of our hotel."

As Becker rose, which took a while, Juliette waited to see if he would recognize her. "Larger than life" was the term invariably employed to describe him in magazine profiles, a man with famously huge appetites—at one time for drugs and fights and prostitutes. But now that he was father to a two-year-old and four-month-old, he confined his encounters to the culinary variety. He had even quit smoking, though he made up for this by chewing Nicorette by the pack, eating mints and Life Savers by the fistful. Still, he remained one of those Industry types who never remembered a name until he needed something specifically from the person to whom it belonged. The fact that she had just recently overseen his now-famous fountain photo shoot would certainly not have registered. Over the years, Juliette had been introduced to the producer no less than twenty times, and each and every time it was an utterly new experience for him.

"Nice to meet you," he said now, holding out his hand, his eyes passing vaguely over her face.

Beside him, Andrea Chapman, the talent coordinator for the Oscars, rolled her eyes and enfolded Juliette in a silent embrace. Producers might come and go, but the Oscars could not happen without her. Andrea was the one who decided who would present and who would perform, Andrea was the one who dealt with all the neurotic demands and concerns, who made sure no one felt like they were being passed over even when they were. She knew everything about everybody and had a phone list that, rumor had it, was insured for one million dollars. She and Juliette went way back.

"You look great, kiddo," Andrea whispered as the two women hugged. For a moment, Juliette was afraid she might break down, but, raising her eyes, she saw Arnie give her a smug smile and that flushed any real emotion from her system. Pulling away from Andrea, she found herself face to face with Forrest.

"Juliette," he said, taking her hand in both of his. "I am so sorry about Josh. I know you two were . . . well, but still, it must be such a shock. It is such a loss, a real loss. He was a deeply talented man. I mean, his work speaks for itself."

Something about the way his mouth twisted as he said these last words made Juliette look sharply into his eyes, but whatever she sensed quickly disappeared. For a moment she thought she would laugh, so sincerely sympathetic did he look. Instead she smiled politely. "Thank you very much," she said, withdrawing her hand. For just a second, for less than a second, Hughes resisted, pressing his thumb into her wrist so hard it would have been painful had the moment lasted longer.

"It's so nice to see you back at the Pinnacle," she said with perhaps a bit more meaning than she had intended.

"Oh, wild horses couldn't keep me away," he answered in a similar tone. "I intend to spend lots of time here."

Becker, hearing something lurking beneath his host's words, returned his attention to Juliette. "I cannot tell you how devastated we were," he said, his wedge of gum visible through his ever-chomping teeth. "It's such a loss, such a great loss." For a moment, the table fell silent. "But I know," Becker added after a full three beats that Juliette could practically hear him counting out in his head, "that the best way we can honor him is to honor the industry in which he has left his mark." Everyone smiled, relaxed, their faces open in agreement.

Juliette dutifully thanked the producer and embraced him; she could feel her name sliding out of his memory as she did so. Two women in cotton tunics jangly with silver and turquoise approached Forrest, drawing near like children approaching Santa Claus. "We're your biggest fans," they said in unison. "We think it's so great you're hosting the Oscars this year," continued one. "But we hope you won't have to water down your material," said the other.

"Talk to this man here," the comedian said, motioning to the president of the Academy. "He's the boss."

"Not me, talk to the producer," he said in turn, pointing to Becker.

"A producer?" Becker said. "In the Pinnacle? Someone take a picture. No, you don't have to worry, ladies," he said. "This year's show is going to be just as out of the box as its host."

"I can't imagine," one of the women exclaimed. "Could you"—she motioned to Juliette— "take our picture with him?"

"Come on, gals, cozy on up," said the comedian, sliding a mint into his mouth and standing dutifully between the two while Juliette took two shots with a tiny digital camera.

"Oh, thank you," said the women. "We're from Dallas, Texas, and this has just made our day."

"No kidding," said Forrest under his breath, smiling and waving as the women moved away. "Why do they always tell you where they're from? Do they honestly think anyone gives a shit? Sorry," he said, glancing at Juliette. "Of course, I'm forgetting: those of you in the service industry have to give a shit."

Before she could say anything, Juliette found herself neatly steered away by Devlin, who suddenly had to speak to her about an urgent matter.

"Gently, J.," he said into her ear. "Gently. The man just lost sixty million in three failed movie deals. A fact which thank God none of us can change."

By the end of the day, everyone was treating Juliette just as they had always treated her, though Devlin seemed to feel moved to stroke the back of her neck with alarming regularity.

"I like this sweater," he said, when she finally asked him what exactly he thought he was doing. "Is it angora? It suits you."

"I'd lend it to you," she said, "but you'd just stretch it out with those broad shoulders of yours. Are you working out?"

"All right, all right," he said, catching the mocking tone in her voice. "I was just trying to be nice."

"You are nice," she said. "You don't have to try."

She went to check on Michael, but he was asleep. "Tell him I'll see him tomorrow," she whispered to Rory in the doorway before she turned away and tried not to feel disappointed.

On the drive home, Juliette steeled herself for whatever emotions might overtake her as she entered the house—how upset Josh had looked when she mentioned selling. It did seem more secretive than ever, a gleam of white buried behind bird-of-paradise and ivy. Listening to her footsteps on the gravel walkway between the garage and the house, Juliette felt a chill drape itself over her. She turned around, certain someone was behind her; nothing was there save the shadow of fig and lemon trees. Putting her key in the lock, she was surprised at how much mail she had. A bulky package had forced a cascade of bills and letters to fall to the ground. In the dark entryway, she cursed as things slid from between her hands. Reaching for the light, she heard a sound in the living room, or *felt* a sound was more like it, a shifting in the dark. Her shoulders tensed and she took a step toward the still-open door.

"Who's there?" she said, one hand tightening on her keys, the other hovering over the light switch—the darkness somehow felt safer than the light, but she hit the switch anyway. The living room blazed to life, empty, though she couldn't shake the feeling that someone was hovering just out of sight.

"Josh?" she whispered, then felt foolish. He was gone, had been gone for so long now. His spirit would have no business here. What would he have to say to her anyway?

"Juliette," said a familiar voice. Stifling a scream, Juliette leapt backward, banging her head against the wall. "Oh, God, I'm sorry," the voice came from a shadow in the dark, "I didn't mean to startle you. I know you must hate me, should hate me, but I just wanted to tell you that I never meant to hurt you."

Running her hand along the wall, Juliette finally found the switch. Light flooded the entryway and David Fulbright took a step backward, a hand thrown in front of his eyes.

"Shit, David," Juliette said, her hand tight around her keys. "What the hell are you doing here?"

He looked down with such sheepish charm, all tousled hair and blinking eyes, that some of her fear slipped away. "Jesus," she said a bit more calmly, "how did you get in here?"

"You left the bedroom window open," he said. "Up the oak tree, over the wall, onto the balcony, and here I am. You really should be more careful," he said, marking a pause with a small strange smile. "If I could do it, anyone could."

"I don't remember opening the bedroom window," she said, feeling fear jockey with irritation—had someone broken in before David? She hurried upstairs and into the bedroom, but everything was as she had left it—there was the television, the stereo, the jewelry box, all undisturbed. "That's weird," she said, turning to find David right behind her.

"God, it's good to see you," he said, towering over her. His hands came up and rested on her shoulders; tensing, Juliette pulled away, slid around him, and headed quickly down the stairs, toward the open front door, the telephone.

"I'm sure you meant well, David," she said, her hand on her

phone, "but breaking and entering is not exactly the standard method of apology."

"You wouldn't return my calls, you didn't acknowledge my flowers. I was too afraid to show up at the hotel, figured Devlin would have my head. I waited outside in my car for hours. Because you have to forgive me," he said. "Really you do. I never meant for you to be involved . . . and then Josh. I never meant for you to be hurt."

"What do you mean, 'and then Josh'?" Juliette asked sharply. "What do you know about Josh?"

"N-n-n-nothing," David stammered. "Except what everyone knows. I just felt badly that you had to deal with that on top of my little stunt . . ."

"Stunt?!" she said. "You had no pulse. I felt it. How did you have no pulse?"

The actor grimaced. "Well, I did," he said, "just not much of one. They gave me a drug that slowed everything down. Not very pleasant."

"You could say that," Juliette answered sharply. "Why would you do something like that?"

Fulbright shrugged, his face drooping like a schoolboy's. "I thought it was a laugh. Becker paid me loads of money and I'd just gotten sacked, so I was feeling very anti-institutional. By the time I realized it was you, it was too late; I couldn't afford to fuck up another job."

"Well, I'm sure you and Mr. Becker will be very happy together," she said.

Now it was Fulbright's turn to look at her sharply. "Why do you say that? What have you heard?" He took a step toward her and Juliette felt all her nerves go on full alert.

"Nothing," she said blandly. "Just I'm sure he has rewarded you for a job well done."

After scrutinizing her for another few moments, the actor's face relaxed. "It will all be ashes if you don't say you forgive me. I couldn't bear it if we weren't still . . . friends."

"Of course we're still friends," she said, anxious now for him to leave, if for no other reason than she wanted to figure out why he was so upset by being linked to Becker. "I forgive you," she said, kissing him gently on the cheek. Sweating, she thought, he was sweating profusely even in the cool evening air. "Go," she said, motioning to the door, "and sin no more."

"Angel," he said, his face brightening. "Can I take you to dinner? Or shall I perhaps stay . . . ?"

"Go," she insisted, softening it with a laugh. "It's been a very long day."

Juliette waited until she heard the car door slam and the engine start and fade away before she moved from the door. It did not seem probable that David Fulbright had broken into her house at night just so he could apologize, but she could not for the life of her figure out what other motive he could have had. *If I could do it*, he had said, *anyone could*. Had he been trying to warn her? From what? From whom?

She looked at the stack of mail and sighed. First she picked up the package. It had no address, no postmark, just her name in block letters. She frowned; had David left it? It was sealed with packing tape, so she rummaged in the desk drawer to find scissors and opened it. A cell phone fell out into her hand.

Juliette stared at the small silver rectangle, half expecting it to ring and then transmit hollow-voiced instructions. She looked again at the manila envelope—just her name on a computer-generated label. She flipped open the phone and turned it on.

"Josh Singer," said the halting electronic voice. "You have . . . six . . . messages."

11

"I should take it to the police," she said the next morning, looking at the phone sitting, banality itself, in the middle of the coffee table in Michael's room.

"Well, maybe," said O'Connor. "But if you were going to, you would have already. And you haven't."

"He called me that night," she said dully, flipping open the phone and opening the call log. "Three times. Here, then my cell, then at home. Those are the last calls he made. At nine-thirty."

"And he left no messages."

"He didn't," she said passionately, hearing doubt in O'Connor's carefully expressionless voice. "He didn't. And you can tell, actually, if you look at the time on these calls," she said, realizing this even as she said it. "They're all less than a few seconds apart—hardly enough time to dial, much less leave a message."

"Let me see that."

She handed O'Connor the phone. She had called him at six-thirty in the morning to tell him about the phone, had woken him up—where was Rory? she wondered. "Well, you had

157

better come over, then," he had said calmly. By the time she got there, he was sitting on the sofa, in pajama bottoms and a T-shirt. He did not have quite the glow he'd had the morning before, but his eyes were bright and alert.

"He also called Anna," he said. "But earlier. Looks like just after she left. Now let's see who called him." He pushed a button and scrolled down. "Anna, Anna, Anna, Anna—all before she says he arrived at dinner."

"All six messages were from Anna, except one from his agent the next morning—clearly before he knew Josh was dead."

"You listened to his messages? How did you manage that?"

Juliette flushed. "He always used the same passcode: 696969."

O'Connor snorted. "And yet you married him anyway. No accounting for taste. But here's one, a call he got at nine forty-five . . . (310) 555-6729. Do you know that number?" She shook her head. "Well, call it. Did you call it? It isn't listed under 'missed calls,' so he must have answered it. He must have talked to someone. Someone who hasn't come forward yet. The last person to speak to Mr. Josh Singer."

Her hands shaking a little, she dialed. The phone rang, once, twice, almost three . . .

"Academy Awards," trilled a young female voice.

Juliette and Michael stared at each other and then she hung up the phone.

"Becker?" said O'Connor after a minute.

"Probably some flack called him to make arrangements for something, for the luncheon, maybe?"

"No, that was the production office. It's not even in the Academy offices. There would be no reason for them to be calling a nominee unless they wanted him to present, and why would they?" He closed the phone and tapped it against the table. "More important, why would someone send this to you? There's no reason to believe you wouldn't just turn it over to the police. Why didn't you?" he asked.

"I don't know," she said. "I was just so freaked out to get it. To think that Josh's murderer might have gotten through my gate, which is supposed to be a security gate, by the way, and onto my porch . . . and David said one of the bedroom windows was open—"

"David?"

Quickly, she told him the whole story of the evening.

"Fucking hell, Juliette," he said. "And did it not occur to you that perhaps the man who broke into your house, the man who was part of the original Becker murder hoax, might have been the person who put the phone in your mailbox?"

"David?" Juliette said. "David isn't a murderer. He's too . . . flopsy to be a murderer."

"Too *flopsy*?"

"You know," she said, shaking her hair into her eyes, pushing it back with a twitching grin and a series of prolonged blinks. "Flopsy."

O'Connor burst out laughing, which then turned into a bout of coughing. Juliette rushed to get him some water. The man was still hooked up to an IV, after all, still thin and shaky if not actively vomiting into her hands.

"I'm going to call the police," she said, after Michael caught his breath. "This is ridiculous, the two of us playing Nick and Nora. I will, I'll call them now. Better late than never . . ."

"Actually, I don't think that's such a good idea, Juliette," Michael said softly, watching her from beneath half-closed eyelids.

"Why not?"

"Because I got ahold of those two scripts Josh was writing for Paramount; you know, the ones he wanted you to 'talk through' with him." He paused, so obviously for dramatic effect that she wanted to slap him.

"And?" she said impatiently.

"Did he tell you what they were about? No? Well, it turns out one is the famous Becker/Diamond project, though I'm not sure who Diamond's supposed to play, since in this version the lead is about thirty-five."

"Which is probably why Josh wanted me to look at it; Becker wouldn't go for that, not if he wanted Max." She shook her head.

"The other one," O'Connor continued evenly, eyes on her, "is about a beautiful heroin junkie/jewel thief. While casing a posh hotel, she comes to the aid of the general manager, who hires her on the spot and turns her life around."

So here it was, after all these years. Juliette kept her eyes focused on the space just above Michael's left ear because she had learned that this was the safest place. It was neither too aggressive—which made people uncomfortable—nor too evasive—which made them mistrust you. It also bought her time to think. Here it was, the truth after all, and no amount of sickbed kisses would push it into nonexistence.

"See, that was Josh's biggest weakness as a writer," she said after a moment. "He didn't pay attention to detail. It was cocaine—how could a heroin addict be any kind of a jewel thief? Heroin addicts drool too much." She moved her gaze onto the actor's face to see what exactly was there. Not triumph, as she had expected, or malicious amusement. Concern. Wariness. Something like anticipation.

"It was a long time ago," she said quietly. "And it was never the big time, never *To Catch a Thief*. Not really script material."

"Did you do time? Would there be warrants?"

She drew herself up. "Hardly."

"Oh, my," O'Connor said. "So you were that good, were you?"

Juliette inclined her head modestly. "The only reason Josh knew is because I told him. Back when I thought honesty was the bedrock of a relationship."

"Thank God you've learned that lesson," Michael murmured. "Did Alex know?"

Juliette thought of her old boss, his wise and lovely face, those gray eyes that saw everything. Everything. "From the moment he saw me," she said. "I was getting a little sloppy. Too much coke, it was time for me to get clean, not that I knew it. But he did."

"So the *Cats* story I was so pleased I knew and remembered . . ."

"Complete bullshit."

Michael looked at her expectantly and she sighed.

"I was in the lobby and I saw this pickpocket working the room. Fine with me, right? Except he starts to lift the wallet of this old guy. I had seen him come in, with his granddaughter, showing her the Plaza, telling her how he had worked there as a bellman years and years ago. They probably couldn't have afforded a cup of coffee there now, but he's telling her how maybe one day she can stay in a place like this when she's grown up, and she's looking around like she's in a fairyland . . ." Juliette shrugged. "So I alerted security, who grabbed the guy and shook, like, six wallets off him. Alex asked me what I wanted as a reward. I said let this guy and his kid stay here, on the house, meals included, for a weekend. He hired me on the spot. 'To keep the criminal element at bay,' as he said. And he knew who I was, what I was, the whole time."

"I think you're wrong," O'Connor said softly after a moment. "That's got blockbuster all over it. I'm thinking Jennifer Lopez, I'm thinking Julia Roberts—"

Juliette made a sound of disgust. "Please. It would only work if I were somehow tempted back into a life of crime. Or maybe if the government hired me to break up some big *Ocean's Eleven* kind of gang . . ."

"Forget the police, let's call it a pitch meeting," O'Connor said, laughing again. "And you say you never discussed this with Josh?"

"Well, 'never' might not be the best word," she conceded. "Anyway, I can't imagine the police would even think to get his scripts, or if they did, make the connection."

"Call them and tell them you have somehow wound up with Josh's cell phone, now liberally smeared with your finger-prints, and you'd be surprised at the connections they will look into."

"But there's no real connection to make. There's nothing to prove that it wasn't wholly a product of Josh's imagination."

"Maybe," he said. "But close your eyes and think about the innuendo on E! and *Entertainment Tonight* and our own KTLA. Think of the lovely chats you and the detectives would be having about why you were so angry that he wanted you to read his script."

She looked at him sharply. "How did you hear about that?"

"Oh," he said, eyebrow arched, "I have my sources."

"If it became an issue, I'd have to leave," she said, shrug-ging. "I'd have to resign and, you know what, that doesn't sound so bad to me right now."

"You leave and Devlin will be out on his ear in five weeks, guaranteed. Not that I care all that much, but could you at least wait until I've finished my chemo and officially returned from Morocco? And anyway, I think going to the police is exactly what the killer wants you to do. I think he, or she, wants the police to think that someone at the Oscars is involved in Josh's death. Think about it: that leaks and it will wreak havoc. It's bad enough now with the talk of this Oscar curse. No one wants an Oscar badly enough to die for it. Okay," he amended in response to her skeptical look, "*most* people don't want an Oscar badly enough to die for it.

"The question is," Michael said after a moment, "who benefits from screwing up the Oscars?"

"Certainly not anyone working for the Pinnacle."

"Spoken with admirable loyalty; ten points for Gryffindor. So that lets you and Devlin off the hook."

"Not Becker; it would destroy him."

"I can think of a few people who would cross a busy street against the light to destroy Becker."

"Not the Academy, not any of the nominees . . ."

"Now, wait, wait, let's not be hasty. We're down at least two nominees, which alleviates the competition. And Ms. Stewart, in her basic black, has now moved to odds-on favorite."

Juliette was shocked. "I don't think she would kill Josh to increase her chances of winning an award."

"Maybe not," he said. "Maybe not. But there are many people behind Ms. Stewart, many people who would benefit from her winning."

"That's what Josh said," Juliette murmured. "That he couldn't believe how many people made money off her, that she was her own small economy. That Arnie . . ." she said, her eyes opening wide, "that Arnie Ellison was determined she would win because she had been nominated twice before. Arnie hated Josh, and I know Josh tried to get Anna to defect to PMK. You don't think Arnie . . . he's a *publicist*, for God's sake."

"Think of the publicists you know," Michael said.

"Yeah," Juliette said. "But murder?"

"Okay, then what about that actress who was staying here, who everyone thought would get nominated?"

"Therese?" Juliette said. "Have you met her? She's the sweetest girl in the world; too good for Hollywood. That's what one of our staff said anyway."

"She was from Colombia, right? And her family background was sort of shady, right? I remember hearing rumors that the studio was having a hard time figuring out a way to spin her. Isn't that why they installed her here—didn't you think it was odd she had no family with her? A young girl like that?"

"What, you think because she's Colombian her family's part of a drug cartel? That is now going to bust up the Academy Awards? You have lost your mind."

He leaned back against the couch and shut his eyes. "Okay, okay, maybe not the most likely scenario. I think we should hang tight and see what happens," Michael said. "Force whoever is behind this to make another move. Meanwhile, maybe you should take Devlin up on his offer to move in with him for a few days." Juliette looked up at him, startled. "Aha," he said with a small smile. "So he did offer. Or there's my Brentwood place—complete with trustworthy caretakers. And of course you're always welcome here. It's not much, but it's home, and it has a few pleasant memories . . ."

"Why do I have to go anywhere?" she asked, standing because she couldn't just sit there while Michael looked at her like that, like he knew everything about her and took great satisfaction in that knowledge.

"Because, Juliette, my darling, my sweet, I'm afraid we can be certain of one thing: Josh's killer knows where you live."

*

Leaving Michael's room was like entering another world, one in which it was difficult to believe for a moment the things they had talked about. The hotel was full of photographers and movie stars in town for the Academy luncheon the next day—two entire floors were devoted to photo shoots. In the morning, those nominees staying at the hotel would be shuttled downtown to the Music Center; no press was allowed at the actual event, which meant all the magazines and newspapers and television shows were trying to create the flavor of the event beforehand. Moving from suite to suite, Juliette caught occasional whispers of Josh's name, of Natasha's name, of a shivery sense of concern, but mostly it was business as usual. Publicists lined the corridors, with their cell phones and their clipboards, room service carts rattled by in twos and threes, while groomers and stylists moved like shadows behind the stars, silently pinning back a baggy suit jacket, smudging on a thumbprint of rouge here, a smear of concealer there.

"It smells like the makeup counter at Robinsons-May," said Devlin as he got off the elevator for which Juliette was waiting. "Did you see Meryl? Is she here yet?"

"Holding suite 1435," Juliette said. "I'm sure she'd love to see you."

Watching his well-tailored back recede down the hallway, Juliette thought about what Michael had said. She didn't believe Devlin would fail if she left the Pinnacle—people underestimated Eamonn Devlin, something she had never done since the day he hired her.

"I have followed your career with much admiration," he told her moments after she had finally agreed to join his staff. "Your entire career," he added with a grin. He held up his hand as she started to speak. "We all of us have secrets," he said. "Just as we all have our special talents. In fact, it is rare that you find one without the other."

Over the years, she had learned some of those secrets—Louisa had been a business manager in a former life, for a high-profile Hollywood madam. (Devlin swore she never did anything she couldn't do from her Culver City office, but Juliette was not sure she believed him.) When the woman had finally gone down in a hail of criminal charges and made-for-TV movies, Louisa decided it was time for a career change, and Devlin agreed. Hans had learned his culinary magic in a Serbian prison; Juliette didn't know the details and frankly did not want to—it seemed impossible that such a gentle man could have any dealings in a vicious war. Gregory had a more traditional background—a modeling career destroyed by crystal, the eleventh-hour rehab, and Juliette never really knew quite where Devlin himself came from, but she did not think it was from the international business school he mentioned in casual conversations.

These were details she had not mentioned to O'Connor, though she imagined he would enjoy knowing them. That the Hollywood elite was being curried and cared for by a group of people who knew a thing or two about role-playing was one of the secret joys of her profession. Dev said he had the most trustworthy staff in town because everyone he hired had already learned their lessons the hard way. But now she wondered—could there be someone here who hadn't learned his or her lesson well enough?

"What?" asked Louisa, making Juliette aware that she had been staring across the lobby at the concierge as she sorted through her thoughts.

"Nothing," Juliette said. "I like your hair that way; it makes you look so . . . sleek."

Louisa rolled her eyes, but her hand automatically crept to the back of her head. "Well, thanks. Look," she said after a moment's hesitation. "I wanted to say I'm sorry. You've been having a pretty rotten time and I think you are handling it beautifully."

"Well, the show must go on," Juliette said, motioning to the lobby, where a luggage trolley full of roses trundled by. There was an awkward silence during which Juliette thought how strange it was that in three years she had never spent five minutes socially with Louisa.

"Did you hear the news about that reporter?" Louisa asked abruptly. Juliette shook her head. "Apparently she was wearing one of those nicotine patches and smoking at the same time. Gave herself nicotine poisoning. That's what caused the heart attack. So it wasn't the doughnuts after all."

"Well, that's a relief," said Juliette. "As well as a cautionary tale."

"Sometimes I wonder what it would take," Louisa said. "Does anything besides war ever trump the Oscars?"

"Not so far," Juliette said. "Remember the year everyone was so afraid the Pope would die on the day of? Suddenly there was no such thing as an atheist in Hollywood."

Glancing at the concierge desk, she noticed a bowl holding the small tins of Pinnacle mints. "So," she said, taking full advantage of Louisa's goodwill, "I see you've got the mints out already. How are they moving?"

Louisa laughed, a throaty sexy laugh that took Juliette by surprise. "People are grabbing them by the handfuls," she said. "If we're not careful, we're going to run out before Oscar night. Free stuff," she added. "The rich and famous cannot get enough of it."

"No worries," Juliette said. "I can always order more."

Out of the corner of her eye, she saw Dog walking a tall, thin man out the door. The man's shoulders were laden with cameras and Dog's hand was underneath the man's elbow despite his usual friendly manner.

"What was that?" she asked, wandering over.

"Oh, just a freelance photographer who didn't know that we don't allow cameras at the pool."

"How far'd he get?"

"To the spa. Phillip stopped him and called me, and I regretfully informed him of our policy." He looked at his watch. "All over and done in four minutes flat."

"Had to wait for the elevator, did you?" she teased. "Listen, do me a favor. Can you just take a stroll along fourteen and twelve this afternoon? There are a lot of people up there. I know, I know, but still. Just keep your eyes open for anyone you don't know or who doesn't look right. Maybe bring in your extras now instead of waiting till Oscar week—I'll square it with Devlin."

"You think there's something to that Oscar curse?" Dog asked.

"I don't believe in curses, but I do believe in criminals. And I'd like the only ones in this hotel to be the ones I know personally." She flashed Dog a grin.

"Well, in this place that narrows it down to pretty near everyone, doesn't it?"

12

The next day, Anna Stewart came out of seclusion to attend the nominees' luncheon. She was wearing pink Prada and a very brave expression as she walked through the lobby with her good friend Kenneth Branagh, who had flown over from London after Josh's death to comfort her. She passed Juliette as if she were not there.

"Hold steady, my girl, hold steady," said Gregory, sliding up behind her as the management ranks fell out to wish their guests a good luncheon. But after seeing several of the stars shoot her glances, some quizzical—"didn't she used to be married to . . ."—some just uncomfortable, Juliette realized she should not be standing there. She caught Devlin's eye and saw confirmation in his raised eyebrows. She was just about to withdraw when she saw Alicia Goldstone approach Anna with tears in her eyes. Alicia, who stretched almost six feet of implanted, Botoxed, and Pilates-perfected womanhood between her stiletto heels and a mane of perilously blond ringlets, towered over the British actress, all but engulfing her in an embrace that could not be avoided. The subtlety of her nominated performance—of a careworn mother who turns to prostitution to support her

Depression-stricken family—had surprised everyone. Watching her now, Juliette could not believe she had pulled it off.

"You're so brave," Alicia said, just loud enough for everyone to hear. "Such an inspiration to us all. I can't imagine how difficult it must be for you to even appear in public. I don't know how you'll get through it."

"Oh, my God," Gregory said, "it's the ultimate girl-psych."

Anna said something quietly, bowed her head.

"I have a house in Santa Fe," Alicia said, "if you need to disappear for a while."

Nodding her thanks, Anna allowed herself to be led from the lobby, which was filling up with women in Chanel and Stella McCartney and men in Gucci and Hugo Boss as the limos circled around front.

"Nice to see that some people don't change," said Louisa, who had sidled up beside Gregory. Juliette was surprised; Louisa rarely commented on the behavior of guests—she confined her cutting remarks to her colleagues. "Ol' Alicia," Louisa said, jerking her chin at the actress who had somehow latched on to Shirley MacLaine as she passed with Warren and Annette. "We used to call her Tonya, like Tonya Harding. Don't you remember?" she said, as Gregory and Juliette looked at her blankly. "Well, I guess you wouldn't; it's not like it made the papers. Remember, like, ten years ago, when she was divorcing what's-his-face at Warner Brothers? A few weeks after she found out he had formed . . . an *attachment* to a certain . . . *escort,* a couple of goons jumped the girl in a parking garage. Broke both her legs. Police didn't touch it—what's another hooker-bashing, more or less?—but rumor had it Alicia was behind it. Paid for it out of her divorce settlement."

With a small savage smile, Louisa headed back to her bank of ringing phones.

"Well, I never," said Gregory, eyeing her as she departed. "You know, now that you mention it, our Louisa does have a slight limp." Turning a deadpan expression toward Juliette, he moved away to help with the growing limo line.

Leaving the lobby, O'Connor's suspicions ringing in her mind, Juliette considered Alicia Goldstone. Was it possible she would hire someone to kill Josh in the hopes that Anna would . . . what? Remove herself from the race? That didn't make any sense—Alicia would be the last person who would want the Oscars disrupted. Even if she didn't win, the nomination had already put her back in contention for roles that a year ago she could only dream of. In a way, a nomination was better than a win—you got the same window of opportunity, but you didn't have to do all the follow-up press.

As Juliette passed the library, someone caught her by the elbow with a force just this side of rough. Sally Gardens, O'Connor's ex, was looking around the room, taking in the contents of the shelves with a sort of grim amusement. "My," she said. "These look familiar. Why would that be? Because they are all from my house. Or one of my houses. The contents of which were not to be touched until the lawyers gave their final approval." A smile played on her lips, which Juliette had no idea how to read.

"I'm sorry if you see something that upsets you," she said carefully. "These were a gift to the hotel and if they are indeed your property, they will certainly be returned."

The woman's eyes narrowed, but then she let out a sigh and rolled her eyes. "They're not mine, they're his. And I don't give a good goddamn about any house but the apartment in Paris anyway. Not that I want that information broadcast to certain parties." Her smile, Juliette thought with a shock, was just as sudden, just as disarming as her ex-husband's. As she had on that other night, she looked Juliette up and down, taking in the soft light blue sweater, the pearl pendant necklace, the black pencil skirt.

"Listen," Sally said suddenly. "Here's some genuine advice from an unexpected source. You look like a nice girl. Everyone I know says you're a nice girl. So when you're dealing with Mr. O'Connor just remember not to do anything you wouldn't do if you knew *for a fact* he was lying. Don't eat his food, don't take his gifts, don't suck his cock—which, by the way, you will be expected to do hourly when he is between films—don't listen to anything he says unless you would do it knowing that it's all a lie. Because that man has forgotten how to tell the truth. If he ever knew. Honest to God"—she lowered her voice and drew Juliette closer—"I'm not sure that he even has cancer. He could just be upset that *Bluebird* bottomed out. He only took the role because he thought it would get him a nomination."

Juliette quietly took a series of deep breaths to fight the flush she felt rising along her belly, up the back of her neck, and onto her cheeks. As if she knew exactly what Juliette was feeling, Sally smiled again, this time a little sadly.

"You don't believe me," she said. "And it's okay. I understand. I've been there. It's hard—those eyes, that smile. Oh, honey, I know. And I'm sure he's heart-melting on his sickbed. Why do you think I split? So do what you want—he's a sweet lover when he wants to be. Just don't let it matter. Because it won't. Not to him." Sally took one more look around her. "Enjoy the books anyway," she said, touching Juliette's arm again. "And I'm sorry about your ex. Why does it always happen to the nice ones?"

According to all press accounts, the nominees' luncheon went off without a hitch, with the exception of a ten-foot-tall, gold-painted plaster Oscar statue almost falling on John Travolta as he passed through the Music Center door. Fortunately, Bill Murray, nominated for his directorial debut, managed to catch it just as Travolta and his daughter jumped out of the way. Because it was outside, the photographers all got a front-page shot—the deadpan Murray, holding what looked like a swooning Oscar in his arms.

"Thank God it was Murray behind him and not some squirt like Cruise," said O'Connor when he heard the news. "How heavy are those things?"

"Pretty heavy," Juliette said. "Bill apparently sprained both wrists catching it, though that won't make the papers. And in the news Travolta was acting like it was a joke, but I heard he wrenched his daughter's shoulder almost out of its socket getting her out of the way. She's going to be fine, but Travolta's out for blood."

"Well, someone is, that's obvious. Do they know how it happened?"

"The base wasn't level, is what I heard. And it was on a platform that shook when people walked by—Travolta was just one shake too many."

"Uh-huh," said O'Connor.

"I don't think it would have killed anyone," Juliette said.

"Probably not," said O'Connor, his eyes closed.

"It seems like it was just an accident."

"Probably so. Or maybe Murray's publicist staged it. You just can't buy that kind of coverage."

"Murray doesn't have a publicist."

Juliette fell silent. Michael was back in bed; he had had another dose of chemo, and it had been a wearing day. As much as she consciously dismissed Sally's "advice" as the predictable rant of an ex-wife, she found herself watching the actor, looking for signs of actual health, trying to tell if he was, indeed, conjuring all this, or exaggerating it, to hide while still getting full attention.

"I heard you exchanged girlish confidences with my ex-wife today," he said, his eyes still closed. Then he opened them and they were amused more than anything. "My agent saw you," he said. "In case you suspected that I myself crept from my bed and hid behind the planter. Did she send me her best 'get well soon'?"

Juliette looked away, unsure how to answer.

"Oh, it's all right," he said. "I know you know she knows. How's that for a line right out of Noël Coward? Why else would she be talking to you . . .?" He sighed. "It sent my agent into a tizzy, though. He's sure those cops are going to spill the beans. I don't think so; they both sent me flowers, did I tell you?" He gestured to two of FTD's medium arrangements, dwarfed by a bouquet now automatically sent up twice a week when the hotel changed its main floral arrangements. Irises and jonquils were the theme this week. "Did she say anything remotely nice at all?"

She wanted to tell, she wanted it to be out in the air, to see his face when she told him what Sally had said, to see in his face the absolute refutation of what she had said. Surely he would be able to defend himself, to utter words that would prove she, Juliette, could trust him. Because she had to trust him—he knew so much now. But he sounded so tired, looked so resigned, steeled almost for the words he knew had been used, that she couldn't do it.

"She said she hoped you were getting better," Juliette said. "And that I should tell you she said hello."

O'Connor looked at her and she knew that he knew she was lying. But he smiled and patted her hand. "We need to figure out what we should do," he said. "I don't like the idea of anyone's daughter getting hurt. And I don't think the accidents are going to stop happening anytime soon."

Between David Fulbright's unexpected visit and Michael's warning about the killer knowing where she lived, Juliette had been approaching her front door each night with extra caution, scanning the front of the house for a pulled-out screen, a bit of broken glass, any sign of disturbance. Tonight, once again, everything seemed as it had that morning, but before she could put her key in the lock, she heard a car door slam and footsteps on the walk. After bending over to pick up the doorstop—brass, in the shape of a hedgehog, it had been a wedding gift—she whirled, expecting to see—who? Certainly not Detective Harrison, who was surveying her with a solemn face.

"Detective," she said, "you startled me." She put the hedgehog down, thinking that she sounded like a suspect from an old *Columbo* episode.

"Sorry," he said. "I just came by to see if you had anything else to tell us about the night of Mr. Singer's death, about the conversation you had with Mr. Singer . . . If you . . . remembered anything else at all about that night."

For a moment Juliette hesitated, her mind racing as she tried to think what it was, exactly, that she was supposed to have experienced that night. She covered her lapse by fumbling with the key in the door. "Won't you come in?" she said. "I just got home, so let me just turn on some lights."

Hearing her heels on the hardwood floor gave her a little balance. She had stayed with O'Connor, had fallen asleep in the chair. Of the several nights she had now spent in O'Connor's room, any details would do.

"I think I told you everything I could about my conversation with Josh," she said. "Was there something in particular you wanted to know? Would you like something to drink?" she asked, figuring if she was going to play it like a scene from a TV show, she might as well play it big. The detective shook his head, ignored Juliette's attempt to usher him into the living room. He put his hands together in front of him and rocked a bit on his heels.

"I'll be frank with you, Ms. Greyson. Ms. Stewart seems to think that perhaps your conversation was not just . . . friendly. She seems to think that you still had, have . . . feelings for Mr. Singer. Which would not be unusual," he added with an attempt at fatherly warmth. "And perhaps he had . . . feelings for you. Perhaps that's what's at the bottom of Ms. Stewart's . . . concerns." Here the detective shot her a sharp glance, and it took all her self-control not to roll her eyes. If this was the best the LAPD could do, try so blatantly to play one woman's feelings off another, she thought, then no wonder this city was such a mess.

"Our marriage was quite over, Detective," she said, back on steady ground. "Of course there was pain, and regret, as there is in any divorce. But if Ms. Stewart thinks there was any residual . . . intimacy on either side, well, she is just causing herself more pain than she ought during this very painful time."

The detective nodded. "Ms. Stewart says she knows he called you, several times, during the course of the evening, that she assumes the two of you had plans to meet later. Which is why Mr. Singer didn't pursue her when she left the restaurant so abruptly."

Juliette said nothing, kept her eyes on the detective's face.

"Did Mr. Singer call you after the two of you parted?"

"I got no call from Mr. Singer," she said. "There was no message on my BlackBerry from him. If he called, I missed it and he didn't leave a message. When Devlin, Mr. Devlin first heard he was missing, my BlackBerry was the first thing we checked. You can look yourself." She motioned to her purse.

"Mmm-hmmm," he said. "That won't be necessary. We're getting his phone records tomorrow. One last thing, Ms. Greyson, and then I'll leave you to your evening. You said he asked you to look at a script he was working on . . ."

"Scripts. Two scripts."

"Yes. Did he send them to you, or have them sent to you, before he met Ms. Stewart?"

"No."

"So you never saw them." Juliette shook her head. "Did you, do you, have any idea what either of them are about?"

"No," she said. "He didn't talk about them. He did say I would have to be discreet. But that is not unusual; people in the business tend to be highly secretive. As you probably know."

"Ah."

"Why?" Juliette asked. "Why do you ask?"

"Oh, nothing," the detective said. "He had a half dozen scripts in his office. I was just curious which he wanted you to look at. Just curious, you know. My wife really liked that *Touch of Summer,* you know," he said with a smile. "A little romantic for me. Hard to imagine a man would write a movie like that."

Juliette surveyed him coolly.

"A man wrote *Romeo and Juliet,* Detective," she said.

"I guess you're right, Ms. Greyson," he replied. "Though as I understand it, Shakespeare has had some credit issues himself over the years."

13

As Oscar night drew near, Juliette held another summit meeting. In previous years, the gathering was to take a deep breath in the calm before the storm, make any last-minute adjustments, and generally pump up morale. This year, so much had happened, actual business had to be discussed.

"We still need to change out the chairs in the lounge and the back garden," Juliette said as an opening. "If I see that white wrought iron in one more photo I am going to scream. The photographers are complaining and I don't blame them. We also need to get some new planters—I saw the same palm frond in both *Entertainment Weekly* and *The New York Times*. Two different actresses, same damn palm frond. Not good, people." Feeling the tension in her voice reflected back in the faces around her, she consciously leaned back in her chair. Devlin wasn't there; he had a meeting off site that morning, he said, and Juliette saw many appraising looks among her colleagues. Even if no one believed she killed Josh, there was still a general discomfort whenever she walked into a room. Though there were behavioral guidelines for many things in Hollywood, no one quite knew how to treat a woman whose ex-husband had been killed during Oscar season.

Juliette decided to just tough it out. "Look," she said. "I know things have been crazy, but we need to stay on top of the basics. If we don't, there are plenty of hotels in town who will."

"I've already run out of the Xanax in my little fanny pack," said Gregory. "I was going to ask you for more, but I'm guessing you've run out too."

When Juliette laughed, the room relaxed. They went around the table, each manager listing the extra personnel—from room service runners to aestheticians to bellmen, the staff of the Pinnacle doubled during Oscar week—and assuring Juliette that there were no new faces, no unchecked backgrounds. The new menu was complete. "We have chosen a palette of green this year," Hans said. "Lime, chile, lemongrass, lots and lots of wilted greens. It's healthy, it's vibrant, it's the color of success." And the signature Oscar week dessert— a winding staircase of chocolate praline topped with a cloud of hazelnut mousse—was almost perfected.

Security was in place all over the hotel and reporting nothing at all unusual, "though it's so difficult to define unusual here at the Pinnacle," said Gregory, an obvious reference to an incident the day before in which two young publicists were caught lounging around one room smoking a joint and watching porn. They apparently didn't realize that Alicia Goldstone had another two interviews to give in the suite until she, the *Daily News* reporter, and the photographer walked in.

The gift baskets were being assembled in a Culver City warehouse "even as we speak," said Louisa. "We went back and forth on including makeup or face cream after the rumor about that *Grey's Anatomy* actress, but after she denied it on *Ellen* I think we're okay."

"She had a lot of pancake on," observed Gregory. "And did you notice how she kept her right side off-camera the whole time?"

Louisa ignored him. "I think I can say with some satisfaction that these are the best baskets we've ever had—Nina and Audrey worked very, very hard on them."

"She seems unnervingly, I don't know, good-natured," Juliette remarked to Gregory as the staff filed out of the dining room and dispersed to their respective parts of the hotel. "I've never known her to give credit where credit was due before."

"Well, Dev finally fucked her in the ass," Gregory said. "So I guess all her pale tiny dreams have come true."

"Jesus H. Christ, Gregory," said Juliette, stopping dead in her tracks and putting her hand on her heart. "There are limits, you know. Like I need that visual floating in my head all day."

"Tell me about it. I'm the one who walked in on them." She stared at him. "I heard a bunch of crashing around in Devlin's office," he said with a careless shrug. "I wanted to make sure he was all right. In these perilous days, you can't be too careful. I backed out, if you'll pardon the expression, before either one of them saw me," he added as if this made it all right. "But if he were a real gentleman, he would have locked the door. I always do."

If we survive the next two weeks, Juliette thought, *it will be a goddamn miracle.* Because she knew Devlin well enough to realize that if he was engaging in that sort of behavior this close to Oscar night, he was pretty disturbed about something.

"You aren't going to believe this," said Devlin as he fell into step with her later that day.

"You would be amazed at the things I have been expected to believe in the last few days," she said.

"I've gotten calls from two studio heads, three directors, and someone working for the Olsen twins," he said, not even acknowledging her remark, "all wanting to know if we were offering eating disorder interventions and could they sign their daughters/wives/clients up the day after the Oscars."

"God forbid they start before; the vintage Valentino might need to be let out."

"I guess the Prophet guy spread the word about his daughter gaining five pounds and now we're miracle workers," he said. "It's a potential gold mine. We've got to get Rick and Hans working on a menu as soon as they have a few free minutes. And maybe we could send Phillip over to Cedars to pick up some, I don't know, intervention-speak or healthy exercise program. But in any case, we need to jump on this before someone else does."

"I'll get right on it," Juliette said, keeping the sarcasm in her voice to a minimum.

"Great," he said. "And I think it's fine that you go with O'Connor down to Palm Springs. Do you good to get out of here for a day or two, though don't make it any longer, mind. You need to be back by Monday, first thing."

"Palm Springs?"

"Yeah, he said he's getting a Lifetime Achievement Award at the Palm Springs Film Festival this weekend and he needed you to go with him. What?" he said, taking in her look of utter surprise. "I thought you knew. I thought I was doing this fine and generous thing by saying yes. But if you don't want to go . . . although he seemed pretty insistent and we're going to need him to give up that suite—Lily's agreed to stay with us provided we have enough room for the triplets and their nannies. So I was hoping, if he was feeling a bit better . . . and then he said Palm Springs, and I thought great—"

"I'll have to get back to you on that, Dev," she said, heading toward the elevators.

"Palm Springs," she said as she strode in the door. "You're going to accept a Lifetime Achievement Award at the Palm Springs Film Festival."

O'Connor was watching television; on his lap was a script, but his eyes were focused on the screen. They did not stray her way when she spoke.

"Yes, indeed," he said. "I am cutting short my stay in Morocco to accept the award they have so generously, and so often, offered. It came as quite a surprise to them; I imagine they are scrambling to get the press release out and add tables to their venue even as we speak."

"What about your treatment?"

"I'm taking another little break," he said.

"What is this? Self-administered chemotherapy?"

"If nothing else, this should prove my devotion to you," O'Connor said, waving her words away. "I mean, a Lifetime Achievement Award? What do they think, I'm ninety or something?"

"Your devotion to *me*? How does going to Palm Springs prove your devotion to me?"

"We have already established that you do not watch movies or television, but do you read the papers? Have you seen who's going to be down there? For reasons even the *Los Angeles Times* is at a loss to explain, half of fucking Hollywood is going to be there this year, either receiving or presenting some trumped-up award to an Oscar nominee hoping to wedge in a few more photos before voting closes. I know you won't want to miss it because your pal David Fulbright will be presenting an award or two. In fact, I understand that all of our favorite people will be in attendance. Becker's going to be there, and our Miss Stewart, which means the always delightful Arnie Ellison should be on hand. Also Alicia Goldstone, Eddie Izzard, and the other Best Actor dark horse, what's-his-name, William Rudnick. He interests me very much, that guy—you know he's a former Marine? *Vanity Fair* did a big profile on him and apparently he was reading Mamet in some tent in Afghanistan when he decided what he heard above the lashing of sand and wind was the call of the muse."

"Did you just make that up? Or was that in the article?"

"Which part?" he said, finally taking his eyes off the television and turning them innocently toward her.

"The lashing sand and wind part."

"Made it up. Did it move you? Did it create an indelible visual footprint in your varied and lovely mind? Do you not find it interesting that there might be a Special Services spook with an agenda smack in the middle of this highly dangerous Oscar race? It interests me," he said, looking back at the screen. "In fact, many of the people I have just named interest me in a way they haven't for years. Too many connections among too many previously unconnected people." His voice had taken on a certain timbre; although it wasn't a British accent precisely, there was something a bit too measured about his speech, as if he were playing a part. Or preparing to play a part. Juliette tilted her head to one side and prepared to say something cutting, but O'Connor didn't notice or even pause.

"So I thought it might be useful for us to go and see what happens. I have a feeling something will. Something that might actually be worth preventing. You and me and Rory makes three. Now, if you'll excuse me," he said, rising and limping toward the bathroom, "I have an appointment with a sunlamp."

"I'll send up a bronzing kit from the spa," she said absently, watching him limp. "Our sunlamps suck. And I didn't say I would go," she added, raising her voice so Michael could hear her.

"I know," he said, his voice muffled through the door. "But you will." The door opened and his head appeared. "After all, Devlin said you could. And when was the last time you had breakfast in bed during Oscar season?"

Twilight was rising as Juliette paced the garden. For a few moments anyway, everything seemed still. It might have been any evening in spring or early winter. In the dusk it was hard to judge the blurred lines of seasons. Always, always there was the ring of silverware on china, the murmur of voices, the steady pulse of distant traffic, but Juliette was far away from all of this as she walked. So much had happened in the last two weeks, so many extraordinary thoughts and conversations, all woven over and among the already heightened activity and emotion of Oscar season, that she was beginning to feel choked by her own thoughts. So, strand by strand, she was trying to pull apart the events, separate them, see what actually had happened, and what had happened only in Michael's imagination. In O'Connor's room, she felt sometimes as if she were an audience of one, watching as he conjured a plot from thin air. Perhaps he did know more about Hollywood than most people, but it seemed absurd, to draw the connections he was drawing.

Josh was dead, that was real. And he had been murdered. And someone had put his cell phone in her mailbox. And David had broken into her house. And Natasha Coleman had overdosed, that reporter had indeed died, and every time she turned around, Bill Becker, Forrest Hughes, and Arnie Ellison were in the hotel, walking around as if they owned the place, as if they owned the town. Not to mention the whole Anna situation. Why hadn't she gone back to London? If it had been Juliette, if Juliette's lover had had his throat cut, she would not have stayed around to see if she had won some stupid award. She would be home, pulling down the curtains of her grief. Why had Anna deliberately set the police on her? Anna had won, there was no need for jealousy. Or had Josh meant to pursue something more than a script consult, had that been an excuse after all to see Juliette again, had Juliette misread the entire situation and now it was too late?

"Stop," she said aloud, leaning against one of the Doric columns, pressing her hot forehead against the cold stone. "Just stop."

Before she could reconsider, she walked purposefully to Devlin's office, went in, and shut the door behind her.

"Do you think there's a plot to ruin the Oscars?" she asked. Her boss looked up from his laptop blankly. "Do you think all of the things that have happened are connected somehow? That Josh and Natasha's deaths and even that reporter's were in some way orchestrated?"

Devlin's eyes narrowed. "What makes you say such a thing?" he asked. "Sit down and tell me what it is you think you know."

Juliette put a hand over her eyes, breathed in the familiar scent of Devlin's office—leather and lilies, the dark green scent of his aftershave, the wool of his suit jacket. It all seemed so normal. Suddenly she wanted to tell him everything—about how Michael had lied to the police, about the cell phone and David's visit, Anna's accusations and what Josh said about Arnie, about the fear she felt every time she approached her front door. She wanted to tell him everything that she had told O'Connor and everything O'Connor had said to her, but looking at Devlin's face, his strong and healthy face, she couldn't. Unlike O'Connor's room, this was not a place for spinning plots or premises; Devlin was real, vibrant, he would do something, take action, make inquiries. Or he would look at her as if she were crazy, his opinion of her would shift, their relationship would change. He would talk to Michael, shatter the intimacy of their hours together. Or he would tell Juliette to stop spending so much time with him, would put Louisa or Gregory in charge of O'Connor. He certainly wouldn't let her go to Palm Springs.

None of this could Juliette bear, not right now. So, taking her hand away, she smiled a self-effacing smile.

"I don't know," she said. "The rumors. Everyone, Sasha, so many of the guests have all these crazy theories, all these grim ideas. I just wondered"—she slid down in her seat as if exhausted—"what you made of it all." She half closed her eyes; he was looking at her so steadily, she thought she might cry.

He continued to look at her and she could see that he was tense, that something like anxiety held his shoulders straight, kept his hands still. For a moment she was almost afraid of what he would say, though she did not know what that would be.

Then he relaxed, and smiled gently at her.

"I think we have experienced a most unfortunate series of events," he said. "The greatest of which is, of course, Josh's death. This town is built on gossip and drama, J., so it's not surprising that even what has happened isn't enough to satisfy the local appetite. But if what people are saying bothers you, it is completely understandable. I think"—he returned his gaze to his laptop—"this trip to the desert could not come at a better time. Get you away from all this insanity. Take your mind off things."

14

The best part of the limo ride to the desert was remembering the looks on people's faces when they found out she was not going to be in the hotel. According to Pinnacle policy, no one was allowed to take vacation during the month between the nominations announcement and the awards ceremony and, although taking a weekend off wasn't technically a vacation, it still caught everyone by surprise.

"They really think that hotel is my life," Juliette said as the tall and stately buildings of downtown gave way to the squat and beige supermalls that lined the Santa Monica Freeway east. "Like I couldn't possibly have something else to do on a weekend."

"Whose fault is that?" O'Connor asked, taking a swig from the largest sports bottle Juliette had ever seen. "Gatorade," he explained, noting Juliette's bewilderment. "Have to keep my electrolytes up."

Getting Michael out of the room had taken some doing—they had left at six a.m., in hopes that there would be no other celebrities using the parking garage exit. When Dog showed up to keep an eye out and lock the service elevator so it would not stop at any other floor, Juliette realized he must have known O'Connor was in the hotel the entire time. Indeed, the two men had an easy rapport with one another that must have been cultivated over time.

"Looking good, chief," Dog said in greeting, taking in O'Connor's tall figure standing with only the help of a dapper ivory-topped cane.

"Think I'll pass, Dog?" O'Connor said. "Think anyone will believe this old geezer is Michael O'Connor?"

Dog shook his head in admiration. "The day I look as good as you do right now, I'll be a happy man."

Juliette had been relieved at how easily O'Connor walked, shaking off all attempts to help him, how he used the cane with nonchalant grace, as if it were for decoration rather than utility. But when he had finally situated himself in the limo, he had let out a long, rather shaky breath.

Now, watching him pull at his sports bottle as if it contained the nectar of life, Juliette eyed him narrowly. "Are you sure your doctor signed off on this little jaunt?" she asked.

"I said it was doctor-approved," he said. "I didn't say by *my* doctor."

"Great," she said. "Fabulous. Listen, could you just please not die during this trip? Because, frankly, I have had enough drama in the last few weeks."

"I would never die in Palm Springs," O'Connor said with a shiver. "That's redundant."

"Where's Rory, anyway?" asked Juliette. "Or are we completely winging this?"

"He's joining us out there. Don't worry, I can manage two hours in a limousine without having a seizure. Why, I haven't vomited on you in days."

"Which really is what I look for in a man," Juliette said.

"That explains a lot."

"Yes, well, not all of us can have your luck in mates."

"She's something, isn't she?" he answered with irritating equanimity. "Sally Gardens. Do you know, I don't think that's her real name. I bet she gave you an earful."

"She said you lie," Juliette said softly. "She said I shouldn't do anything I wouldn't do if I knew for a fact that you were lying."

O'Connor nodded and looked out the window.

"I'm beginning to think it is impossible to tell the truth to someone who's in love with you," he said. "Or who thinks they're in love with you. And I mean literally impossible in the biological sense." He turned his face back toward her. "I have lived my life as publicly as a person can, I have been as obvious about my numerous character flaws as a person can be. And when I am courting a woman, I always make it clear that I am who I am and that this is not necessarily the sort of man someone would want to marry. But it's like they don't hear me. It's like they're too busy spinning some fantasy of who they want me to be. Sally said she loved me, but the moment we got married, she wanted me to be someone else."

"You mean she thought, shockingly enough, that since you were married, you might consider not sleeping with other women," Juliette said.

"No," said O'Connor sharply. "I actually don't have a difficult time being monogamous," he said more quietly. "And Sally certainly could not have cared less if I was banging someone else; hell, she encouraged it. No, it was more about the work. She didn't understand about the work."

"What about the work?" Juliette said doubtfully.

"That it takes me away," he said. "Physically and emotionally. That it's important, that it takes a lot of effort. That when

I'm working, I am not available for parties and trips and telling a woman every five minutes she's the most beautiful thing I've ever seen. That I'm actually not doing it for the fame or the money or awards or . . ." His voice trailed off. "Oh, never mind."

"What are you doing it for, then?" she asked.

"I don't know," he said, looking out the window again, watching the landscape grow drier, browner, more bleak. "Probably because it's the only thing I know how to do."

Juliette considered saying something cutting; it was difficult to reconcile what she was feeling in this moment with the man sitting across from her—rich, successful, with every resource at his fingertips; even with his illness, he was more powerful than pretty much anyone she had ever met. So sympathy over his failed marriages, over his inability to be understood by members of the opposite sex, was difficult to conjur.

"Maybe," Juliette said, "you should try choosing a woman who is capable of understanding such things."

Almost immediately she wanted to take it back. She waited for his slam-dunk rejoinder, but the moment twisted back on itself and it was he who looked away.

"A woman who really understood wouldn't want to be with me," he said to the window. "And besides," he added, because he absolutely had to, "I like them young and greedy. The sex is hotter that way."

Juliette rolled her eyes. O'Connor laughed and used the remote to turn on the flat-screen that emerged at the push of a button from the ceiling of the limo.

"So what are we watching?" Juliette asked.

"Six minutes of everything," he said, pulling out a stack of DVDs and an official-looking form. "I am a voting member of the Academy, if you will recall. And ballots are due tomorrow."

Rory was standing outside with the hotel general manager when the limo pulled up. The Metropolis was a brand-new hotel, owned by a Las Vegas–based chain. The lobby was a very credible re-creation of the restored Grand Central Station, down to the sky-blue star-spangled ceiling and the famous clock. As cheesy as it had sounded, Juliette had to admit the first impression was, well, impressive. Though not quite as utilitarian as the actual train station, all the style notes were there—the reception and concierge desks were wood, with delicate gold grillwork reminiscent of a ticket booth; bench-back sofas and chairs were scattered throughout the lobby; the sundries store looked like a newsagent's from the fifties; the café was a warm and inviting diner.

"Look at that," O'Connor said, gesturing to a line of wooden phone booths along one wall. "Those can't be actual phone booths. I haven't seen an actual phone booth in years."

"They are computer stations," said the GM, a young German who had been taken aback to see Juliette emerge from the limo. In his mind, she represented as big a pressure to perform as the movie star. "Or they will be—they are not fully functional yet. We barely got open in time for the festival," he admitted, with a nervous glance at Juliette.

"It really is gorgeous," she said, looking around. "Perhaps you'll give me a tour later on . . . Peter? Is it Peter? But I think we should get ourselves up to our rooms just now. Mr. O'Connor has just flown in from Morocco, and I'm sure he'd like to rest a bit."

"Mr. O'Connor" was just that moment signing autographs for a trio of young women and shaking hands with the men who were either their dates or their agents, Juliette really couldn't tell.

"I'm actually wondering if there isn't another, perhaps less public way for us to come and go," she said, though Michael looked steady enough, his color high, his smile attracting onlookers from ten thousand paces.

"Of course, of course," Peter said. "If you had called ahead, I could have directed you . . ."

"No, that's fine," she assured him. "But perhaps you can help me—he is just too amiable," she said, lowering her voice. "You really have to do the dirty work for them . . . but then why am I telling you? You were at the Ritz in San Francisco, weren't you? So you know."

Peter nodded, and the two of them, with Rory's help, managed to disengage Michael from the crowd growing around him and get him safely on the elevator.

"What?" he said. "That was the most fun I've had in months."

They had been given a suite with two adjoining bedrooms and a room down the hall. Bouquets of flowers stood on every surface, a tray with sandwiches, coffee, and champagne waited on the coffee table, and gift baskets and bags lined the bed. Peter was very apologetic that it was not the penthouse, "but Ms. Stewart's people booked last week and in light of the sad circumstances . . ." He looked right past Juliette as if he didn't know. And perhaps, she thought, he didn't. *Why should he?* she thought. *Josh and I were ancient history.*

"It's fine, just lovely," Michael said, vaguely directing Rory's bags to the room down the hall. "I'm happy you were able to find us any room at all, considering the scandalous lateness of our reservation. Perhaps you would join us for a drink before we leave this evening. Or afternoon, rather—what time does this thing start? Five?"

"Six," Juliette said. "But you're scheduled to walk the red carpet at five-thirty. Which means you'll show up at five fifty-five."

"She knows me too well, my Juliette," he said, with a complicit glance to the general manager. "So perhaps we could meet in the bar at, say, five?"

As soon as the door closed, Michael collapsed on the sofa.

"This is going to be harder than I thought," he sighed.

"You don't have to do it," Rory said, helping him take off his jacket. "We could say you got some sort of Moroccan flu . . ."

"Oh, I'm going to do it," he said. "Jesus, did you see that lobby? I felt like I was in a soundstage—like Kevin Costner was going to come leaping out, machine guns blazing." Rory was busy clinking bottles, handing Michael several pills and a glass of water. "Look at all these flowers. I didn't know they had this many flowers in Palm Springs. Would you give me, like, one minute?" he said to Rory, who was preparing a syringe. "Juliette, my dearest, my darling, pour us some champagne, just to take the sting out of the stinger here."

When they each had a glass, he said, "So, here's to a lifetime of achievement. Whatever the fuck that means."

After putting away the few things she had brought and sending her dress out to be steamed, Juliette knocked lightly on O'Connor's door.

"He's asleep," Rory said, coming in through the front door of the suite. "I gave him a sedative. It should put him out for a few hours, which he will need if he's going to go through with this. Not that I can even begin to comprehend what he is doing out here." The nurse looked at Juliette with intense, almost angry speculation.

She shrugged. "I go where my boss tells me to go," she said

truthfully. "And my boss said to go with Michael to Palm Springs."

"Well," Rory said, throwing his hands in the air after a moment, "then we'll chalk it up to artistic insanity and make the best of it, I suppose. But it's going to take more than a little bronzer to make him presentable. Fortunately," he said, looking out the window, "it's clouding up. Nothing as unkind as direct sunlight, is there?"

Unable to deny her curiosity, Juliette gave herself a tour of the Metropolis, which—from the two-hundred-seat screening room to the bars on the twelfth, seventh, and fourth floors, the conservatory on the mezzanine, and the underground pool and sauna—was more like a cruise ship than a hotel. With an hour to kill before she had to get ready, she had ordered a cappuccino and a piece of pie at the café's perfectly reconstructed counter, when she heard a familiar voice cry out her name.

"I heard you were here," said Max Diamond, spinning her around on the swivel seat and embracing her where she sat. "Though why you're here with O'Connor, that I don't know. Are you two an item now? Lovely man, but not very nice in divorce court. Or so I have been told. By several women. But how long are you down for? You have to come out to the house—I just brought down the Chagalls. Are you coming tonight? Or are you just here for a little sunshine, not that it looks like we're getting any?"

Juliette nodded. "Yes, I'll be there. Are you going? Are you getting an award?"

Max laughed and shook his head. "No, no. They reserve their awards for nominees and old standards like Michael. No, I'm hosting. Yeah, I know, like I need it, but you have to understand the community down here is very tight and everyone's expected to pitch in. Two hours on my feet beats handing the festival committee a half a mil anyhow. And they're good people, all of them, really good people. This town is on the upswing; you should buy something down here. If you want, I can take you around tomorrow or Monday . . ."

"I'm heading back to L.A. tomorrow morning," she said. "It's a big week coming up."

"Right, right," Max said. "Oscar week. God, I am so glad to be out of that craziness. This"—he gestured to the lobby, to Palm Springs in general—"is much more my speed. They start on time, dinner is served, people get their awards, and boom, you're back home in time for *CSI*. No limo lock, no Governor's Ball, no Graydon Carter, just a nice time."

Seeing his round, friendly face, filled with genuine affection but still managing to keep an eye on the lobby, the bar, the front desk, Juliette had to smile. "Well, maybe we could have breakfast tomorrow," she said. "I'm sure Michael would love to see you. Or can you sneak away before the show? We're having drinks downstairs at five."

"Too late for those of us in the working class," he said, pinching her cheek. "But maybe breakfast, if you make it brunch. I'm an old man, I need my sleep. And so does himself, it seems. I called the moment I heard the eagle had landed, but his assistant said he was asleep. Strange, to have brought a beautiful woman to a lovely hotel and then fall asleep on her. Not the Michael O'Connor I know." The comedian was watching her carefully now. *All these years in the business,* Juliette thought, *and still he's not tired of the gossip.*

"It's not like that, Max," she said flirtatiously. "We're just good friends. And he flew in from Morocco today; he's totally jet-lagged."

"Must be, must be," said Diamond, putting his hand on her knee. "I'd never let you wander around eating pecan pie and talking to wild-haired comedians if you were my date. Is he back in town for good, then?"

"He's flying out tomorrow, or the next day, I think," Juliette said vaguely.

Max nodded. "Long way to come for a silly award," he said. "But I guess Michael's not getting any younger either. Last time I saw him, it looked like he had lost some weight."

Juliette kept her face still and shrugged. At that moment, Max's cell phone rang—the opening strains of the theme from *The Godfather*, which made Juliette laugh. "Well," he said after a curt conversation, "I am reminded that I should be getting home. Got to iron my hair and curl my shirt, as they say. See you later, gorgeous. And don't let that man fuck with you. I mean it. You tell him I'll cut his balls off, he fucks with you."

With a kiss and a grin, Max Diamond was gone.

At four o'clock, when Juliette got back, the suite was silent, the door to O'Connor's room closed. When she emerged from her own room an hour later, showered, changed, simultaneously slipping on her heels and closing the clasp of her necklace, nothing seemed to have changed. Glancing at her watch, she knocked tentatively on his door. "What?" the actor snapped from what sounded like the bathroom. She took a half step backward, the black tulle of her underskirt rustling as she did.

"Nothing," she said. "I just wondered . . . would you like me to make your apologies to the GM?"

"Yes," said Rory.

"No," said O'Connor. "Jesus, man, give it a rest. The face is what it is. And it was never much to begin with."

He threw open the door and strode into the suite, limping heavily, with Rory right behind him, hands full of concealer and pancake and mascara. O'Connor poured two glasses of champagne, then drank both of them before he even glanced in Juliette's direction. "Well, you look lovely," he said angrily. Standing in her low-cut forest-green gown, with its full skirt and tight bodice, she suddenly felt ridiculous. No one should be dressed like this at five o'clock in the afternoon.

"I told you we should have brought in a groomer," Rory said, making small stabs at the actor's face with a makeup brush. O'Connor grabbed his wrist and smiled.

"Touch me again," he said, eyes flashing. "Go ahead. Touch me again."

Rory shrugged, rolled his eyes, and backed away.

"It's your funeral," he said.

"And I've got the makeover to prove it. How bad is it?" He turned to Juliette. "Seriously."

You look fine, she could have said, and meant it, because he did look fine. In person, many actors looked more ordinary than they did on-screen: they had makeup lines and clothing that didn't fit quite right, just like ordinary people. The difference was that somehow, once they got on camera, all the imperfections smoothed away; a woman coated with pancake wound up looking like something carved from alabaster. But tonight wasn't about the camera. Tonight was about in person. And Juliette had sensed from Max's questions that maybe the Morocco plan had not gone unnoticed, that rumors were beginning. Sighing, she went back in her room and returned with her Oscar Night Survival Kit.

"Somehow I knew I would need this," she said, steering O'Connor out onto the terrace, into the full terrible light of the desert.

"Jesus," he said, blinking. "Not even Ashton Kutcher looks good in this light. I am over forty, you know."

"We get you presentable in this light," she said, wiping away about half the matte Rory had applied, "and you'll look gorgeous in any other. What is this?" she asked curiously, her fingertips touching something bumpy at the top of his forehead, under his hair. His hand shot up and circled around her wrist as if to pull her hand away, but then he did not. Instead, he looked at her sideways and she saw the same expression she had seen on the day Devlin had brought her to him—the double-dare of anger and fear. "Of course," she said, realizing one second too late what she should have just assumed, "the chemo. Wow, it's a good one." She ran her hand through the wig's thick hair. "I didn't even notice . . . before. It feels just like your real hair."

"It is my real hair," he said. "I mean it," he added as she prepared her professional "whatever you say, sir" face. "Before I went into treatment, I had them shave my head and make the piece from my own hair. It cost me a fucking fortune. More than the Bentley."

The bit of prearranged vanity made Juliette laugh out loud before she could think; he looked abashed, then grinned.

"Well," she said, tugging on a curl, "it's certainly sexier than getting the hair from some Ukrainian novitiate."

"I don't know," he answered, cocking an eyebrow. "Ukrainian novitiates can be pretty sexy."

Juliette turned his face back to the full sun, picking up the conversation as if nothing had happened. "It's like ladies' dressing rooms," she said, working concealer into the corners of his eyes, removing the eyeliner and most of the mascara. "If you can even stand to look at yourself under those overhead lights, whatever you're trying on will look just fabulous when you get it home."

"Clearly," he said, voice strained somewhat as she held up his arms, pinned back the seams of his jacket along the side, under the sleeves, "you and I shop at very different establishments."

Juliette smiled. "Mr. O'Connor, you haven't lived until you have experienced the Loehmann's dressing room." She let his arms drop and surveyed him critically, giving the tuxedo jacket a sharp tug at the bottom.

"Is that where you got this little number?" he asked, running his index finger down the side of her neck along her shoulder to the small black strap that held her dress in place.

"Well, no," she said, dipping her pinkie in a pot of lip balm and smoothing it carefully along his top lip, then his bottom lip, trying not to think of the last time she had been this close to either one. "My friends at Armani sent this over."

"And I would bet," he said, following the strap on its inevitable descent, "it looks like nothing at all on the hanger." His hand hovered over the tops of her breasts; Juliette could feel its heat like a warm shadow over them.

"We'll be late," she said, laying one hand on the side of his face, examining the results of her handiwork.

"They'll wait," he said, doing the same to her, and dipping his head just a bit closer to hers. "They always do."

"I told that Peter guy you wanted to go out the back entrance," Rory said, appearing suddenly from nowhere, puffing slightly. "So he's going to join us up here for drinks. I hope," he said, suddenly taking in the tableau on the patio, "that's okay."

"Fine," said Juliette, pulling away, piling all her makeup items back in the fanny pack.

"You look so much better," Rory said with admiration as Michael watched Juliette disappear back into her room. "She really does know what she's doing." From outside the door came the discreet rattle of a drinks cart and a light knock on the door. O'Connor rolled his eyes. "Well, then, let's get this party started," he sighed.

But in the limo on the way to the awards ceremony, Juliette began to have second thoughts. Just a half hour chatting with the general manager and his wife had left O'Connor silent and listless. Getting into the limo, he looked from behind like an old man and whatever had stirred on the balcony was long gone; he sat across from her, staring out the window. She could see from the rise and fall of his white tuxedo shirt that breathing was a bit of an effort, but his silence was so obvious, so complete, that she withdrew her gaze and watched as Palm Springs rolled past through the tinted glass.

Through the miracle of cell phones and an excellent limo driver, they arrived at the red carpet entrance to the convention center at 5:55 precisely. Juliette could see the throngs of people pressed against police barricades, a host of photographers in tuxedos and formal dress, and anxiety ballooned in her stomach, filled her lungs. *How do they do this?* she wondered. *How do people face this kind of attention over and over again?* She remembered once hearing a crowd at the Golden Globes screaming Sarah Jessica Parker's name. They were fans but still it had not been a friendly sound.

The driver opened the door and a muffled roar filled the car. O'Connor did not move. After a beat, Juliette gathered her skirts, figuring she was supposed to get out first, offer him her arm, make the transition smoother. At her movement, O'Connor held up his hand. His head was still turned away, he was still staring out the window; she could see the shadows under his eyes, the pulse beating in the hollow of his temple. He looked so thin. So thin and so ill. Of course they would see, everyone would see, this was stupid, they had been so stupid, he had cancer written all over him. She opened her mouth, but before she could speak, he dragged his gaze away from the window and looked her square in the eyes. "Don't forget that we're here for a reason, my Juliette," he said. "Someone killed Josh and I'll bet my lifetime achievement that someone is here."

He pulled himself from the limousine. By the time Juliette joined him, by the time he reached in, took her hand, and helped her out into the cool twilight that popped with a thousand flashes and seethed under a wall of voices calling his name—"Michael, left; Michael, right; Michael, over here, over here!"—the man she had just seen, the sick and fretful man, was gone. In his place, miraculously broad-shouldered and tall, striding like a well-groomed warrior through the forest of cameras and notebooks and outstretched hands, was Michael O'Connor, a force of nature radiating white teeth, impossibly blue eyes, and all the magic Hollywood could muster.

The transformation was surreal, almost frightening. Unconsciously, Juliette took a step away from him. "None of that," O'Connor murmured, putting his arm around her waist and drawing her into the shelter of his shoulder where she had no choice but to wind her own arm around his waist. "Keep your eyes peeled," he said, kissing her chastely on the cheek for a photo op, then taking her hand and leading her through the gauntlet of the red carpet. "This will take a while."

15

Thirty minutes. It took the two of them half an hour to walk a hundred feet because O'Connor would shake every outstretched hand, take every business card, answer every question from every journalist from *People* to the *Palm Springs Weekly,* kiss every preternaturally tanned cheek of every Palm Springs matron who shimmied up to him all sequins with impossibly deep cleavage. Suddenly here was Kevin Spacey and Scarlett Johansson, Eddie Izzard and Chris Rock and Bill Murray and Alicia Goldstone, Forrest Hughes, and, of course, Bill Becker. And here was the obligatory phalanx of publicists acting as part tugboat, part offensive guard, moving their people through the crowd, offering them to certain journalists like so many pieces of ripe fruit. Arnie Ellison hovered in the background, his eyes pinned on Hughes and Becker, who seemed joined at the hip. Anna, Juliette realized, had probably already been deposited inside—it wouldn't look good for her to be walking the carpet, at least not the carpet in Palm Springs. "I have Sharon Stone," one young man announced to the crowd of reporters with all the subtlety of a ballpark peanut vendor. "I have Sharon Stone." O'Connor only had Juliette, who drew looks of confused half recognition—without the context of the Pinnacle, even stars she knew weren't sure how to place her.

"But where, oh, where is Ms. Stewart?" O'Connor murmured in her ear as he exchanged punches in the arm with William Rudnick, the former Marine. "Beautiful work, man," he said to the actor. "Just fucking brilliant work."

Juliette smiled to keep from snorting. They had watched exactly seven and a half minutes of Rudnick's film in the limo on the way down. O'Connor had concluded that Becker must have bought at least the SAG portion of the Academy—with two exceptions, he said, declining to name them, everyone had been chosen for their shock value.

Rudnick, a big bull of a man, stood staring, hanging on to O'Connor's hand for dear life. "I can't tell you what that means to me," he said. "I mean, oh, man, *Red Water*? Or *Elliott*? Those were like gospel. You just speak to me every time. It's just an honor . . ."

"Well, maybe I was wrong," O'Connor said as Juliette steered him onward. "Obviously a man of great intelligence and genuine artistry."

"Explains why things are going so well in Afghanistan," Juliette muttered.

"Don't mutter, darling, it isn't polite. Does Kevin Spacey *own* Palm Springs now or something?" he asked, watching the actor be enveloped in yet another throng of admiring locals. "Or is this still left over from that Bobby Darin movie?"

When they finally managed to get into the ballroom, O'Connor gave Juliette a small shove. "Circulate," he hissed. "We're looking for pickpockets, jewel thieves, and other miscreants. And if you see anyone with a single malt scotch handy," he added, "send him over here."

"Are you supposed to be drinking?"

"I'm not supposed to be doing a lot of things," he said, winking suggestively. "But I still plan on doing them, my Juliette."

Juliette drifted into the crowd, just in time. Anna Stewart threaded her way directly toward O'Connor, working her face into a portrait of patient sorrow as she went, then all but falling into his arms when she "accidentally" bumped into him. Juliette tried to find some small, tiny kernel of pity for her—if nothing else, it must be a shock to have your lover killed like that—but it really was beyond her. Watching Anna allow herself to be ministered to by O'Connor, Juliette wondered if the actress was capable of murder. If, as O'Connor seemed to think, Natasha's overdose and the reporter's poisoning were somehow related, she could certainly see Anna having a hand in that. Poison, even in the form of mismarked narcotics, seemed right up Anna Stewart's alley. But to cut a man's throat? She simply couldn't imagine Anna allowing her hands to get so dirty. Unless she got someone else to do it for her. That, Juliette thought, as Anna allowed herself a small laugh into Michael's handsome face, she might believe.

"Having fun?" said a familiar voice at her elbow. Juliette jumped guiltily as if her thoughts had been somehow broadcast, and turned with surprise to face Gregory Bridges.

"What on earth are you doing here?" she asked. "Does Dev know you're here?" She couldn't believe Devlin would let the two of them out of the hotel at the same time.

Gregory shrugged. "I have a long-standing date down here, unlike some who just zipped down on a whim. Eric's on the festival board," he said, nodding toward a tall blond holding court two groups to their left. "He asks for so little and he gives so much in return . . ." Gregory grinned. Eric was the son of a famous producer, "exhaustingly rich" was how Gregory described him, and the two had been living together for more than a year now, though neither Juliette nor any of the Pinnacle staff knew Eric very well. "So," Gregory said, shouldering his way closer to Juliette, "what are you doing with Michael O'Connor? He isn't even one of ours."

Juliette shrugged and lied. "I've known him for years, since the Plaza, actually. He called and asked if I wanted to join him. Dev said sure because, I think, he's hoping I can bring him over from the dark side."

"Hmmm," Gregory said doubtfully. "There must be more to it than that. This is not exactly the best time to be *recruiting* someone. God knows where we'd put him. From all accounts, he's a fairly demanding guest, is Mr. O'Connor." He scanned her face thoughtfully.

"Well, I don't think he's coming this year," Juliette said, reaching out to brush an imaginary something from Gregory's shoulder just to keep her face from flushing, "but you know Devlin—he's the big-picture guy. I just go where I'm told, so here I am."

"Uh-huh," said Gregory, still looking at her skeptically. "Oh, well, there goes Max. Can you believe he's *living* down here? It's like the whole world has gone mad. Or maybe he's been secretly gay all these years . . . Did you see our Alicia? She's got this body stocking on and no drawers to speak of. Save me a dance anyhow," he said with a wink, and headed back to Eric and his crowd of bodybuilders.

People were beginning to take their seats, but, surveying the room, Juliette realized that all the stars were still standing, so it would be a while before Max actually took the stage. The interior of the civic center had been done up rather well, she thought, with dark satin draped along the walls and pale tulle from the ceiling. On each table a centerpiece of roses and cornflowers and lilies of the valley stood, easily two hundred a pop, she thought. There were three open bars and at least twenty servers circulating with drinks and hors d'oeuvres. *This must cost as much as the Governor's Ball,* she thought, remembering what Max had said about how the Palm Springs community was small and powerful and expected everyone to pitch in. No wonder so many A-listers were here: apparently there was money to burn in the desert. Josh would have loved it.

Thinking then of what O'Connor had said—that Josh's murderer might very well be in this room—Juliette grabbed a drink from a passing tray, not much caring what it was.

"Will the age of the mojito ever end?" said Sasha Curizon, helping herself as well. "Apparently not in Palm Springs."

"How are you, Sasha?" Juliette said. "You look lovely."

The reporter snorted. "Had to take the Oscar dress out two weeks early; now I'm going to have to buy a new one for the actual event. And will the paper pay for it? Not those skinflints—the guys get their tux rentals reimbursed, but the women just have to eat it. Nothing new there. So what are you doing down here with Mr. O'Connor, who I heard was in Morocco recovering from something a bit more serious than another divorce, though he looks pretty good from here . . . ?" Sasha turned a guileless smile on Juliette. "Are you two dating?"

Juliette choked on her drink, coughing so hard Sasha had to slap her on the back a few times. Heads swiveled around them and for a moment a small cone of quiet descended. "Not to worry, not to worry," Sasha said loudly as Juliette straightened her breathing out. "Just a mojito malfunction, no one's been poisoned, nothing to see . . . yet," she added under her breath.

"Do I take that convulsion as a yes or a no?" she asked, returning her attention to Juliette.

"A no. A definitive no. We are old friends," Juliette said. "From the Plaza days. He called and invited me, I think to be nice," she added in a burst of inspiration. "He had heard about Josh, of course."

"Of course," the reporter said evenly. "And you came down to an event where your ex-husband's lover is going to receive some stupid award and no doubt cry on cue while receiving it because you had nothing better to do."

"I guess I didn't think of it like that," said Juliette, regarding her just as evenly. "I guess I thought it was a chance to get out of town with someone who is a good friend and take a break before the madness of Oscar week."

"Uh-huh," Sasha said. "Look, Juliette. I'll level with you. I'm not here to write color on this stupid festival. I think there's a good chance someone is trying to sabotage the Oscars—I know, I know, very Internet conspiracy theory, but still. We've got a dead reporter—and no matter what the police are saying publicly, Marie wasn't smoking. Why do you think she got so fat? There was something in those doughnuts; a few people said they felt weird after eating them. What she *was* doing, however, was working on a story about Bill Becker. Who had just signed Natasha for that film of his. Which seems almost too coincidental to believe. This," she said, leaning in and lowering her voice although in the din of the party there was no need, "is Pulitzer material. I figure out who did this and I never have to cover another awards show. In. My. Life. So if you know anything, and you always do, tell me. We could get whoever slit Josh's throat together. Think," she added, taking a sip of her drink and watching the effect of her words, "of how good that would look for your hotel."

Stunned by the ambition she saw in the other woman's eyes, Juliette swallowed hard. If *The Times* was pursuing this line of thinking, then the police must be as well, which meant what? Were they still watching Juliette, watching O'Connor, wondering now if his sickbed alibi was all a scam? She hadn't even thought about that when she agreed to this little trip—why, oh, why had she let him lie for her? Lies always backfired, and the unnecessary ones backfired the loudest.

"Sasha, if I knew anything at all," she said carefully, "I would tell the police. And then," she added with her own conspiratorial smile, "I would call you."

Glancing to her right, she saw O'Connor deep in conversation with Becker; the producer looked very happy. As he slapped O'Connor on the shoulder, O'Connor caught her eye and winked.

"Okay, everyone," said the voice of Max Diamond, squeaking slightly with feedback. "If you're not in your seats in five minutes, I'm rolling tape of my grandson's circumcision. The uncut version."

Amid laughter and groans, the well-dressed multitude began to make their way to their tables.

"I read in the *Los Angeles Times* that this festival is becoming the mini-Oscars," Max said when most people had taken their seats. "Here's how you know that isn't true. There is no VIP green room, we will all be fed before midnight, and Bill Becker isn't screaming at anyone."

When the laughter died down, he continued, raising his voice slightly over the sound of chairs scraping back from tables, of people setting down their glasses, pulling their napkins from beneath their silverware. "No, I love Bill," he said, moving side to side a bit like a boxer, fighting the eternal battle with his small infectious grin, "and I worry about him. So much stress could give a man a heart attack. I mean, look at the guy. Every other producer and studio head I know is suddenly a toothpick. Have you noticed this? Brian Grazer weighs, what, ninety-five pounds? And that includes hair product. Bob Shaye could wear my daughter's jeans. But Bill, he doesn't care. They get smaller and he gets bigger. Sometimes"—he lowered his voice—"I think that's his plan—he's waiting until the rest of them are so thin they can't fight back and then he'll just eat them."

From the middle of the room, Becker grinned and gave Max the finger. For the next three hours, Max did his best, but it was still a long evening. First there was the video montage titled *Tiffany's Goes to the Movies*—Tiffany's being a proud sponsor of the event. Then there was the video montage of *The Magic of the Movies*. Watching clips from *The Guns of Navarone*, *The Bishop's Wife*, and *Psycho*, O'Connor leaned in and whispered, "Did they just lift this from Turner Classics?"

"You need to eat," Juliette whispered back—dinner had been served promptly, but O'Connor's plate, with its selection of chicken, beef, and salmon, was untouched. Absentmindedly, he picked up his fork and took a few bites. While everyone else was watching the screen, O'Connor was watching the room. Turning in his chair, he caught various peoples' eyes and waved or winked a greeting, but Juliette could see his eyes moving from table to table, carefully, appraisingly.

"What are you doing?" she whispered finally. He smiled at her slowly, sexily. He dropped his arm around her, cupping the far shoulder with his hand, then brought his mouth close, very close to her ear, and for a moment she forgot what it was she had asked him. "I'm trying to figure out who the most desperate person in this room is," he said. "I mean," he added, and this time his lips grazed the spot just behind her earlobe, "besides me."

Three hours later, Juliette would have had to admit it was a toss-up. For a few moments, things looked up when Spacey, a gifted mimic, came out and did a Max Diamond impersonation and then Max came out and did a Kevin Spacey impersonation, and then the two of them engaged in an evershifting monologue featuring all of the celebrities present, including O'Connor. But then the awards process began and the various acceptance speeches were long and, with a few exceptions, quite strange. Alicia Goldstone spoke rather drunkenly about the work she was doing with the victims of river blindness; Bill Murray just stared at the award for almost three minutes before saying, "Thank you for the tallest, most pointy award I have ever received"; William Rudnick spent almost twenty minutes thanking his "real true family," who turned out to be his agent, his lawyer, and his personal publicist; Chris Rock made some uncomfortably funny jokes about black people in Palm Springs; and Anna Stewart managed to choke out a brief thank you to the "greatest writer I have ever known, my beloved Josh," before virtually collapsing onto Max's shoulder. Eddie Izzard, in long silk skirt and tunic, was hilarious in discussing his plans to galvanize an actiontransvestite movement in Hollywood, and Michael was brief and sincere, thanking the film festival organizers for "keeping storytelling alive and the storytellers honest," offering his sympathy to those who had been affected by the "odd and unnerving tragedies" that had beset the community of late. "I certainly hope," he said with a wry, sexy smirk, "that we can put all this behind us and return to what we're good at— deal making and backstabbing."

As he spoke, Juliette watched the room. Framed in the

doorway a hundred yards from the stage, William Rudnick, who had all but kissed O'Connor's ring earlier that night, was talking into his cell phone, and Anna Stewart had finished her dessert and was leaning over to finish the one in front of the woman beside her. A few tables over, Forrest Hughes had his hand down a blond woman's dress; clearly a local, she looked to be all of seventeen. As Juliette turned her attention back to the stage, she accidentally caught Arnie Ellison's eye—the calculating look on his face took her by surprise. She stared at him and saw again the small strange smile. Gregory, she noticed with a start, was deep in conversation with Bill Becker.

Onstage, O'Connor was finishing up. He thanked his "good friend Juliette" for accompanying him tonight. And with a final heart-stopping smile, he disappeared into the shadows.

After a few more jokes from Max, it was over. O'Connor allowed himself to be steered into a series of local television interviews as the rest of the winners and A-listers beat a hasty retreat to their limos. Juliette searched the crowd for Gregory, but he seemed to have vanished; she thought about calling Devlin but decided against it. The two men obviously had their own set of issues to deal with—Juliette was beginning to wonder if what Gregory had told her about Dev and Louisa was even remotely true. Sighing, she looked around the room. She did not feel like she was any closer to understanding who had killed Josh and if it was in any way connected to the deaths of Natasha and Marie Stanton. *Why did I come down here?* she thought, shifting her weight to keep her feet from aching. *What did I think would happen?* Remembering Michael's lips against her ear, the sudden flush of heat she had felt at the center of her body, she stamped her foot to interrupt her own unwelcome thoughts.

"You're mad at me already? I haven't even done anything yet," said Max, appearing to her elbow. "So dance with me anyway." Without giving her a chance to say no, he led her to the dance floor, where a few die-hard couples were making the most of the big band sound.

"You were hilarious," Juliette said after a moment of marked silence. "The absolute best thing of the evening."

"Which isn't saying much. God, things can get weird down here. That's what happens when there are no cameras; some of these people just go haywire or something."

"Well," said Juliette diplomatically, "I think the atmosphere is a bit less formal, so maybe they feel comfortable enough to—"

"Act like complete morons. Like I care about river blindness. I mean, I care, I don't want to get it, I don't want anyone I know to get it, but over dinner this is not what I want to hear about. She was just trying to show what a model citizen she is, not that she has a chance. The pity votes are all going to Anna."

Unconsciously, Juliette stiffened. Max looked at her quickly, slid a reassuring hand onto her back. "It's just something that happened to someone you used to love," he said. "You have to think of it like that. You can't let it get to you. You certainly can't let her get to you. She'll be gone and forgotten in two weeks. You can get through that easy, kiddo. You've gotten through worse."

Juliette smiled down at him. He was so handsome in his funnyman way, trim and solid in his tux. "You're right," she said, thinking of those first weeks after Josh had left. "I have, actually."

"Thataway," he said, executing an adroit turn. "Now, if you'd just run away with me to Greece, you'd understand what happiness really is."

"Max," she said, "don't disappear into the desert. Make some more movies. I couldn't stand it if you didn't."

Max looked at her and for the first time she could see something dark and sad in his eyes. But he then smiled his gap-toothed smile and it disappeared. "For you, darling," he said, "I would do anything."

"Mind if I cut in?" said O'Connor, appearing out of nowhere. "You moving in on my date, Diamond? Though as good an impression you do of me, she might not even notice."

"Wouldn't dream of it, dreamboat," said Max. "Though you don't deserve her, napping the afternoon away. But she has just coaxed me out of early retirement. Someone should call the trades."

"It's too bad you didn't just buy the rights to that Salinger thing," O'Connor said. "The movie would be made by now. If it lies around any longer, Becker will eat it too."

The two men laughed. "He's going to have a heart attack one of these days, I keep telling him," Diamond said. "But does he listen? Maybe he'll listen to you; he likes you. Tell him to lay off the carbs. He's gained, like, thirty pounds in the last few months."

"It's good to see you, Max," O'Connor said. "I hear you killed them in New York. I bet the Academy is wishing they had convinced you to host again. Saved everyone a lot of trouble." He looked at the comedian with a small smile.

Max snorted and looked away. "Maybe, maybe not. Well, I've got to toddle off, early hours down here in the desert. Juliette said something about brunch and there's actually something I'd like to talk to you about."

"Great," said O'Connor. "I look forward to that."

In the limo on the way back to the hotel, O'Connor was silent, his face again to the window.

"You all right?"

He nodded.

She told him what she had noticed during his speech—especially Anna's dessert consumption. "That woman normally does not eat anything. I mean nothing. So clearly she was stressing about something. And I couldn't believe Arnie was just sitting there while Forrest mauled a teenager. That man is going to land in jail if he doesn't watch himself." She related the conversation she had with Sasha. "If you were looking for the most desperate person in the room," Juliette said, "she'd be on top of the list. I could definitely see her knocking off a co-worker or two if she thought it would win her a Pulitzer, but I don't see her killing Josh. I don't see anyone killing Josh, at least not the way they said he was killed."

"It's a cutthroat business," O'Connor said absently. "Sorry," he said, turning toward her. "Unfortunate choice of words." He turned his attention back to the window with no other comment.

"So," said Juliette after a pause, "did you see whatever it was you thought you might see?"

"I don't know," he said, and his voice bouncing off the glass sounded flat and somehow distant. "I think . . ."

"You think what?"

He pulled his gaze away from the window. His face was disturbed, as if he couldn't believe his own thoughts, but still he wasn't looking at her. "I think I need to think about it some more," he said. Then his eyes focused on her and his face softened, grew so tender Juliette felt her throat close tight. Every character he ever played seemed to come together, so much talent, so much complexity. For years she had watched him, for years she had known him. And here he was. "Later," he said, pulling her off her seat and onto his lap. "Much, much later."

They made it through the lobby barely brushing shoulders, up ten floors in the elevator with another couple hip to hip, down the hall past a room service runner holding hands. Watching him fumble with the key card, Juliette felt her breath grow ragged and wondered if Rory was inside. "I sent him to bed down the hall," O'Connor said as if he read her mind. Then the door was open and they were inside, enveloped by sudden dark as the door closed, her back against it hard and his mouth on hers harder. She couldn't see or hear anything, couldn't breathe even, but it didn't matter because all that mattered was the body pressed against hers, shoulder and knee and hip, the mouth that tugged at hers and stroked, the fingers cupped around her face, her shoulders, tracing the soft skin on her arms. Her own hands touched his cheeks, his hair, burrowed inside his jacket, pulled the shirt from his waist until they found the warm sudden flesh of his back, his belly, his chest.

"Off," he murmured into her neck, into the soft hollow between her breasts as his hands slid down her back, along her sides. "How does this come off?"

"Back," she said, tugging off his jacket, yanking open the bow tie, unbuttoning the shirt. "Hook, then zipper." As she said the words, it was done and the dress fell around her and he groaned softly, pulled her against him so there was nothing at all in the room but darkness and flesh pressed together, and if she had been able to think about anything at all but the wonder of his mouth and the pleasure of his hands she would have realized the dress had worked out just like in the movies.

218

"Bed," he said, deep into her mouth, kicking off his shoes as she undid the cummerbund, the button, then the zipper. "Which bed?" he said, stepping out of his pants and rearranging his grip on her so she could feel him, so he could imprint himself against her.

"Mine," she gasped. "Mine." They moved across the room and her mouth never left his, even as she felt herself fall, felt the cool sheets against her back, even as he reached out and turned on the nightstand light.

"I need to see this," he said, unsnapping the front of her bra, "I need to see you. Finally."

His mouth was on her, all over her, and she could not believe how good it felt, better than good, better than better than good, his fingers here and there and buried deep until she couldn't stand it. "Can we," she said, remembering vaguely what she knew from a time before she had begun kissing him, remembering vaguely that maybe he shouldn't be doing this. "I mean, are you okay to . . ."

His mouth was on hers, making things go deep and silent again, and he was all around her in the dark behind her closed eyes. "Juliette," he breathed into her ear as she rose against him. "I would rather die than stop."

And she knew exactly how he felt.

Later, when things had calmed down, when she lay curved against him on the disarranged bed, she was able to clarify this remark.

"That was just rhetorical, right?" she said, tracing the shape of his mouth, his chin. "I mean, you didn't go off your treatment just for this."

"Just for this?" he said mockingly. "Why, not five minutes ago you were heard to remark—"

She put her hand over his mouth and laughed, embarrassed. "I know very well what I remarked; I was here at the time. What I mean is . . ."

"I know what you mean. And partly, yes, I did. Sorry," he said, rolling onto his side and looking into her eyes, "but there are things you can wait for and things you can't." She held her breath and waited for the moment to pass, afraid of what might happen, what she might say. "I also meant what I said before," he continued. "Things are very strange just now and I would rather be able to think clearly for two minutes put together. I will finish the treatment," he said, holding up three fingers in a Boy Scout pledge, "the minute Best Picture has been announced and no one has been murdered onstage at the Kodak." She laughed, but still tears pooled in her eyes and she leaned toward him and kissed him, finding as much pleasure in the familiarity of it as in the pleasure itself. "I'm not going to die, Juliette," he whispered into her hair, "not now anyway."

A sob threatened to choke her and she kept her face hidden for a moment while he stroked the back of her neck, as if she were a child. "Tell me a secret," he said, pulling the hair from her face.

"I don't have a secret," she said, wiping her eyes with the sheet.

"Tell me about your exploits as a jewel thief, then. Now, now, now," he said as he saw her face grow distant, "I have bared my rug, my illness, my very soul. For chrissake. I have vomited in front of you, passed out in front of you, and walked the red carpet in Palm Springs in front of you. You know me," he said, his voice slowing a bit as the words sank in, "better than just about anyone ever has." He stared down at her, bent, and kissed her softly on the side of the mouth. "So tell me," he said, "about your wicked past."

"I was living in New York and I fell in with a bad crowd," she said, pushing him away.

"I was living in New York and *I* fell in with a bad crowd," he said. "But I became a movie star. What happened to you?"

She shut her eyes and tried not to remember that the last time she had told this story, the only time she had told this story, had been under very similar circumstances, only the man lying naked beside her had been Josh.

On the other hand, what O'Connor had said was true; she did feel like she knew him well. Right now. What that meant in the long run she didn't let herself consider because she knew, from experience, that six months from now, he could be air-kissing her in the lobby while looking over her shoulder for someone interesting. That's how it went in this business.

"I fell in love with my drug dealer," she said. "I had dropped out of NYU and I was hanging with some punk types down in Alphabet City, smoking a bunch of grass and shooting a little speed."

"Parents?" O'Connor asked gently.

"Out of the picture." Juliette paused. "Dead. Car crash when I was nineteen. Which is why I dropped out. And that," she said, feeling him stir, "is all I will say about that. So I fell in love with this coke dealer, named, I wince to report, Viper. Coke dealers are, as I came to find out, as expensive a habit as the coke itself, of which I was becoming increasingly fond as well, and as I had no visible way of supporting myself I came up with this ingenious scam."

"Which was . . ."

Juliette sighed. *In for a penny,* she thought. "Well, remember back in the late eighties, how it was all Louis Vuitton and Gucci luggage? I mean, everyone had the same damn bags. So I bought myself a set of knockoffs and I would dress in what was left of my Connecticut prep school finery and saunter into the lobby of the Waldorf or the Helmsley and swap my empty bags for someone's full ones. You would be amazed," she said, turning to him, animated despite herself, "how easy it was. Half the time I'd get nothing but shit—clothes, shoes, once I picked up a satchel full of sex toys—but usually there'd be something good—jewelry, drugs, cash. A lot of women keep their cash in their big bags because they think it's safer than in their purses. Though sometimes I'd take the purses too, especially when I realized that most people can't remember what their room number is, so there would be the key or the card and a slip of paper with the number on it. Up I'd go—it only took me a week or so to learn how to spring a room safe—most room safes are for shit. They're just there to make the guests feel better. A baby could crack them. Or I'd get some friends in on it, they'd create a diversion in the lobby—like this one girl would come in all bloody, her clothes ripped up, and of course everyone including the guy at the front desk would run to help and I'd slip behind and help myself. For a while there I was pretty slick," she said, the energy slipping out of her voice replaced with disgust. "Pretty slick for a fucking cokehead thief."

"And then Alex hired you."

"And then Alex hired me. Viper thought it was great, the ultimate inside job, but I told him to get lost. For one thing, it would have been so obvious. For another . . . well, I liked Alex. He reminded me of people I used to know." She fell into silence, remembering the relief, the knee-weakening relief of sitting in that office, surrounded by polished wood and warm leather, talking to someone who wasn't stoned or strung out, or just young and stupid. Someone who seemed to have a plan for his life. For her life.

Beneath her head, O'Connor moved his shoulder, prodding her to continue. She sighed. "Of course, Viper didn't like being told to get lost, so he had two of his buddies beat me three ways to Sunday, left me for dead in an alley. Literally. Left for dead. In an alley. Unbelievably cliché. But Alex found me, I never did figure how, showed up in a taxicab like the cavalry, got me a doctor, took me home, and sat with me while I got clean. Made me eat, made me sleep, made me laugh, and all for no good reason that I could see. I asked him once, you know, *why*, and he said, 'You never know when you might accidentally save someone's life.'"

Again, she trailed off into silence.

"What happened to Viper?"

"Alex got them all put away for a few years. Viper OD'd in jail, I stayed put at the Plaza, Alex got AIDS and died along with half of fucking New York, and the rest, as they say, is history."

Juliette stared at the ceiling. She hated her story, hated that it sounded so melodramatic. When she had told Josh, he had been shattered (his own word), full of fear for her and of her. They had to "process" the whole thing for weeks, for months. She looked at O'Connor to see what he would say. He too was gazing at the ceiling.

"That's a good story," he said finally. "Any of it true?"

This being the last thing she thought she would hear, Juliette could only laugh. "All of it, as a matter of fact," she said, punching his shoulder. "Aren't you going to dissolve in protective tenderness? Or flinch away in shock and horror?"

"I remember you back in the eighties," he said. "You looked like you were pulling through pretty good then and you look like you're pulling through pretty good now. Shit happens to everyone who goes messing around in the back alleys. Believe me, I know. But soft lives make soft people, and you, my dear," he said, palming her belly, her breasts, the side of her neck, "are well-tempered steel."

"Careful you don't cut yourself," she said, pulling herself up and straddling him.

"That is one way of putting it." He grinned as she settled herself. "But wait, wait," he said as she began kissing his neck, the hollow of his throat. She sighed and sat up, hooked her hair behind her ears. "So how good are the room safes at the Pinnacle?"

"There are no room safes at the Pinnacle," she said primly. "There is a bank of safe-deposit boxes in a room behind the concierge desk, which is never, ever unmanned, and each guest receives one key, no key cards, and they are impossible for even a professional safecracker to break into in less than an hour. I know this for a fact because I had to hire the best in town just last year when a couple left their Oscar tickets locked in the box, took the key, and called from the Kodak. We also have two doormen, one inside, one outside, and the one inside does indeed open the door but he is really security, scanning for anyone who might "misplace" their luggage and pick someone else's instead, or try to pick up someone else's mail or packages, or even reporters who might be trying to read the cards on the flowers to see who's staying with us. In the three years I have been there, we have not had one incidence of theft and no unauthorized photograph taken inside the hotel."

"Just a body in the pool."

"I am still trying to figure out how they did that," she sighed, slumping a bit. "I didn't want to give David the satisfaction by asking him. I think it may have had something to do with me being preoccupied by a certain high-maintenance guest."

"Who has not even begun to reach the pinnacle of his demands," he said, rolling back on top of her.

"That," she said many minutes later, as he turned her gently onto her belly, "is one way of putting it."

16

Somewhere a phone was ringing. From a heavy dark sleep, Juliette raised her head—the clock read three-thirty a.m. She felt O'Connor get out of bed, heard him move quickly toward the suite's living room and pick up the phone. "What?" he said. "What, *now*? Can't you just come . . . oh, for fuck's sake. Yeah, all right, all right. I'll be there in two minutes. Jesus." He put down the phone. When he returned a few minutes later, he was pulling on pants and a T-shirt. "I'll be right back," he said, kissing her, smoothing her hair. "Don't let anyone take my spot."

When she opened her eyes again, the clock read five, but she was still alone in the bed. "Michael," she called, wondering if he was in the bathroom. "Michael," she said, walking out into the living room area, which was still dark. Visions of him passed out on the floor flashed through her brain and she began turning on lights, peering into his bedroom, his bathroom. Nothing. No one. Where had he said he was going? He hadn't. The only person she could think of who would call him at that hour was Rory—had Michael missed some shot or pill or something? She quickly dialed Rory's room. There was no answer. *I'll be right back,* he had said. An hour and a half ago. How strong was he anyway, after a night like this?

She pulled on some clothes and hurried down the hall to Rory's room. After a few minutes of banging on the door, she heard a groan. "Rory," she said through the door. "Rory?" Finally, the door opened a crack and the nurse's face appeared, puffy and squinting against the light.

"What?" he said. "Jesus. I feel like I've been hit by a truck. What?"

"Is Michael in there?"

"Is Michael . . . You're kidding, right? What time is it? What the hell are you doing here anyway?"

"I can't find him," she said, panic rising in her throat. "Someone called in the middle of the night—I thought it was you. He said he'd be right back. More than an hour ago."

"He probably got hungry, or went for a swim, or something."

"I don't think so," said Juliette, declining to explain why she didn't. "Okay, well, if you hear from him, tell him I'm looking for him."

The hotel was filled with the chilly early morning silence that Juliette never liked, not even at the Pinnacle. She checked the pool first—empty, as was the spa and the steam room. There was a library/TV room on the fifth floor—on one of the leather sofas, an old man snored over a Tom Clancy novel. Down in the lobby, the only thing moving was the fountain; the night manager stood at attention behind the front desk, but Juliette could see he was reading a magazine.

"Hi," she said, approaching him. "I was wondering, have you seen Mr. O'Connor? Michael O'Connor."

The young man dropped his eyelids just a fraction. "I'm sorry," he said, "we don't reveal the names of our guests."

"Oh for God's sake" she said, "I'm staying with him. I'm Juliette Greyson. Where is your GM? Peter . . . whoever."

"I'm afraid Mr. Rivers is not here at the moment. If you leave your name and room number—"

"Oh, never mind," she said, turning from the desk and reaching into her pocket for her cell phone. "Dev?" she said after a minute. "Listen, something weird . . . What? Well, yeah, well, I'm in the middle of something too. Something weird is going on down here. I think I've lost O'Connor. I know, I know, but I woke up and he was gone. Not gone, *gone*. His stuff is here, but I don't know where he went and, well, he said he would be right back and I, well, I have reason to believe he meant it. Do you have a number for Peter Rivers? He's the GM of this monstrosity—can you call him? Thanks, yes, yes, big time. Many favors. 'Bye, Dev."

At an unexpected and unusual loss for what to do next, she began pacing the lobby, looking to see if there was any nook or cranny she might have overlooked, hoping to find O'Connor stretched out asleep with the newspaper or, as Rory had suggested, eating a piece of pie. As she turned a corner, out of sight of the front desk, she could see no one, which, she mentally noted, was a very bad thing because it meant that anything could happen in this space between the closed café, the closed newsstand, and all those telephone booths, and the guy at the front wouldn't even notice. *At the Pinnacle,* she thought, casting her gaze around, *we'd never stand for this layout.*

Sighing, she turned to go. Maybe Michael was in the room right now wondering where the hell she was. As she turned to go, a figure caught her eye. One of the telephone booths was occupied. Juliette took a step forward, thinking she would ask whoever was in there if a man had come down this way, when she suddenly remembered the GM telling her the phone booths were computer stations. As yet unfunctional computer stations. An icy hum began in her head and she walked toward the closed booth. Through the frosted glass she could not make out much, just a shoulder and a back pressed against the door. She knocked once, though she didn't expect a response, and pulled on the door. When the body of a man fell against her, she was not so much surprised as relieved—this was an old man, with very little hair and a mottled round face. Lowering him carefully to the floor, she realized he was still breathing—heart attack, she thought calmly. She was just about to run to the front desk for help when she saw the cord wrapped around his neck. Shivering, she pulled it away; it had been yanked so tight it cut into the man's neck in places. The man's hand came up to rest on her hand—his eyes were closed and she could not tell if it was an intentional action or just a muscle spasm, but she recognized the hand. With a gasp, she looked again at the face and saw what she was looking at.

Michael O'Connor, without his hairpiece, garroted beyond recognition, fighting for breath. Juliette knelt down beside him and screamed.

Many things happened then, though Juliette could not tell if they happened quickly or slowly. Her attention was riveted on two things: the feel of O'Connor's hand in hers and the shallow rise and fall of his chest. If she took her eyes from him for one second, she thought, she would look back and he would be gone. Although it had been the snarky night manager who had first responded to her screams, by the time the paramedics arrived, the general manager was there, and so Juliette was able to explain, eyes still on O'Connor, about the necessity of keeping this absolutely quiet.

"No one must know it's him," she said. "I mean, the police will and the doctors, but no one else. Do you understand?" She tore her gaze away long enough to see understanding and compassion in the man's dark eyes.

"Devlin explained everything," he said quietly. "The situation will be contained."

For a moment Juliette almost smiled. She could hear the ambition in his voice—if he proved himself, there would soon be a new member of the Pinnacle staff.

The paramedics lifted O'Connor onto the gurney. There was an IV in his arm, an oxygen tube under his nose; for a moment, Juliette had a flashback to that horrible half hour at the pool when she thought David Fulbright had been killed. Impulsively, she leaned over and whispered in his ear, "If you are faking this, I will kill you." But there was no response, not a flicker of an eyelid, not a flutter of a finger. Pressing her lips against his clammy forehead, she said, "You can't die." Tears thickened her voice. "Not now."

Gently, one of the paramedics pulled her up and they rolled the stretcher away. She moved to follow it, but then here were the Palm Springs police and in a daze she realized they were going to ask her questions. The hotel was beginning to wake a bit and Rivers appeared, steered her and the police into his office; she passed Rory in another office, talking to what looked like a detective—the nurse looked at her defiantly, even angrily, when she passed. She explained what had happened, recounted the phone call, what O'Connor had said to her.

"Why did you go looking for him?" one of the officers wanted to know. "He had only been gone, what, an hour?"

"An hour and a half," she said. "And he said he would be right back. He's not been feeling well," she said, "and I was afraid maybe he had passed out somewhere, or gotten sick."

"He looked pretty good getting that award last night," said the other officer. "Not sick at all."

Juliette put her hand to her forehead. "You'll have to talk to his nurse," she said. "I see someone is talking to Rory."

After a while, they let her go, having taken all her information. Lurching out into the lobby, she stared at the breakfast crowd bustle. It seemed impossible to her that life was going on as usual for so many people, just as if nothing had happened. Where had they taken him? She cursed herself for not getting the name of the hospital. Rivers would know, she thought, and she headed toward the front desk when someone caught her by the elbow.

"Come on, sweetheart," said Gregory. "I'm taking you home."

She stared at him dumbly.

"Dev called. I've gotten all your stuff together." He motioned to her bags alongside the wall. "There's a car outside."

"But Michael . . ." she said.

"They've airlifted him up to L.A.," he said. "Back to Cedars. At his agent's request. So there must be a pretty good chance he's going to pull through," he added with a tiny grin, "otherwise why would his agent get involved?"

Juliette nodded, tried to smile, but she felt tears running down her face and she couldn't think for the life of her how to stop them.

"It's all right, honey," Gregory said, putting his arm around her. "You cry all you want."

When they were about twenty minutes out of town, Gregory reached into the back seat and pulled out a large envelope, which he put on Juliette's lap.

"This is from Devlin," he said carefully, keeping his eyes on the road. "He said I should take you wherever you wanted. No questions asked."

Juliette looked at Gregory with frowning surprise, but he kept his gaze straight ahead. In the envelope was a plane ticket from LAX to St. Croix, ten thousand dollars in cash, and a silver-plated .45.

"Is he out of his mind?"

Gregory shrugged.

"Does he think I tried to kill Michael?"

Gregory didn't say anything.

"Does he think I killed Josh? After somehow flying to New York and switching Natasha's coke for heroin?" Juliette's voice was verging on hysteria and she didn't care—she felt it was about the only appropriate response at this point.

"He thinks your ex-husband is dead and now your, well, the man with whom you have become quite close, and who I am told was *your alibi,* has been attacked . . . Dev just wants you safe." Finally he turned to look at her. "We all want you safe. No matter what."

Juliette slid the gun and the money and the ticket back into the envelope and shook her head. "Why should I be safe when apparently no one else is?"

Gregory took her directly to Cedars. O'Connor had been given the Elizabeth Taylor Suite, but no visitors were allowed. Not even Juliette. Especially not even Juliette. She was stopped at the door by O'Connor's agent, a 350-pound, white-haired man named Lucius Taylor, whose resemblance to Santa Claus ended at the beard. "What the hell were you playing at?" he said by way of greeting. "What the hell were you doing, letting him go down to Palm Springs, much less poking his nose around in your ex-husband's murder?"

"He told you that?" Juliette asked, taking comfort in the implication that Michael could at least speak.

"No," said Lucius, "you just did. He's not saying anything. He may never say anything again. Fuck me, woman, the man is in the middle of chemotherapy—you don't take him out for a jaunt with some murderer running around."

"I didn't take him anywhere," she snapped, figuring if Michael were truly on death's door, Lucius would not be wasting his time yelling at her—he'd be holed up somewhere with O'Connor's lawyer and a copy of the will. "He took me. And I would think you of all people would know how difficult it is to sway him once he has made up his mind."

"Sway him?" the agent said, leering. "Is that how you'd describe it? Here's what I know: since he started hanging out with you, he's off his treatment, blowing down to the desert with me having barely enough time to logistically get him 'home from Morocco,' accepting some lame-ass award that is going to set his career back five years, and on top of all that, someone's practically decapitated him."

"How bad is it?"

"Bad e-fucking-nough!" he shouted. "So being no relation by blood or marriage, you are, until further notice, off the list of visitors, not that there will be any visitors because I don't even know who this guy in that bed is—my client, Michael O'Connor, being on his way back to Morocco to finish preproduction on *Two Thieves*."

Juliette nodded. "Can I see him?"

The agent's face flushed.

"Please," she added softly.

"One look," he hissed. "One short, tiny look. No talking, no touching."

Juliette nodded again and slipped into the room. Behind a curtain, Michael lay so still it was frightening. His face was a normal color and back to its normal size; there was a bandage around his neck and Juliette could see the blood that had seeped through. She reached out and took his hand and squeezed. "Michael," she said. But there was no response. Glaring, Lucius motioned her back out the door.

"I will stay away," she said firmly, "if you will call me the minute he wakes up."

Flushing and sputtering, the agent nodded curtly.

"And if he asks for me, you tell me," she added.

"Out," Lucius said, "before I call security."

On the elevator down, Gregory said nothing. Juliette stared at the ice-cube-tray formation of the lighting above her—why did hospitals go out of their way to make everything as hideous as possible? she thought, wiping at the tears that ran steadily down her face. Wordlessly, Gregory handed her a large linen handkerchief. When her BlackBerry rang, she dug for it frantically, wildly wondering if perhaps in the five minutes since she had left, Michael had come to, had asked for her. But it was Max.

"You stood me up," he said in a hurt voice. "When I called over, they said you had checked out. Early."

"Oh, God, Max," she said, as the elevator doors opened and the phone line crackled. "I'm so sorry . . ." Her voice wavered and she swallowed to steady it, putting a hand on Gregory's arm to keep him from walking out onto the street. "Something just . . . came up," she said. "And I just, well, I don't know how else to say it, but it just slipped my mind . . . I had to come back to L.A. earlier than I thought and . . ." It was all slipping away, all the hotelier poise, all the years of calm, of perfect pitch, falling around her right here in the lobby of Cedars-Sinai.

"You don't say another word, kiddo," Max said kindly. "I understand. I told you, didn't I? I told you that guy can't be trusted. Great actor, don't get me wrong, and I love him like a brother, but I wouldn't want him dating my sister, if you know what I mean. You know what? Next time I'm in town, I'm going to bring my nephew by. He's a great guy, close to your age, an orthopedist. You'd like him."

"Oh, Max," Juliette said, laughing and crying all at once.

"I know, I know," he said. "You call me when you're feeling better. And I'll be back in L.A. one of these days. Maybe sooner than you think."

"Max Diamond thinks I blew him off for breakfast because Michael dumped me," she said to Gregory as they stepped into the mist-dimmed light.

"Well," said Gregory, "in a way he did."

Juliette shot him a look.

"Well?" Gregory said. "It would have been nice if someone had bothered to tell me Michael O'Connor was in our hotel. What am I? The Pinnacle taxi service now?"

When Gregory finally took her home, Juliette stared at her house like she had never seen it before. Inside, it smelled cold and stale; grapes and apples rotted in the bowl on the kitchen table and a half-drunk latte was curdled in the sink. Walking out onto the patio where she and Josh had once spent an entire day stringing the oak trees with fairy lights, she lay down on a leaf-coated chaise and tried to remember who exactly she was anymore and why all this was happening to her.

The sound of the doorbell woke her hours later; the light was gone and she was stiff and chilly, damp in the winter twilight. Padding toward the door, she remembered the gun Devlin had given her. It was still in the envelope on the table by the front door. She thought for a moment about pulling it out, but looking through the peephole she saw that it was Devlin himself standing on her front porch.

"These are yours, I believe," she said, handing him the envelope when she opened the door.

"I'll certainly take the cash, and the ticket if you insist," he said, not missing a beat, "but you're keeping the gun whether you like it or not." Then, with no warning at all, he gathered her in his arms, tucked her head beneath his chin, and just stood there. She wanted to push him away, but she found she could not. The sound of his heartbeat steadied her, the soft cotton of his shirt, the silk stretch of his tie, the familiar soapy smell of him comforted her. There were no kisses, no exploratory caresses this time; he just held her tightly and she allowed herself to be held.

"Do you think I killed Josh?" she asked his shirtfront.

"No," he said quietly. "And I don't think you tried to kill O'Connor. But it all seems too close by half and it frightens me. I don't want it to come any closer. I don't want anything to happen."

"Things have already happened," she said, looking up at him. "Horrible things. Dev, if you had seen him . . ."

"I don't want anything to happen to *you*," he said simply, looking down at her. And for the first time since she had known him, she saw something that looked like a flicker of possibility in his eyes. It was just too much for her to bear.

"Oh, Dev . . ." she said, helplessly, hopelessly.

"How could I afford to lose you?" he asked, his sideways grin quickly back in place. "This close to the Oscars."

"Christ," she said, pushing him away then, not because she was annoyed with him but because the thought of Oscar night brought her up short—was it possible such a thing still existed? "Are they still going through with it? After what's happened?"

Dev looked at her quizzically. "As far as everyone but you, me, and six or so other people know, nothing has happened. Michael O'Connor is on his way back to Morocco— paparazzi caught him at the Palm Springs airport. The press is too busy dissecting the MDB restructuring and picking over the latest Forrest Hughes scandal. Apparently there are photos all over the Internet of him with five girls, all in various stages of undress, none of whom are even legally able to drink."

"But the police—"

"Have their own reasons for keeping it under wraps. And anyway, they think they've found their man. They arrested him a few hours ago, which is actually why I came over, well, the main reason I came over." Juliette stared at him, her mouth open. "It was the nurse," he said gently, "that Rory fellow. They've got him dead to rights; the phone call O'Connor got last night came from his room. The hotel has a record of it."

Juliette could not believe it, but Devlin swore it was true. Apparently, police had searched Rory's Hollywood apartment and found all sorts of photos and clippings and assorted "signs of an unhealthy obsession with Michael O'Connor." A smear of O'Connor's blood was found on the wall in Rory's room, and a swatch of hair from his wig in the hallway just outside the door.

"That doesn't make any sense," Juliette said, sitting down, allowing Devlin to pour her a glass of whiskey. "Rory adores Michael."

"Or hated him," Devlin said. "Envied his success. Saw a chance to get even."

"But why would he strangle him when he could have easily poisoned him? Jesus, he was shooting him up with dope hourly."

"Yeah, but O'Connor went off his meds, right? So maybe Rory figured he'd have to do something quick. Or maybe he saw what was going on with you and O'Connor and he just went mad. Makes sense to me," he added, with an indecipherable look.

"Dev," Juliette said.

Her boss held up his hand. "I don't need to know," he said. "I don't want to know."

She looked at him fondly for a moment, but then shook her head. "But do they think Rory killed Josh? Or Natasha? Do they think he pushed over that Oscar statue? Or poisoned the *Times* reporter? Not to mention Lisa Javelin—"

"Whoa, whoa, whoa," said Devlin, "one dastardly deed at a time. Not all of those things are necessarily connected. But yes, he could have killed Josh; he was off that night, remember? You were with O'Connor, after all." Juliette glanced at him; the Irishman's face was unreadable, though she thought she saw a brief flash in his eyes.

"But why would he kill Josh?"

"To get to you? To sabotage the hotel? To screw up the Oscars? I appreciate your confidence that I can second-guess a sociopath, but really, maybe the best course is to wait until the police have done their duty. Wait, and find a little comfort in knowing that O'Connor's attacker, at least, is behind bars."

Juliette looked at him; he seemed very confident, like he always did. And she wanted to believe, not that it was Rory so much—she had liked Rory—but that it was over. She thought of Josh's cell phone—of the calls he had received. Clearly he had been away from the hotel for some time when he died, away from Jar where he had met Anna. Had Rory followed him the whole time, waiting for an opportune moment? She shivered, remembered the night she had spent in O'Connor's room, with Rory just a few yards away, how he had come in with bags of clothes from Saks. Had he been jealous? Had he killed Josh to somehow get to her? It didn't seem possible. But then none of it did when she sat down and thought about it.

"Are you fucking Louisa?" she asked suddenly.

Devlin started, stared, then laughed. "Why? Should I?"

"Gregory said you were. He said he walked in on you last week."

"Gregory has many fine qualities, but veracity, at least when it comes to things of a sexual nature, is not one of them. Gregory," he added, his voice softening just a bit, "has a fantasy that someday you and I will get married and he can live in the safety of the Pinnacle family forever."

"He doesn't."

"He does. He probably told you that to make you jealous."

Juliette laughed. "He has a very warped idea of what would make me jealous."

Devlin looked at her strangely and she found she could not meet his eye. *Uncharted territory,* she thought, the phrase presenting itself neatly in her mind. *We are entering uncharted territory.*

"Did you know he was going to Palm Springs?" she asked, partly because she wanted to know but also to diffuse whatever she felt building around them like static before a storm.

"Yes," Dev said. "Things may be . . . taking an odd turn, but I do still know what my staff is up to."

Juliette nodded. "I was just surprised you would let both of us be gone," she said. "I mean, it's not exactly policy."

"I had my reasons," Devlin said, his jaw tight, his eyes steady. But before she could even ask, he smiled and stood.

"Now let's talk about dinner, shall we?"

17

Impossibly, things went back to normal. When Juliette
returned to the Pinnacle the next day, she found what she had
left—an extraordinarily well-run hotel in the midst of its
busiest time of year. And within an hour she herself was so
busy she simply did not have time to think about murder and
poison and the possibility of some grand conspiracy. She
didn't even have time to worry about Michael. All the nominees from outside the U.S. were already ensconced, or
checking in that day—the American Film Institute luncheon
was on Thursday, the DGA and SAG awards Friday and
Saturday night, the Foreign Press dinner on Sunday, and the
week before the Oscars was crowded with parties and dinners
at the Malibu compounds and Brentwood mansions of producers and directors and studio executives. Soon the hotel
would be fully booked, the restaurant and bar filled with stars
and Industry bigwigs—every nook and cranny of the lobby
would be jammed with reporters trying to have "quiet" chats
with nominees, while the back garden would be a revolving
photo shoot.

Meanwhile, the jewelers and designers and stylists were

taking up their suites, offering an elite corps of invitees—mostly-nominees but also some high-placed Academy members—the chance to view, and borrow, finery from the top of their lines. Racks of couture—gowns and tuxedos—rattled through the lobby, carts stacked high with bags full of makeup and handbags and perfume and footwear jockeyed past each other. The Brink's truck began its daily drop-off, heavily armed men clomping through the lobby to leave paper sacks full of velvet boxes with the concierge, usually only marked with a single name.

"I love this part," Louisa said, signing for the day's sixth delivery from Harry Winston. "They have guns just to walk this stuff through the door. I'm expected to sit on it until the stylists pick it up, and what do I have to defend myself? A ballpoint pen."

"But oh, how you wield it," said Devlin. Lousia looked up at him shyly and Juliette was struck by how happy she actually seemed when Devlin was around. And Devlin was suddenly around a lot, chatting with guests in the lobby, leaning against a stool in the bar, even taking a seat now and again at a lunch table. He always kept a high profile during these weeks, but this kind of presence was unusual. When he had left her house after eating Chinese food, he had again refused to take the gun—"I've got one, thanks," he had said with a wink—and Juliette had remembered something her old boss Alex had told her a few weeks before he died. "If you get to a point when you need real protection, you call Eamonn Devlin and tell him to bring in his boys." When she had pressed for details, Alex had only smiled faintly. Alex had great fun on his deathbed when the morphine was working, dispensing bits of wisdom and plans for everyone's future, making cryptic comments and dramatic overstatements. Most of which Juliette had forgotten.

If Devlin was so sure that the danger was over, Juliette thought, why was he so clearly keeping an eye on things?

But as he had predicted, there was not even a whisper about O'Connor in the press. Not that a whisper would have been heard over the gleeful roar surrounding the Forrest Hughes photos. Although a police check revealed all the women involved to be over eighteen—one was even twenty-three—there was the predictable discussion over whether Hughes would still host the Oscars, was he suitable to host the Oscars, was he using the Oscars to rekindle his career, was Becker using him to attract a younger and raunchier demographic, and on and on. Sasha wrote a story that suggested the whole thing had been staged, to give the Oscars yet another bump in the press and also to divert attention from the deaths of Josh and Natasha.

Juliette found this last hard to believe until she watched as Forrest swaggered into the hotel for an interview with *Rolling Stone* on the day Sasha's article appeared. With Arnie seemingly attached to his elbow, he ignored the *Rolling Stone* stringer for a full twenty minutes—despite the fact that she was about twenty-five, with her well-toned midriff and well-inflated cleavage obligingly revealed—while he made the rounds of the bar and the restaurant. Juliette watched Forrest mug and flirt with one of the waitresses and, standing firmly in the doorway, willed him to touch the girl. *Just once, just one touch,* she thought, because if he did she would have him thrown out of the hotel, Oscars or no Oscars. As if sensing her thoughts, Arnie whispered something in his client's ear. Forrest smirked but moved away, making the rounds once more before walking past Juliette close enough for his shoulder to just miss brushing her breasts.

"Ah," Forrest said, breathing vodka and cigar smoke into

her face, "Juliette. Fancy seeing you here. I would have thought with all that has happened you might take a few days off. But you are in fact one tough broad."

"And I could say the same to you, Mr. Hughes," she said with a gracious smile. "Certainly the last few days have not been as traumatic for me as they must have been for you."

"Haven't they?" he asked, with a knowing look. "Haven't they really?" But before Juliette could ask him what he meant, Arnie, without a glance in her direction, hustled him off.

"What do you think he meant by that?" Juliette asked Devlin, who had appeared silently beside her in time for the comedian's last comment.

"I have no idea," he said. "But that's another one who will never stay in this hotel again if I can help it. Do you know Arnie Ellison had the cheek to suggest that you were acting as if you were general manager of this hotel?"

Juliette's neck tightened. Devlin's words sounded like a reprimand. Arnie might be an asshole, but he was now one of the biggest publicists in town. And fond as Devlin might be of her, his goal was to keep the people Arnie repped firmly ensconced at the Pinnacle. She glanced sideways at her boss's face. For a crazy instant she wondered if he was going to fire her.

"I told him he had uncovered one of the best-kept secrets in Hollywood," Devlin said, his eyes on the lobby, a grin tugging at the corners of his mouth. "And so now I'd have to kill him. That shut him up." And with a light pat on the small of her back, Devlin glided away.

"I bet it did," Juliette thought. Watching him go, she realized that of all the people involved in whatever sort of drama was unfolding around her, the person she least understood was Eamonn Devlin.

*

Yet against Devlin's direct orders, she visited Rory in jail. It was horrible—the drive to downtown Los Angeles alone had reminded her of how unreal her life was, only moving in the small comfortable radius of the Pinnacle. The judge had set bail at one million dollars; Rory couldn't get it—the only person he knew with that kind of money was O'Connor. When the officer brought him out to the visiting window in his prison grays, Juliette was struck by how criminal he looked. But he seemed so gratified to see her that she just didn't know what to think. According to Rory, he had fallen asleep early that night and didn't wake up until Juliette was pounding on the door. His theory was that he had been drugged. "After you guys left, I had maybe two glasses of champagne and some of those chocolates that had been sent to the room. And it was like I just passed out, like someone had slipped me a Mickey Finn."

But police had tested all the food and alcohol they had found in the suite and Rory's room and it was clean.

"Did Michael miss a dose of meds?" she asked. "Because that's what it sounded like when he was talking on the phone. Like it was you telling him he needed to come get his pills."

"Like I would tell him to come get them? Does that sound like something I would do?" Rory asked. "And yes, he did miss a dose, but shit, he was playing so fast and loose with every-thing at that point, I couldn't have gotten him to walk across the room, much less down the hall. It wasn't me. I was asleep. I swear, Juliette." His eyes filled with tears. "I would never hurt Michael. I love him. You must see that. You must believe that."

Juliette had no idea how to respond to this. "Sociopath" was the word Devlin had used. Surely many killers thought they loved the people they harmed, surely many killers lied their heads off to whoever would listen.

"But who else would call him?" she asked. "Who else could get him out of the room?"

"You mean, besides you?"

Juliette looked at him quickly. Behind his eager expression, his eyes were hard.

"I was right there beside him," she said. "I was the one who went looking for him, the one who found him."

Rory said nothing and Juliette remembered what she had read in countless mystery novels—that nine times out of ten, the person who found the body was the one who made the body.

"I'm going," she said, rising from her chair—why was Devlin always right?

"Wait," Rory said quickly, his eyes going from steely to desperate, his hands pressed against the thick Lucite. "I know you didn't kill him. You love him as much as I do. But see how easy it is, see how it could look like you did? That's what's going on here. Someone has set it up so it looks like I did it. Who knows? Maybe he was strangled in my room. I felt like shit when you woke me up. I could have been so out of it I wouldn't have heard a thing."

Juliette nodded slightly, but still she stood. This had been a mistake. He was manipulating her and she had put herself into a position where that was possible. She glanced at the guard, who indifferently rose from her seat to unlock the visitors' door.

"Please," he said, his voice a whisper through the shield that separated them. "Just tell me if he's going to be okay."

"I don't know, Rory," she said quietly. "I don't know if he's going to be okay."

And in fact, there had been no word from the hospital. Juliette had no idea at this point if this was real or just an informational blackout—she believed that if O'Connor was capable of getting in touch with her, he would, but she didn't trust Lucius to tell her what was going on, really, and none of the doctors would talk to her.

"There's nothing you can do," Gregory said to her, when he caught her hissing into her BlackBerry at some nurse who was telling her nothing. "Just try not to think about it and throw yourself back into the chaos that is this hotel at this moment. Do you know who I saw this morning?" he said, lowering his voice to gossip level. "That Therese girl. You know, the one we thought was going to get nominated but wasn't? Well, she's here. In this hotel. She checked in yesterday. I think she's here to see *Ricardo*."

Juliette smiled her gossip-received smile, then quickly excused herself, all but tripping over Dustin Hoffman and his wife to find the assistant room service manager. Ricardo was at his post, surrounded by a sea of carts dripping linen, festooned with flowers and fine china. The wall behind him was covered with computer printouts listing guests and their likes and dislikes—crustless toast, white peaches over yellow, brown eggs over white, FIJI rather than Evian. Yellow Post-it notes, with newly discovered quirks, dotted the list and the window across from it like so many peevish butterflies. At first glance, it seemed impossible that the hundreds of breakfasts-in-bed delivered every day during Oscar season could emerge from such a small, crowded space. For a moment, Juliette treaded water at the edge of the frenzy, watching the complicated and graceful, if very loud and clattery, dance. Servers and runners and cooks buttered toast and covered plates, filled thermoses and found just the right sort of jam, the right kind of honey for each cart. Of all the miracles that occurred at the Pinnacle during Oscar season, she thought, the breakfast rush was the most spectacular.

Still, it did not dim her anxiety—she remembered how Michael had floated his theory about Therese and the drug cartel connection, how she had ridiculed him. But now . . . "Ricardo," she said, tugging him away from the ringing phone. "Listen, sorry. I know you're incredibly busy, so I will get right to the point. Why is Therese Salvatore in the hotel?"

The young man flushed, and shrugged. "She is shooting another movie, in Burbank, and she wanted to stay here. She's only here for a few days," he added.

"Do you know her family?" Hearing the harshness in her voice, Juliette smiled. "Sorry, it's so loud in here. I meant, I remember her saying her sister knew your sisters, or something like that. Did that turn out to be true?"

"Yes, yes," said Ricardo eagerly. "Her sister went to school with mine, at St. Agnes in Bogotá. Her mother is a teacher there. Her father is a cook at one of the hotels. They are very nice people. Why do you ask me?"

Juliette shook her head, suddenly embarrassed. "It's such a small world sometimes," she said, "I just wanted to see how it turned out."

"It is not a problem," Ricardo said, "if I see her sometimes? It is not against the rules?"

Technically, Juliette thought, it was against the rules. The hotel had a policy against fraternizing with the guests, but considering her recent behavior, she did not feel she was in any position to point this out. "Just not so much flirting in the hotel," she said kindly. "I know you won't have much free time in the next week or so, but after, you should take some vacation and then you can see whoever you want. You are," she said, glancing again at the organized chaos around her, "a wonder, Ricardo. We could not do it without you."

I am losing my mind, Juliette thought as she hurried back to her office. *If I keep jumping at every shadow I am going to completely fall apart. I have just got to accept that Rory did what he did and Josh just got mugged and Natasha was too stoned to tell what she was snorting and that reporter was a nicotine fiend.*

For a moment, she allowed herself to stand still, to watch as the guests for the New Line luncheon began assembling on the garden patio, the men handsome and well tailored, almost all the women impossibly beautiful. *I have just got to make it to next Sunday without having a nervous breakdown,* she thought, smiling as Ewan McGregor winked at her from across the room. *How hard could that be?*

Ten days before the Oscars, champagne began arriving by the truckload, the main restaurant's menu officially changed, the spa hired four extra aestheticians and still was booked from seven a.m. until ten p.m. The Foreign Press called at the last minute to change the dessert on its annual dinner from éclairs to flourless chocolate cake, which meant that Rick and his staff pulled an all-nighter and for several hours one of the private dining rooms was literally covered in small chocolate cakes. "I think they wanted to avoid the cream filling," said Hans, surveying what the staff was calling *le chamber du chocolat.* "Which is insulting! No one ever got sick from something out of my kitchen. No one."

"It's not just us," said the pastry chef as he and his staff sifted powdered sugar carefully over each small cake. "It's everyone. My friend at Sugar Plum says no one is sending anything, no cakes, no tortes, no éclairs. Only cookies. He has been making more cookies than at Christmas."

"They're sending flowers," said Louisa, who was also standing in the doorway watching. "The florists are so overwhelmed, they're sending business down to San Diego, up to Santa Barbara. No one wants to take a chance of someone even getting a tummyache after what happened at the *Times*."

"Next," sniffed Hans, "someone will die from some poisoned flower, like in that Batman movie."

"Okay, break it up, break it up," Devlin said, coming up behind the group. "Oscar week has officially begun. What are you all doing standing around? J.," he said, "a word."

As they walked down the main stairway, he explained, "Lily's arriving day after tomorrow with the babies. I want you to settle them in. And Anna Stewart," he added quickly, "would like you to stop by her room sometime after seven this evening, if that's convenient."

"Any idea why?" Juliette asked, determined not to break her stride, not to give away any more than she had lately.

"None," Devlin said, waving to Robert De Niro as the actor passed. "And if it becomes unpleasant," he said, "you should just take your leave. There are limits, after all, to the services we provide."

"First I've heard," she said with a grin. Then, catching sight of a familiar face heading into the lounge, crowded already at just before five, she broke away from Devlin and hurried across the lobby.

"Andrea?" she said, gently touching the shoulder of Andrea Chapman, the Oscar talent coordinator. "What on earth are you doing here? It's six days till Oscar. I didn't think they let you out of the Kodak at all this week."

"Oh, I haven't been in the Kodak this week," Andrea said flatly. "Didn't you hear? Becker fired me."

"What?" Andrea Chapman had been the talent coordinator for the Academy Awards, as well as just about every other awards show in town, for as long as anyone could remember. With her low and lovely southern accent and trademark white-blond hair, she was the terror of the press corps and publicists alike—if she felt someone was in any way interfering with the talent, a glance from her and a reporter's credentials were yanked or a publicist escorted off the red carpet. She was as much a fixture of the Oscars as the statue itself.

Realizing she was actually gaping, Juliette steered Andrea to a reserved table. "Do you have one minute?" she asked.

"Honey, if you're buying, I have all night," Andrea answered.

"What the hell happened?" Juliette motioned at the bartender to make the martinis extra-big.

Andrea shrugged. She was impeccable in black linen, her makeup exquisitely applied, but still Juliette could see the lines around her eyes, her mouth. What was Becker thinking?

"I told Mr. Becker I didn't think some of the things he was planning were in keeping with the spirit, or safety, of the awards," she said. "And he said if I felt that way, I was welcome to leave. They bought out my contract and I left." She shrugged, but the pain showed in her eyes and in the small twitch at the corner of her mouth. Juliette took one of Andrea's hands in both of hers.

"I just can't believe it," she said. "He must be going insane. How is he going to pull this off without you?"

"I don't know, and frankly I don't care," she said, recovering herself. "He's making a mockery of the whole thing—all he cares about is ratings. He's got some of the nominees faking fights in the audience, he's designed the set to look like the Colosseum and he wants to rig it so columns fall down. In the middle of the show! He's even got someone who's going to pretend to kidnap a trophy model. Onstage! It's like he thinks it's the Keystone Cops or something."

"Well, he can't get people to agree to that . . . can he?"

"That anyone is still speaking to him after the stunt he pulled last month is a mystery to me. But look at who's nominated this year," Andrea said, throwing up her hands. "Some of these people will do anything if they think it will expand their fan base. Oh, and he's having Forrest Hughes make his entrance from a hanging cage. Like a Cher concert. The Academy Awards! As if Hughes wasn't bad enough on his own. For the life of me, I cannot understand why Becker picked him. They don't even like each other. It's like," she said, lowering her voice, "Hughes has something on him. Something really bad."

"Can't you talk to the Academy? How can they be okay with all this?"

Andrea finished her martini in two gulps; Juliette motioned for a second round. "They're panicking. You know what would happen if they cut the show down to two hours? Every union but SAG and the DGA would be picketing and the event would just be another celebrity showcase. I mean, the whole point of the Oscars, in my mind anyway," she said, leaning forward, "is to show people the faces they don't see, the people who put their hearts and souls into the movies and don't get the big paychecks and the free diamonds. I mean, you can see Brad and Angelina on the cover of every magazine nowadays, but don't you think the cinematographers and visual effects people, the screenwriters, deserve the same amount of glamour and dignity, even for just one night? I do." She spoke with an earnestness Juliette found almost heartbreaking before diving back into her martini. "But Bill Becker, all he cares about is if he can get a bunch of thirteen-year-old boys to watch. What's next? *Academy Awards: the Video Game?*"

Juliette, shocked at such an outpouring from a woman known for her reticence and consummate diplomacy, could only shake her head and pat Andrea's hand.

"You know what I think?" Andrea said. "I think Bill Becker is trying to sabotage the Academy Awards."

18

Later that day, Lucius left a message saying that their "mutual friend" had regained consciousness briefly. That he was, however, unable to vocalize yet, that he had quickly fallen asleep, and that at this juncture it would not be in anyone's best interest for her to try to contact him, but that things looked "promising." "Perhaps you can visit in the next few days," he finished with more gentlemanliness than Juliette thought possible.

Filled with an enormous sense of well-being, Juliette paused for a moment in the ladies' room, brushing her hair and reapplying her lipstick and perfume before heading up to Anna Stewart's room.

A young blond woman answered her knock, smiling briefly and holding up one finger before disappearing back into the room. "Have her come in," echoed Anna's voice. Juliette stepped through the door and into a place she barely recognized as a Pinnacle suite—velvet and silk was draped everywhere; Tiffany lamps had been brought in; several very fine, small paintings, including, she thought, a Vuillard, hung on the walls; there were books and papers stacked and strewn along the floor; and the desk shone with a large collection of crystal paperweights. "I am to be Colette," Anna said in a bored, distracted voice, not rising from the overstuffed chair by the window. "In a week and a half. Can you believe it? They will not push back the schedule. Not even now. I do not see how I can be expected to do this. But I am. So there you are."

"I'm sorry to hear that," Juliette said. "It must be difficult."

Anna stared up at her with her big dark eyes, which seemed even more shadow-ringed than ever, or perhaps it was artfully applied kohl.

"Please sit," she said, gesturing toward a chair facing hers. Her voice was low and, Juliette had to admit, just as thrilling as it was in films. Feeling as if she were in a play, Juliette sat. "I was surprised to see you in Palm Springs," Anna began. "I did not realize you and Michael were . . . so close."

"We have known each other a long time."

"So it seemed." She paused for a moment and played with the bracelets that clattered around each arm. Juliette felt impatience rise—was she here to watch Anna channel Colette? "I felt then," Anna said finally, "and again when I returned here, a certain awkwardness between us that I think we need-n't feel, sharing, as we have, such an awful loss."

Juliette inclined her head and tried to adopt the tone of her hostess. "I certainly do not want to make you feel awkward in any way," she said. "Josh and I had not seen each other in almost a year. The more immediate loss, of course, was yours."

"And yet you spoke with him for several hours on the . . . that night," Anna said. "I wonder if you will tell me what you talked about."

Juliette considered the actress—what did she want really? Surely not to share memories of Josh.

"We talked about many things," she said. "His work, my work, the Oscars, mutual friends, you . . ."

"Why didn't he answer his phone when I called him?" Anna asked abruptly. "I called and called during that time and he never answered. Why not?"

Juliette shrugged, a little taken aback by the anger that surged in Anna's voice. "I don't remember his phone ringing; he must have turned it off."

"He never turned it off when we were apart," Anna said accusingly. "Never. He certainly wouldn't have turned it off if you were just chatting away about this and that. It makes no sense."

"I couldn't tell you," Juliette answered, trying to remain calm, remembering Devlin's words. "I didn't hear his phone, that's all I know. Perhaps he left it in his room."

"Or perhaps you were doing more than just talking," Anna said fiercely. "I know he was angry with me that evening. We had just had a fight, we had been fighting for days . . . it happens. I get anxious, I get fearful, and he always needed me to be so strong . . . but it was only nerves, it was only an argument. About my publicist, for heaven's sake. Josh and I were happy, we were very, very happy. He didn't regret leaving you, no matter what it might have seemed like; he had no intention of coming back. We were going to be married. Oh, we hadn't formally decided, but it was inevitable, no matter what he might have said to you that night. No matter what he might have done. He loved me. He loved *me*."

Anger poured through Juliette's body, lighting up the tips of her fingers, the backs of her knees. Many things she could take, many remarks she had taken over the last few weeks, but this she was not letting go.

"Then why did you feel it necessary to imply something

different to the police detective?" Juliette asked coldly. "If you were so certain of Josh's feelings, why would you bother to suggest that I still had feelings for him? And if I did, what would it matter to you? Why would you go out of your way to throw suspicion on me? *I* didn't benefit from Josh's death. As you say, I had already lost him. But then maybe," she added, speaking carefully, enunciating her consonants in a way she hoped would make Michael proud, "so had you."

For a moment the actress's face froze. Slowly, slowly, she began shaking her head.

"No," she said. "No. We were happy. *Happy.* He was just . . . overwhelmed at times. By the pace, by the people, by the life we were living. It began to affect his work, his ability to work, but all writers are like that," she said with a dismissive gesture, "aren't they? I mean, they all have writer's block now and then, they all go through drafts that maybe aren't as good as they might be."

She was clearly looking for a response, for some affirmation, but Juliette just stared. Josh couldn't write and Anna couldn't help him. Which explained why he had returned to the script about the jewel thief, his desire to have Juliette read the Salinger project.

Taking her silence as anger, Anna adopted a more placating tone.

"I'm sorry about the detective," Anna said, her voice suddenly warm and confidential. "I . . . wasn't myself and it was Arnie, really, who wondered if maybe there was something still . . . if maybe the police should be aware of . . . the circumstances of the divorce."

Arnie. Juliette came back to herself with a start. Again, here was Arnie Ellison. Hovering at the elbow of virtually every aspect of . . . what had Devlin called it? This series of unfortunate events.

"Arnie and Josh never did get along," she said, watching Anna's face. "Josh did tell me he had suggested you switch agencies. Did Arnie know that?"

Anna stood up quickly, turned away, and moved across the room as if there had been some commotion outside the window that she simply must see. Though she could not see her face, Juliette watched the tension gather on the actress's shoulders.

"I have no idea," Anna said lightly, her face still toward the window. "It wasn't a serious discussion, after all. And as much as I loved Josh, I make my own career decisions and always have done. For better or worse. Which," she said, turning to face Juliette with a small smile, "is something I'm sure you understand."

The two women surveyed each other coolly. Anna must have had a motive for wanting to talk with Juliette, but now she was clearly on the defensive. As Juliette continued to regard her, she was filled with curiosity more than anything else. How small the actress was, how narrow her shoulders were, how light and prominent her bones. How old was she anyway? Twenty-eight, twenty-nine? What sort of life did she envision for herself, in the end? And where on earth could someone like Josh have fit in?

"What exactly do you think is going to happen next?" Juliette asked, mostly because she just wanted to know. "I mean, honestly." Anna's eyes widened and Juliette was surprised to see real fear in them. Not emotional angst, but real naked fear. But before Juliette could think or say anything to follow up, Anna collapsed onto a chair. Her head fell into her hands, her shoulders heaved. Juliette sat absolutely still, astonished, until the actress raised her face, streaky with tears and kohl, and whispered, "Oh, Juliette, I just miss him so much. I just want to go home and they won't let me. They keep telling me to be strong for Josh, to remind the world what a wonderful movie he wrote, but I know it's all bullshit. They just want the publicity for the fucking DVD sales, they don't even care if I win. I don't care if I win. I just want to go home where my friends are, where I don't have to keep seeing these streets, this city, thinking about what happened here."

She gave herself over to sobbing. When Anna could again draw breath, Juliette handed her some tissues and helped her wipe her face. "Christ, I look like a Welshman," Anna said as the tissues came away black. "I guess I'm overdoing the eyes. I'm sorry," she said. "I meant to get emotional, just not this emotional."

Juliette handed her another tissue. "That's the trouble with emotions, they don't respond well to plans." Anna sniffed, and tears threatened again. "Listen," Juliette said quickly, hoping to stem them, hoping to cut this shorter than she feared it might wind up, "for the record, Josh did not give any intimation of being unhappy with you. What he really wanted was for me to read his screenplays. He wanted me to give him *notes*," she added, with a little more anger than she had intended. With little satisfaction, she saw that this perked Anna Stewart right up.

"Really?" she said, eager and self-centered as a child. "He just wanted you to give him notes? You're not just saying that to make me feel better?"

Juliette rose. "Why on earth would I want to do that?" she said. Anna had her public face well back in place; Juliette knew she would accidentally reveal nothing more and Juliette didn't begin to know what to ask to pry anything else out of her. "Well, I really should be going now. I hope you feel the air is clear between us; I know it will be difficult, but we want the rest of your stay here to be as pleasant as possible."

"Thank you," the actress said, standing and holding out her hand. "I'm sure it will be."

Devlin just happened to be waiting for the elevator when Juliette left Anna's room.

"Oh," he said as if he were just remembering the appointment. "How did that go?"

"I don't even know what *that* was," she said. "Either she is actually and truly heartbroken that Josh is dead or she deserves the fucking Oscar already." On the elevator, she leaned against the wall. "Michael came to, for a minute anyway," she said dully; her encounter with Anna had somehow taken the shine off the news. What did it matter to her anyway? Of course she hoped he would be all right, but once he was, what use would he have for her? Never had a night of passion been more a product of mutual need for reassurance—a month from now, her life would be just as it was. Michael O'Connor had more in common with Anna Stewart than he ever would with Juliette.

"I heard," Devlin said. She looked at him quickly. "I called Lucius and told him if he ever spoke like that to you again, his life as he knows it would be over. Because I have photographs," he said as the doors slid open.

"How did you know he yelled at me?"

"Gregory told me. Listen, my darling—" He was interrupted by a ringing BlackBerry. "What?" he said. "Yes, yes, I understand. Well, tell them we're working on it . . . We can't exactly build a new wing between today and tomorrow, can we?" He sighed and shoved the phone into his pocket. "Russell Crowe wants a room for his nanny and kitchen space for the kid's chef, Spielberg suddenly needs two suites, though he won't say for whom, and the president of Tiffany's has decided that his children will be joining him and his wife. Fortunately, Angelina has decided to leave the children behind, which frees up one nanny room, and Gwyneth has decided to stay with friends."

"Do you ever wonder just how long you'll be able to do this?" Juliette said, heading over to what she could see was a tense moment between Dog and an *Entertainment Weekly* photographer.

"As long as it takes me to convince you to run away to St. Croix with me," he said gallantly. "I still have those tickets . . ."

"Tickets?" she said. "I only saw one."

"I was going to meet you there," he said. "You don't think I'd send you off to an island paradise on your own, do you? And the Four Seasons is opening its newest resort . . ."

Laughing and no longer listening, Juliette hurried over to Dog.

Lily, her husband, her triplets, and their nannies arrived early the next morning, just walking into the hotel as if they were normal people.

"Oh, we rented a car at the airport," Lily said when, as the troops quickly assembled, Juliette apologized for not having gotten their arrival time from the limo driver. With her dark hair pulled into a ponytail and her wide, ready smile, the twenty-million-a-picture star could easily have been the nanny herself; she had one of the little girls hitched on her hip, the other two were resting comfortably in their father's arms. "I'm afraid we have far too much luggage," the actress said in an embarrassed tone. "You can't believe how much crap there is for babies these days, and people send us everything. The only thing I really liked was the stroller you all sent; when all else fails, we put the girls in and they fall right to sleep. Like magic."

"I'll tell Gregory," Juliette said. "He had it made to order."

Lily laughed. "Of course he did. Why do gay men always know more about baby accoutrement than straight ones?"

From the corner of her eye, Juliette could see that people coming out from breakfast were beginning to hover around the edges of the lobby, hoping to make eye contact with Lily or get a good look at the babies. So when Juliette saw Devlin, surreptitiously straightening his tie and hurrying down the main staircase, she began leading the group toward the back elevators.

"May I?" Devlin said, falling into step with them and holding out his hands for the child Lily was holding. "Oh, aren't you a little beauty?" He leaned in and kissed Lily on either cheek, held out his hand to Gavin, the second-grade teacher Lily had, to the shock of the Western world, married after a nine-week courtship.

"That one's Rose, that one's Heather," Gavin said. "And this is Buttercup. I think," he added with a laugh.

"Well, what a lovely garden you have," Devlin said. "And you both look well yourselves for all that. I'm guessing you haven't been sleeping much."

Lily laughed. "Much? You mean at all. We're hoping the Pinnacle will work a little magic. My people have me booked into the spa for I think three hours straight in the hope that they can make me presentable."

"Nonsense," Devlin said. "If it weren't our people, I'd say that was wasted money. But at least it ensures you'll be off your feet for a few hours."

Watching him deftly cradle a baby in one hand and orchestrate the procession that now included an armful of gift bags,

Juliette was amazed—how did Eamonn Devlin come to be so comfortable around infants? As the group headed toward the Presidential Suite, she felt her stomach turn over—she had not been up here since O'Connor had left. She had given the housekeeping staff concise directions about how the room should be prepared for the new guests, down to hiring the woman who had done the bedrooms for Jodie Foster's children, but she hadn't been able to bring herself up to check on the finished project. She looked at Dev guiltily, but he was busy opening the door.

And she needn't have worried. The room she stepped into was utterly different than the one she had left. None of the original furniture remained; everything was done in soft garden colors. One large corner of the living area had been recarpeted in soft cotton with all sorts of interesting squares sewn on—letters and animals and bits that crinkled and others that squeaked, all of it sectioned off by a low soft wall. The master bedroom was quietly colonial, reminiscent of Lily's Virginia home, and the other room had been transformed into Pooh's Hundred Acre Wood, with three cribs and two double beds for the nannies. The top of one bureau was lined with new baby bottles, and tucked discreetly in the corner of the master bedroom was a breast pump.

"God bless your souls," Lily said when she saw the pump. "This portable one I have is good for nothing. That looks like the real thing."

"We got it from Cedars," Juliette said. "All the attachments are new, of course, and in the drawer. And this," she said, tapping a night table, "is a little refrigerator, so you can keep things separate if you'd like."

"I guess we could have left all our junk at home, Lil," said Gavin as the porter rolled two carts in, each stacked with portable playpens and toys, car seats, and dozens of pieces of luggage.

"Would you believe that only the two big bags are ours?" Lily said. "It's ridiculous. If we changed those kids' outfits every hour on the hour we couldn't use what we've got. But we couldn't leave it behind, honey. Half of Hollywood is going to want to see the girls this week, and they'll want to see the stuff they sent too. Which is fine," she said, watching as Devlin lowered little Rose into her new play corner. "But maybe," she whispered to Juliette, "you could help me find a place to donate a few things when we leave. I just feel so guilty . . ." She looked around at the splendor. "And I worry what it's going to be like for them"—she motioned to the babies, who were sleeping, oblivious to the mobiles that hung down from an ingenious contraption attached to the wall—"growing up with all this."

"Oh, but it doesn't matter," said Devlin, standing from his paternal crouch. "Things never matter that much to kids. Not if they don't have them, not if they do. They see the fine, decent people their parents are and that's all that makes any difference."

Looking at him, the actress's eyes filled with tears. "Someone should marry you, Dev," she said. "And quick. Before those good looks go. What about you?" She looked at Juliette. "With that red hair, you'd make a lovely couple."

Juliette's face froze, but Lily looked at her calmly.

"I know," Lily continued. "And I am sorry. It's hard losing someone even when . . . well, either way it's hard." And Juliette remembered then that part of the actress's mythology included a college sweetheart killed in a riding accident. "Life goes on, though," Lily said, looking at her babies. "Sometimes that seems like a punishment, but mostly it's a gift. Christ," she said with her famous rough wide-open laugh, "I'm halfway to the Lifetime Channel. Hormone rush, I guess."

Devlin stepped into the small silence and began to make their farewells. "Whatever we can do to help," he said.

"Oh, I'm sure we'll think of something," Lily said as she leaned in to give Juliette a hug. "We always do."

"Such lovely, lovely people," Devlin said as he and Juliette moved down the corridor.

"Isn't it nice," she said, "when you can say that and for once actually mean it?"

19

By Thursday, everyone and their brother-in-law and their brother-in-law's personal assistant had checked in to the Pinnacle. Five extra bellmen were on duty and still Louisa, her staff, and at times Gregory and Juliette spent most of their day delivering gift bags and flowers and gowns and jewelry and even, occasionally, carts full of luggage. Some Industry types found a solution to the general food fear by simply ordering trays of goodies from the hotel kitchen to be delivered to their favored guests. Rick wound up hiring his friend from Sugar Plum and half his staff just to make sure that guests weren't receiving repetitive sweet trays. Security had trebled, with one agent assigned to the kitchen alone, while three patrolled the pool area and another was stationed outside the back door to the kitchen—earlier in the week a pair of young men had slipped into the lounge through the kitchen, leaving DVDs of their student films on each table. By two o'clock so many bottles of champagne and jars of caviar had been ordered through room service that they had to send a runner out to the Beverly Regent to pick up more.

Bill Becker swaggered in for lunch as if he hadn't a care in the world. True to form, he paused to chat with Devlin, then turned to Juliette as if he had never seen her before in his life. He looked flushed and heavy, but he had reserved the most visible table on the back patio so everyone coming into the hotel would see him as he sat with two nervous-looking men who Juliette assumed were his assistants, and a tall, gorgeous Asian woman who she'd bet money was a trophy model.

"I wonder if she's the one who's going to get kidnapped," she murmured to Gregory as he passed.

"Probably," he said. "And it wouldn't surprise me if Becker himself showed up onstage to do it, he's such an old ham. Will the last fat man in Hollywood please turn out the lights?"

Working off an intricately coded list loaded into her BlackBerry, Juliette, Devlin, and Gregory met the various VIP guests as they arrived, showing them to their rooms, smoothing over any problems as quickly as they could. One Supporting Actress nominee complained that her suite smelled of cigarette smoke and would not be assured that it was a nonsmoking suite, so a last-minute switch had to be made; William Rudnick dressed down his publicist right in front of Juliette for not getting him a room that faced east, but mercifully was willing to take a smaller room with better *feng shui*. Three dozen last-minute dinner parties were requested, either en suite or in the various private dining rooms, and several guests informed the concierge that they hadn't ordered their limos for Sunday and could someone do that please for them?

"Yeah, like every limo from here to Nebraska isn't already booked," said Louisa. "What do these people think? That they can hail them like cabs?"

"It is going to get worse before it gets better," said Gregory.

"I am guessing at least a third of the men don't have their tuxes yet. Who'll take the odds?"

Strangely enough, Juliette was soothed by the familiar chaos—the exhaustion she felt as the day crept toward evening was a sweet distraction from the anxiety that seeped into her shoulder muscles and stomach whenever she had a free moment. What if Rory was innocent? She still could not shake from her mind his pleading eyes, or how drugged he had looked that morning—but he was an actor. All that makeup he had certainly could have made him look bleary and drugged. Still, what if it wasn't him? What if someone had tried to kill O'Connor because of something he said or something he saw in Palm Springs? It could have been anyone who was there, and that was pretty much everyone. Anna, Arnie, Forrest, Becker, even Gregory. Had he been sent by Devlin? Access, ability, yes, but motive? Why would Devlin kill Josh?

"Stop," she told herself. "You will drive yourself insane." She squeezed her eyes shut, listened to the clattering business of the hotel. "And that's silly, when you can just let this place do it for you."

Tales from the Kodak were making their way through the hotel—bad luck seemed to plague the production. Fuses blew and lumber fell and all the press credentials somehow vanished and had to be remade, irritating about five hundred journalists and costing several thousand dollars. Hundreds of yards of red carpet were laid down before someone realized it was the wrong color red. Rumor had it that two boxes of the Oscar statues were missing.

Gregory was just relaying this last bit of information when Devlin appeared at Juliette's elbow.

"Call for you in my office," he said.

Juliette looked at him with a mild sense of shame as she

headed down the hall. Whatever Devlin was, he wasn't a murderer.

"What?" he said, sensing her stare.

"Nothing."

In the office, she picked up the receiver, as Devlin hovered, his back to her, staring out the window.

"Well, you certainly know how to show a fella a good time," said a soft, harsh voice she didn't recognize. For a minute she thought it was a practical joke, then she heard an intake of breath and realized that the raggedness she heard was pain, pain and perhaps damaged vocal cords.

"Michael?" she said, as the wall she had built around her anxiety collapsed. "Oh, my God, it is so good to hear your voice."

"Don't make me laugh," he wheezed, "it could quite literally kill me."

"Are you all right? Do you remember what happened? Can I come see you? Can I come now? I'm coming now." She looked toward Devlin, who nodded with an unreadable expression on his face.

"Slow down, honey," O'Connor said, his voice dwindling to a whisper. "I'm not at my best—"

"I'll be there in ten minutes," she said, and hung up the phone. "An hour," she said to Devlin, "I'll be back in an hour."

"I'm not worried about the time, J. Just remember . . ." He looked at her with something close to pity on his face.

"What?" she said defiantly. "Just remember what?"

"Nothing," he said, turning back to the window. "Give him my best."

O'Connor looked terrible. He could barely speak, could barely move his head. He tried to smile when he saw Juliette, but it wound up a grimace of pain. "Don't," she said, stroking the side of his face. His hair, what was left of it, lay in wisps on his skull. His eyes were still so bloodshot they were almost completely scarlet. When Juliette bent to kiss him, he held up his hand, but she just dodged it, laying her cheek against his.

"I have been so scared," she whispered.

"I'm sorry," he said. "We were wrong to go down there."

"You thought you could do some good. You thought you could find the murderer."

O'Connor grimaced. "I was playing a game, Juliette. I was playing a part. God forgive me, I was having *fun*. I didn't really think, I mean not really . . ." His voice faded to a strangled whisper. "But it looks like I was right. It was . . . one of us."

He did not remember the phone call—along with being strangled, he had apparently suffered a concussion during the struggle. He could not believe Rory would try to kill him, but he had no alternative to offer.

"Who else could call you in the middle of the night and get you to leave the room?" she asked.

He moved his head slowly from side to side. "The last thing I remember is you," he said.

"Which part?"

He smiled, a real if small smile. "The good part."

"Do you remember us talking? Do you remember the story I told you?"

"The last thing I remember is falling asleep beside you," he said. Something in his voice made her look up.

"You don't think . . ." She couldn't even bring herself to say it.

"No," he said. "I don't think . . ." He smiled drowsily. His eyes began to droop.

"I'll go," she said as he squeezed her hand. "But I'll come back tomorrow."

"It was odd," he said, not opening his eyes, "that Forrest Hughes was in Palm Springs. And that Becker would allow it."

"Why?" Juliette asked sharply. "Why do you say that?"

But Michael was almost asleep now. "Keep your head down," he murmured. "My Juliette."

Lucius was standing outside the door. "He's not going anywhere for a long time," Michael's agent said when Juliette asked about the medical report. "The doctors have to decide if he needs surgery on his larynx, and even if he doesn't, he needs to rest before he can start chemo again. He may never sound the same," Lucius said, "he may never look the same. And while he was able to face the whole cancer thing with a to-hell-with-them attitude, I don't know about all this. It could just ruin him, you know?"

Surprised and touched by what seemed like an actual display of emotion from an agent, Juliette laid a hand on the man's shoulder. "You know what I think? I think he's going to be fine. Seriously. A year from now, it'll be like it never happened."

"A year?" The agent's face fell. "You know how much his asking price will go down in a year?"

At nine o'clock, Devlin called Juliette on her BlackBerry and told her to meet him for dinner in his office. "This is an order," he said. "Because I have this peculiar feeling that you are running on last night's caffeine and breath mints."

She was happy enough to sit down in his office, to take her time over a salad, a glass of white wine. The exultation she had felt since she had spoken to Michael fueled her like a drug. He was alive, he would get better. Rory would just disappear and nothing else would matter. She had flown through the rest of the day, organizing and problem solving with an efficiency that surprised even her.

"It's way too late in your life to become a tweaker," Gregory had said after watching her flit from one needy guest to another. "It's like ballet—you have to pick it up by the teen years or you'll just blow your joints out."

Now, savoring her risotto, Juliette told Devlin everything Lucius had said, but somehow, in her mind, these were just challenges, challenges she was certain Michael would overcome without breaking a sweat.

"It will work out perfectly," she said. "He'll be ready to come back by the time all this Oscar craziness is over, and without all the distraction, we can really help him get better."

"After all this Oscar craziness is over," Devlin said, pouring himself another glass of wine, "I want you to take a vacation. Far away from here. Three weeks. Minimum."

Juliette laughed. She had never taken a three-week vacation in her life; no one at the Pinnacle took a three-week vacation.

"I'll take some time off, sure," she said. "But I don't want to leave. He might need me."

"He won't need you, J.," Devlin said curtly. "You are not his doctor or his nurse or his wife or even his girlfriend. He was a guest at this hotel, an important guest at this hotel," he amended, nodding, "but still just a guest. Obviously the two of you formed some sort of . . . attachment, but I think you might be getting ahead of yourself to think—"

"To think what?" she asked, her voice dangerously low. "That he might actually care about me? That what happened might actually mean something?"

"Juliette, my darling, no one knows better than I the power of your many charms," he said. "But he is who he is and if our experience in this Industry, in this town, has shown us nothing else, it has proven the often temporary nature of . . . intimacy."

"You're jealous," she said, realizing the moment she said it that she must be a little drunk. She had never said such a thing in her life.

"Perhaps," Devlin said surprisingly, swirling the wine around in his glass. "Or maybe I don't like seeing you falling in love with the idea of having someone to take care of. Again."

"He is going to get better," Juliette said.

"He'll still need to be taken care of," Devlin said impatiently. "Just like they all do. You deserve better than that," he added with a kind but level look. "You deserve someone closer to . . . real."

If I had any gumption at all, Juliette thought, *I'd get up and walk out of here. I'd get up and quit and then I would never have to think about any of this crap again.* But looking at her boss, she realized she could not sustain her own anger. Devlin's face was kind and so familiar; his voice, the set of his shoulders, even his mocking ways were as well known to her now as her own face. She had been listening to his advice for years and it was the rare case in which he was wrong. When he had shown up at her house the other night, when he had held her in his arms, she had felt safe, more than safe. She had felt herself. Devlin knew the best and the worst, she never had to pose around him, which made him a very rare person in her life. She pushed the last of her risotto around on her plate and felt a lump form in her throat; hadn't Michael said almost the same thing? *You're the type of woman who can't love a man unless he has to lean on her every single day.* Hadn't her anger at him been mostly at the stinging truth in his words?

She thought of how Lucius's words had filled her with concern but also, she had to admit, a shameful sense of relief—O'Connor couldn't dump her from a hospital bed. She wouldn't have to face seeing him wink at her from across the lobby while he embraced some long-legged twenty-five-year-old. *Shit*, she thought miserably. *Shit, shit, shit, shit.*

"J.," Devlin said, taken aback by the look on her face, "I didn't mean—"

"I know exactly what you meant, Dev," she said. Then she raised her gaze from the plate and smiled at him sadly. "Point taken."

He stared at her for a full minute and she stared right back.

"Sometimes," he said, "you take my breath away."

20

By ten o'clock on Friday morning, every chaise at the pool had been claimed, even though by Los Angeles standards the morning was freezing at 60 degrees. Phillip was negotiating with the wife of a nominee over the meaning of a "no save policy" while he and two pool attendants tried to squeeze a few more lounges in around the Jacuzzi. Stylists were pouring into the hotel and one of the guest elevators was used to accommodate the overrun of room service carts. Calls were already coming down to the concierge desk about missing gowns and tuxes. Shoes and handbags and runners were being dispatched, while Louisa and Juliette emptied their car trunks of all the wraps and necklaces and bags, shoes, and earrings they had brought from their own homes—inevitably someone's mother or a nonconnected Academy member needed something. The men on the staff began bringing in their formidable collections of shirt studs and cufflinks and bow ties for the inevitable requests on Oscar night. A buffet of fruit and sandwiches and many types of caffeinated beverages was put out in the staff dining room. Gregory distributed large bowls of chocolate-covered espresso beans. The staff began wearing their survival kits and eyeing the Xanax covetously.

Everything was going so smoothly that Juliette was actually surprised to get a message from Sasha Curizon. It took her an hour or so to return it and when she finally reached the reporter she was shocked at the hysteria in her voice.

"I need a room," she said. "I know you're booked, but I also know you keep a room or two free and I need one of them. Some guy shot at me. I was stopped at a light on La Brea and Third and he pulled up beside me, this guy in a rubber mask, and shot at me. Blew out my side window, cracked my windshield, and drove off. The cops are trying to make it seem like it was a carjacking or something, but I know it's about the murders."

"Murders?" Juliette said, to buy a little time, to insert a pause in the woman's tirade.

"Yes, murders," she said. "Your ex-husband, our reporter, that Russian actress in New York. I even heard some guy was almost strangled to death down in Palm Springs, that's how they nabbed this Rory guy. A nurse, a former drug addict, and an actor. He even worked with your buddy Mr. O'Connor. Which is why I think you may know what I'm talking about. My editors have taken me off the story. They want me to take some time off, but I'm afraid to go anywhere. Something like this happened three years ago with another reporter and it turned out some mob guy had hired someone to kill her. You need to let me stay at the Pinnacle. Because if anyone is going to break this story, it's going to be me."

"Sasha," Juliette said, "I'd like to help. You know I would. But there are no rooms here. You can come stay with me if you'd like . . ."

"You? You think you're safe? Jesus; your ex called you, like, three times just an hour before someone slit his throat—oh, yeah, we got his phone records. If I were you, I wouldn't stay alone either."

"Be that as it may . . ." Juliette prepared to hang up.

"I know O'Connor has cancer, Juliette," Sasha said quietly but firmly. "And I know what kind of cancer. And if you don't do me this one favor, I will put it on the front page, then call *Entertainment Tonight* myself."

Juliette was silent.

"I think something terrible is going to happen on Oscar night. And," she continued, comprehension dawning in her voice, "I think you do too."

"Sasha, I don't know what you're talking about regarding Mr. O'Connor, who, as you said, seemed fit as a fiddle just last weekend, but," Juliette said evenly, "I also think I know you well enough to trust your instincts. Come over. We'll find you something."

When she hung up she sat for a long time in her office, trying to think. Had she just invited a viper into the nursery? Sasha had as much to gain from a violently disrupted Oscar ceremony as anyone—other journalists had invented people and events in the quest for glory. How many times had Sasha complained about the lack of respect her paper showed entertainment journalists—cracking an Oscar conspiracy, even one of her own making, could give her the satisfaction she was looking for.

But somehow, Juliette didn't believe it. She didn't believe it because the same fear had been nagging at her since the moment Devlin showed up to tell her that Rory had been arrested. Josh had not been killed by a mugger—a mugger wouldn't have left his cell phone in her mailbox. His death and Michael's attack were related—somehow the murderer must have felt that O'Connor knew something, just as he had known David Fulbright wasn't really dead in the pool. But why would Rory kill Josh? Or send poisoned doughnuts to the *Times*? He had nothing to gain from it; it seemed a bit extreme that he would do such things simply because of a grudge against the entertainment industry.

So who would be next? The accidents in the Kodak had all been far from fatal; the only real casualties were those in the public eye. Who was in the public eye? With a hotel full of Oscar nominees, that wasn't particularly easy to narrow down. Who under this roof was the most high-profile person? Whose death would cause the greatest stir?

When the answer came to her, she stood as if she were shot and ran to Devlin's office. He was on the phone. Juliette reached out and hung it up.

"I think there is a chance someone is going to try to take Lily's kids," she said.

"What on God's green earth are you talking about?" he said, hurrying over to shut the door.

With resolute calm, Juliette relayed what the reporter had said to her and what her thought processes were. "I could be completely wrong," she said. "I hope I'm completely wrong. But I think we have to do something. We have to call in some extra security. Some special security. You need," she said, remembering Alex's words, "to call in your boys."

She watched him to see what he would do. Until she said the words, she had no idea what they could mean, but watching as he stood there, framed against the window, so tall, so assured, able to persuade almost anyone to do almost anything, she realized in a flash what she should have known for years, if she had just thought about it hard enough. Such a good Irishman but always moving, all over Europe and the

States but only where the real money was, where real money could be raised.

"My boys, eh?" he said with a twinkle. "Is that what Alex told you to say in times of dire emergency?" She flushed and he chuckled. "But that was years ago, love. Things have changed a bit since then. There's been a cease-fire, you know; the boys have agreed to lay down their arms. Myself, I was decommissioned long ago. Poor you," he said, pinching her chin. "Thinking I was so much more glamorous than ever I was. But," he added, "there are still some people I can call on if you think the situation warrants. Besides the ones I already have in place. Have had in place since I got here."

"Dog is . . . ?" Juliette asked, shocked.

"Was, dearie, was. None of us 'are' anymore. Well," he said, sighing deeply and giving her one last quizzical look, "we have certainly had the oddest assortment of conversations. And I think you're wrong, by the way," he added. "Not about some-thing happening, but about the babies. It doesn't fit. If something happens, it will be at the ceremony itself, I'm almost positive. But almost is never good enough here at the Pinnacle, so if I have to watch 'em meself," he said in his broadest brogue, "no harm will come to those wee girlies."

"Just stop," she said. "I feel like I'm down the rabbit hole already. I don't need you going twee."

When he began humming "Danny Boy," she left the room.

O'Connor called Juliette midafternoon, this time on her BlackBerry, catching her as she was counting Oscar tickets.

"I realize I fell asleep on you the last time you were here," he rasped. "But I seem to remember you saying you would come back anyway."

"I know," she said, trying to keep her tone cool, both

because of Louisa's proximity and Devlin's warning. "But it's just insane here and I haven't had three minutes to myself."

"I understand. And it isn't like I've got much to offer, is it? The police still haven't found my damn hair, even. Compared with my current condition," he added bitterly, "vomiting was at least exciting."

"Oh, don't," she said. She walked away from the concierge desk and found a quiet corner in the library, surrounded by the books he had sent—could it only have been a few weeks? It seemed so long ago. "Please don't. You know it isn't that. Things are insane here and, well . . ." Because she couldn't help it, couldn't stand to have him feel lonely or forgotten, she told him what Sasha had told her, what she herself was afraid of—that Rory wasn't behind the murders, the attacks, and that if he wasn't, surely something else was going to happen, something huge and terrible.

"Did you tell Devlin what you just told me?" O'Connor demanded. "And is he . . . taking steps?"

Jesus, she thought, *even he knew about Dev.* But then her boss knew about O'Connor, and Sasha, now ensconced in the small single behind the linen pantry—Juliette realized the reporter was truly frightened when she didn't even complain about the location—knew about O'Connor, and O'Connor knew about Juliette, and yet they would all meet at a party sometime and pretend that none of them knew anything at all. Hooray for Hollywood.

"He is," she said, hastily changing the subject. "Do you remember in the limo you were looking out the window, and I asked you what you were thinking, and you seemed so disturbed, but you said you had to think about it some more . . . Do you remember that?"

"Vaguely," he said. "I mostly remember kissing you."

284

"It was very memorable," she said. "But you have to think. Someone must have figured you were onto something. Why else would they attack you? You have no impact on this year's Oscars."

"Thank you very much," he said. "I'll have you know I was asked to present Best Picture, but unfortunately I am too busy filming in Morocco to do so—"

"Best Picture? Maybe that was why you had to be gotten out of the way—maybe someone thought your being in Palm Springs meant you changed your mind. Maybe something's going to happen at the Oscars. Who replaced you?"

"Beats me. I've been a bit out of the loop, if you remember. Call Becker. Or look in the *Times*—they usually do a write-up on those things."

"Not this year," she said. "This year, everything's a big secret. Even Andrea Chapman doesn't know what's going on except that apparently someone's going to kidnap a trophy model." She relayed to him what Andrea had told her. When she was done speaking, there was a long silence on his end of the phone.

"Michael," she said finally, "you still there?"

"Yes," he said, his voice even more harsh than before. "Much good it does me. I can't even fucking take a piss on my own. Listen," he said after another minute. "I am torn between putting you on a plane and getting you backstage Sunday night. Though I don't even know what you'd be looking for.

"Listen, sweetheart," O'Connor said after a moment. "I want you to do me a favor. Don't go home tonight. Go over to Devlin's. Spare me the protests," he added quickly. "I want you to be safe and you'll be safe with him."

He sounded miserable, both physically and emotionally. "I don't want to stay with Devlin," she said. "I'd rather come over there and sleep on the sofa. I've never spent the night in the Elizabeth Taylor Suite."

"It has little to recommend it," he said, his voice brightening just a little as she hoped it would, "but given recent events, I don't consider myself such a safe companion."

"What are you talking about? Lucius has security all over that place."

"Yes, well," he said, "I also don't want to draw more attention to the situation than I already have. I still have some pride," he added, "strange though that might sound. To you."

Juliette swallowed. After all that had happened, she wondered if a relationship, a friendship could survive. In her experience, the more a person revealed, the more he or she punished you for having seen it.

"Go to Dev's," he said lightly. "I may want to see you, but not on the next hospital bed down from mine."

She didn't even have a chance to ask Devlin; when they fell into step beside each other as they moved through the lobby checking on the dinner crowd, he said, as if they had already arranged it, "I'm leaving in a half hour. We can stop at your house and pick up some things on the way home if you'd like."

She stopped in her tracks. "What, did O'Connor call you?"

"O'Connor? No. What does he have to do with it?"

"He told me I should stay with you. To be safe."

"Oh, he did, did he?" Devlin narrowed his eyes. "Big of him, I must say." Then he laughed appreciatively. "He's a canny man, our Mr. O'Connor."

"What's that supposed to mean?"

Devlin just laughed again. "Half hour," he said, moving toward a table headed by David Geffen. "My office."

*

Juliette had never been to Devlin's house. No one at the Pinnacle had been to Devlin's house. Rumor had it that he didn't have a house; he just stayed with whomever he was sleeping with, or came back to the hotel. Pulling in to a private drive in Hancock Park, Juliette expected some modern monstrosity, or an Italianate villa sprawling up a hillside. Instead, the house was more like a large cottage, with a deep front porch and a stone floor in the entryway that gave way to warm wood floors throughout, covered here and there with braid rugs and large pillows occupied by a pair of Irish setters. "The supermodels of the dog world," Devlin said as they pushed their noses into Juliette's hand. "Gorgeous but bred into almost sheer stupidity."

"I don't know why, but I saw you as a chrome and black leather guy," she said, setting her bag at the bottom of the stairs and following him into the kitchen. She settled herself with great pleasure in one of the low, overstuffed chairs that flanked the stone fireplace where, miraculously, a fire was burning. "And instead, here I am in Killarney. Although I do wonder about the welcoming blaze; is this one of those fireplaces that work on remote?"

"Hardly." He laughed. "I have a housekeeper—do you think I'd leave my girls alone all day? And it's Westport Town, if you please," he said, clattering pans onto the stovetop. "In the shadow of Croagh Patrick."

"Which is?"

"The mountain where St. Patrick sat during forty days of prayer before coming down and founding his first church in Ireland—there's a pilgrimage you can take, fourteen miles . . . oh, never mind. Eggs and sausages all right with you? Or did you have your heart set on dim sum?"

"Eggs are fine. It must be beautiful there . . ."

"It is."

"Do you ever want to go back?"

"Sometimes," he said. "It's changing, changed. And so have I. I don't know if it would feel like home any longer. What about you? You're from back East . . . do you miss it?"

"I've lost track of where home is anymore," she said, settling farther into the chair. "I guess the Pinnacle's the closest thing." She accepted the glass of whiskey he handed her. "Which is pretty pathetic."

"That it is. Stay put," he said as she rose to help him set the table. "You make a nice enough picture as it is." One of the dogs came and rested her head on Juliette's knee. Devlin snorted. "She's not on remote either, in case you were wondering."

Later, as she washed her face and prepared for bed, Juliette could hear Devlin humming from the bathroom just off his room. She thought that of all the odd things that had happened lately, this was perhaps the oddest. In the many years she had known him, she had never seen Devlin in a situation where he wasn't, at some level, working. Never had they shared a meal that did not include talk of the hotel, of other hotels, of the guests and the town and the business in general. Never had she enjoyed a conversation with him that did not, at some point, come down to a problem that had to be solved. But tonight, with all that swirled around them, with all the strange events in play and the apprehensions they both had, she felt she had spent the evening with a man she had only just met. A man who read, who preferred Manet to Monet, Siena to Rome, Barcelona to Paris, a man who laughed until tears formed in his eyes, who had slippers singed at the edges from holding them too close to the fire on a rainy evening. A man who had *slippers*.

When the clock chimed eleven, he had shown her upstairs, to the guest bedroom, without a word, without so much as a lifted eyebrow or an inviting glance. Having found a Dorothy Sayers on the bookshelf, she debated knocking on his door, but decided against it. Suddenly, inexplicably, she felt shy. "Night, Dev," she called down the hallway, and, heart pounding, quickly got into bed.

A few minutes later, he appeared in her doorway with a water pitcher and a glass, which he placed on the nightstand. "You look comfortable," he said.

"Full of eggs and toast," she replied. He was wearing a T-shirt and a pair of pajama bottoms. The sight of his throat, the small wings of his collarbone, made her ears grow hot; she had never seen him without a shirt and tie before. She put the book down.

"A murder mystery?" he asked. "Isn't real life exciting enough?" He smiled and for the life of her she could not think of what to say, did not know what she would do when it became apparent he was leaning down to kiss her. Her breath caught in her throat as his lips brushed her cheek lightly and pulled away.

"We are long past the point of my trying to seduce you," he said. "And while I may not have many standards by your lights, I do draw the line at making love to a woman while her heart is full of another man."

He smiled at her again and put his hand on the top of her head. "Sleep well, J., and if things go bump in the night, I'm right down the hall."

He left, and for one wild moment, Juliette hoped something would go bump. Then she shut off the light.

21

Devlin knocked gently on Juliette's door at six-thirty. At seven, she came down to find him eating yogurt and granola, immaculate in his Savile Row suit. "Eat," he said, pushing a bowl her way, not lifting his eyes from the *Times*. "We've got about fifteen minutes. I have a breakfast meeting."

"You're eating before a breakfast meeting?"

"That's the wonder of breakfast meetings, isn't it? You never actually get to eat." He grinned at her. "I haven't watched a woman have breakfast at this table in years. It feels so domestic."

"Domestic hasn't worked out that well for me," she said. "I do better with room service."

"Liar. You were born to wield a wifely coffeepot. You just haven't found the right one yet."

The day before the Oscars was usually subdued at the hotel, except for room service, which ran continually from six a.m. until two in the morning. While some guests headed out to do last-minute shopping or meet friends for lunch, most stayed in, at the spa, in the gym, or by the pool. A steady stream of friends and admirers came to visit and the concierge desk called in favors for last-minute tuxedos, hairstylists, makeup stylists, and pharmaceutical needs, but overall there was a strange stillness, like the sky over the ocean before a huge and devastating storm.

"I'd wear the Kevlar if I were you," Gregory said, passing Juliette as he went to help out with the lunchtime valet backup. "Louisa saw you and Devlin walk in together and I thought her eyes would literally jump out of her head like some Merrie Melodies feline. Max Diamond was standing there in the middle of one of his never-ending monologues and even he noticed something was wrong. If you think she isn't capable of knifing you in the back as you chat with Meryl or Glenn, then you haven't been paying attention."

"My car's in the shop," she said, her stomach sinking—why hadn't she taken her own car to Devlin's? That had been stupid. "He had to be in early for a breakfast meeting so he gave me a lift."

"Sounds good," he said. "I'll throw it against the wall and see if it sticks."

Seeing Devlin heading up the staircase, she timed her steps to catch up with him without looking like she was catching up with him. "Go ask Louisa if she's had lunch, and if she hasn't, have some lunch with her," she said as she passed him.

"Louisa?" he said, startled. "Why would I do that?"

She eyed him coolly. "Because tomorrow is the Oscars and she saw us come in together. Even though, as I just told Gregory, it was simply a matter of you giving me a lift because my car's in the shop."

"Christ," he said. "Now I'm lying because I *didn't* sleep with someone. The world has gone mad."

Devlin sent as many of the staff as could be spared home early that evening. The next day would be the longest of the year at the Pinnacle and he wanted everyone fresh. "Think of it as the Super Bowl," he said, "and behave accordingly. No drinking, no sex . . . or at least no drinking or sex after midnight."

Driving her own car this time, Juliette stopped at Cedars on the way to Devlin's. O'Connor was asleep when she arrived, but she persuaded the hospital nurse to allow her to sit quietly in the room for a while. He looked better, more like himself, though someone had completely shaved his head. When, after about a half hour, he began to murmur for water, she was there to guide the straw to his lips. Happiness was not the first emotion his face registered when he saw it was her, so she held up her gift—a black Pinnacle baseball hat.

"I brought you this," she said, settling it on his head. "Until they find your hair."

"I always swore I'd never wear a goddamn baseball cap," he rasped with a faint grin. "Brad Pitt's always wearing a goddamn baseball cap."

"I'm not even sure you need it, though," she said. "The cueball look suits you."

"I should have done it weeks ago. Then you would have been spared the sight of the Crypt Keeper."

His mood seemed so foul that Juliette didn't dare answer. Pulling her chair closer, she told him stories from the hotel—about the poor valet who didn't know to call Ben Kingsley "Sir Ben," about how Chris Rock walked through the lounge last night nodding at women and saying, "Hooker, hooker, trophy wife," almost, but not quite, under his breath, about how the Academy still couldn't find an entire box of Oscars, and UPS insisted it had been signed for, but no one could read the signature, about how nice and normal Lily and her husband seemed, how they had a real Virginia barbeque sent down to the staff dining area.

"She's a class act," O'Connor said, finally responding. "A little rocky there at the beginning, but once she kicked the heroin, she turned into somebody who was really somebody. So it can happen. Even in Hollywood." Then he once again fell silent.

At nine, another nurse came in and told Juliette she would have to leave, standing there so Juliette didn't have a chance to do much but squeeze his hand.

"I'll see you on Monday, maybe," he said, his voice flat and listless.

"I'll call you tomorrow. If I can get away . . ."

"It's okay, Juliette," he said bitterly. "I'm getting tired of having my hand held. You have better things to do. And if you don't, you should."

Leaving, she felt worse than when she had arrived. She knew he was angry at how helpless he was, at what still had to happen before he could resume his real life, if he would ever be able to resume it. But still she felt hurt and frightened—by how much she had wanted him to seem happier when she was there, by how important it was that she make him feel better.

Driving to Devlin's house, she remembered all those years with Josh; how frustrated he was, how often depressed, and it was always Juliette who talked him through, coaxed him out. That was how they had begun their courtship; she had seen him reading pages on a park bench in Central Park, then balling them up and throwing them away. He had seemed so young and handsome and unhappy; she fished them out of the trash and ran after him. "You shouldn't do that in New York," she said when she caught his elbow. "Otherwise someday you'll open a magazine and read an award-winning story that seems so strangely familiar."

He always said he had fallen in love with her on the spot. It had been one of her favorite stories. But thinking about it now, it made her cringe. Why wouldn't he have fallen in love with her on the spot? She saw herself standing there, having just rooted around in the garbage, so eager that he would see what she had done, and smile, reluctantly and then with a growing appreciation. And so it went for ten years—her working all day to support them financially, then coming home to support him emotionally: encouraging, suggesting, critiquing, editing. Christ, she had typed two novels out for him. And she really didn't care about there not being much money, or no time to have a child, all she wanted was for him to love her back, to be happy with her, to bloom a little under her hand so she could feel worthwhile.

She had spent most of her adult life taking care of people because she was afraid that if she didn't, no one would love her. And if no one loved her, she would just . . . disappear.

"And here I am doing it again," she said out loud, parking alongside Devlin's BMW. It would never be enough, she thought. No matter what she did. You couldn't *make* someone happy any more than you could make someone love you. But you could die trying.

She sat for a few minutes in the car, her forehead against the steering wheel, trying to gather enough strength to move, to walk and talk and pretend she was the same person she had been two hours ago. But somehow, she thought, that wasn't quite true. Some little piece of herself had shifted, like a rock in a stream, changing the flow of water and the path it carved into the earth forever.

She was on the porch and reaching for the doorbell before she realized the front door was ajar.

She pushed it open. "Dev?" she called, anxiety beating in

her throat, subsiding only slightly when she heard the scrambling of the two dogs running across the floor.

"In here." His voice came from the kitchen.

"You left the door unlocked?" she asked accusingly.

He lifted his eyebrows. He was standing at the stove, stirring something in a pot. "You don't have a key," he said. "And I didn't know how late you'd be. I've made pasta," he said, turning toward the counter, exposing the gun he had tucked into the back of his pants.

"You're carrying a gun? To make pasta?"

"I've been carrying a gun since you asked me to bring in my boys," he said. "Have you met them, by the way? The new janitors? Lovely men, the carpets outside the Presidential Suite have never been cleaner."

"You're carrying a gun in your own house?"

Hearing the strain in her voice, Devlin stopped grating cheese. "I asked you to stay here so I could *protect* you, woman. And not being James Bond or Harrison Ford, I need more than my fists and a good script to do it. But the gun's not what's bothering you, is it?" He looked at her more closely. "What is? What happened?"

She shook her head. "Nothing," she said. "Nothing that hasn't happened a thousand times before." She didn't even have to see his face to know he understood. Dev always understood. Why was that? Instead, she looked at the steaming pot, the bread sliced on the breadboard, the bottle of wine on the table, and she felt utterly weary, sick of herself and her inability to see things clearly until it was two beats too late. "I'm sorry, Dev," she said, looking now at her feet. "I'm just not hungry. I think I'd better just go to bed."

As she turned to go, he caught her by the shoulders, tipped her chin up, and looked into her eyes. "You're going to get through this, J.," he said. "I promise you. We will get through this."

Looking up into his face, she wondered how she had managed to work with him for so long, to know him for so long, and not see the sadness that was there, deep and unrelenting. Somewhere in Eamonn Devlin was an old, old heartbreak glossed over many times.

Without even thinking about it, she kissed him. Lightly at first, for a thank-you, but then the feel of his mouth was such a relief she found she couldn't leave it. The kiss deepened and time slowed like it does, she thought, with kisses that matter. She felt his sudden intake of breath; his hands tightened on her shoulders as if he would push her away but could not bring himself to do it and she would not let him. "Show me," she said, winding her arms around his neck, her eyes closed, her cheek against his, "show me how we will get through this."

Without a word, he scooped her up and carried her, as if she weighed nothing, down the hall and up the stairs. On his bed, she could think only of how softly he kissed her, how tenderly he touched her, hesitant, his hands trembling, so different from what she thought it would be like that she found herself touching his face again and again to make sure it was really him. When he finally slid his hand into her blouse, they were both wide-eyed, holding their breath, as if neither of them had done anything like this before. Fully clothed, she felt more naked with him than she ever had in her life. Something warm and light rushed into her chest, something sweet and thrilling that she didn't want to leave, so she reached out, pulled him on top of her, pulled his mouth onto hers. "Stay," she said, wrapping her legs around him. "Stay," she said again, not sure what it was she meant, but it didn't matter, for right now there was this, the weight of him on her, the familiar smell of his hair, the sight of his dark eyes so close to her, eyes that would not look away.

"Always," he said, and she could feel his lips move against hers as he said it. She tightened her hold on him, on the fine sturdy mass of him, and tasted his breath in her mouth, the salt of his skin.

But suddenly, he tensed. "What?" she said, but his head was turned now so she couldn't see his face. "Shhh," he said, rolling off her. There was a thump on the porch, and the dogs began barking, low and furious. Devlin pushed her onto the floor between the wall and the bed, grabbed the gun off the nightstand, and crouched in the doorway. "Stay put," he said, moving quietly down the hall.

Juliette pulled herself onto her hands and knees, looked around for a weapon, settling on the nightstand lamp with its marble base. Unplugging it and removing the shade, she wound the cord around it and followed Devlin, hefting it till it settled right in her hand. She saw him standing at the door; swiftly, he moved to look out the window, jumping back as it shattered. He threw open the door and Juliette could hear footsteps running, a door slamming, tires squealing as a car gunned down the driveway in reverse.

"Are you all right?" she asked, putting her hand on his shoulder. He whirled and almost struck her; she in turn automatically countered with the lamp, which he caught easily, leaving them staring at each other, panting. "Not a bad choice," he said, hefting it. "If the attacker had been bending over my lifeless body."

"Or strangling you," she said defensively.

"Right," he answered, seeing her point, steering her back into the house. "Mind your feet," he said, "it's all-over glass."

"Gunshot?" she asked.

"No," he said, bending over to pick something up from the floor. "Oscar." Turning on the light, he squinted at the base of the gold statue. "Winner, Best Original Screenplay. But alas, no name," he said, looking over at Juliette. "I believe we have found one of the missing Oscars."

"But Dev," she said. "The Oscars aren't ever engraved until after the show."

"I know," he said.

And indeed, the rest of them were blank, a boxful shoved under the oleanders beside Devlin's porch. They decided it would be better not to call the police, better instead for Devlin to "find" the box in the morning in his office disguised as a box of Pinnacle stationery. The reason they decided this they didn't discuss, though they both knew it: someone had gone out of his or her way, had made up the Best Screenplay plaque, chosen it as a projectile for a reason. Someone knew Juliette was there.

The window was not the only thing the Oscar had shattered. When they finally went up to bed, Juliette followed him into his room without thinking. But there was no chance of recapturing whatever had moved them, and neither of them tried. Instead Juliette laid her head on his chest, staring into the dark.

Almost without thinking, she began to tell Devlin everything. Everything she knew had happened, and everything she thought had happened. That she hadn't been in O'Connor's room the night Josh was killed, that she hadn't called the police about the cell phone, how Arnie Ellison had sicced the police on her, how Forrest Hughes had seemed to know something bad had happened in Palm Springs, that Michael thought it was odd Forrest was there in the first place, that

Sasha Curizon seemed way too involved in everything that was happening but wasn't actually writing about it, that Juliette had begun to wonder if maybe someone on the staff was involved somehow because so much of what was happening seemed to revolve around the Pinnacle. She waited for Devlin to react, to berate her at least for keeping so much of this information from him, but he didn't interrupt, just kept breathing steadily and stroking her hair. "Curiouser and curiouser," was all he said.

She raised her head and pulled herself into a sitting position beside him. "But I just don't see it," she said. "There must be some connection somewhere, but I just don't see it."

"Don't you?"

"I just don't see why any of these people would want to *kill* anyone. It doesn't make sense."

Devlin laughed, a low bitter sound in the dark. "You would be amazed what people will kill for, J. Considering the sort of people involved in the entertainment business, I have long been astonished that there aren't more murders. Money, power, and ego—that's really all it takes. And, of course," he added softly, "revenge."

In the silence he left behind a night bird twittered outside the window. Juliette sat perfectly still considering the sort of past Devlin might have had—if there were people he had killed or caused to be killed.

As if reading her thoughts, he reached for her hand.

"I'm not involved, J," he said. "At least not yet."

He pulled her back toward him and after a moment's hesitation, she went.

"I know you're not," she said, and she did. It was just about the only thing she was certain of at this point. God, what she wouldn't give to be able to stay here, right here, with Dev in this placeless dark for hours, for days. Without any of this, without the Oscars or the Pinnacle or Los Angeles or any of the people who still crowded her mind. She closed her eyes tightly and willed them away, but two at least would not leave. The only two who knew she was staying with Devlin: Gregory and O'Connor. The only two who would know enough to dump the Oscars on the doorstep. Was Gregory somehow involved? Or had he just opened his mouth to the wrong person?

The one thing she had kept from Devlin was the fact that only O'Connor knew that she had helped Josh with the script. *Tell me you didn't write at least half of that script,* he had said. O'Connor, she thought now, didn't have an alibi for the night Josh died—he had given Rory the night off. Why would he do that? Leave himself companionless for an entire night? *I'm not even convinced he has cancer,* his ex-wife had said. *He could just be mad he didn't get nominated for Bluebird.* Was it possible the whole thing was a setup? Everything Sally had said described a person completely different from the one Juliette knew, or thought she knew, but so many things she thought she could take for granted were shaking themselves loose, disappearing. Could O'Connor be the sociopath? Money, ego, power, revenge. Three out of four, those he had easily. Could he have faked his own strangulation, getting the doctors and his agent to sign off on it with some extraordinary story that he would have no problem making them believe?

Her mind spinning, Juliette glanced at the clock. Midnight. And the busiest day of the year beginning in six hours. Maybe she should try to reignite whatever had happened with Devlin, maybe he could at least fuck her mind clear, her body calm enough to sleep. Maybe that could, somehow, take care of everything.

301

Lifting her head, she glanced up at him to see if he was thinking the same thing, but his face was full of worry and something else, something she couldn't begin to contemplate. All she could do was lay her head back down. Whatever else had happened tonight, they had crossed some line with each other that would not bear crossing back.

22

"It's raining," Devlin said as he shook her awake.

"Don't be silly," she said, not opening her eyes. "It never rains on the Oscars."

But it was, and peering out into the fine mist that filled the back garden, Juliette couldn't help but feel better—whoever was planning whatever they were planning could not have counted on the rain. The rain would change everything; Los Angeles always overreacted to weather. There would be fewer crowds, shorter red carpet time, tents and awnings that would obscure the view from nearby rooftops, which would mean, perhaps, some of the SWAT teams usually stationed there could come down, be repositioned—more security inside than out. The rain would make everything seem much less dramatic.

It also meant, she realized, the guests would wake up and panic—hairstyles would be rethought, and shoes, wraps, and jackets would be added. Even British and European guests were undone by rain in L.A. The hotel's umbrellas would have to be unpacked, counted, and checked. The loading time would double—no one would want to get there early, which meant the lobby would be more crowded with people ordering drinks and food, and the limo line would go 'round the block, then 'round the block again.

She threw off the covers and rushed into the shower.

But by nine a.m., about an hour before the guests began their collective stirring, the rain had stopped and the gray skies were pulling themselves apart like cotton batting to reveal a clear blue winter sky. The Academy, expressing great relief, sent a stagehand to the hotel to collect its statues. Spares had been ordered, but no one could seem to find them either. Sasha was up and about when the police came by, and as they questioned Devlin, she cornered Juliette.

"So he found them where?"

"In his office. He thinks they may have been there a few days; the box was marked 'stationery.' It must have been some weird delivery mix-up. Or someone's idea of a joke."

"He was opening new stationery on Oscar morning?"

"He sends up a personal note with each breakfast this morning," she said, not missing a beat. "That requires a lot of stationery."

Sasha squinted at her skeptically, but Juliette just smiled. The reason she and Devlin had decided on this line was that it happened to be true, and, as Devlin said this morning, lies were always easier to tell if they were mostly true. "And we don't have to mention that I wrote those notes a week ago," he'd added with a grin.

"I think it must have been Becker," Juliette added. "I mean, it kept the show on the front page yesterday. What more could he ask for?"

Sasha nodded reluctantly, her eyes shifting toward the closed door to Devlin's office. "Is he going tonight?" she asked. "Your boss?"

Juliette laughed. Did Sasha think Devlin was involved? Of course, Juliette herself had considered the same thing as recently as two days ago, but now, after last night, she felt a rush of defensiveness. "No," she said. "Unless someone has forgotten their tickets or their earrings and there is absolutely no one else who can be spared. Then I guess he'd go. But for the most part, we just heave a gigantic sigh of relief when the last person is out the door, enjoy a huge dinner, try not to drink too much, and get ready for the winners, and the losers, to come swarming back in the wee hours."

A look of irritation crossed the reporter's face. "That is exactly what you said last year," she said. "When I was report- ing the story about this place. Exactly what you said." Now she was looking at Juliette with skepticism.

"Because that's exactly what happens," Juliette answered. "You'll see for yourself this year."

"Not hardly," she said. "My editors may have pulled me off the story, but the Academy doesn't know that. I still have my credentials. In fact, I'm heading out there in one minute—as of eleven p.m. they still hadn't finished the set. Becker was tear- ing his hair out."

Watching Sasha go, Juliette wondered if she should have tried to find out what the reporter thought might be going to happen. But she still wasn't entirely convinced that Sasha was not involved in some way; if nothing else, Sasha had her own agenda, which was clearly very different from Juliette's.

By ten-thirty, room service was so busy that Juliette pulled Phillip off pool duty and Rick from the pastry kitchen to help run carts. She herself delivered breakfast to Eddie Izzard, Meryl Streep, Hugh Grant, and Lily Mathews.

"Hey," the actress said as Juliette wheeled the cart in. "Things must be pretty busy if they've got you on room service duty." She was sitting in the rocking chair in front of the doors that led out to the terrace, nursing one of the babies.

"Crazy busy," Juliette said, flipping open the table wings, taking the plastic wrap off the juice glasses, the pitcher of milk. "Can I bring you something?"

"Water," Lily said. "Can't get enough." Juliette filled a glass and handed it to her; she drank it thirstily. "All I do these days is nurse, drink, and pee. I know girls on TV shows who go back to work after a few weeks; I do not see how they do it. If I make it through this evening, it will be a miracle. So," she said, shifting the baby from one side to another, "who are the new shadows in the hall?" Juliette looked at her quizzically. "The guys," Lily said. "The extra security. They on every floor, or just ours?"

"We always increase our security staff during Oscar season," Juliette said automatically.

The actress laughed, disturbing the baby for a moment. Once she was settled again, Lily looked straight into Juliette's eyes. "Don't give me the company line, missy. I know security and I know *security* and I ain't never seen security that looked like that. Things have been a little strange and I guess I'm just wondering if there's a specific reason those two are where they are."

It wasn't anxiety that Juliette saw in her face, but a simple need for information. Lily and Gavin would spend the next twenty years of their lives making decisions about the security and privacy of their children that other parents would never even have to consider—it had started days after they were born, when Lily invited the paparazzi who had haunted the Richmond hospital and followed the car home, onto the lawn of their home. There she cradled each baby and allowed the cameras to go wild, the agreement being the shooters would leave them alone for at least three weeks. Not for the first time, Juliette was grateful that whatever moved people to be actors had never, not once, stirred within her.

"Being a new parent is hard enough," Juliette said, then caught herself—company line again. "Devlin didn't want you to even have one second thought during your stay here. We want you and Gavin to try to actually have some fun tonight."

Lily looked at her levelly and gave a small nod. "Thank you," she said. "We'll try. To have as much fun as we can while working. Poor Gav. He just hates this crap."

"Oh, Juliette," she called as the other was slipping out the door. Juliette stopped. "Tell Michael I said 'Hey,' wouldya? He's a good guy and I hope he feels better soon." For one second she flashed her impossibly wide smile and then she turned back to her baby. Sighing, Juliette withdrew. She was no longer surprised at the nonsecrecy of secrets in Hollywood. It really was like some elite club, complete with code words and handshakes. She just took comfort in the fact that at least four people in this hotel were, at the moment, very happy.

Stopping by the pool, she saw Devlin making the rounds of those guests determined to soak up the sun until the last minute. Just seeing him gave her a sudden rush of pleasure, something even deeper than pleasure. The watchful set of his shoulders, the way he squinted when he smiled, the easy way he moved from person to person. Graceful, she thought, how had she never noticed that? Just seeing him relaxed her somehow and with surprise she realized it almost always had. What would it be like to love him? To tear down that wall, or at least open a door, a window, and invite the possibility?

Catching her eye, Devlin gave her that cool, professional "all well?" look she had seen so many times before and Juliette felt her face get hot. She wondered if she should share with him her thoughts about O'Connor. A second later, she decided against it. Things were confusing enough, and she was being paranoid, just as she had been about the appearance of that Colombian actress—she was still embarrassed about that. *All we need to do is get through this day,* she thought. *Just get through this day.*

Automatically, she lifted the corners of her mouth in an "all serene" smile, registered his answering nod, and moved on.

By noon, the hair and makeup people began arriving. Juliette was always surprised by the general motley appearance of those in charge of beautifying the beautiful people. In twos and threes, they headed to their clients chewing gum, hair yanked up in untidy tails, men and women alike in banged-up jeans, biologically attached, it seemed, to their grande lattes and mochaccinos. Flowers arrived by the bushelful, champagne by the cartload. By two o'clock, the hotel was well on its way to full-throttle, well-organized chaos.

"With three hundred and seventy-eight stylists in this building," said Gregory as he hustled from one room to another for the sole purpose of tying bow ties and settling French cuffs, "you would think we'd be able to take it easy."

"Not every nominee can afford a stylist," reminded Juliette, who had spent the last twenty minutes picking handbags for a sound mixer's wife. "Pity the documentarian."

"If they can't afford a stylist, then the state of California should appoint one for them," Gregory answered. "It's the Oscars, for crying out loud. And really, next year I'm going to demand the stylists wear uniforms. If I see one more pair of flip-flops or one more ill-fitting camisole, I'm going to throw them all out."

"Then," Juliette sighed, blowing a piece of hair out of her face, "we'd really be screwed."

One guest decided she wanted her full-length gown to be shortened; she had heard that Charlize Theron was going above the knee this year. That required the full attention of a seamstress for several hours, so the head of housekeeping was enlisted to join the other two seamstresses as they flitted from room to room, taking straps off gowns, or adding them, finding clever ways to fold scarves and shawls to conceal unsightly back bulges or flabby arms, hemming pants and skirts, and in one case, taking a swath of material from the hem of a dress and adding it on either side of the back zipper—when trying on her dress in the morning, one nominee for Best Short Film discovered she had not quite lost the ten pounds she swore she would lose before the big day.

"Next thing you know, we'll be doing last-minute lipo," muttered Louisa. She was supervising the zipper procedure, all the while assuring the sobbing woman that it happened all the time and "if I told you to who, you just wouldn't believe it."

Five separate guests called down to the concierge desk, frantic because they could not find their tickets, only to be reminded that the tickets were downstairs in their room safes—it was Pinnacle policy that tickets remain in the safes until the guests were ready to leave. And since the safecracking incident, Juliette had brought in an extra concierge whose sole job was to make certain no one got in their limos without their tickets.

At three o'clock, Juliette slipped into her office and changed into a black cocktail dress and a chaste, though quite good, diamond necklace with matching drop earrings, kicked off the comfortable flats that made Oscar day bearable, and stepped into her heels. She added a bit of lipstick, a smudge of eye shadow, spritzed her pulse points with Chanel, and rejoined the staff. Gregory and several of the male concierges were already hurrying from room to room tying bow ties and inserting cufflinks. Juliette, Louisa, and the female concierge began circulating among the rooms, helping those women who did not have personal stylists, and occasionally those who had.

"It's just like a big prom or something," said Holly Hunter as Juliette shuffled through the packages of panty hose they kept on hand.

Juliette smiled at her in the mirror—for a few hours it was, indeed, something like that.

Some of the guests—various Academy members, nominees in the less glamorous categories as well as a few nominee spouses, began to gather in the lounge. It was the bartender's job to ensure that no one left the bar noticeably drunk, even if it meant watering the drinks of those guests who were ordering in quick succession. But since they had a new bartender now, Juliette stopped by to see that everything was going smoothly.

She noticed that Lily's husband was one of the men sitting at the bar, looking slightly dazed. Gesturing at Gregory to join her, Juliette walked over to him.

"Your first Oscars?" she asked kindly. He nodded and laughed. He was a nice-looking man, not so much handsome as nice-looking. With all the men in the world at her feet, Lily had chosen someone she would have been lucky to get if she had never left her hometown. They seemed very happy, so maybe that was the secret—marry someone who understands where you came from rather than where you happen to be or want to go.

"We had just gotten married this time last year," Gavin said. "So she let me off the hook for our honeymoon. It's all so crazy," he said, glancing around the hotel. "I mean, everyone is very nice, you all are very nice, but all this . . ." He shook his head. "It's hard to believe any of it's real."

"It isn't," said Juliette. "That's the trick of it. It's all just a bunch of people doing their jobs. Just like you do yours. They, we, just maybe take ourselves a bit more seriously than you do."

"And dress better," Gregory added. "I assume," he added tactfully, taking in the man's gray trousers and dress shirt, "you'll be changing soon."

"I'm not putting that thing on until the absolute last minute," Gavin said. "I haven't worn a monkey suit since my junior prom."

"Tell me," Gregory said, his eyes closed, "that it wasn't powder blue."

"Well, I'd like to"—Gavin laughed—"but . . ."

Gregory made a sound of pain in the back of his throat.

"Okay," Gregory began, "I am going to give you a red carpet primer. First of all, you think no one is going to be looking at you, but they are. And nowhere near as kindly as they will be looking at your wife. You have to give her enough room that the fans don't think you're possessive, but not so much that they think you are jealous of her fabulousness. Think Matthew Broderick and Sarah Jessica rather than Prince Charles and Diana. Lily's publicist will probably want her to spend the minimum amount of time on the red carpet, so she'll hustle you along. But that will be a mistake. And anyway, Lily probably won't let her—she's big on stopping and chatting with the press."

"Don't I know it." Gavin groaned.

"Here's what you should do," Gregory said, and Juliette could see from the light in his eyes that he had a sudden inspiration. "There are really two red carpets—a big rope divides it into two sides. One for the A-list and the other for the boring old Academy members. While Lily is chatting up the press, glad-hand some of the people on the other side of the rope.

That way you not only win the love and affection of voting members, you also don't stand there trying not to look bored when you really are."

"But why would they want to talk to me?"

"Because they will talk to anyone if it gives them a chance to stand still for a minute—I mean, they want to see what Angelina's wearing as much as I do. And if you're not on the A-list side, the red carpet's a cheat—they've got these big, burly red-carpet sheriffs hustling everyone along so fast you might as well just stay home and watch it on TV. That's why I never go to the Oscars."

"That, and the hotel would collapse without you," Juliette added.

Gavin sighed. "Maybe I should just stay home and watch the babies."

"You'll be fine," Juliette said. "It'll be fun. Just don't forget to eat something—it's a long time between arrivals and the Governor's Ball."

"And you better get back up to the room," Gregory said. "It may have taken you twenty minutes to get ready for the junior prom, but we'll turn you back if you don't meet our standards."

"He will," Juliette said with a grin. "I've seen him do it."

Outside, paparazzi and onlookers gathered on the sidewalk across from the hotel. Although the high hedges and relatively long drive prevented anyone from really seeing the entrance from the street, there were plenty of telephoto lenses. Fans held huge signs that they flashed when the limos passed by in hopes that a beloved star might glance their way. Dog had four guys posted on the main entrance alone, two facing the door, two facing the drive, while he walked his own complicated path around the hotel. Six miles he walked on Oscar day, he had told Juliette a few years ago. "Wore a pedometer just so I'd know. Guess the place just gets bigger with all those famous folks in it."

By four o'clock, people were beginning to come down from their rooms in earnest. Limousines wrapped the hotel. The city closed off side streets in a two-square-block radius. Barney, the head doorman, had his earphone on. Gregory stood by with a clipboard and a list of all the guests and their ETAs—if a star was late in hitting the red carpet, he would hear about it within thirty seconds from that star's publicist. As the elevators disgorged group after group of famous people in their designer finery, Louisa set out a line of her people to give each guest a last-minute once-over, under the guise of nodding and wishing everyone a wonderful night. Visible bra straps were caught, tags were clipped off or turned in, last-minute hairpins offered, spots removed instantly from lapels and shirtfronts. Gregory caught one man who had split the back of his trousers; without a word, Louisa turned him around and marched him into Devlin's office, where several spare tuxedos hung.

Devlin himself stood just inside the front door, speaking to each of the guests as they left, shaking hands, kissing cheeks, offering compliments so accurate and specific that Juliette would have thought he'd stayed up the entire night thinking of them—if she hadn't known this was not possible.

"Where are the mints?" she asked Louisa, who shrugged.

"Gone," she said.

"I thought we ordered more."

"We did order more, but they just flew out of here. I'm serious," Louisa added, catching Juliette's doubtful look. "They were very popular."

Juliette sighed and turned her attention back to the crowd. It would not surprise her to find five unopened cartons of them shoved somewhere in a few days, but now she wasn't going to get herself into a sweat over breath mints. Unzipping her survival kit, Juliette offered one guest who had just realized she had forgotten lipstick a fine assortment, another who was complaining of a headache an Advil.

"Where do I get one of those?" asked Victoria Beckham, catching a glimpse of the contents as Juliette zipped it up. "Forget this thing," she said, shaking her lovely but useless sequined clutch, "I need one of those."

Juliette smiled and made a mental note to send a freshly stocked bag, sans Xanax, to the Beckham's room the moment things settled down. She also made another note to consider making something like these up for next year's gift basket.

By four-thirty, the lobby roiled with chatter and nervous laughter, with the smell of a thousand perfumes, the clatter of high heels, and the shimmer of a billion dollars' worth of borrowed gemstones. Impossibly, miraculously, everyone made their way out the doors, Barney and the other doormen making sure the full skirts, the beaded trains, all made it into the limousines without accident.

"I'm out of Xanax again," Gregory murmured as he passed her. "The cast of that bird-watching movie were all atwitter."

Juliette dutifully groaned at the pun. The crowd was beginning to thin. Lily came down with her husband. Gregory spun Gavin around and gave him a manly slap on the back. Juliette had to admit he cleaned up very well. She did not like to think, however, what Lily would have to do to keep her nursing breasts in her blue gown all night. Lily had refused toupee tape because, she said, she needed them to be mobile. "First time I've had to take a breast pump to the Oscars," she said, hefting a silk sack. "My publicist better be happy. She seems to think people will have forgotten me despite all her hard work. Or something like that. Here are our numbers," she said, handing Devlin a piece of paper, "and the feeding schedule, which the nannies know is a joke—the little suckers eat all the time."

Catching Juliette's raised eyebrows, she laughed. "Didn't Dev tell you? He asked if he could sit with the babies for a while. Seems he's gone all paternal on us."

"What?" Devlin said when Juliette looked at him as Lily and Gavin climbed into their limo. "It was your idea. And really, can you think of a better way to spend Oscar night?" Then, glancing past her shoulder, his face changed; Juliette turned and saw Anna Stewart, in lacy black, come out of the elevator, accompanied only by an assistant who was clearly not dressed for the Oscars. Swallowing hard, Juliette walked directly up to her, held out her hand. "You look lovely," she said. "I hope the evening goes well for you."

"Thank you, Juliette," Anna said, wincing slightly. "I just wish I had different shoes. I'm breaking the cardinal rule and wearing new ones."

"What size are you?" Juliette asked.

"Seven and a half."

Louisa, answering Juliette's glance, shook her head slightly—they had already lent out all the spare shoes they stored for the Oscars. "We could get a few other pairs brought over to the theater," she said.

"Here," said Juliette, stepping out of hers. "Try these."

Her face a study in conflicting emotions, the actress stepped out of her shoes and into Juliette's; relief and suspicion both crossed her face.

"Take them," Juliette said. "They're not poisoned or anything."

Just then, Alan Rickman and his wife hurried through the lobby. "So sorry, darling," he said, kissing Anna on each cheek. "The traffic is horrendous. As usual. You look gorgeous, are you ready? Let's go, then." And with a nod to Juliette, they were gone.

"Is that it?" Louisa whispered to Juliette, surveying the empty lobby.

Juliette sidled over to Gregory. "Is that it?"

"Not quite," he said. "William Rudnick and Russell Crowe—" As he spoke, the elevator opened and the two actors with their wives hurried across the lobby. "Tickets, tickets," Juliette called after them. The men rushed back, laughing, in a cloud of aftershave, bourbon, and cigar smoke, grabbed the tickets, and disappeared out the door.

"That's it," said Gregory. "Until someone realizes they've forgotten something."

As if on cue, the concierge phone began to ring.

"So far, so good," said Devlin, walking up behind her. But putting her arm lightly around his waist, she could feel the gun was where it had been last night. "I'm going to perambulate for a few minutes," he said. "Care to join me?"

"I need to make one phone call," Juliette said. "I'll catch up with you."

Taking a deep breath, she stepped into the library, pulled out her BlackBerry, and dialed Cedars. She asked for the Elizabeth Taylor Suite. After a few minutes she got the nursing station and a woman informed her that the occupant of that room had been moved, and no, she couldn't, it was not hospital policy to discuss such changes. She could try to call the patient's doctor in the morning, but there was nothing to be done now. "It's Oscar night," the nurse said, as if somehow this would explain everything.

She found Devlin pacing the perimeter of the back garden.

"All seems well," he said as she fell in step with him. "I've got my boys posted upstairs and I will check in on the babies in a bit, but everything seems in order."

Juliette took a deep breath. "O'Connor's checked out of Cedars," she said, as if revealing a huge and telling secret. Devlin stared at her.

"So?" he said.

"Well, when I saw him last night, he didn't look like he was going anywhere anytime soon. But when I just called, they said he had been moved and they wouldn't tell me where."

"Ah, well, you know, he could have just switched rooms and figured you were too busy to call . . ."

Juliette shot him a "how stupid do you think I am?" look.

"Or maybe the press got wind of it and his people moved him to a different hospital."

"He would call me," she said.

Devlin watched the shadows of the willow leaves dance against the soothing gold of the walls and said nothing.

"I still think something's going to happen," she said. "Tonight. Something bad."

"J., the Kodak is crawling with security," Devlin said, putting his arm around her. "There is nothing you or I could do that isn't already being done."

"Do you believe that?" She turned her face to his, prepared to surrender her anxiety if she saw that he had surrendered his.

After a moment, he rolled his eyes. "Almost," he said. "But what do you want me to do? Call the police and tell them we think something 'bad' is going to happen? It's been all over the news—they've doubled the police presence. Do you want me to go over there and stand backstage to make sure the thing goes smoothly?"

Yes, she thought. *Yes, that is exactly what I want.* Somehow, she felt like if he were there, if they were there, whatever was going to happen might be prevented.

"No," she said, realizing how idiotic it all was—when had she started to think of Devlin as some sort of superhero? "No, you're right. I know you're right."

"Go have a drink and watch the arrivals," he said. "It'll make you feel better. Maybe Anna will trip in your shoes and break an ankle. I know that would make me feel better."

"She's not that bad," Juliette said.

"She most certainly is. You're just too soft," he said. "But then that's why we all love you so."

Juliette couldn't even bring herself to meet his eyes when he said that. She wasn't ready to see the old joking twinkle in them. Not just yet.

But she couldn't shake the feeling of dread that crept along the back of her skull. If O'Connor weren't involved, where would he go? To another hospital? To another hotel? On the bar's television, she watched the stars parade up the red carpet and strained to catch a glimpse of him, though she couldn't imagine he could make it up the red carpet and didn't know what she would do if she did see him. There they all were, the people she had just seen filling the lobby of the Pinnacle, now chatting with Joan Rivers and Isaac Mizrahi, squinting into the late afternoon sun, waving up at the roaring stands. No one was assassinated, nothing blew up, everything looked exactly as it did year after year, and yet . . . And yet, her stomach grew heavier, the back of her neck colder. The music swelled and the trademark golden statue swirled onto the screen, Forrest Hughes made his descent from the ceiling of the Kodak in a cage, as promised, and the only disruptions were the seven bleeps the network censors inserted into his opening monologue.

Utterly restless, Juliette walked out through the lobby, where she bumped into Gregory carrying a Tiffany bag, a Hugo Boss bag, an Armani bag, and an envelope that looked suspiciously like tickets.

"Don't ask," he said, jangling his keys. "Last-minute deliveries—no, not to the ceremony," he said, seeing her eyes on the envelope. "The Governor's Ball. We need to add that to the rule book."

Juliette nodded absently, then made an executive decision. "Give me those," she said, taking the tickets. "And that, that, those, and especially this," she continued, relieving him of his bags, his car keys, and finally his backstage pass to the Kodak—the Pinnacle got one every year for just this sort of emergency. Someone always forgot something and often remembered it minutes before heading out onstage.

"You are not taking my Porsche," Gregory said, hanging on to the car keys.

"Fine," Juliette said, "you can drop me. Even faster."

"Devlin isn't going to like this," Gregory said as they pushed out of the hotel doors into the fading sunlight.

"Then let's not tell him," Juliette replied.

23

Three entire blocks of Hollywood Boulevard were closed to accommodate the red carpet and the fifteen-foot-high walls of stands alongside it. Fans lined the other side of the street, where the neon of the El Capitan blinked crazily and shops sold T-shirts and fake Oscars, held in check by police barricades and many forms of security. The red carpet itself ran along the sidewalk before turning in to the entrance of Hollywood and Highland, the shopping mall in which the Kodak was ensconced. Black curtains hung in front of the shops that lined the entrance, TV personalities had carved out small interview spaces, and pillars held up enormous bouquets of flowers every few feet. But still it was possible to see slivers of the Nine West store, the crystal shop—the Kodak anchored a mall, after all.

The show was a half hour in when Juliette made her way up the red carpet. Some of the press still perched on the bleachers, hunched over laptops or cell phones, transmitting pictures, or calling in copy. A few photographers took her picture as she walked by, for color or just in case she turned out to be someone. By now the red carpet was littered with gum wrappers and water bottles, call sheets and empty packages of mints and breath strips, which publicists carried by the fistful. There were flowers crushed underfoot, along with a few stuffed animals, thrown by adoring fans.

Walking as fast as Anna Stewart's shoes allowed, Juliette made her way into the entrance of Hollywood and Highland and then through the security station in front of the side door of the Kodak. Opening her purse and the bags to the uniformed officials, she was allowed into a small lobby, swiped her pass at the electronic station, followed a corridor down and around, went up a short flight of stairs, and came out backstage.

Much of Oscars' glamour wilted under the fluorescent light that bathed the backstage. Here were many famous people in lovely clothes and makeup, but all of them were clearly working, greeting each other with the careful hugs, the manly handshakes of conference attendees. On monitors hung or propped in key locations, the show unfolded, effortlessly it seemed, as if on another planet, while backstage no one sat or even stood for very long, everyone seemed to have a clipboard and to be carrying on two conversations at once. Becker had delivered on his promise—almost every big star was present and accounted for tonight, many of them contributing, in one way or another, to the show. Juliette paused for a moment to watch Meryl Streep kiss George Clooney before the two of them presented the nominees for Best Adapted Screenplay.

"Thank God," said Robin Williams, taking the Hugo Boss bag; someone had spilled red wine down his front at the cocktail party and he was on in ten minutes. "Do you mind?" he said, cutting off Hugh Laurie as he was about to enter one of the two bathrooms. "Wardrobe malfunction."

"Ah," said Laurie as he stepped aside.

"Look who's here," said a familiar voice. "And bearing gifts. Who left what and where?" asked Max Diamond, kissing Juliette on either cheek.

"Max," she said. "I thought you were giving this year a pass."

"So did I," said Max. "But this guy"—he tugged at the arm of a large man in black, who turned and became Bill Becker—"convinced me I should be here. We've got a bit of a surprise in store for our friends out front." In a stage whisper Max added, "I'm kidnapping a trophy model."

Becker looked down at Max patronizingly. "I figured if I didn't give you something to do," he said, "you'd wind up onstage anyway. Wild horses couldn't keep you away from this show, and you know it."

The two men laughed, though Max's smile seemed strained. "Have you seen Alicia Goldstone?" Juliette asked Becker. "I've got her earrings."

Becker looked at her with irritation. "Why don't we ask someone whose job it would be to know that?" He grabbed a young woman in a blue jacket. "Honey, see if you can help this lady. Now siddown and enjoy the show, Max," he said, heading back to the production trailer. "You're not on for forty minutes and you're making everyone back here nervous."

Juliette, smarting under Becker's dismissal, quickly explained the situation to the page. Glancing up at Max as Becker passed, she saw her own feelings reflected on the comedian's face in a way that shocked her. Her own feelings, magnified. Not frustration or even fury, but something else, something primal and disturbing. Max hated Becker, really and truly hated him. It was gone in a second and she was just able to get her eyes back to the page as he glanced her way. "Great," she murmured to the girl. "Thank you so much.

Now," she said brightly to Max, "I just have to find Lily Mathews and I'm done."

"I think she's in the green room," Max said, nodding toward the lavishly appointed, cordoned-off space where the presenters, winners, and A-listers gathered during the show. "Holding court. God, she looks terrific. Just terrific."

"I know," she said, kissing his cheek, thinking about how sad it was that he could not, in the end, let go of this. "Come by tomorrow if you're up to it."

"I'll do that," Max said.

On the monitors, Billy Crystal mugged with Forrest Hughes, who, for some reason, had stripped down to his underwear. The sound was turned down so Juliette couldn't hear what the joke was, but she had to admit that for a complete and utter asshole, Hughes had a pretty nice body.

When the guard passed Lily's parcel through the green-room door, Lily called out for her to come in. "Breast pads," she whispered to Juliette, opening the Armani bag. "I asked Louisa to put them in something respectable. I've gone through three sets and we're less than an hour in. Lord. Have a seat." She scooted over on the divan to make some room. "Don't you love this getup?" She motioned round the room full of gilt and dark silk and white orchids trailing everywhere. "They say *Architectural Digest* designed it, but it looks like pure Alabama cathouse to me. You want something to eat? Champagne?" Juliette shook her head. Sitting here somehow made her feel better. Here were the stars doing what they were supposed to be doing—looking glamorous, chatting as if they were all part of some genetically gifted family, undisturbed in their couture and diamonds.

Outside, men in tuxedos rolled heavy lights and props down the hall. Young and pretty pages in blue jackets and gray skirts greeted the winners as they came offstage and steered them through the warren of hallways and elevators that led up to the pressroom, where reporters would shout questions at them until the next winners materialized.

The laughter of the audience was audible from the large flat-screen TV that dominated the room and from the stage itself. Becker had indeed convinced Robert Downey, Jr., and Johnny Depp to face off in a mock-fistfight that was bringing the house down.

"You missed the best part," Lily said. "They had Gwyneth sitting next to Jack Nicholson and at one point she stood up, told him to keep his hands to himself, and slapped his face. I don't think Jack knew that was part of the script. Pulled it off pretty good too. Becker's plain all-out nuts; I told him if he pulled any crap with me, he'd wish he had gotten jail time. And the way he's got poor old Max and Forrest competing for that damn movie of his is just crazy. I understand why Forrest is after it—he needs a bounce pretty badly. But I don't know why Max is bothering at all—with all the hype it's getting, there's no way the film is not going to bomb. But he wants it so bad you can smell it—utter desperation, you know? And that's never pretty."

The word leapt out at her: *desperation*. That was what she had seen on Max's face just now—hatred and desperation. What Michael had said he was looking for in Palm Springs— the most desperate person in the room. Max had been in Palm Springs, and in the hotel the night Josh died. In fact, Max really had been around a lot, in town and at the Pinnacle, much more than usual, much more often than made sense considering he wasn't up for an Oscar, wasn't even hosting.

Her mind was so busy sorting and resorting words and

images that it took her a moment to realize Lily was still speaking to her.

"Do you want some?" the actress asked, holding out a large bowl crammed with candy and gum and mints. Including, Juliette noticed, a tin of Pinnacle mints.

"How did this get here?" she asked, pulling it out.

"Didn't you put them there?" Lily asked. "They're all over the place—in the bathroom, by the back elevator. A product placement coup—it had Juliette written all over it."

Juliette shook her head. "No, it wasn't me. It must have been Devlin."

But even as she spoke, she knew it wasn't—Dev would never do something like that. Nor would anyone else on the staff, at least not without asking her. So why were they here? *Death by breath mint,* Josh had said all those weeks ago. *You know, I just used that in a script I just finished.* A script, the script, the one that had been all over town. The one Max had read, and Michael, and Forrest, and who knew who else.

The sense of calm was whisked away; excusing herself, Juliette quickly phoned her boss, almost bumping into Catherine Keener, who had just won the award for Best Supporting Actress. "Can't I just go home now?" the winner was pleading to her publicist, holding her Oscar upside down.

"You'll be home before morning," the young woman answered. "Do you need a mint?"

Panicking, Juliette followed them, scooped out two tins of Pinnacle mints from a basket by the elevator. When Devlin answered, Juliette hissed, "Did you have someone put our mints backstage at the Kodak?"

"What the fuck are you doing backstage at the Kodak?" he said, angrier than she had ever heard him. "I want you back here. Right now. This minute. Or I will come drag you out of there by the hair, my girl, and I mean what I say."

"I'll take that as a no," she said. "Because they're all over the place."

"Hell," Devlin said after a small pause. "That's not right."

For a brief moment, all Juliette could hear was the sound of him breathing, hard, as if he were walking quickly. Poison, everyone thought there had been poison in the doughnuts, but it was only the nicotine from the reporter's patch that caused her heart attack, though Sasha didn't believe it. *In Sherlock Holmes,* Rory had said, *it was always pure nicotine—looks just like a heart attack.*

"'He'll have a heart attack if he's not careful,'" she said.

"What?"

"That's what Max said about Becker, like, three, four times. Shit, Dev," she breathed into the phone.

"So it would seem," Dev said. "Well, don't just stand there talking to me. Pick 'em up, get 'em out before someone keels over with our logo in their hands. Find out who put them there."

"I know who put them there," she breathed, as Jake Gyllenhaal bumped past her.

"What?" Dev said as the noise level rose. "Listen, I'll be right over. Try not to get killed meanwhile, if you don't mind."

The show hit a commercial break and suddenly backstage flooded with people, heading for the green room, the coffee islands, the bathroom. Where did Lily say she had seen the mints? The bathroom. One was empty. Pulling the liner from a trash can, Juliette grabbed three tins off the counter. Pounding on the door of the other bathroom, she pushed past a very annoyed Halle Berry and collected three more. From the green room to the back elevator, up and down the backstage area, she hurried from tabletop to tabletop, eyes scanning frantically for the familiar logo, scooping up tins where she found them. Pushing into the production trailer, she saw out of the corner of her eye Becker's outraged face turning from a bank of about thirty TV screens. "What the fuck . . . ?" someone said, as she quickly looked over the desks, the table loaded with food, including a pile of pastries Juliette recognized as being from the Pinnacle with a sign saying PROPERTY OF BECKER, HANDS OFF, but, mercifully, no mints.

She dashed back outside, watching everyone who passed to see if they had a tin in their hand, in their pocket. Security, she thought, she should tell security, or maybe she should just scream. Just bring the show to a halt while they figured this out. Behind her, she saw one of Becker's assistants looking around wildly, no doubt for her; she'd be thrown out of the backstage area before she could even tell anyone what was happening. In her mind the body count began . . . Were the mints outside, backstage, in other bathrooms, on any of the Kodak's many bars? Were all of them poisoned? Could someone really do that? *No*, she thought, *no. Just calm down. Just calm down and think.*

She stepped behind some curtains as Becker himself clomped past. Standing in the wings stage left, she ignored the hustle of the crew shifting the scenery and tried to steady her mind, tried to think of what was the best thing to do next. Against the glow of the stage lights, she saw Max appear from nowhere, lay his hand on Becker's arm, force himself to laugh when the producer threw it off. "Jesus Christ," Becker said. "Would you give it a rest? I'm in the middle of something here, if you hadn't noticed."

"All right, all right," Max said, digging into his pocket. "Relax. Remember your blood pressure. Here, have a mint."

Shaking his head, Becker dragged his hand through the tin Max offered, clawed up a handful, threw them in his mouth, and chewed. Juliette made a choking sound and rushed toward them, waiting for the producer to clutch his arm and fall to the floor, for his face to flush and his eyes to roll up in his head, or whatever happened when a fat man had a heart attack.

But nothing happened. Max glanced at her, his face composed, his eyes concerned. He too popped a mint in his mouth. Then he smiled at her and tears sprang to her eyes—God, he looked so nice, so warm, so funny and familiar. What had she been thinking? How could Max hurt anyone? She felt the muscles in her back unclench—she had been wrong, of course she had been wrong. As discreetly as she could, she put the bag of mint tins on the floor behind her, kicking them under a curtain.

Suddenly Becker gasped and Juliette whirled, saw his eyes widen and his mouth drop open. "Oh, my God," she said, gauging his weight, hoping she could catch him as he fell, wondering if she still remembered how to do CPR. But then Becker's face twisted itself into a grudging grin and she skidded to a halt, following his gaze—walking toward them, slim and tall in tuxedoed splendor, although completely bald, was Michael O'Connor. Beside her, she heard a small gasp; out of the corner of her eye she saw something like horror flash over Max's face. In her purse, her BlackBerry buzzed furiously—Devlin. Reaching in with minimal movement, as if she were afraid of startling a wild animal, she turned it off.

"Jesus," said Becker, grabbing O'Connor's hand, slapping him on the back. "A fucking cue ball. I didn't even recognize you. What the hell are you doing here? You told me you weren't going to be in town."

"Change of plans," O'Connor said, pulling himself from Becker's embrace. "Max," he said, turning to the comedian, speaking in a soft voice that almost disguised the hoarseness, "you're looking a little pale. Must be a strange feeling . . ." He paused for a moment, took Juliette's two hands, leaned in and kissed her cheek. "How are you, darling?" he murmured, but she could see his eyes were on Max, who flicked his eyes from O'Connor to Becker, clearly waiting to hear what would come next. She squeezed his hands in warning, but he didn't seem to notice. "To watch the show from backstage, I mean," O'Connor finished, offering the comedian his hand.

Max shrugged. "Nice change of pace," he said.

"I bet," O'Connor said with a contagious grin. "Seems like you've got a winner," he continued, turning to Becker. "All that murder and mayhem looks like it's paying off—even Forrest is holding his own out there."

"We'll see," said Becker, his attention divided suddenly by a voice in his ear phone and the show schedule in his hand. On the monitor above his head a man with a bushy beard won for Best Art Direction. "We'll see when the numbers come in." He barked orders at some nameless unfortunate, his gaze blankly passing over O'Connor's face for a moment. "Hey," he said suddenly as he came back in focus. "You want to present? Seriously. That'd be great. A total surprise."

O'Connor made a sound of demurral.

"No, it'd be easy. Why don't you go out with Max? Forget the trophy model bit, the two of you could just riff. The lighting guys will kill me, but what the hell, it's my show. Keep it fresh. That's what you always did, right, Max?"

O'Connor tilted his head toward the comedian, watched him from the corners of his eyes. A smile tugged at his mouth.

He's enjoying this, Juliette thought. *How could he be enjoying this?* Tension rose to fill the moment, humming.

"Sure, Becker," Max said after a moment. "You gotta keep it fresh." He bounced on his toes and Juliette saw his hand slip into his pocket. For a moment she was certain he would draw a gun; she took a step backward, looked around in search of security. As if he sensed her thoughts, O'Connor began edging the group out of the backstage shadows toward the light of a well-traveled corridor, but Max merely produced a handkerchief and blew his nose. A stagehand approached Becker with pages. Becker surveyed them, grunted his approval. "Get me a Coke," he told the man. "A real one, none of this diet shit. Whaddya say, O'Connor? Want to take the stage? Show there's no hard feelings for *Bluebird*." Becker grinned savagely.

"Nah," O'Connor said. "Leave the show as it is. It's going good; I'd only spoil it. I've got a frog in my throat; you probably noticed. Besides, I don't want to get in Max's way. I mean, he's already tried to kill me once." He said the words lightly as he walked, one eyebrow raised as if he were amused. "The question is," O'Connor continued, still speaking in an easy, friendly way even as he turned and planted himself in front of Becker, "did you know about it?"

Becker laughed, at first wholeheartedly, and then more uncertainly. He looked from Max to O'Connor, then even at Juliette, his face baffled but wary.

"I don't know what the hell you're playing at," he said. "But I have to get back to the truck—"

"Not just yet," said O'Connor. He wrapped one hand around the producer's wrist, with the other he loosed the collar of his high-necked dress shirt. Even with a prodigious amount of makeup, the marks of the garroting were clear and ugly. "This is a little something I picked up in Palm Springs, courtesy of our friend here." He nodded at Max. "Oh, I don't think he did it himself, not our Max. You're not a brutal guy, are you? And, not to brag or anything, but I'm pretty sure I could take you, if it came down to it."

If O'Connor expected a reaction, he didn't get one. Max stood, bouncing on his toes, his face unreadable. "Still," O'Connor continued, "there's only one mimic I know who's good enough to make me believe it's my nurse on the phone. Which is why I was so surprised, when I got to Rory's room, to see him sound asleep on the bed and some goon standing in the doorway. But next time you hire a hit man, Max, make sure he's not a movie fan. That way he won't chicken out at the end."

Juliette watched as what might have been fury flashed briefly across the comedian's face. Then Max's eyes widened and his shoulders sagged. He held his hands up in wounded surprise. She wondered at the sense of déjà vu that flicked through her, then she remembered the comedy in which Max had played a small-town con man who preyed on lonely women. His shoulders had sagged in that role too.

"I have no idea what you're talking about," said Max, his voice hurt. "Last I heard you were on your way to Morocco. You're not well, Michael. We all know you're not well. You shouldn't even be here—I mean, look at you. You're a mess. But still, why would you say such things? About me? We're friends. We've always been friends."

He looked at Juliette appealingly.

Julia Roberts and Gwyneth Paltrow, with two pages in attendance—one was fiddling with Roberts's back zipper as she walked—brushed by. There was a flurry of greetings and air kisses, but the women hurried on. Max began to follow them. O'Connor moved slightly so his shoulder was blocking him. A minute later, the two women walked arm-in-arm onstage to present the Thalberg to Robert Redford.

"I'm on in twenty minutes," Max said, in the same aggrieved tone. "I have to get into makeup."

"You've got time," said Becker.

"But this is crazy," Max said, throwing up his hands again. "Do you believe this? He's trying to derail your show. Michael, why are you doing this? Because you didn't get nominated? Can't we deal with all this after?"

"I don't know," said Becker quietly. "Can we, Max?"

A chill went down Juliette's back; there was something so complicit between Max and Becker. She remembered they had been sitting together the night she had spoken with Josh, heads together, watching him leave just as she had watched him leave. Had Becker been in on it all along?

"The way I figure it," O'Connor said, turning his attention back to Becker, "Max wanted the Salinger part—"

"It isn't Salinger," Becker said automatically. "We established that in court."

"Whatever," O'Connor continued. "Max wanted Salinger and you wanted a successful show. At first I thought someone was trying to ruin you by wrecking the Oscars. But they're pretty hard to wreck, aren't they? A dying Pope couldn't do it, the invasion of Iraq couldn't do it, so what's a few nominees, give or take? And when I gave it some thought, I realized that if someone really wanted to bring you down, there are easier ways than that. Aren't there, William?"

The last sentence was spoken in that quiet tone actors reserve for moments of great danger. For a minute the two men locked eyes.

"How's the chemo going, Michael?" Becker asked softly. "Next time you'll have to put a special clause in the prenup."

O'Connor laughed grimly. "See, this is why I tend to think you didn't know about Palm Springs," he said. "Blackmail has always been more your line. You must really miss Pelicano."

"So then it had to be something about the victims themselves," said Juliette, as things fell into place in her mind. The three men started, as if they had forgotten she was there. "Josh had rewritten the Salinger script for a much younger man. The reporter was doing a story on Becker, so she must have known that Max wasn't the shoo-in he was pretending to be. But what about Natasha? Didn't she want to do the movie?"

"She wanted to work with Mr. Dreamboat here," said Becker. "Or Heath Ledger. She was a bitch. But she had a lot of buzz and came cheap, even after the nomination." Becker shrugged. "I can't say I was too upset when she died. Or your ex," he said, glancing at Juliette. "He was a prick, and a rotten writer. Someone else must have written that damn *Summer* movie."

O'Connor snorted. "Yes, well, I can't imagine you were too upset when any of them died," he said. "But maybe that was part of Max's plan—to prove that he could play a sociopath. A little overly Method, but hey, whatever works."

"Listen, you asshole," Max said, that trademark grin unable to soften the fury in his voice. "If I wanted you dead, you'd be dead. How hard would it be? You and me, we can still get someone to do pretty much whatever we want in this town. Isn't that right, Juliette?" he said, his eyes still on O'Connor.

Watching him, Becker laughed, tucked another wedge of gum into his mouth; Juliette could see in the way he looked at Max a combination of irritation and admiration. Max saw it too, and his face relaxed. When he stirred to speak, Juliette wondered if he might not confess to all, brag even. Instead, he clapped his hands together and rubbed them.

"You know what?" said Max. "This has been interesting, I definitely want to hear more, but I, and perhaps I am the only one, have a show to do. So maybe we can pick up Michael O'Connor as Ellery Queen or Nick and Nora or whatever you're doing here a little later." He turned to go.

"What you don't know, Mr. Becker," said Juliette quickly, not even sure it was true anymore, but knowing that she couldn't let Max leave, not yet, "is that Max planned to kill you too. Because it didn't work. The show didn't stall, you weren't cowed, and even if Michael turned down the part, David Fulbright would take it in a heartbeat. Isn't that right?"

For the first time, Becker looked surprised. Juliette pushed her advantage.

"So the only thing Max could do was kill you and then buy the rights to the film from your grieving widow."

Max turned and laughed out loud, but now his face was flushed and rumpled with anger. "And how was I going to do that, Juliette? Poison him with breath mints? I saw you practically have a heart attack back there, but look, there he stands, hale and healthy. I'm sorry," he said, taking a step toward her, rearranging his features into concern, "that your husband left you—it must have been unbearable to have him killed and watch while all the sympathy went to another woman. And I'm sure you have formed a deep, er, attachment to Michael, who, as we all know, specializes in that sort of thing. But this is all a bit much. You need a vacation, Juliette," he said, laying a hand on her cheek. "That's all. This is craziness," he said, waving it away as if it were smoke. "We'll forget all about this. Why don't you come out to the house in Malibu sometime? Promise me you'll do that."

For a moment, she was confused. All around them glowed the blue light of the stage. She could hear the murmur of the presenters speaking onstage, could see in the shadows stage-hands leaning against bits of sets; one was eating an apple while he followed the action on a monitor above his head. It all seemed so unreal. She was suddenly aware of how much her feet hurt in her shoes, how her zipper bit into the soft flesh beneath her arm. She could smell on Max citrus and cigars, and again doubt assailed her—she remembered all the times he had been so nice to her, made her laugh, she remembered Becker in the fountain, Max taking off his sweater and handing it to the girl, the photographer growing impatient, she remembered wheeling away the cartful of pastries that Becker couldn't keep his hands off—

"The pastries," she said, as it dawned on her, and Max jerked his hand away. "In the production truck." She turned to Becker and O'Connor. "There are those raspberry pastries from our kitchen, specially for you." Becker looked at her, confused. "Have you eaten any yet?"

He shook his head. "I'm saving them for after the show."

"When you'll eat them, one after the other," Juliette said softly. "Who would be surprised if he had a heart attack? So much pressure, and look at all the weight he's gained."

Becker blinked, remembering perhaps Max's jokes in Palm Springs. He looked from Juliette to Max to O'Connor.

"Okay," he said. "That's enough. This has gone far enough."

Max tensed, began to speak in protest; Becker held up a hand. Juliette took a step closer to O'Connor and wondered what would happen next. She gripped her bag; weighted with her BlackBerry, it would make something of a weapon.

Then the sound of applause squirmed into the silence, split it open. It was a commercial break. All around them tuxedoed stagehands swarmed, starlets fluttered by, people spoke into headsets, a cart rattled past stacked with the gold statuettes themselves.

"You need to get into makeup," Becker said to Max, as if nothing had happened. "And I need to talk to some people."

"But—"

"I know," Becker said. "Don't worry," he said when Max still hesitated. "Plan A, we're still going with Plan A."

Reluctantly, Max withdrew. Becker spoke quietly into his headset, Juliette caught the words "goddamn pastries." Then he looked at O'Connor. "I'm not saying you're right," he said. O'Connor nodded. "But if you are," Becker said, "I'll take care of it." O'Connor nodded again.

"Now," Becker said, "I would appreciate it if you would sit down and stay seated for the rest of the show." A look of understanding passed between them. Becker turned and walked away, leaving a sense of vacuum in his wake.

"That's it?" Juliette said after a minute. "Aren't we going to call the police? Shouldn't someone, I don't know, arrest Max? Or Becker? Or both?"

"On what charge?" O'Connor asked, looking down at her sadly.

"Well, he tried to kill you, for one."

"I'm sure Max has an ironclad alibi for the time of my attack, as I am sure he has for each of the deaths."

"The pastries—"

"Are being disposed of, even as we speak. And who knows if there's anything even in them? Who knows if Max was trying to kill Becker? Becker doesn't seem too worried. And we've got no proof. Of anything."

"Even so," Juliette protested, "there needs to be an investigation. Maybe they can find whoever he hired to kill Josh, or attack you. I mean, he pretty much confessed."

O'Connor continued to look down at her.

"I didn't hear anything that sounded like a confession," he said.

"You don't *want* an investigation," she said accusingly. "Because then they might find out about the cancer. But you can't, you can't just let him get away with murder. Just because you're worried about your image—"

"Think about it, Juliette," O'Connor said softly. "Think about what you know. Max is probably on the phone right now with the meanest, toughest lawyers in the world, and they will tear everyone involved apart before anything approaching the truth gets touched. And people will eat it up. Do you want police and reporters and the motherfucking entertainment media sorting through Josh's life? Through your life? It won't be just you or me, it'll be everyone you know, everyone you care about. Do you think Dev could survive that kind of scrutiny? Could any of you? Think about it, Juliette. Think about what it would be like."

Juliette opened her mouth, then shut it. It would be horrible. It would be worse than horrible. *This is how people win Pulitzers*, Sasha had said. The greed in her tone had been frightening, and that from a journalist with some integrity. But still she couldn't believe this was how it was going to end, that this was how Michael was going to let it end. Shouldn't he follow it through, guns blazing, to see that justice was done?

"But what about Max?" she said finally. "We can't just let him go . . ."

"Max isn't going anywhere," said Michael with a strange tone of disgust in his voice. "Because he's got nowhere to go. This is his life. Right here. His palace and his grave."

A young woman in a blue blazer approached them, blushing furiously. "Mr. O'Connor," she said in a small voice. "Mr. Becker asked me to see you to your seat."

Michael made a small kind gesture and the woman retreated slightly.

"You coming?" he said to Juliette. She shook her head. Glancing at the monitor, she saw Anna Stewart making her way to the stage, tears streaming down her face, then Josh's face filled the screen—he had won for Best Screenplay. There was no way she was going out there. She was not an actor. She could not sit there and smile for the cameras while Max mugged from the stage and ruthless people gave speeches thanking God and their mothers. "Get Devlin to take you home," he said. "I'll call you later."

She nodded and looked at the ground. Disappointment swelled in her throat until she thought she would choke.

"Juliette," he said softly. Reluctantly she looked up at Michael; his features were blurred by her tears. "I promise you it will turn out all right in the end. You'll see. Lovely," he said, leaning toward her, his mouth moving from her cheek to her ear to her neck. "You are so very lovely."

She put her hands on his shoulders to push him away and was shocked at the amount of padding there. She looked closely into his face and could see how strained it was, how thin and tired and ill he was, how much effort it must have taken just to get here, to remain standing.

"I'll call you later," she said.

Walking out of the front entrance of the Kodak, Juliette shivered. It was cold and dark, the red carpet empty and eerily silent, like three a.m. after a long sleepless night. Hollywood Boulevard was still blocked off, she realized. There would be no cabs. To the left, fans still stood, hoping for some glimpse of a star, any star, so she bore right. *So where do I go now?* she wondered, knowing she was thinking both literally and figuratively. She certainly didn't feel like going back to the hotel just yet. She didn't feel like doing anything. For a moment, she thought longingly of that one evening when Dev had made her eggs and sausage and they had sat in front of the fire petting his dogs. That was about the only nice, uncomplicated thing that had happened to her in months. And then, of course, she had gone and complicated it. Now she would have to tell Dev what had happened, what Michael had done, what she had done. Which was nothing.

Shit, she thought, realizing she would have to walk to the Renaissance, where, she assumed, there would be a taxi stand. If it were up to her, she thought, she would just lie down here and let them roll her up and take her away with the red carpet.

Exhaustion washed over her as she thought about everything she was going to have to get through in the next few days just to keep up with regular life. Tomorrow was going to be hell; the day after the Oscars was even busier than the day of, what with all the late breakfasts, the celebratory brunches, the racks of dresses being returned, the mountain of jewelry, not to mention the sensitive losers lurking about.

Her feet hurt so much that Juliette contemplated walking barefoot, but the sidewalk was so dirty she couldn't quite bear the thought of it. Instead, she turned in to a small parking lot wedged behind one of the souvenir shops that lined the street beside the Kodak. Immediately, the lights of Hollywood Boulevard disappeared. Sighing, she tried to walk a little faster and stumbled, bumping into a pair of young men, one of whom was just ending a call on a cell phone.

"Sorry," she muttered.

"No worries," he said, and the next thing she knew the other had her left arm pinned behind her back—he yanked it so hard she heard a snap and felt a cold dart of excruciating pain move toward her shoulder.

"I said I was sorry," she gasped as they yanked her toward a black Volvo parked in the alley.

"Not as sorry as you're going to be, Ms. Greyson," said the other, opening the door and shoving her toward it.

Taking a deep breath, Juliette planted her feet and prepared to scream, but she never got the chance. As her head was banged with great force against the roof of the car, she heard a familiar voice.

"That, my friends," said Devlin, "is something you will now and forever wish you hadn't done." Strangely, the two men took their hands from her and froze.

"Devlin?" one of them said. "We didn't know . . ."

"Well, now you do. And you have ten seconds to show me the backs of you." Without a word, the men turned and fled.

"I've been looking all over for you," Devlin said calmly as he stepped out of the shadows. "You really need to turn your BlackBerry back on."

In his hand was a gun with a silencer attached; he managed to get it into his belt in time to catch her as she fell.

Devlin took her back to the Pinnacle; a doctor was in his office by the time they got there. "Look," she said when Devlin helped Juliette through the door, "it's Boo and Jem." She set Juliette's arm, wrapping it in an impossibly thin cast that was black and shot through with silver threads. "It's a new polymer," the doctor said. "Very popular. Comes in hot pink too, but that didn't seem very Pinnacle." She also diagnosed a mild concussion. "Take her home, but don't leave her alone," she said. She gave Devlin a sidelong, knowing look. "Not that you ever would. If she vomits or passes out, call me." Devlin thanked her and hurried her out.

"Do you have a plumber in your harem as well?" Juliette

asked when he returned. Devlin had a rollaway brought in, along with countless pillows. She didn't bother to ask why he wasn't taking her home or to a hospital; she knew. Michael might think everything was fine, but Devlin clearly did not. She watched her boss make tea. His tie was off, his shirt-sleeves rolled up, but other than that he looked as he always did—quietly polished, darkly handsome. She remembered the fear in the men's faces when they had seen him, how quickly they had run. Clearly they knew him from some other life.

Behind him, the Oscar telecast rolled silently to its conclusion. There was Anna Stewart accepting her second Oscar of the night. The camera cut to the losers; Alicia Goldstone smiled tightly, clearly furious. Juliette leaned back against the pillows, closed her eyes, and fought nausea. "What are we telling everyone?"

"That you fell off those damn shoes and broke your arm," he said. She nodded, eyes still closed, but then a thought sent her bolt upright. "Michael," she gasped. "It must have been Max who sent those guys, unless it was Becker. But whoever it was, he'll send someone after Michael too."

"Quietly," Devlin said, handing her a cup of tea. "Quietly. Mr. O'Connor is quite safe and will be escorted back to the hospital"—he looked at his watch—"just about now. And he should be grateful I'm not doing the escorting or he might find a few more bruises than he already has."

"It wasn't his fault," Juliette said, "or at least not really. I could have . . . I should have . . . Oh, Dev," she said, tears bursting from her eyes, streaming down her face, "my head hurts so much and my arm hurts so much. If you hadn't been there, God knows what would have happened, and I don't even know if it's over yet."

For several minutes, she simply sobbed, images hurtling

through her brain—Josh so smooth and satisfied, O'Connor's face purple and convulsed, all the gowns and the flowers and the gift baskets and the money and the calm way Bill Becker had nodded. *I'm not saying you're right,* he had said. *But if you are, I'll take care of it.*

She cried until she choked and at last Devlin put a hand on her shoulder. "Shhh," he said, "shhh, you'll make yourself sick, and we can't have that. We've had everything else, God knows, but we can't have that."

Turning down the light, he slid next to her so that somehow he was sitting behind her and she was lying against him. "It's over," he said. "We're safe as houses here. Now," he said, tucking her head under his chin, "you tell me what happened and then we'll see where we are."

Taking a deep breath that ended in a hiccup, Juliette told him everything that had happened backstage, how Michael had just let Max walk away as if his image were more important than the people Max had killed.

She was dry-eyed by the time she finished, but still her voice shook. "Why do I never see them for the liars they are?" she asked. "You would think Josh would have taught me something. Never believe anyone in the Industry. If their mouths are moving, they're lying."

Devlin laughed quietly. "I don't think you're being quite fair," he said. "There wasn't much O'Connor could have done that minute, given the circumstances. Not that he should have let you go tripping out the door. But he was right—there isn't much evidence and a lot to lose looking for more."

"So we're just supposed to live in fear of Max and Becker for the rest of our lives?"

Devlin leaned his head back, away from her. Where she had been warm, now she grew chilly. She nestled down against him, so he would pull her closer, and he did. "I wouldn't worry about them," he said into her hair. "I wouldn't give them another thought. They won't bother you again, anyway."

Juliette grew still. She could feel Devlin's breathing, his heart beating against her back. When he spoke, the sound of his voice rumbled in her ears, rang down through her shoulders. But still she saw him as he had been, stepping from the shadows, the gun in his hand, two men quaking in fear.

"Did you kill them?" she asked finally. "Did you kill Max and Becker?"

Devlin laughed again, loudly this time. "You flatter me, J. Scaring off a couple of hired thugs I can take care of—a movie star and a mogul, that is well beyond me, I'm afraid. Let's just say that in the course of finding you, I made certain that the parties involved know there will be . . . consequences should anything happen to you or any of our guests. We do have a reputation to uphold, after all. Here at the Pinnacle."

For a while, for a long while, they sat in silence together. Juliette was exhausted. She listened to sounds of the hotel, the guests trickling in from their parties, some loud, some quiet, the shouts of congratulations, the music from the bar, which stayed open until four on Oscar night. It seemed so familiar but no longer safe, no longer comforting. On Devlin's flat-screen, Eddie Izzard looked with amazement at the statuette in his hand. He was wearing a tux, but his lips and eyes were to die for.

"I don't know if I can stay here," she said, breaking the silence. "I can't imagine it will ever be the same now. I always knew people here were ambitious and greedy, desperate sometimes in their own way. But all this . . ." She stared into the dim light that surrounded them. "You should have seen Michael and Becker, their faces. It didn't even faze them, or at least not much. I never knew that there was such ugliness underneath it all, such violence . . ."

"Ah, well, that's people, isn't it?" Devlin said. "Wherever there are people, there's deceit and betrayal. And murder. It's no different here than anyplace else. Just the weather's better, and the food." Juliette laughed in spite of herself. "The trick is to figure out who or what is really important, protect that with all your might, and let the rest play out."

For a moment, she thought he might say more. She felt his breathing stop. In the silence she could hear the tick of his wristwatch. On the television screen, the producers of *A Touch of Summer* embraced on the stage.

"It's a sweep, then," Devlin said finally, pulling himself from behind her. "You should probably try to sleep now. Don't worry," he said as she protested, "everything will be exactly where you left it in the morning."

24

When Juliette finally slipped out of Devlin's office, having helped herself to suitable clothes from his morning-after closet, the sun was high and the hotel in full roar. Fuzzy with painkillers, she hadn't gone two steps before Gregory was at her elbow, flapping the trades and informing her that it had been the highest-rated Oscars in history, TiVo'd more than the Pope's funeral.

"And if that weren't enough," he said, opening a copy of *Variety*, "Becker took the stage at the New Line party to announce once and for all that Max Diamond will play J. D. Salinger in the movie that isn't about J. D. Salinger."

"What?" Juliette grabbed the tabloid. The words swam in front of her eyes.

"Yeah," Gregory said, "I guess Becker figured if Max could fool a room full of movie stars into thinking he had really lost his rocks and kidnapped a trophy model, he could play a genius recluse turned Internet predator. Did you see him? Max, I mean. He was amazing. I was completely taken in. I thought for a minute he was really going to kill her. Right there at the Oscars. He was deranged. I never knew he had it in him. Oh, they send their best, by the way," Gregory said. "I guess they heard about your little fall—so embarrassing, darling, you really should have come up with a better story, like you were mugged or something."

Juliette looked sharply at him; he gave her a Cheshire grin.

"Are they here?" she asked. "Max and Becker? In the hotel?"

He nodded, still grinning.

"Does Dev know?"

"What kind of question is that?" Gregory asked. "Our fearless leader has been up since dawn, glad-handing and schmoozing like nobody's business. I guess he feels like he has to turn on the charm without our Miss Julie around. Last I saw, he was pouring Max a glass of champagne."

Juliette shoved Gregory away with her good arm and strode off.

Entering the lobby, it took her a moment to adjust to all the light and noise and movement. People, so many people, moving in and out the front doors, flowing into the dining room, out to the garden, forming a small eddy at the entrance to the bar. Oscars glinted gold from tables on the patio, where the odor of cigar smoke rose above the fragrance of lilies and roses, like the very smell of success. *Today,* Juliette said to herself as she headed to the patio, *I just have to get through today. After that, who knows?* Downing another Vicodin, she put on her best day-after-Oscar smile and prepared for the possibility that she would have to make animated small talk with the men who quite possibly tried to have her killed.

Slowly she made her way through the bar and out to the garden patio, where laughter and greetings rang above flowers and pitchers of mimosas. Across it all, she saw Devlin rising from a table that did not contain either Max or Becker. When he caught sight of her, he excused himself and made his way over. Watching him walk, Juliette tried to see in his carefully pleasant expression, his easy stride, the man from the night before. The man who had saved her life, the man who had calmed her fears. It was as if there were two Devlins—the man she saw and the man she now knew, or was beginning to know.

"You don't have to be here," he said into her ear, drawing her aside behind a stand of bird-of-paradise. "Though I am glad to see you on your feet."

"Gregory said Max and Becker were in."

"They were, and now they are gone."

"Gregory said Becker made an announcement about the Salinger movie."

"He did. And more that that." Devlin's mouth twitched as he gazed out at the sea of famous faces, the endless dance of service and the served. "He and Mr. Diamond are forming a production company, it seems. They're partners." Juliette looked at him, frowning.

"Eamonn," she said earnestly, laying her hand on his arm. "We have to do something. They can't just . . . We have to tell someone . . ."

"Not today, love," Devlin said, smiling still and nodding across the room. "Today we keep our guests happy, today we congratulate the winners and comfort the losers, today we celebrate the wonder that is Hollywood." He laughed again and pinched her chin. "Don't look so worried, J. These things have a way of righting themselves. Oh," he added, putting his hand in his jacket pocket. "Mr. Diamond asked me to give you this." He handed her an envelope. Frowning at him again, she opened it. On a single piece of Pinnacle stationery were the words: *No hard feelings. Love, Max.*

"Unbelievable," Juliette said. "These people are simply unbelievable."

"I know," Devlin said happily. "Me, I can't wait to see what happens next."

"Oh, I can," said Juliette, having just caught sight of Anna Stewart doing a stately promenade among the tables.

"Juliette, darling," she cried, two Oscars gleaming in her hands. "Oh, those rotten shoes. Look at you. I feel terrible."

"It's nothing," Juliette lied, automatically downplaying the drama of her own life as she had always done. "Just a sprain. Gives me an excuse to take it easy and look pitiable. Congratulations," she said, acknowledging the statues.

"Thank you," Anna said with a small beaming nod. "This one is, of course, Josh's," she said, allowing her face to dim just so. "I hope you don't mind . . . that is, I thought . . . they look well together, don't they?"

"Like bookends," Juliette said.

"Would you like to hold it? For a moment?" Anna asked, as if conferring a great favor.

A dark and wild laugh rose in Juliette's stomach. "I don't think so, Anna," she said. "But thank you all the same."

"I don't suppose you're going to tell me what really happened," said Sasha, falling into step beside Juliette a few hours later as she made her way through the lounge. Whether it was due to the bump on her head or the actual events, Juliette wasn't quite sure at first what the reporter meant by "what really happened."

"Not that it matters," Sasha was saying. "I'm leaving the *Times*." Juliette stopped and looked at her; the reporter nodded and shrugged. "I got a three-project deal over at HBO. One's a movie about a plot to wreck the Oscars." She grinned. "Becker's producing it. Come on," she said, taking advantage of what she saw in Juliette's face. "I'll buy you a cappuccino."

"So," she said, picking through the muffin basket after they found a small table in the lounge, "it turns out Marie was smoking after all. Marie Stanton," she said, responding to Juliette's blank look. "The reporter who died? Yeah, I know what I said, but I started asking around and apparently Marie's idea of stopping smoking was to cut down to a pack a day." Sasha shook her head. "But she got hooked on the patch too. According to her sister, heart problems run in the family. Chalk one up to natural causes. So," she said, "what did you think of Anna Stewart's speech on behalf of your ex? Pretty ballsy, I thought . . ."

For the next fifteen minutes, Juliette smiled and nodded, murmured agreement when it seemed appropriate. But as soon as the reporter paused for breath, Juliette reached over and gave her hand a squeeze. "I'm so happy things are working out so well for you," she said, making small leave-taking movements.

"Well, thanks," Sasha said, taken aback slightly. "I know you're busy," she added quickly. "And I just wanted to thank you for, you know, putting me up and putting up with me. It was a crazy time, wasn't it? I'm glad it's over. Oh," she added, and suddenly there was nothing chatty about her. "I heard downtown that they caught the guy who killed Josh. Or rather, they found him. Some junkie who'd overdosed. But he had Josh's watch and a blade they think . . . well, they're running tests. So that's good, isn't it? To have closure."

"Yes," Juliette said, rising with finality. "Yes, it is. Thank you for telling me, Sasha. And you know you're one of the family here at the Pinnacle, anything we can do for you, just let me know. Here," she said, holding out her hand, "let me take care of your parking."

As soon as she could, Juliette backed Devlin into his office and told him what Sasha had said. "So," she said, feeling foolish, confused, and inexplicably angry at her boss, "did we ever find out who put our mints all over the Kodak?" The blurriness that had shrouded the last two days had somehow been yanked away; it wasn't over, it was merely taking a different form, the people involved doing what they did best—lie and charm and spin. And Devlin seemed the most calm and charming of the lot.

Devlin shut the door as Juliette spoke. "And who, come to think of it," she asked, her voice rising, "were those two guys who attacked me? The men who seemed to know you so well?"

"What two guys?" Devlin asked. His face was a mask, and for a moment Juliette felt uncertainty crowd her. Then he winked. "To answer your first question: Louisa, as it turns out, was the brains behind the mint distribution. It seems"—he straightened his jacket sleeves, settled his cuffs—"she was trying to impress me. As for the gentlemen you met the other night, I have no idea who they were and I cannot help it if my reputation, like yours, precedes me." Devlin could not quite conceal a small satisfied smile. "As for the rest, well, we all have our opinions, don't we? But the dust seems to be settling and the dream machine grinds on."

There was a detachment in his tone that baffled her, but also exhausted her.

"Clichés don't become you," she said.

Devlin laughed.

"Which reminds me," he said. "Mr. O'Connor has requested the pleasure of your company this afternoon for tea. Why he felt he had to go through me, I do not know. I hope you aren't toying with the affections of a guest. That certainly wouldn't do."

"Stop it," Juliette said, not knowing if she should laugh or scream. "Whatever this is, Dev, it isn't funny."

"No," Devlin said, putting a hand on her shoulder. "It's not. I know it's not."

"How did he sound?" she asked, not really listening. "Did he sound all right?"

Devlin's hand fell away. "He sounds fine," he said. "Just fine."

O'Connor looked pretty good too, or at least Juliette thought so when she watched him enter the lobby. Catching sight of her, the actor smiled, but first he had to greet the dozen people who came out of nowhere to shake his hand and embrace him, or to simply edge a bit closer, staring, hoping to catch his eye. He wore the black baseball cap Juliette had given him and leaned on a cane, though it was difficult to tell if he needed it or was just affecting a look. She could hear him explain to the circle of admirers that he was preparing to play a POW "and of course they want to shoot the last scenes first."

When O'Connor finally reached her, he glanced at her arm and his smile fled. "I don't know what to say," he said quietly, keeping his distance. "Juliette, tell me what to say."

It only took a moment for Juliette to give way. Warmly, publicly, she kissed his cheek, threaded her good arm through his. "Say, 'I'm sorry to hear about your accident, Juliette,'" she said. "And stop looking like you accidentally ran over my dog. I don't even have a dog."

"How did I live all these years of my life without you?" he said, smiling and nodding various greetings as they made their way to the garden. But when they slid into their seats at a table made private by several rose trees, he took her hand.

"You have to know how sorry I am," he said. "You have to know I had no idea he would try anything like that."

"I know," she said, and she meant it. Still, she couldn't help adding, "It's just a good thing Dev showed up."

"Yes," O'Connor said with a dark laugh. "The real hero will out in the end."

"I didn't mean it that way," Juliette said, though that was precisely how she had meant it. "How are you, anyway?" she added quickly. "I mean, healthwise. Are you okay?"

O'Connor nodded, allowing the moment to pass. "To the shock of my doctors, I am all right. I still need another round of treatment, which I am almost ready to begin. And that is why I'm here."

"Oh, Michael," she said, as the image of him back in the hotel, attached to tubes and vomiting into a basin, rose in her mind and filled her with misery—could he go through that again now? Could she?

He held up his hand. "No," he said, "I'm not here to beg accommodation or nursing. I'm here to tell you that if you want to go to the police, if you think we should go to the police, I will. I mean, I actually have already," he added hurriedly. "I had to spring Rory, after all, poor guy—but my lawyer, God bless him, figured out some story that cleared Rory without going into too many details. I just gave a table reading. But," he said, looking at her, his blue eyes dark and serious, "I want to do the right thing. Whatever you want, Juliette," he said, putting his hand, large and warm, over hers. "I will do whatever you want."

Looking at him, Juliette felt almost suffocated by emotion—gratitude, tenderness, desire—they were all there, fighting their way up her throat, jockeying for control of her heart, of her brain. But at the same time, a small cool voice in the back of her head wondered if that wasn't precisely what O'Connor was counting on—that Juliette cared too much about him to let him sacrifice himself, even for justice. *How do you tell*, she asked herself, *how do you tell when they're lying when they may not even know themselves?*

"I can't take that responsibility," she said finally. "You need to decide for yourself. You're the only one in possession of anything like facts—all I have are theories and guesswork. And," she added softly, turning her hand so her palm pressed against his, "faith. I do still have some of that."

He looked at her and she wondered if it was love or just confusion she saw on his face. Either way, it was gone in a flash, replaced by cool amusement.

"Perhaps Mr. Devlin can offer us some guidance," he said, turning his head slightly, and there, indeed, was Dev, standing beside the table. Juliette could not think how he had gotten there without her noticing.

"Guidance, no," said Dev, taking note of their clasped hands, which they each withdrew immediately. "But news I can give you. Sad news, alas. It seems our good friend Max Diamond is dead." Juliette gasped, but Devlin didn't blink. "He was found in his home early this afternoon. Heart attack."

Juliette and O'Connor stared at each other, then turned to Devlin. Seeing the look on Juliette's face, Devlin laughed sharply. "No, J. I didn't do it."

She turned to O'Connor.

"Well, I didn't do it," he said. Both men looked at her speculatively. She felt her face flush. "I certainly didn't do it," she said.

"Becker," said O'Connor.

"Becker," said Juliette.

"Mr. Becker," said Devlin, "would like to have a memorial for his good friend and partner. At the Pinnacle. Early next week. So when you are through, J.," he added, "we'll begin making the arrangements."

25

The memorial for Max Diamond looked like the Oscars, Part II. A-listers from the theater world and Hollywood old and new descended on the Pinnacle for an afternoon ceremony that would last well into the evening. For the Pinnacle staff, the impact was immediate—upon hearing the news of Diamond's death, Devlin had called an emergency Diamond Memorial Summit at which Juliette supplemented each Oscar Night Survival Kit with more Xanax, a refreshing facial spray, and three very nice linen handkerchiefs.

The limos began arriving shortly before noon, dispensing one luminary after another. Watching the various Redgraves and Gyllenhaals climb out of their town cars, Juliette couldn't help feeling that it was too bad Max wasn't there to enjoy it.

"I'm going to miss him," she said to Devlin as Paul Newman and Joanne Woodward moved past. "I really am."

"As will we all," Devlin said. "I don't think he was a bad man, J.," he added, dropping his voice. "He just wanted what he wanted and, like so many people we know, he had become far too accustomed to getting it."

She and Devlin and Gregory stood along the back wall in

the hotel's largest banquet room, listening as star after star rose and spoke, watching as film clip after film clip chronicled the career of a brilliant and very funny man.

"He should have won an Oscar for that," Gregory whispered after a particularly hilarious scene from one of Max's movies, the story of a man who can see into the future, but only a few seconds into the future. "It really is a shame they didn't even give him at least an honorary Oscar."

Now came Billy Crystal, now came Steve Martin, then Warren Beatty, and, of course, Jack Nicholson. Michael O'Connor spoke movingly of how Max always made whatever he was doing look easy, how he never stopped trying to improve his game, never gave up on his craft. Tears came to Michael's eyes when he spoke and Juliette could not help but believe that, despite everything that happened, they were real. Indeed, when the final montage of Max as Oscar show host rolled, Juliette found herself weeping, not only for the man she thought she had known but for the fear and pain that must have driven him, that seemed so visible now.

"I'm not just a comedian," he said from the screen as the final images of him holding the tall and lovely trophy model at gunpoint rolled. "You think it's easy to be this funny? I'm an actor," he said, as the camera caught the faces of the famous and the sound of laughter swelled. "An actor. Which maybe now you'll understand."

Juliette understood—all the fame and money in the world wasn't enough to make Max feel like a success. After fifty years in the business, he was still looking for his big break, and he had been willing to do just about anything to get it.

"Pull yourself together, love," Devlin said, handing her a handkerchief as the lights came up and the crowd began to rise. "It's showtime."

Murmuring compliments and condolences, Juliette and the rest of the staff began moving the guests into the rose garden, where tables of food and several bar stations were set up. A string quartet played tastefully in the background and boxes of cigars were on every table, in memory of Max. Soon laughter echoed from group to group, Juliette received several compliments on her cast, and woman after woman broke away to flirt with Devlin. It could have been any party, any sort of party during Oscar season.

About an hour into the festivities, Bill Becker appeared at Juliette's elbow.

"I need to talk to you about something," he said, nodding toward the back of the hotel. "Inside." Her heart racing, Juliette steered him through the French doors into the library. Becker carried a thick manila envelope. It looked suspiciously like the one that had held Josh's cell phone, but then all manila envelopes looked alike.

"So I hear you're the person who can fix this," he said abruptly, handing the envelope to her. "O'Connor's agreed to play the guy who isn't Salinger, if you do the rewrite. And we've got a couple of girls in mind for the female lead. Give it a read, tell me what you think is wrong. I know there's something wrong, but I can't put my finger on it. I bought the one about the jewel thief too." he added. "It's in there. I thought you might like it." For the first time since he began speaking, he looked her full in the face. "For old times' sake. O'Connor's interested in that one too."

"For what role?" she asked, saying the first thing that came into her head.

"Good guy, bad guy, he doesn't care. It's the female lead's picture. He just thinks it should get made. For some reason." Becker looked at her again and inserted a cigar in the side of his mouth. When she raised her eyebrows, he laughed. "My doctor okayed two a day," he said. "That nicotine gum was killing me."

Juliette laughed in spite of herself and Becker's face relaxed into approval.

"I don't know," she said, weighing the envelope, feeling the two screenplays pressing into her hand. "I don't know if I could, after everything that's happened . . ."

He nodded, took another puff on his cigar. Said nothing. Waited. For all his infamous temper and pushiness, Bill Becker had mastered the art of waiting. Juliette tried to match his unflustered countenance, to wait right along with him, but fidgets crawled up her arms, along her shoulders, and she found herself longing to see something but that look of amused expectation on his face.

"Why did you send David Fulbright to my house that night?" she asked suddenly. "Why did he put the cell phone in my mailbox? Just a poetic flourish?"

Becker raised an eyebrow. "Ah," he said, and took a seat, throwing his arm along the back of the chair, exposing his chest, his formidable gut, a gesture that said he had nothing to hide.

"That kid is a loose cannon," he said with a chuckle. "Talented, but we'll see. A lot of those Brits are talented, but they've got no balls. He was trying to show me he had some balls. Breaking and entering, into the home of a, shall we say, professional."

Juliette kept her eyes on the space just to the left of Becker's ear.

"What, you're running a frat house now? You dared him to break into my house?"

Becker leaned forward, tapped his cigar into a small dish

full of wasabi-coated almonds that someone had left. "He wanted the part. In the movie about the jewel thief." He nodded toward the envelope still clutched in Juliette's hand. "I told him I didn't think he was . . . menacing enough." Becker blinked his eyes several times. Again, despite herself, Juliette laughed, remembering her own David Fulbright impersonation.

"So why put the cell phone in my mailbox?"

"That I couldn't tell you. What cell phone?" For the first time, Becker sounded genuinely curious.

"Josh's cell phone. Someone left it in my mailbox. After he was killed." She watched him closely; if she had to put money on it, she would bet this was news to him. Then a smile edged onto his face, the first real one she had seen anywhere near Bill Becker. It was sad somehow, weary, but there was pleasure there too.

"You know what I think?" he said. "I think Max had a thing for you, Ms. Greyson. And I'm not the only person who figures you're better off without your ex around. Maybe he thought he had done you a favor. Maybe he wanted you to have . . . a memento."

"You're saying Max had Josh killed for *me*?" As if her knees had given way, she sat suddenly in the chair across from Becker.

"It's always difficult, isn't it?" he said, and his voice was surprisingly gentle. "To learn what people are really capable of. Let me ask you something." He gestured with his cigar like a man trying to close a deal. "What did you feel when you found out Josh was dead? I mean, after the initial shock. Did you feel sorrow? Or was it more like relief?"

For a full minute, Juliette looked straight into his eyes. They were black, she realized, the pupils barely distinct from the irises. She had never seen someone with actual black eyes before. Perhaps that was why they seemed so detached, so utterly lacking in judgment or sympathy. She swallowed hard and shook her head; in the end, it was he who looked away.

"I heard you're selling your house," Becker said, standing up as if to go. "Nice house. You might get two mil. But you'll be amazed how fast that goes, what with realtor fees and taxes, moving expenses. You fix that script so O'Connor signs off and you can buy a better house, a better life, as far away from here as you like. If that's what you want. Fix that other one up, and who knows? You might win your own Oscar someday." He put the cigar back in his mouth. "You call me when you decide; we're scheduled to start shooting in six months. So call soon."

He turned to head back out into the garden.

"Did you know?" Juliette asked. Becker stopped, turned around. "Did you know what Max was doing? Did you have him . . ." She couldn't bring herself to say the words, they didn't seem to fit. Not here, in this nice hotel, speaking with one of the hottest producers in Hollywood.

There was a long pause, which Becker occupied by looking at her thoughtfully. "You were right about those pastries," he said with a smile. "Chock-full of nicotine." He shook his head and chuckled. "That crazy sonofabitch. If only he hadn't tried to kill me, we would have gotten along just fine." He laughed, then focused on her once again. "I look forward to working with you, Juliette."

And, nodding at her cordially, he strolled back into the garden.

Late that afternoon, Juliette told Devlin she was taking him up on his offer of a month-long vacation, that she was leaving in two weeks. He looked surprised, but nodded. "I understand," he said. "You don't need to convince me. You take whatever time you need."

They were standing in the rose garden, watching staff members strip tables of their cloths, balance enormous trays of dirty glassware, fold up tables and chairs. Something at least finally felt over. Juliette tried to think of a way to say what she had to say gently. But she couldn't.

"I don't know that I will be coming back," she said finally. "I don't know if that would be a good idea. Too much has happened. I feel too exposed here, too uncomfortable."

He looked up at her, startled. "Oh, come now," he said. "This is Los Angeles. In six months, no one will remember what happened."

"I will," she said. "I will remember."

It wasn't easy to even think of leaving him. For a month, much less longer. Looking at him, she wished they were somewhere else, anywhere else, meeting on some dim winter street in another city entirely, another life entirely. Leaning over, she took his hand. "Too many things turned out to be completely different than I thought they were, and I feel . . . all hollowed out. I'd be no use to you."

"I don't need you to be of use," he said.

"*I* need me to be of use."

He squeezed her hand and nodded. After a moment he cleared his throat. "Well, come to think of it, I only signed a three-year contract," he said, "which is up in December. So what do you reckon?" he asked, eyes twinkling. "Paris? Tokyo? Madrid? There's the new resort about to open in Cannes. The company has to realize at this point that we're a pretty good team . . ."

Juliette smiled; there were other things she wanted to say to him, that she would say to him, but not now, not even close to now. "We'll see," she said.

Devlin leaned back against the wall, a simple movement that shocked Juliette as much as anything that had happened. She had never seen Devlin lean on anything; perfect posture defined him. "You need to make a choice, you know," he said quietly. "About what sort of life you want to live. And with whom."

There were violets in the grass at her feet. Looking at them, she remembered the wonder she had felt when she first came to Los Angeles and discovered that violets bloomed almost year-round. It had seemed miraculous. She thought about that night in Devlin's bed when for a few shattering moments it seemed that something wonderful might happen.

"So do you, Dev," she said softly.

He stood there, hands shoved in his pockets, and she wondered if she knew him at all; he seemed impossible, the sum total of too many parts. But then he smiled and was Dev again. "Point taken," he said. He looked up over the tops of the trees and pushed himself away from the wall. "I do love you, Juliette," he said to the twinkling twilight sky. "For what it's worth. You just give me a shout," he said, pinching her chin. "When you're ready to get on with it." And then he walked away.

"I will do that, Dev," she said softly to his perfectly apportioned retreating back. "I most definitely will."

It did not matter that he had not heard.

Juliette caught up with O'Connor as he sat in the lounge surrounded by a coterie of young directors. "Will you excuse us?" Juliette said, with unaccustomed firmness, drawing him in to one of the private dining rooms that had been closed off during Max's memorial. Closing the door behind her, Juliette tossed the envelope Becker had given her onto one of the dining tables; it made an ominous thunk.

"You're taking the Salinger role," she said.

"It's not—"

She held up her hand. "Spare me. Was this what it was about all along? Was Max right? Were you stealing the part?"

"Stealing the part?" he said. "I don't call being pursued by Bill Becker to the ends of the earth 'stealing the part.'"

"Don't you have any hesitation, any feelings about making this damn movie? Jesus, Michael. Think about everything that has just happened. Or didn't any of it matter to you?"

O'Connor shrugged. "It's a really good script. Or could be, if you fix it." He raised his eyebrow at her. "What do you say, Juliette? You ready to jump in the game at long last? Or are you going to stay here making sure everyone's toast is done to their satisfaction?"

Juliette turned to go, but O'Connor had risen and stopped her. "Come on," he said, his arms around her. "If nothing else, it would be fun. You deserve a little fun. What happened, happened. Walking away now isn't going to undo it. Or prevent bad things from happening again."

"I don't know," she said. "I don't know if I'll ever even be able to go to the movies again. I'd be too busy wondering what the body count was."

O'Connor laughed out loud. "Well, then maybe you should become a producer," he said. "Look, forget the movies, forget Becker and Max and the damn script. Think about what it is you actually want, for once in your life."

His words so closely echoed Devlin's that she stared at him. Mistaking her look, he ran a self-conscious hand over his scalp.

"On a lighter note," he said, "they found my hair. In some Palm Springs dumpster. Could have been worse," he added. "It could have turned up on eBay. But I think I like the shiny look. Which is good, since it'll be falling out again in a few weeks.

"I'm doing it right this time," he continued, when she didn't speak. "Checking in to a private facility in an unnamed state. Rory's coming, of course. After all he's been through, I imagine he will be a permanent member of my staff, whether I like it or not." He grimaced. "But it'll be good to have someone I know with me."

"Where are you going?" Juliette said, because she could not bear not to ask. "Maybe I could visit you . . ."

O'Connor smiled, shook his head. "No," he said. "Not this time. God willing, I'll be done in six weeks. I better be done in six; I'm scheduled to be on set in seven and I can't afford to punt because the divorce is killing me.

"The thing is," he said more quietly, "and I don't want you to take this the wrong way, but the next time you see me flat on my back, I would like it to be poolside. Or," he added, lifting an eyebrow, "more along the lines of Palm Springs, less along the lines of the Presidential Suite."

Juliette put up her hand again. "Palm Springs," she echoed, shuddering.

"It was the best of times," he said softly, "it was the worst of times. But mostly, I think, it was the best of times."

Tears filled Juliette's eyes; quickly she looked away.

"Don't cry, my Juliette," he said, taking her hand, pulling her close to him. "Not now. For one night, let's pretend. For one night, surely we're allowed to pretend."

"Pretend what?" she asked. "That none of this ever happened? That you're well? That I'm well? That things are even remotely normal?"

He looked at her with such tenderness that she regretted the sharp tone of her words. "Let's pretend," he said, "that we are two people who, though confronted with a series of alarming obstacles, might just be falling in love."

And he said it so well that it didn't matter if Juliette could almost see the words written on a page. There he was, with the face of a thousand magazine covers, a hundred billboards, a face that she had seen unfold in every emotion, as familiar to her as her own. More so. It wasn't real, how could it be real? She closed her eyes and tried to remember the last time her life had felt normal. She thought of the look on Josh's face just before he got on the airplane—then, maybe then, but of course six weeks later, he was gone, so that hadn't been real either.

With something like a sigh, she leaned into the kiss she knew would be there, now, right now, in this moment. She slid her hands along the stern graceful bones of Michael's neck, along the shocking bareness of his skull, and as the kiss widened, and deepened, she noticed that it didn't feel like pretending at all.

Two days after it went on the market, Juliette sold her house to a screenwriter and his wife. They requested a twenty-day escrow because he had to fly to Toronto for a film. For a moment Juliette hesitated, but decided that marital advice was almost never welcome and it wasn't any of her business anyway. She signed the papers and began boxing up her clothes, the art, the books, most of which she put in storage. Everything else she sold to the new owners or gave away.

She left Los Angeles on a Thursday afternoon. That morning, she packed what little remained of her belongings in two cardboard boxes; Dev had said he would come by in the evening to pick them up. He hadn't offered to drive her to the airport and she hadn't asked. Juliette had told everyone at the Pinnacle that she was going on a long-overdue vacation; she and Dev had said their goodbyes over the phone, and that had been difficult enough. She had not heard from O'Connor since the night of Diamond's memorial, unless you counted a postcard from Heathrow with the words, Will call, if not dead, in six weeks. M., scrawled on it. And that was fine too; for the first time in she couldn't remember how long, she felt no obligation to anyone. It was unnerving and at the same time exhilarating, like being launched into someone else's life.

After she packed the boxes and her bags, the only thing left of

369

hers was the manila envelope Becker had given her—still unopened. She hadn't even looked at the scripts, hadn't allowed herself to think of looking at the scripts. Standing now in the dusty silence of the house, waiting for her taxi, she told herself there was no point in taking them. She had promised Becker nothing; had, in fact, made it very clear she wasn't keen on getting involved. She didn't want to burrow deeper into Hollywood, she wanted to leave it, possibly forever. Working on Josh's scripts would be too damaging, emotionally and spiritually. She'd be right smack in the middle of the people and place she was going to great lengths to leave. It was absurd.

She picked up the envelope with every intention of putting it in the box for Devlin to pick up. It was heavy in her hand. Without thinking, she opened it, took out one of the scripts, and flipped it open. Minutes passed. God, she thought, poor Josh. He always seemed to just miss the mark. And it was so easy, really, scenes like pieces in a puzzle, characters like people that you knew. Outside, the taxi arrived and honked. A few more minutes passed. The second act was a mess, the third not much better. She'd have to start from scratch, basically. She'd have to give O'Connor a real challenge—that could be fun. To see if he still remembered how to actually act. The taxi honked again. Coming back to herself, Juliette slid the script back in the envelope and stood there. She went to toss the envelope into the box, but found herself stuffing it into her carry-on bag.

It will give me something to do on the plane, she thought as she finally headed out the door. And what was the worst that could happen? It was only a movie.

ACKNOWLEDGMENTS

I would like to thank the following people, without whom this book would not exist: first, my husband and children—Richard, Danny, Fiona, and Darby—for their patience, support, and inspiration. My agents, Lauren Pearson and Joe Regal, for their wonderful editing, pep talks, and hand-holding. My editor, Kerri Kolen, for her great eye and for loving my characters as much as I do. Mark Lee, for all his wise counsel and advice. Early readers of the book—Suzann Papagoda, Paul Brownfield, Betsy Sharkey, Rich Nordwind, and Kelly Scott—gave me great notes and encouragement. Sarah Cairns and the folks at the Four Seasons Los Angeles showed me how a fine hotel works during Oscar season, while the people behind the Academy Awards telecast continually amaze me with their dedication and brilliance.

Finally, I'd like to thank the Academy of Motion Picture Arts and Sciences for each year giving us such a glorious spectacle to write about, talk about, and dream about.

POCKET
BOOKS

Karen Quinn

Holly Would Dream

Fashion historian Holly Ross often wishes she lived in a simpler time, when the clothes were glamorous, the men debonair and the endings happy. But, about to be married and with a big promotion promised, her own happily-ever-after seems assured.

So where does it all go wrong? How in the space of one day does Holly find herself homeless, jobless, penniless – and fiancé-less? Why is she cruising on the ultra-luxurious *Tiffany Star* in pursuit of dashing property tycoon Denis King? And how come she's trying to track down a case full of priceless Audrey Hepburn gowns before Interpol tracks *her* down?

With the sparkling Mediterranean and the eternal city of Rome as the backdrop, this romantic fashion caper is filled with intrigue, comedy and plot twists galore.

'A slick, stylish caper for fans of *Ugly Betty*' *Eve*

ISBN 978-1-4165-2765-7
PRICE £6.99

POCKET
BOOKS

Nicola Kraus & Emma McLaughlin

Dedication

What if your first love left town, without a word to anyone, days before graduation? What if he went on to become one of the biggest recording stars on the planet, and every song he's famous for is about you? What if, after thirteen years of getting on with your life – walking past his face on newsstands, flipping past his image on TV, tuning him out on the radio – you get the call that he's landed back in your hometown for an MTV special two days before Christmas? What if you finally had the chance to confront him? What would you do?

This is the dilemma faced by Kate Hollis, a woman on the threshold of her thirtieth birthday, who discovers that the only way to embrace life as a fully-fledged, well-adjusted adult is to re-visit seventeen.

'Hilarious and heartbreaking in equal measure – a must-have read'
Woman

ISBN 978-1-84739-124-7
PRICE £6.99

POCKET
BOOKS

Paige Toon

Johnny Be Good

**Lots of girls fall for their bosses . . . but how many work
for the hottest rock star on the planet?**

I'm Meg Stiles. This is my leaving party. And that song we're
making a mockery of? That's written by one of the biggest rock
stars in the world. And I'm moving in with him tomorrow.
Seriously! I am not even kidding you. Well, maybe I'm misleading
you a little bit. You see, I haven't actually met him yet . . .

No, I'm not a stalker. I'm his new PA. His Personal Assistant.
And I am off to La-la Land. Los Angeles. The City Of Angels –
whatever you want to call it – and I can't bloody believe it!

Celebrity PA to wild boy of rock Johnny Jefferson, Meg's glam
new life in sun-drenched LA is a whirlwind of showbiz parties and
backstage passes. Cool, calm Christian, in town to write his famous
friend's biography, helps keep Meg's feet firmly on the ground. But
with Johnny's piercing green eyes and a body Brad Pitt would kill
for, how long will it be before she's swept right off them again?

'Wonderful, addictive, sharp and sexy' COSMOPOLITAN

ISBN 978-1-84739-044-8
PRICE £6.99

**POCKET
BOOKS**

This book and other **Pocket Books** titles are available from
your local bookshop or can be ordered direct
from the publisher.

978-1-4165-2765-7	**Holly Would Dream**	£6.99
978-1-84739-124-7	**Dedication**	£6.99
978-1-84739-044-8	**Johnny Be Good**	£6.99

Please send cheque or postal order for the value of the book,
free postage and packing within the UK, to
SIMON & SCHUSTER CASH SALES
PO Box 29, Douglas Isle of Man, IM99 1BQ
Tel: 01624 677237, Fax: 01624 670923
Email: bookshop@enterprise.net
www.bookpost.co.uk

Please allow 14 days for delivery. Prices and availability
subject to change without notice